LIA ANDERSON
DOG PARK MYSTERIES

LIA ANDERSON MYSTERIES
by C. A. Newsome

A SHOT IN THE BARK
DROOL BABY
MAXIMUM SECURITY
SNEAK THIEF
MUDDY MOUTH
FUR BOYS

SWAMP MONSTER

LIA ANDERSON DOG PARK MYSTERY 7

C. A. NEWSOME

TWO PUP
PRESS

SWAMP MONSTER

Copyright © 2020 by Carol Ann Newsome
"Gypsy" Copyright © 2019 by Carol Ann Newsome
Cover Design by Elizabeth Mackey

Two Pup Press
1836 Bruce Avenue
Cincinnati, Ohio 45223

Version 1.03 February 13, 2021

Newsome, C. A.
Swamp monster: a dog park mystery/ C. A. Newsome
Pages cm
ISBN 9781947085053 (paperback)—ISBN 9781947085046 (ebook)
1. Murderers—Fiction. 2. Murder Investigations—Fiction 3. Cincinnati (Ohio)—Fiction. 4. Mill Creek Valley (Ohio). 5. Crime—Kentucky—Newport—Fiction. I. Title.

For everyone who ever lost a furry soulmate
and everyone brave enough to raise a puppy

SWAMP MONSTER

WATER

SATURDAY, MAY 16, 1987

INCHES OF WATER SEPARATED ANDREW FROM LIFE, BLURRING the face he'd opened his door to hours earlier. Pressure built in his lungs, screaming for a release impossible while a size-eleven boot pinned him to the bottom of his claw-footed tub. The brass studs on his costume ground painfully into his chest. He allowed his eyes to bulge and calculated: he had ninety seconds, two minutes tops.

Ninety seconds. Lifetime to an impatient punk. *I may be old, but I can still wait you out.*

He thrashed weakly, a panic play for an audience of one, designed to bring an early end to the current dunking. Counted to three, released a whisper of breath. Closed his eyes to slits. Went limp. Counted ten, fifteen.

The last breath of air escaped, rising in a cloud of tiny bubbles, obscuring what little he could see. The boot vanished. Hands dove into the water, jerking him into a sitting position.

Water, rolling off his face, streaming out his nose. He convulsed, coughing his insides raw, the intake of air like fire. No point trying to run. His opponent was much younger, too strong. He wouldn't make it out of the tub. It pissed him off, this nobody punk catching him with his guard down.

Thank God Jenny isn't here.

"Ready to talk, old man? I'll let you live." The punk sat back on the closed toilet lid, one sodden work boot propped against the rim of the tub, dripping on the puddled floor as he flipped a coin lazily in the air, waiting.

Andrew forced the words out in a voice ragged from repeated drownings. "You're a fool chasing a chimera. I'm not who you think I am."

The coin fell, bouncing on the floor as the sneering face thrust forward. "I'll kill you and pull this house apart."

"That coin," Andrew croaked, "is all you'll get."

The punk stood. The foot returned, poised against Andrew's sternum. "Last chance. Raise your hand if you change your mind."

Andrew sucked in air as water closed over his head for the seventh time. The need to breathe built under that oppressive leather boot; pressure, and pain like knives. He'd been certain the punk would realize the stories weren't true when he almost drowned the last time. His only chance was to finesse, buy time with promises until he could escape.

He'd escaped before.

But I had Rose that time.

What was the point? How long before the punk realized he was being played? An hour? Two? Then what? At sixty-eight, he no longer had the reflexes to exploit the openings inexperience would provide. His current predicament proved that.

He wished he believed in God. If there was a God, if he could see Rose again…. But the world was too cruel, too selfish to be under the auspices of a benevolent intelligence. Hypocritical to call for divine intervention now, while facing eternal nothingness.

Andrew's lungs exploded. Bubbles rushed to the surface, a school of fish in a feeding frenzy. The boot stayed. Oblivion crept along the edges of his vision.

Encroaching darkness brought awareness: whatever waited in the void, he wasn't ready to confront it. He struggled—and failed—to lift an arm exhausted by repeated torture.

In the last moments of Andrew's life, Rose occupied his mind. Rose and what had never been.

INTERLUDE

TUESDAY, MARCH 5, 2019

LIA ANDERSON STOOD IN THE ENTRY CORRAL OF THE
Mount Airy Dog Park, staring into gloom unrelieved by
the sun rising behind a solid wall of cloud cover. The
park, a repurposed picnic area surrounded by more than a
thousand acres of urban forest, was empty.

The leash looping her wrist tugged. Her silver
schnauzer hated to wait. Chewy was a simple dog, always
living in the present. Beyond the gate, there were smells to
smell, squirrels to chase, trees to mark.

She couldn't go in, not yet.

The white metal canister she held weighed less than
two pounds. There was something wrong about this
container—one that held fourteen years of love, loyalty,
and adventures; the sum total of a dog's life, a very good
dog's life—something so wrong about it weighing so little.
Worse for the container of that life to be bland and sterile,
suitable for a stash of cheap ribbon candy, the kind that

hangs around forever until it forms an ugly mass as hard as concrete.

Honey had been her center for all of her adult life: the one she counted on, her one constant through college, starting her own business, through disastrous boyfriends and the terrifying beginning of her relationship with Peter. Her heart, her rock, a better mother than her own had been, now reduced to ashes. She wondered if there would ever be anything big enough to fill the hole.

She couldn't bear putting Honey in one of the schmaltzy urns available at the crematorium, so she hadn't bought one. Bailey suggested painting the can. But her talent was for design, not emotion: pleasant arrangements of shapes and colors that some found evocative but were never intended as such. Painting the depth of her feelings for Honey was beyond her. She was left with this blank white can that showed nothing and contained everything.

Chewy tugged again.

"You don't linger in the past, do you, little man?"

He barked, leaning against the leash.

Honey's death had been almost without warning. Her healthy, happy dog stopped eating. A visit to the vet and a diagnosis of pancreatic cancer—so common in golden retrievers—days before that one bad day when she looked so miserable, couldn't be tempted with favorite treats or even hamburger, wouldn't drink water, wouldn't get up, wouldn't move at all. Then a quiet death in her sleep before Lia could decide if this was the day she had to put her down.

A blessing, not having to make that final decision, not having to watch Honey suffer the way some dogs did. But

Honey's passing drove home an important truth: Everyone leaves you. The only one who doesn't is the one you leave behind when you die.

The sound of a motor in the parking lot below drew her attention to a small, familiar truck with a cab on the back and almost as much rust as Lia's ancient Volvo 240. The woman and bloodhound who emerged were of a pair, tall and lanky and beaky, with red hair (though Bailey's retained its glory with chemical assistance), easygoing and difficult to ruffle.

Lia could never decide if Bailey's defining feature was her hands or her eyes. The hands, nicked and calloused from her gardening business, were an extension of her thoughts, mobile and fluttering and graceful as a pair of pet birds. But her eyes—large, luminous, bulging slightly —looked into you with old-soul compassion, and love that saw you as you were meant to be.

Lia waited for woman and dog to hike up the curving service road to join her. Chewy and Kita sniffed noses. Bailey said nothing, just put a warm arm around Lia's shoulder. Lia turned, folding into Bailey's embrace.

When Lia's hiccuping sobs stopped, Bailey rubbed her back. "You don't have to do this now."

Lia kept her cheek pressed into Bailey's jacket. "She wants to be here, with her friends. Not stuck in this stupid can."

"Do you want me to go with you?"

Lia turned her head from side to side, wiping tears and snot onto Bailey's jacket. "I need to do this alone."

"Okay, then. If anyone shows up, I'll shoo them away. Can I buy you breakfast afterwards?"

"I don't know if I can eat. I'll let you know when I'm done."

Bailey opened the gate. Inside the corral, Lia bent down and unclipped Chewy, stuffing his leash in a cargo pocket. She set the canister on top of the trash bin and struggled with the lid. Bailey moved in, pressing strong, scarred thumbs under the rim, pushing just enough to loosen it. "There you go." She held the inner gate open.

Lia stepped into the park. Chewy bolted, leaving long streaks in the heavily dewed grass. Lia followed behind, dribbling bits of ash and bone as she said goodbye to her dog.

DAY 1

SATURDAY, APRIL 20, 2019

TERRY DUNN SPOTTED THE PROSTHETIC LEG JUTTING FROM a branch overhanging Mill Creek. He laid his paddle across the bow of his canoe and adjusted his bifocals. Canoeists and kayakers cut around him, their snarky comments audible on the water.

He squinted at the leg, a relic of last week's flood left high by receding waters. Made of wood and corroded metal and rotting leather, it was an archaic, fantastical thing.

The tree limb and its faux-human counterpart formed a whimsical juxtaposition, as if a steampunk superhero leapt into the branches. In the next instant, the leg would whisk from view as this mysterious hero continued on a mission to prevent the assassination of President Harrison or the bombing of the New York Stock Exchange. *Danger, and the fate of the free world resting on his shoulders. At the center, a beautiful, enigmatic woman with glossy sable hair, skin like pale silk, and midnight pools for eyes.*

Terry wanted it.

In the stern, his roommate, Steve, said, "What's the problem?"

Both men were in their sixties and of similar build—though Steve was round versus stocky, had a Van Dyke instead of a brush mustache, and protected his bald scalp with a white Panama instead of the camo ball cap Terry wore over his buzz cut. Diametrically opposed in mindset, no one—including Terry and Steve—understood why they hadn't killed each other.

Terry flapped a hand in dismissal as he calculated the best path through the flotilla of canoes and kayaks participating in the Mill Creek Yacht Club's spring float.

"Hold up a minute."

Mill Creek was a glorious slice of secret wilderness, cutting invisibly through the city at the bottom of a deep gully bordered by industrial properties, railways, and highways. Captains of industry once dumped toxic waste into the waterway with impunity—a state of affairs lasting more than a century, until reclamation efforts began in the nineties.

The creek's hidden nature also meant few people were aware of the recent flood. Today's float trip—the first of the year—had been up in the air due to the fast-running water. They'd made the final decision that morning, with Commodore rubbing his chin and Dick poking his tongue in his cheek until they decided the superb weather pushed the odds in favor of proceeding.

The creek had yet to return to normal levels, spilling

over banks and climbing up the gully. Muddy tree trunks rose out of the swollen waters like columns in a forgotten temple dedicated to an ancient deity.

"Treasure, two o'clock." Terry shoved his paddle hard, fighting the current and ignoring the protests of other paddlers as he cut across their path.

Steve added muscle to the task. "I can't believe Commodore didn't spot it first."

"Too close to 666. Everyone wants their rest stop."

"Watch the rocks."

"Water's too high. It's not a problem. When we reach the tree, swing around so you're downstream."

They worked silently, maneuvering the canoe under the prosthetic. Steve jammed his paddle into submerged rocks to hold their position. The canoe rocked.

Terry laid his paddle aside. "Hold 'er steady while I stand up."

"Capsize us, and you can forget watching *The Expanse* on my Prime Video account."

Terry waved the threat off, mentally crossing his fingers that it wouldn't come to that. He stared into the canopy and planned his attack. Even a man who'd been robustly active all his life had to pay close attention to logistics when he reached the age of sixty-seven.

He positioned his feet to maintain balance, planted his hands on the bench and rose slowly, shifting to counteract the boat's movement. The leg remained four maddening inches beyond his outstretched hand.

"Too bad we didn't come last week. I could have pulled it out of those branches without standing."

"Last week a stunt like that would have put both of us

in the water with your drowned body caught in a strainer next to mine and that leg laughing at us."

"Hand me my paddle, will you?"

Steve grunted. Terry felt the paddle tap his kidney. He reached behind for it, never taking his eyes off his prize. If he nudged the leg just so ...

"I'm going to drop it in the water on the lee side. Don't let it get past you."

He ignored the eye roll most likely happening behind his back and reassessed his balance. The canoe wobbled as he raised the paddle. He edged it higher, inserting it between the prosthetic and the most likely branch. A slight twist of the blade and the leg popped out, neat as an extracted tooth. It splashed into the creek, bobbed, and drifted. Terry returned to his seat as carefully as he'd left it while Steve fished the hunk of flotsam out of the water.

Leg in hand, Terry bumped his bifocals up on the bridge of his nose and examined the fine grain of the waterlogged wood, the detailing in the metal, the elegant line where the shin swooped into the foot. He grinned at Steve. "An exceptional find."

Steve removed his panama and wiped the pink skin on top of his head. "I hope it was worth the effort. What the hell do you want with it, anyway?"

"He's a dragon, not an it. He'll make a perfect figure-head. Better than Commodore's, better than Dick's. I shall name him Smaug."

"Whatever you say, Bilbo."

Terry drew two fingers delicately along the length of the shin. The finish was long gone, but the wood was sound. He made a moan of pleasure.

"You call that thing 'Precious' and I'm dumping both of you in the water," Steve said.

"Commodore's bear will hide in shame after Smaug takes his rightful place."

Terry retrieved a tangle of bungee cords from the waterproof bag in the belly of the boat and applied himself to mounting the leg upside-down to the bow in imitation of Viking longships.

"Ahoy! What do you have there?"

Commodore, founder and longtime president of the Mill Creek Yacht Club, pulled his canoe alongside. The aqua teddy bear strapped to Commodore's *Mud Turtle* was number five, one through four having rotted off over the years.

Terry leaned back so Commodore could admire his new acquisition.

Sun glinted off Commodore's glasses as he examined the artificial limb. "A gift from the storm gods. It's been outside a long time. Wonder where it was hiding."

"Who knows? He's mine now," Terry said.

Commodore pushed off. Terry and Steve followed, rounding a bend to see the last of the kayaks turning into 666. The apocalyptically named dog leg—which terminated at Metropolitan Sewer District culvert number 666 —was a popular rest spot and the location where Commodore's second in command lectured about Mill Creek history to paddlers.

Steve rested his paddle across the gunwales and swiped a sweaty hand across a sweatier brow. "Ready for a break?"

"I could recite Dick's talk in my sleep. Push on."

13

"You just want to find any junk before everyone else."

"I'm looking for Smaug's lair. The storm may have uncovered it."

"Your dragon swam upstream?"

"It happens."

"If I don't get a break, you're buying when we get to Boswell's. Or we can trade places."

"Sure, whatever."

Terry avoided Dick Brewer's lectures because neither Dick nor Commodore appreciated his frequent interruptions and corrections. That, and he enjoyed having this part of Mill Creek to himself.

Creosote-soaked pilings introduced the final stretch to the barrier dam and the Ohio River. Giant truck tires and shopping carts marred the view, impossible to remove after decades mired in mud.

Decommissioned bridges and unidentifiable concrete structures lifted his geek heart. Here he was Samwise, encountering ancient ruins as the Fellowship of the Ring floated down the Great River Anduin.

As they rounded the next bend, a dozen heron rose from the trees. Terry followed their flight into the sliver of sky above the gully.

Steve's voice intruded. "Will you look at *that*."

A fallen cottonwood spanned the channel. Debris piled on the partially submerged crown, narrowing the waterway to a dangerous degree. The resulting funnel forced a waterway carrying several times its usual volume to more than double its already accelerated speed.

Millions of gallons passed under the trunk with less

than three feet of clearance. Hit the trunk, and it would knock your head off.

Terry stilled his paddle. The current tugged, insistent, dragging the canoe downstream.

"Make for the bank."

"Left or right?"

Slower water on the crown side. Easier portage around the roots. Roots it was.

"Left."

They fought to the quieter water along the bank. Terry steered the canoe between rocks, lodging the aluminum craft in the soft bank.

"This is a fine mess," Steve snarked. "We'll be lucky to get around."

Terry ignored Steve's grumbling and calculated. The ground was a mire that could suck your boots off. Beyond the crater, a thirty-foot mudslide exposed railroad tracks at the top of the bank. Sun shone through the ties, casting long, striped shadows down the bank.

He and Steve might safely portage around the tree, but every person who followed increased the risk of further collapse, sending tons of earth on their heads. Half of the paddlers on today's trip were first timers, not prepared for a touchy situation.

Terry's stomach growled. He could forget lunch at Boswell's. He wondered how long they would be stuck, how they would get everyone out.

Behind him, Steve's grumbling continued unabated. "You know my back. I get the front end."

Steve's back injury only appeared when convenient,

but Terry didn't argue. They wouldn't move the canoe any time soon. "We need to check this out before the others get here."

"I'll do it. I need to stretch my legs."

Terry waited in the boat, rummaging his bag for an abused power bar while Steve slogged around the enormous fan of exposed roots.

"Holy moly. You're gonna want to see this."

Terry's irritation vanished. "Treasure?"

"A find, for sure."

Terry hauled himself up the bank, rounding the rim of the muddy crater until he stood beside Steve. He scanned the wall of muck and twining roots and shook his head. "I don't see anything."

"Step back and shade your eyes."

An image emerged from the depths of the tangle, dark, incomprehensible shapes taking form. Bits of corroded brass in a fan-like pattern, then a spray of the studs— that's what they were—leading downward. He was looking at a jumpsuit nested in and pierced by roots: tiny, organic filaments, meandering tendrils, ancient, fat, snakes.

The jumpsuit might have been black, though who could say? He followed a pant leg downward. Bell bottoms? Hard to tell. He scanned the morass for the other leg and found a shoe. Above the shoe a bone floated, suspended in the roots and stained brown from decades in the earth.

His eyes shot up. A foot above his head, a mottled skull presided over all, tucked between the remains of a collar that must have reached the man's ears when he still had them. Centipedes, beetles, and a variety of unidentifiable insects swarmed the figure, giving it the gruesome appearance of movement and life.

Terry turned away, gagging as he pulled a sweat-soaked bandana from around his neck. He mopped his face with the damp cloth.

"Please don't say it."

"Looks like Elvis got back to his roots."

LIA STEPPED AWAY FROM HER EASEL, NEEDING TO SEE THE canvas from normal viewing distance. The single iris bloom lacked the depth she wanted. *Too blue.*

She looked at the clock. An hour until she and Peter left for the latest Avengers film. Plenty of time to glaze the petals and clean up.

In the corner, Chewy curled in the center of Honey's bed. It was three sizes bigger than he needed and the stuffing leaked from a tear in the side. Chewy had a newer, nicer studio bed, but he preferred this one. She couldn't bring herself to throw it out.

"I know, little man. I miss her too."

Chewy sighed. In the apartment overhead, Peter's phone rang.

She turned her attention back to the painting, loading her brush with acra violet, stroking it along the foreground petal. The canvas would be ready for another layer by Tuesday, Monday if she was lucky. Ten days till her showing with David's new client. Fingers crossed the iris would be finished in time.

She loved her new studio. Northern light filled the octagon sun porch at the rear of the Victorian she'd recently bought. The spacious backyard would soon be a riot of color. By July she'd be harvesting her own heirloom tomatoes. *I can have gazpacho every day if I want.*

Home ownership was an unexpected pleasure after a lifetime of apartment living. Right now she was in the honeymoon phase, with property taxes, repairs, and lawn maintenance yet to materialize. She wondered how long it would take to adjust to the realities that came with taking on the huge Victorian and decided denial was a wonderful thing.

Feet clomped down the back stairs, followed by the murmur of Peter's voice on the phone. Lia gave the painting a critical look. *Too red.* Peter would call the color something like "cherry after a bar fight." She dragged a rag across the surface to pick up the excess paint.

Chewy whuffed.

Viola padded in, a panting, black chow-lab shadow with a blacker temperament. Peter followed, all long legs on a runner's build, phone to ear as he shoved dirt-brown hair out of the midnight blue eyes that kept his face from being ordinary. His face tensed, like Viola spotting a nemesis cat.

She could forget the movies.

She cocked an eyebrow. He held up a finger. Long pause. Peter's eyebrows slowly raised until they disappeared under his hair.

"We're on our way. Don't let anyone near it.... No photos. I don't want to see this on Facebook.... I'll call you back as soon as I know."

He pocketed the phone and ran a hand through his hair again, a sign he was sorting through his thoughts.

"What happened?" Lia asked.

"Terry and Steve found a skeleton dressed like an Elvis impersonator on Mill Creek."

"Oh?"

"I called it in. They want me to handle the scene."

"That's Homicide. Why tag you?"

"Homicide is jammed up and I'm the nearest warm body. I'm hoping you'll come with me."

"Me?"

He flashed her a look, half exasperation, half begging.

"They're your friends. I need you to keep an eye on Terry. You know how he is."

Terry's itch for detectival pursuits—born when Lia's ex-boyfriend turned up dead at the dog park—manifested as an unwholesome marriage between a kid in a candy store and a bull in a china shop.

"They're your friends, too."

"More like inconvenient in-laws. We could be gone a long time. Will you take the dogs to Alma's?" Alma, their septuagenarian neighbor, was Peter's surrogate grandmother and nanny to Viola and Chewy.

"It'll be a wrench, but I'm willing to give Chris Hemsworth a pass. This time."

Peter gave her a solid hug and kissed her forehead. "Not what we planned, but at least we'll spend part of the afternoon together. Get your creek clothes on. We're meeting Cynth at the launch site in twenty minutes."

Lia watched Peter's retreating back. She grumbled to Chewy, "Everything I own is creek clothes."

AN EIGHT-FOOT CHAIN-LINK FENCE SURROUNDED THE CITY garage in Millvale where Terry's group launched their float trips. Lia drove through the gate, the tires of Peter's Blazer biting gravel as she headed for a huddle of vehicles at the far end of the otherwise empty lot. Beyond the vans and SUVs, the overfull creek lapped at the ground.

Cynth McFadden stood up in the back of her Ford Ranger as they approached, waving them over. Her creek clothes consisted of neat khaki shorts, a royal blue golf shirt, and a matching ball cap with "POLICE" embroidered on the front, her long, wheat-colored braid threaded through the hole in the back. At her feet, a trio of kayaks jutted out the tailgate.

Peter ended the phone call he'd been on since they left home. "Water's too high. They never should have gone out in this."

"At least we won't have to climb down the bank. The entire lot must have been under water last week. I wonder what they did with the trucks."

"Garbage trucks have tall wheels. They can handle a foot of water."

As Peter and Lia exited the Blazer, Cynth grabbed one end of a kayak. "You sure have interesting friends."

Peter took the other end. "Consider them job security."

"Lucky you."

The detectives worked in perfect, wordless tandem, sliding boats onto the grass. It was intimidating, the way Peter and his fellow officers intuited need and responded, operating from a kind of hive mind Peter said you developed after you breeched a dozen or so drug houses together. Lia grabbed the double-ended paddles from the bed of the truck and wondered if she and Peter would ever have that near-telepathic rapport.

Kayaks sorted, Cynth pulled a day pack from the cab and tossed it on the grass. "What's the plan?"

Peter grabbed a duffel filled with granola bars they'd picked up along the way and dropped it next to the largest kayak. "The site is approximately two miles downstream—"

"We couldn't put in closer?"

"All fenced industrial property. It'll take more time to find a place to put in than it would to just go. Amanda and Junior are on their way. They'll take one of the club canoes." Peter jerked his chin at a pair of giant aluminum canoes upside down on the grass. "Not an ideal way to carry out remains, but it's the best we can do under the circumstances."

"What's my role?"

"We have three dozen people trapped by a downed tree."

"Crowd management, then. Do you need me to take statements?"

"The organizer has contact information for everyone.

The detective assigned to this can interview anyone he wants later. No need to make work for ourselves when someone else will just want to redo it."

Peter pulled two life vests from the back of his Blazer, handing one to Lia. "You're in the blue kayak. Let's get moving."

FAST, MUDDY WATER CARRIED LIA DOWNSTREAM WITH little effort on her part. Peter and Cynth paddled ahead, strategizing and considering potential scenarios. Their voices mixed with the splashing of paddles as Lia's muscles warmed to the exercise. She relaxed despite their grim destination, taking in the unexpected wilderness and allowing her mind to wander.

Wooded banks grew higher as they paddled south, climbing thirty feet or more. Drowned trees rose eerily out of the water, a layer of mud marking the flood level, bits of trash caught in lower limbs. Above the flood line, the pale green of young leaves dusted the sinuous tracery of branches.

Lia made a career of painting flowers. Flowers made people happy, and she enjoyed the interplay of shapes and colors. But her first love was trees.

Trees were strong and soulful. She felt them in her core, especially in winter and early spring when they were bare of foliage, naked and yearning.

Each tree had its own internal logic expressed in replicating patterns. DNA she supposed, though she preferred to think of it as a defining quality, or even personality: crooked branches with the frayed ends of neural pathways; flowing like tears; stiffly straight and pointed; Machiavellian tangles; sweeping up and inward like hands cupped in prayer.

The way a twig joined a branch and the direction it grew mimicked branch to bough and bough to trunk, until you had thousands of tiny terminations reaching into the future, every one of them expressions of the same idea. And hidden in the earth, a structure equal in size to the crown, boring through obstacles as if seeking the past.

There had to be something profound buried in these thoughts, but her musings always stopped before she was forced to consider her own past and the bits of it she carried forward. She found the hypnotic rhythms of trees soothing. That was all.

Startled flocks of long-legged waterfowl flew up, delighting her. Wooded banks gave way to a section of creek that had been paved from the bed to the top of the bank, forming a giant concrete channel. Lia looked up into the sky, feeling like a leaf drifting in the bottom of a storm ditch.

The trees returned, punctuated by industrial concrete structures: small, blocky buildings and platforms accessible by intriguing steel rungs, something you'd see in dystopian films—*The Hunger Games* or *Logan's Run*. Lia filed the images away, determined to return for plein air painting.

Peter's voice floated across the water. "We're here."

Lia pulled her eyes from an intriguing arrangement of

creosote-soaked pilings lining the shore. Canoes and kayaks dotted the water ahead, spilling around a bend where the creek narrowed between high banks.

They rounded the curve to find the giant tree interfering with everyone's Saturday plans. Upended roots and a mudslide blocked the left bank, the slope a gaping, open wound. The trunk spanned the creek, crown dragging in the water and filling the right bank of the gully to the rim, branches choking with flood debris.

Cheers and applause rose. Lia imagined the boaters were bored, cranky, and ready to leave. Peter and Cynth stopped paddling, waving at the crowd while waiting for her to catch up.

Cynth said, "Quite the party."

"Party's over now," Peter said. "Or it will be."

"What next?" Cynth asked.

Peter jerked his chin at the shore. Terry and Steve manned an aluminum monstrosity with an inverted mannequin leg mounted on the prow. A tall, skinny man with a halo of white hair worthy of Einstein floated in a matching canoe fronted by a bedraggled teddy bear and bearing the name *Mud Turtle*. Beside him, an aquatic version of the Marlboro Man had deer antlers strapped to his boat.

"The guys with Terry must be in charge. I'm hoping they have a plan to get these folks out of here without destroying the scene. Lia's job is to distract Terry."

"Thanks a lot," Lia said.

"Fun for everyone," Cynth said.

Peter handed Lia the snack-filled duffel bag. "Can you pass these out?"

Lia took the bag, heading for the nearest canoe. Paddlers flocked to her granola bars like ducks to bread crusts. A young guy asked if the bars were paleo. Lia offered him a bar and said, "Air is paleo." He shrugged and grinned, then took the bar.

After a brief bank-side conference, Einstein paddled to the middle of the creek, gesturing for the group to gather. His high voice rang loud and clear over the water.

"Thank you for your patience. Now that Detectives Dourson and McFadden are here, we can finish our float. Due to the unusual circumstances, we need to forgo our usual foray through the dam."

The crowd booed.

Einstein continued, "We will still hold the initiation ceremony for new paddlers. Boswell's is expecting us."

A voice from the crowd: "How are we getting out of here?"

"We're shooting the sluice. Neither bank is passable, and paddling upstream in this current is a no go. Unless you want to hike out and find your own way back to your cars, the only way out is through. There's enough clearance if you sit in the bottom of your canoe and keep your paddles inside. I'll direct you in. Dick—"

Einstein nodded at the man Lia dubbed Cowboy, whose canoe had edged next to her kayak while Einstein talked. Dick held up a hand and waved. He was sandy haired, with a healthy mustache. Chiseled bones preserved a face ravaged by sun and time. Late forties, early fifties? A tarnished medallion and the absence of a toothpick in his mouth saved him from being a cliché.

Dick caught her looking at him. He tipped his battered straw cowboy hat and winked.

Einstein, oblivious to Dick's flirting, nodded at a twenty-something man in vibrant sport gear. "—and Paul will be on the far side to catch you. If we have problems, we'll reassess." He pointed at a spot along the right-hand bank. "Line up over there. We'll send you through one at a time."

The crowd muttered, grumbling mixed with sharp sounds of agitation. No one volunteered to hike out.

Lia turned to Dick. "Why the fuss? The creek can't be that deep."

He pointed at the crown. "The tree and debris form a natural dam. You have several times the normal volume of water forced through a fraction of the space it needs. The only way it can respond is to speed up. We're asking people to pass through blind, with no control. You have submerged rocks, pilings. If you capsize, the current is too fast to stand up. You could drown."

"Oh," Lia said.

"If you fall in, don't fight it. Hold your breath and wait for the creek to widen out. The current will slow and you can swim for shore. We're sorry about this. If we'd known about the tree, we would have canceled the trip. Haven't you paddled the creek before?"

Lia shook her head. "I've only been on lakes."

"Different animal," Dick said.

Terry and Steve joined Lia as she paddled to the line forming along the shore. She leaned over from her kayak and hissed, "You could have called 911. This isn't even Peter's district."

"Trust a discovery so portentous to strangers? Certainly not," Terry said.

"We had plans," Lia said.

"Admit it," Steve said to Terry. "You called Peter because you want to poke your nose in."

"The thought never crossed my mind."

"I'm sure it didn't," Lia said.

"Of course, If Peter sees fit to ask for my help—"

Steve snorted.

"—It's an evocative scene. The tree is exceptionally large. I would expect it to be a hundred years old or more."

"That jumpsuit is pure disco," Steve said. "That makes your bony friend a time traveler because you can't bury a body under an established tree."

"You could if—"

A cheer erupted. Dick's canoe and the *Mud Turtle* sat alone in the center of the creek, a safe distance from the sluice. A man in the rear of the *Mud Turtle* fought the current while Commodore held the gunwale of Dick's canoe. Dick pulled his paddle in and lowered himself to the bottom of the boat.

"We'll all have wet pants when this is over," Steve said.

The crowd fell silent. Commodore gave Dick's canoe a shove. The current caught, whipping the canoe under the trunk. Lia counted off the seconds. One ... two ... Three ... Four....

Cowboy Dick shouted from the other side of the tree. "Clear!"

More whoops. Paul's kayak approached the launching point.

"Slick as grease from a goose," Steve said.

More cheers as the second boat passed under the tree.

Dick called from the other side. "Clear!"

Orderly as patrons at a bank, the line inched forward, the passage of each boat punctuated with celebratory whoops.

Lia scanned the shore, expecting to see Peter and Cynth doing something cop-like. The pair stood, watching the procession of canoes. *Probably making sure everyone gets out safely.*

"What are people saying about the bones? Anything interesting?"

"Whiners, all of them," Terry said. "Claimed they had a right to see Elvis. I held them off at great peril."

Lia looked hard at Terry. "You didn't sneak a souvenir?"

Terry's eyes widened in shocked affront. "Moi, interfere with a crime scene?"

"There are no stray bones in your pocket?"

"Certainly not!"

"I may ask you to turn them out when we reach dry land."

"I kept an eye on him," Steve said. "He's clean."

"Okay then."

Terry huffed. "You accept Steve's word and not mine? Outrageous!"

Lia and Steve shared an eye roll.

Lia asked, "Any theories that don't involve Elvis, time travel, or little green men?"

Steve removed his Panama hat and wiped his skull

with a handkerchief. "Commodore started the club back in the nineties. If anyone knows anything, it's him."

"Is he the guy who looks like a cross between Larry Byrd and Einstein?"

Steve guffawed. "That's him."

"What's he saying?"

Terry's face took on a mutinous expression. "He hasn't said a word."

Lia imagined Terry had spent the hour it took for her, Peter, and Cynth to arrive at the site pumping the Commodore for information. "Does Commodore have a real name?"

"He's Bruce. Bruce Koehler." Steve said.

"How long have you known him?"

Terry scratched the scruff on his chin. "First time I went out on the creek was ... when was it? Five years ago, September. I met him at a cleanup in Sharonville."

Commodore gave Lia a reassuring smile as he grabbed the side of her kayak. The boat bobbed, pulled by the current. Commodore was much stronger than he looked.

"Is your paddle tethered to your kayak?"

Lia nodded.

"Hold it lengthwise along the top of your kayak, bend over and relax. Dick will catch you when you clear the tree. Just pretend this is Congo Falls at King's Island."

Lia draped herself over the top of the kayak with her arms extended forward, the double-headed paddle pinned under one arm. She turned her head to the side, one cheek pressed into the top of the boat, giving her a view of Commodore's life vest.

Commodore asked, "Ready?"

Lia took a deep breath, pretended she was doing yoga, and relaxed further into the pose. "Ready."

The kayak jumped forward. Lia's stomach lurched, her heart racing as the bank flew past. One ... two ... Three.... She counted eight seconds. The kayak slowed, then jolted as someone grabbed the side.

"Clear!"

The crowd whooped as Lia pushed herself upright.

Cowboy Dick grinned at her, the sun catching his silver medallion. "You okay?"

Lia ignored the blood rushing in her head. "Yeah, I think so."

He nodded at the boats congregating downstream. "Hang out until we get everyone through. Then we'll head to the dam."

THE REST OF THE TRIP WAS UNEVENTFUL, ENDING IN A lake-sized basin beneath slopes ten stories high. Water moseyed through the retracted barrier dam, exhausted from the frantic pace at the sluice.

A rocky path dove into the water, leading to a submerged landing. Veteran paddlers hauled people and boats onto the bank while younger backs ported boats to the top.

Lia was grateful for the assist. Sweaty, hungry, and drained from exertion and nerves, she barely made it up the hill. She considered skipping Boswell's, but Terry was driving and it was easier to go along for the ride. And if she ate, she might head off a crash.

THEY ARRIVED AT BOSWELL'S ALLEY TO FIND THE YACHT Club invasion in full swing. Creek-worn paddlers milled the pub, shouting above ESPN on the large-screen TV mounted over the bar, sound bouncing off exposed brick walls like ping pong balls.

Someone grabbed Terry and Steve. Lia followed the current of migrating bodies to a back patio, where the first to arrive dragged glass-topped tables together. A small, forty-something woman flipped through her pad, scribbling orders on separate checks.

"What'll you have to drink?" the waitress asked, starting a new page.

Lia looked over the woman's head, searching for Bruce Koehler, A.K.A. Commodore Einstein. "Sweet tea. And I'd like a Boursin burger and onion rings."

"Smart, getting your order in early. I'll have your tea right out."

Lia located Bruce and took the empty seat beside him. "I wasn't expecting to put on a performance when we landed."

The promised initiation had consisted of two rows of old timers clacking paddles overhead, forming a gauntlet. Inductees passed through in whatever manner they desired, the loudest cheers awarded to newbies with the most athletic and imaginative moves. Lia had executed a series of pirouettes while making a mental note to get even with Terry for putting her on the list. At least she got a free T-shirt out of the deal.

Bruce grinned. "You did a wonderful job."

The waitress returned with a loaded tray, setting a pitcher of beer and a half-dozen mugs on the table. Bruce poured, saving the first mug for himself and handing the rest to anyone within reach. He offered the last mug to Lia.

"Thanks, but I have tea coming."

"You're an adaptable woman. I know this wasn't how you planned to spend your Saturday."

"This was more interesting. I pass over the creek all the time but I never think about it."

"Most people don't, and they have no clue how vital the creek is to Cincinnati."

"I talked to Dick Brewer after we landed. He said he met you when you were taking water samples."

Bruce scratched his chin. "That was right after he retired from the army. The club was in full swing by then."

"Why do you take samples?"

"We monitor the creek for the organizations that make up the Mill Creek Alliance. A hundred years ago, the city economized by tying sewer overflow into the storm sewers. In those days, pig carcasses from the slaughter-houses were so deep in our branch of the Erie canal—where Central Parkway is today—people said you could cross the water by walking on them."

Lia wanted that image out of her head before her burger arrived.

While Lia's stomach rebelled, Bruce continued,

"They're slowly separating the lines. Three decades ago, we had raw sewage in the creek every time we got a hard rain. Factories still dumped toxic waste. You saw a chemical sheen on the water every afternoon."

Lia swallowed hard and pushed on. "You wouldn't know it now. Except for the concrete channel, it looks like a nature preserve."

"The concrete was an error in judgment by the Army Corps of Engineers. We've learned that trees and other vegetation do a better job of preserving the banks and are better for the overall health of the creek. Dick caught a trout in the Cumminsville stretch last year. We're exceptionally proud of that."

"You're proud of a trout?"

"This particular species has a delicate constitution. Finding one three miles upstream is evidence of our success. In 1997, Mill Creek was named the most endangered urban waterway in America. Our combined efforts have turned it into one of the cleanest. Sewer water still runs into the creek, but it's treated except in the hardest storms. It's important to have the sewers tied into Mill Creek."

"Why is that?"

"It's the only way to ensure we have water running through the creek year-round. You've got to have running water to support the habitat, or it will dry up and die. The added water keeps the creek alive."

"You've been involved with the creek for a long time."

"Since the early nineties. Back then everyone talked about Mill Creek, but nobody had laid eyes on it. I said we needed to go down and see for ourselves. That's when I started the club. We're the unofficial eyes for the Mill Creek Alliance."

Dick Brewer tossed his straw hat on the table and snagged Lia's rejected mug. He took a long swallow, winking at her. "Hey, Bruce, how long have you been waiting for that cottonwood to come down?"

"Longer than I've known you," Bruce said. "I sat under that tree. Didn't know it harbored an escaped Elvis impersonator."

Lia asked, "You saw the bones?"

"We had to assess the bank."

Terry and Steve dragged chairs over and shoehorned in. "They wouldn't take my word for it."

The waitress arrived with Lia's burger and another pitcher. Bruce poured a mug, handing it to Steve. "Thirty people to think about. Had to make sure. They'll have a job of it, getting those bones out."

Lia took a guilty bite of burger. Peter and Cynth would be stuck on the creek, slogging through mud for hours with only a handful of granola bars.

Terry's hand snuck over her onion rings. She smacked it, earning a wounded look. "Get your own," she said. "How do you suppose the bones wound up there?"

Bruce rubbed his chin. "A more interesting question is whether Elvis was buried there or not."

"What do you mean?" Lia asked.

"Creek banks aren't stable. There's a thing called slippage. Trees at the top of a bank migrate down to the water and eventually fall. That's why we lobby for a sixty-five foot easement along the creek, to allow for new growth to maintain bank stability. That cottonwood might have started out by the railroad tracks."

"Someone buried that poor man by the tracks and planted a tree to hide him?" Lia asked.

"Could be," Dick said. "But if he did, he's stupid."

"Why do you say that?"

Bruce refilled his beer. "Cottonwoods have shallow roots. Every time we run across a downed tree, it's a cottonwood. Should have planted a sycamore. Deep roots, hardly ever fall. I'm glad I don't have to collect those bones."

Terry turned to Dick. "You're the construction guy, how would you get them out?"

"Not my bailiwick," Dick said. "I couldn't hazard to say."

"You need to give Lia your card. She bought a Victorian. Nobody's done anything to it in decades."

"Are you forgetting the painting party?" Steve said. "And the floors?"

Terry waved a hand. "Cosmetics. I bet the wires are shot. The porch could use attention. Then there's the attic—"

"The attic is fine," Lia said.

"Stuffed full of Ruth Peltier's junk?" Terry said.

"Some of it has historical significance."

"If you call Beanie Babies and Hughes High School memorabilia significant."

Bruce raised an eyebrow.

"Ruth owned the house until she died," Lia explained. "We're working our way through the last of her property."

Bruce grinned. "Eye of the beholder. I'm sure she treasured her Beanie Babies."

"They were gifts from students," Lia said.

Terry filched an onion ring. "She put up with hordes of delinquents for thirty years. Why remember them after they're gone? Your brickwork needs tuck pointing."

Lia searched for something, anything to change the subject. Her eyes settled on Dick's medallion, an elegant silver relief of a walking bull mounted in a bronze setting. "That's a lovely piece," she said, tapping her chest just below her collarbone.

Terry waved the stolen onion ring in the air, dripping ketchup. "It's a public service announcement. He wears it because he's full of bull."

Terry was on a roll.

"What you said about slippage," Lia said to Bruce, "Is it possible he was buried lower on the bank and a mature tree migrated over the grave? That would explain how someone dressed for disco wound up under an older tree."

"I'm sure that tree isn't as old as you think," Bruce said. "Cottonwoods grow fast."

Dick nodded. "Faster if it has a body to feed on."

VIOLA MET PETER WHEN HE ARRIVED HOME, A BLACK smudge ghosting down the steps in the darkened hall, a soft woof in welcome, waving her silky mop of tail. He knelt to ruffle her neck fur.

"How are you, girl?"

She ducked out of his arms and headed up the stairs.

Peter followed, peeling off the T-shirt that was now only fit for changing oil. He gave it a sniff and tossed it on the bathroom floor, so as not to contaminate the clothes in his hamper. His jeans and sneakers followed. Viola stood far from the pile, grinning.

"Smart girl," he said. "I know I stink."

Peter stood in the shower as pounding water eased sore muscles and washed the accumulated stress and muck of the day away. Some people meditated. This was better. You couldn't find showers like this in newer houses. He silently blessed Ruth Peltier for never updating the plumbing.

When the water turned tepid, he stepped out to find Viola lapping up a puddle on the floor. She lifted her muzzle and began licking stray drops off his shin. Peter pulled his leg out of reach and grabbed a towel. "Not that I don't appreciate the assist, but that's not proper behavior for a daughter of the house."

He wrapped the towel around his waist and padded barefoot into the kitchen. "Let's find you a biscuit."

Three biscuits later, Peter traded his towel for a robe and turned to the stairs. Viola barked, ran back to the kitchen, turned in the doorway and barked again in a classic Lassie move. There were biscuits trapped in a box, screaming for rescue in a frequency only a dog could hear.

"Not now. I have to see my other best girl."

Viola's tail dropped. Peter thought he heard a canine snort, but she fell in behind him as he went downstairs.

Urban light pollution bled through the windows, illuminating the way. Peter appreciated the ability to navigate the dark without fumbling for light switches, but he missed seeing the stars. He needed to find time to take Lia camping, someplace where you couldn't see your hand at night and the Milky Way dazzled the sky.

Chewy lifted his muzzle as Peter opened the door to Lia's room. Viola settled onto her downstairs dog bed, dropped her head onto her paws and looked away. Used to her moods, Chewy curled back into his favored sleeping position, executing a kind of canine shrug.

Across the room, Lia's moon-pale face rested easy in sleep, hair spilling across the pillow, the swoop of her neck disappearing under her quilt. He sat beside her and brushed a strand of hair off her cheek.

She stirred, blinked, and smiled. "Hey, Kentucky Boy."

"Hey, Tonto."

"Today I'm Tonto?"

"Thanks for having my back today."

"I didn't do much." She sat up and scooted over to give Peter room.

Peter sat against the headboard, drew Lia to him so her back snugged against his chest. He wrapped his arms around her and dropped a kiss on her shoulder.

"It wasn't the day we wanted, but you made it easy for me to do what needed to be done. You always do."

"Glad to be of service."

"Hear anything interesting while you were hanging out?"

"Einstein—"

"Bruce?"

"That's him. He thinks the body was buried up by the railroad tracks. He says trees migrate down creek banks and then fall over. He called it slippage."

"That's a fancy trick, a corpse moving underground."

"You think someone did that on purpose, planted a tree on top of that body so it would move?"

"If the killer planted that tree, I imagine he did it to keep the body from being found. I don't think he would have done it if he knew the tree would fall over. That's counterproductive."

"Dick said Commodore has been watching that tree for years, expecting it to come down. What do you suppose that means?"

"That just means he's tuned in to the creek. If he knew what was under there, I don't imagine he'd say anything about it to anyone, do you?"

Lia yawned. "I'm sure you're right. What time is it, anyway?"

"Almost midnight."

"What took so long?"

It was a question, not an accusation. Unlike Viola, Lia was not in a snit over being neglected.

"Amanda and Junior had to cut the whole mess away from the tree, roots and all."

"How'd they manage that?"

"Like disarming a bomb with a thousand red wires. Surgery with a Sawzall and pruning shears. Amanda cussed a blue streak the whole time."

"Poor Junior."

"I wouldn't worry about Junior. You could hit him with a hammer and he'd just go about whatever he was doing."

"Poor you, then."

"Cynth and I were conveniently banished to the creek

to see if parts of Not Elvis—that's what Amanda calls him —were laying on the bottom. Which was pointless because the water was too muddy to see anything."

"Maybe she wanted you out of the way."

"Fine by me. We spent most of the afternoon on the water, mostly out of earshot. After that we sieved a hundred gallons of muck to make sure nothing important was left behind. Then there was Junior, going over the area with a metal detector."

"Sounds like you needed a bigger team."

Peter sighed. "No room on the site for a larger team and no one else available with all hands processing that club shooting across town. It wasn't ideal, but it was the best we could do under the circumstances. You also have to factor in the quality of any evidence we were likely to get. It's not like we'd find tire treads or fingerprints that needed to be preserved. I would have been home hours ago, but we went into the station to take care of paper-work. I want it in Parker's hands first thing Monday morning."

"Why don't you want the case?"

Lia had become expert at reading between his lines.

"We won't solve it."

"You won't?"

"Cold cases get solved two ways. Technological advances allow us to extract new information from evidence collected at the time. Even if we figure out who he is and where he was killed, any evidence that existed at the time is degraded, has been painted or paved over, or is just plain lost."

"I love a man with a positive attitude. What's the other way?"

"Smart ass. Someone knew all along and finally decides to talk. By the clothes, those bones date back to Jimmy Carter's presidency. Anyone who knew anything is dead or has Alzheimer's."

"Still, it would be interesting."

"Sure. Interesting like Jack the Ripper. Thousands of experts examined the evidence for more than a century, and all we have are a dozen theories no one will ever prove."

"I liked the case Patricia Cornwell made for Walter Sickert."

"Only because you think his paintings stink. I'm betting on the guy who discovered the first victim. Smart money says he was in the middle of butchering Polly Nichols when he heard the cart coming, and covered himself by running out and raising the alarm. But it doesn't matter. There's no way to prove anything.

"Not Elvis has the potential to stall a career and haunt the poor slob who gets him. He'll spend his retirement drinking in the basement while he reviews the file he stole from the department and wonders what he missed."

"Thus the expedited paperwork, to end your involvement before it begins."

"Plenty of crime in the here and now. Solving those means justice for the living and preventing future crimes. I'd rather do work that makes lives better. Not Elvis is only good for click bait and the book someone is bound to write."

"When you put it that way, I see your point. Did you eat?"

"Cynth and I split a pizza. That's one advantage of the move to College Hill. La Rosa's right across the street. It's not Dewey's but it will do."

"Don't ever let the locals hear you say that." Lia turned in his arms, pressed a cheek to his shoulder and ran a finger down the lapel of his robe. "I imagine you're tired."

Peter smiled into her hair. "Woman Who Expects So Little, I'm never that tired."

FIRE

MONDAY, FEBRUARY 3, 1936

THE SIRENS WOKE MAL. THE LIGHT OUTSIDE HIS WINDOW made him get up to look. He lived in a room over a grocery store on Monmouth Street, and with all the neon on all the joints on the strip, the night was never dark. But this was too bright for 3 a.m.

He raised the sash and poked his head into the freezing air. A glow lit the sky, rising behind the storefronts. He sniffed. Plenty of smoke this time of year, but this was acrid and dirty. He dressed, grabbed a quart bottle of beer from under his bed, shrugged on his coat and headed up to the roof.

Old man Morton sat on a crate, hands burrowed in his pockets. He jerked his chin at the darkness.

"Damn shame, that."

Miles south of town, red and gold flames rose from the top of a hill, shooting several stories into the air. The color danced, mesmerizing and alive like the inside of a

43

hot crucible. Black smoke poured into the sky, blotting out the stars overhead. He bet people could see the show from the high places across the river in Cincinnati.

Mal's breath fogged in the frigid air. He stamped his feet to shake the cold and took a pull of beer.

"What is it?" he asked.

"That's the Beverly Hills, son. We won't see her like again."

The Beverly Hills. A gambling palace fit for Hollywood and royalty, where swells from all over threw their money away. Gutter rats like him never made it past the door, though he could handle cards with the best of them.

And someone torched it.

Mal sat on the crate and shivered in the bitter cold. He offered his bottle to Morton, watching dreams burn while the smoke stink sank into his clothes and skin.

DAY 2

SUNDAY, APRIL 21 , 2019

LIA PEERED INSIDE THE LAUNDRY BASKET SITTING ON HER usual picnic table and forgot about the friends crowding around her. Curled in a gray blanket, a tiny ball of splotchy brown and black fur stared at Lia with startled eyes as blue as an October sky. Her hands reached out of their own volition and picked up the puppy, bringing her face to face.

The puppy licked her nose with desperate affection. Tears prickled Lia's eyes as she cuddled the warm body against her shoulder, fur soft as petals, pulsing with the beat of the tiny heart. She inhaled the earthy scent that was paradoxically light and sweet: comforting as baking bread, intoxicating like nothing else in the world, and the reason puppies found homes.

She cleared the lump in her throat. "Where did she come from?"

"Forget where she came from," Peter said. "What is she?"

"She's eighty-seven point five percent Catahoula leopard cur," Bailey said. "The last of her litter. I'd keep her, but Kita is too old and cranky."

"Cata-what?" Peter asked.

"Catahoula, from Louisiana. Her ancestors hunted the bayous with their Native American humans. They climb trees."

"Just what you need," Peter said. "A swamp monster."

Lia stroked the velvet head. "You hush. Bailey wants me to take her so she can still play with her. What's the twelve point five percent?"

"Great-granddad was a husky."

"That's fine," Lia said. "Mixed breeds are healthier."

"You don't need a puppy," Peter said.

Lia lifted the pup again, rubbed noses. "This little girl is exactly what I need."

"How many years since you house trained a dog? Do you remember what you're in for?"

"The polyurethane can handle it."

"Your shoes will never be the same."

"Flip-flops are cheap."

"Do I get any say in this?"

"Not if your answer is no." Lia sat at the table, facing out with the puppy on her lap. "Has she had her shots?"

"Not a one," Bailey said.

Chewy jumped on the bench, muzzle extended to sniff the intruder. Pup backed into Lia's stomach, barking furiously. Viola leaned against Peter, asserting her proprietary rights.

"What will you name her?" Steve asked.

"I don't know her well enough to name her," Lia said.

Jim, a grizzled cross between Saint Francis of Assisi and Treebeard, extended a finger. Pup latched on, chewing. "She has blue eyes like Frank Sinatra. Call her Frankie."

"Her eyes will change," Bailey said. "The left already has a hazel tint in one spot."

"She looks like a chocolate chip cookie," Jim said. "Call her Cookie."

"More like chocolate chunk," Terry said. "C. C."

"Chocolate chunk cookie is three words," Steve said. "That makes her C. C. C."

"C. C. C. sounds like stuttering," Terry said. "Call her Harvey."

Lia huffed, "I'm not naming her after a six-foot rabbit."

"Not the rabbit. Harvey was the demon dog who told Son of Sam to kill people."

"So not funny," Lia said.

"Mulch," Peter said. "That's what she looks like."

She pressed her lips to the pup's ear and whispered, "Ignore them. They're just being jerks."

"She looks mysterious," Bailey said. "If she were mine, I'd name her Tarot or Astro."

"Or Woo-Woo," Peter said.

"Astro like the Jetsons?" Jim asked.

"No, no, and no," Lia said.

"What about artists?" Bailey asked. "Someone who painted in browns?"

"I can't stand the cubists and she doesn't look like a

Rembrandt." Lia bit her lip. "Chiaroscuro might work, but vet assistants would have fits trying to pronounce it."

Bailey tilted her head. "Shorten it. Chiaro."

Lia looked into the blue eyes. "Is your name Chiaro?"

Pup wiggled and sneezed. Lia returned the pup to her shoulder, the tiny nose cool where it nuzzled her neck.

"Guess not."

"You have to call her something," Bailey said.

"She'll be 'Pup' until I figure it out. Can I borrow the basket? You never know where parvo is lurking. My arms will fall off if I have to hold her until we get home."

Bailey reached into the basket, retrieving the gray blanket. There seemed no end to it as she gathered it to her, as if she were a magician pulling scarves out of a hat.

Baffled, Lia asked. "What *is* that?"

"It's a Moby wrap, designed to hold a thirty pound baby. I think it can handle a puppy. That way you can carry her around and not worry about picking up diseases until the vet says it's okay."

"How does it work?"

"Hand the little girl to me," Steve said. "I'll keep her company while Bailey gets you set up."

Steve took Pup, cuddling her in one arm while he tickled the underside of her chin. He crooned, "Vixen, you can sleep with me tonight."

Terry leaned in and inhaled. "I smell puppy. No man has smelled puppy and been unable to love it."

Bailey looked up from the wrap. "What are you two going on about?"

"*Based on an Untrue Story.*" Steve said. "Bad TV movie about bad TV movies. Meta before meta was meta. We watched it because Terry has a thing for Morgan Fairchild. She launches a new perfume designed on the properties of puppy aroma."

"I'll stop showering after my morning run if whiffing dog is an aphrodisiac," Peter said.

Lia stood, exchanging a look with Bailey. "So not the same thing."

Bailey folded the twelve-foot wrap, then pressed the midpoint against Lia's sternum.

"Hold this here."

Bailey gathered the ends at Lia's back, flipped them over the opposite shoulders, crossed her chest like bandoliers, then brought them around Lia's waist to tie in front.

Lia stood in the circle of her friends, staring down at her mummified torso. "Do you seriously expect me to do that by myself?"

"Thousands of mothers do it every day. You'll get used to it."

"Now what do I do?"

Jim now held Pup. Bailey wiggled her hand and said, "Hand her over." Jim kissed the top of Pup's head, then surrendered her.

Bailey stroked the small belly. "Pull the layers out from your chest."

Lia complied and Bailey lowered Pup into the opening. She fussed with the crisscrossed straps, tugging them so they supported Pup's haunches.

"There you go."

Lia took an experimental step forward. Pup swiveled her head, taking in her surroundings. She gave Lia a confused look and pawed at the wrappings. Lia pressed a hand against the little body to hold her in place.

"Give her a day," Bailey said. "She'll enjoy being queen of all she surveys."

Lia reached into a pocket, extracted a treat, held it under Pup's nose. Girlfriend gobbled it down.

"There," Bailey said. "Friends for life."

"How big do you think she'll get?"

"Catahoulas have a wide variation. Could be thirty pounds, could be ninety. I'm betting she falls somewhere in between."

A head butted Lia's leg. Chewy stared up at her. Her independent little guy felt displaced. She stooped to give him a pet and a treat. Mollified, he propped himself on Lia's knee and gave Pup a sniff. Pup retreated into the Moby wrap.

"You'll get used to each other." Lia mentally crossed her fingers. *I hope.*

Viola refused to come anywhere near Pup. When Peter put a leash on her, she balked, digging her paws in and leaning so hard in the opposite direction her collar slipped over her head.

"Maybe later," he said.

Lia returned to the bench, doling out treats to encourage other dogs to meet Pup. Peter surrendered, sitting next to Lia and scratching the moving target that was Pup's head.

She understood the genius in Bailey's Moby wrap. You never knew where parvo lurked, and it would be more than a month before Pup was protected. With the wrap, she could carry Pup everywhere during her formative months, socializing her without risking infection.

Terry rubbed his hands. "Now the main event is over, tell us about Elvis."

Peter shrugged. "You found bones, we bagged them."

"What about clues, man? We need clues!"

"Unless the killer's name is stitched into Elvis' underwear, any clues were gone long before we got there. If there is anything, I won't hear about it."

"Why not? It's your case, isn't it?"

"Just pinch hitting on a busy weekend. Your bones will be assigned to someone in Homicide or Cold Case."

"Outrageous!"

Steve snorted. "You're only pissed because you thought calling Peter meant you'd get to stick your nose in."

Peter folded his arms. "You wrecked date night so you could play detective?"

Terry said nothing.

"It's all he talks about," Steve said. "Elvis this, Elvis that. I had enough of Elvis when I was nineteen."

Terry feigned indifference. "I was never a big Presley fan. Went to Graceland once."

Steve said, "The closest I came to Graceland was the lobby of a roadside Elvis museum. The teaser exhibit featured Elvis' toilet seat cover and the ugliest lamp ever made."

Lia had to ask. "What did Elvis' toilet seat cover look like?"

"Chewbacca on a bad hair day, in avocado. If he was sitting on that, no wonder he died."

Terry's face turned pink. "Bah! Where's the provenance? Probably pulled it out of a dumpster. I bet they were selling vials of Elvis' sweat."

"They sold those at the gas station down the road."

"How could you pass up Elvis sweat?" Lia asked.

"Oh, I bought a vial. I gave it to my girlfriend. She didn't need me after that."

"Poor Steve," Lia said. "Displaced by the King."

"Best five dollars I ever spent. That vial of sweat saved me from a train wreck."

Terry pouted. "I can't believe you let Elvis slip through your fingers."

"I've got plenty on my plate," Peter said.

"Do tell."

"I would, but then I'd have to kill you."

"Not telling him will kill him," Steve said.

DAY 10

MONDAY, APRIL 29, 2019

A WEEK LATER, PUP SNUGGLED IN THE MOBY WRAP, snoozing like the angel she wasn't as Lia drove home from the park. You'd think her new dog could at least *pretend* to be the teensiest bit repentant, after chomping the wires of Lia's forty-dollar earbuds as they'd dangled in front of her muzzle.

That was puppies, meeting the world with their teeth —though Honey had never been so destructive. Since Pup took up residence, girlfriend had sunk her needle-sharp pearly whites into everything she could get her tiny paws on.

Lia's traumatized furniture now cowered beneath the quilted pads she'd duct-taped on after she caught the little demon gnawing the oak arm of her lovely Mission couch. Her collection of artist-made throw pillows hid on the top shelf of a closet. Three pairs of flip-flops were toast.

Peter had taken to alternately calling Pup "Jaws" and

"Weapon of Mass Destruction" and said there had to be gator or shark mixed with the Catahoula—none of which helped her find a name for her new girl.

Lia parked, hoping the destruction of her earbuds wasn't an omen for the rest of her day. David and Zoe were due at eleven. Lia had ninety minutes to feed the fur kids, take them to Alma's, shower, put on something that didn't make her look like a mud-wrestling bag lady, undo the puppy proofing in the living room, and arrange her paintings in an orderly fashion that suggested she was a professional.

Long-time patrons would laugh about her MacGyvered protective measures, but Zoe was new and you never got a second chance to make a first impression. *Better tour the house for puddles. Can't have a potential client dipping designer pumps in dog pee.*

Normally Lia took time to appreciate the architectural details that still dazzled her: the circular tower topped with a slate witch's hat; stained glass transoms and leaded sidelights; wall-climbing ivy planted before she was born; and the wide, wonderful porch—which was fine, no matter what Terry told Dick Brewer.

Today she blew past them, Chewy's legs churning to keep up as she raced up the steps. Lia unlocked the deadbolt and pushed the door open. Pup woke, barking and scrambling as if she was about to take on Mike Tyson. Lia dropped Chewy's lead and struggled to untangle Pup from the wrap.

Pup launched from her arms, leaving behind a flurry of scratches on her way to the floor. Girlfriend raced to the base of the stairs, growling, desperate to hurl herself up the steps she hadn't yet learned to climb.

"Hush! What is it?"

Pup kept up the cacophony. Chewy cocked his head, looking at Lia expectantly. Whatever was wrong with Pup, Chewy wanted his breakfast.

Something thudded upstairs.

Peter should be at work. Lia looked out the sidelights. A white Cadillac—a sleek, pearlized beast in a neighborhood that trended to new Kias and vintage Volvos—sat where Peter's Blazer had been that morning.

She scooped Pup up and grabbed Chewy's leash, scanning the street as she ran out of the house. *No Blazer. No department-issue Taurus.* She stuffed an annoyed Pup back in the Moby wrap, then dug her phone out of her pocket.

Peter picked up immediately.

"Hey gorgeous."

"Thank God. Where are you?"

"Heading to Hughes High School. Why?"

"Someone's in your apartment."

"Get out now."

"Already did. Pup started barking as soon as I opened the door. I heard someone moving around upstairs and ran out."

"Call 911. I'm on my way."

A young, earnest officer named Cal Hinkle pulled up less than five minutes later. Lia was relieved to have someone she knew, though Cal's freckles and haystack hair made him look about as dangerous as Howdy Doody. He rounded the front of the patrol car, hand resting on the gun at his hip.

Pup began a new fit of barking.

"Is your prowler still here?"

"Upstairs, in Peter's apartment. Unless he went out the back."

"The front door open?"

Lia nodded. Cal's face settled into lines of firm resolve as he headed inside. Lia clutched the squirming Pup to her chest as she waited. Chewy whined. *Missing his breakfast.*

In less time than she expected, the front door opened. A petite woman emerged, a poor man's Nicole Kidman with porcelain skin and delicate features a shade short of classic. A sophisticated blonde cut framed her bewildered expression. Dressed in a mauve suit with a patterned scarf, she looked ready for lunch at the museum or maybe the corporate takeover of Avon. Her new client, arrived early?

Cal followed her out, looking sheepish.

The woman talked non-stop in a soft Kentucky drawl as she descended the steps. She arrived on the sidewalk and bent over, her outstretched hand hovering over Chewy's head. "What a cute schnauzer!"

Chewy backed away, hiding behind Lia's legs. The woman looked up, smiling into Lia's stony face. "Honestly, I don't understand what the fuss is. I have permission to be here."

"Permission from whom?" Lia demanded.

She tilted her head. "I'm sorry, who are you?"

"This is my house."

"Your house? Did I walk into the wrong house? ... No, that can't be. I used Peter's spare key and his name is on the mailbox. It says 'second floor,' right next to his name.

That's where I was, on the second floor. Really, this is a mistake."

"How did you get Peter's key?"

"He keeps it in a little fake rock. His uncle makes them. We all have them."

"Even if you had Peter's consent, his entrance is on the side. You had no business entering my apartment."

"He wouldn't have a front door key in his rock if he didn't use it."

Lia blinked. Then she lied. "Peter gave me that rock. That wasn't his key, it was mine."

Faux Nicole huffed, stating the obvious. "You can't expect me to know that."

Lia tamped down a rare surge of temper. "When did Peter say you could waltz into his apartment? Because I just talked to him and he wasn't expecting anyone."

The woman appeared oblivious to the steam now escaping Lia's ears. "I wanted to surprise him."

Cal inserted himself, apologizing. "Miss, I need to see your identification. For my report."

She reached into a vastly overpriced designer handbag and fished out a matching and equally over-priced wallet.

"This is just a silly misunderstanding. I'm sure a report isn't necessary." She looked up, focused on something over Lia's shoulder. "Peter!" Faux Nicole waved, taking two steps toward the street, brushing past Lia.

Lia turned to see Peter exiting his work car two houses down. Pup, roused by the commotion, lunged out of the Moby wrap, snagged the trailing end of Faux Nicole's scarf, and tugged.

Faux Nicole screamed. "Get him off! Get him off me! That's Hermès!"

Peter jogged up the sidewalk, then stopped. "Susan?"

Susan?

"Peter! Get this monster off me!"

Peter stuck his hands in his pockets and did nothing.

Lia pried the scarf from Pup's jaws and slapped it into Susan's hand. "For pity's sake, she was never on you, you twit."

Susan gasped. She wrestled the dog drool-enhanced scarf from around her neck and shook it in Cal's face. "That's assault! Arrest her! That dog needs to be put down!"

Cal turned to Peter, desperation on his face. Peter strolled up and pulled Pup out of Lia's Moby wrap, scratching the furry neck. "This little girl?" Peter said of the creature he claimed was part velociraptor. He held Pup up to his face. Pup licked his nose, desperate for understanding, or perhaps protection from the crazy woman. "Doesn't look like a vicious beast to me."

Cal cleared his throat. "You know this woman?"

"Sure I know her. Susan Sweeney. We used to be engaged. Book her for criminal trespass."

"She says she has permission to be here."

"I don't know how, since I haven't seen her in years."

"Peter Dourson, we've been running in and out of each other's houses since we were in elementary school."

Peter handed Pup to Lia. "Have you searched her purse? Maybe we're talking about breaking and entering, or burglary."

"Honestly, Peter, your mother—"

"Your proprietary rights ended when you broke our engagement to marry the furniture king. Lia, I'm late for a conference and I need you to handle this. Check our stuff to make sure Susan didn't do more than let herself in."

Cal looked miserably after Peter's retreating back. "You want me to press charges, Lia?"

Normally Lia would let it go, if only to save Cal the paperwork. But Susan Sweeney's honeyed entitlement rubbed her like a cheese grater.

"You heard Peter."

"You'll sign a complaint, then?"

"Let me get a pen."

The disbelief on Susan's face made Lia want to laugh.

"What about my scarf!"

Chewy whined.

Lia shifted the squirming pup to her hip. "Cal, what's the difference between criminal trespass and breaking and entering?"

Cal rubbed his forehead. "Two hundred and fifty dollar fine or thirty days, versus six months to a year in jail."

Susan dropped the sopping scarf. Chewy barked at it as it fluttered to the ground.

"You can have the damn thing." She turned to Cal. "Give me my ticket and I'm out of here."

"Sorry ma'am. There's no ticket for this class of misdemeanor. I have to book you."

Susan stiffened, incredulous.

Cal continued, "You have to ride in the back of my car, but I'll leave off the cuffs."

Susan flashed a forced smile. "I guess Peter must have his little joke."

Lia gave her a ferocious grin in return. "Aren't you forgetting something?"

"And what could that possibly be?"

Lia held her palm out. "My key. Hand it over."

FOURTEEN-YEAR-OLD STACY BENDER SAT ACROSS THE conference table from Peter, staring into her lap. Lank dishwater hair obscured a face peppered with acne. He'd had a brief glimpse of eyes wide with panic lurking behind the hair.

Panic inspired by the woman beside her. Prematurely wrinkled skin marked Stacy's mother as a chain smoker, as did the odor of smoke permeating her hair and clothes. Or perhaps the dull, burnt smell was a product of the rage leaking out through Ms. Bender's rapidly tapping fingernails.

He exchanged a glance with Kim Freeman, the Hughes guidance counselor sitting at the end of the table. They'd both smelled Ms. Bender's wake-up beer under the smoke. Tobacco and alcohol aged the skin. Stacy's mother had to be ten to twenty years younger than the fifty plus she appeared to be.

"Sit up, Stacy," Joyce Bender snapped. "I had to take off work to be here. Officer Dourson asked you a question. You'll damn well answer it."

Peter caught a flash of defiance under the curtain of hair and exchanged another look with Kim. Stacy was less likely to tell the truth if it would bring her grief at home, but the law was the law. Children had to be interviewed in the presence of a parent or guardian. Not that Joyce Bender was much of either.

"It's all right, Ms. Bender," he said. "Stacy just needs a minute." It wasn't the first time he'd played good cop/bad cop with a parent. It was a game he disliked because Joyce Bender's bad cop would only turn into worse cop at home, and there was nothing he could do about it.

"Her minutes are costing me money. I have three kids to feed. She's taking food out of their mouths."

Two hours lost pay would be minor compared to Bender's weekly spend on beer and cigarettes.

Peter picked up his phone, tapped the screen several times, then placed it in front of Stacy, face up. A blurry photo of a girl holding a shipping box was visible to everyone at the table.

Stacy gave the phone a quick look. "That's not me. You can't even see my face."

"The hair is unmistakable, Stacy."

Stacy said nothing. Her hand crept up to rub at an acne scab on her chin, then jerked away.

Joyce Bender leaned over, squinted at the photo. "That's the shirt grandma gave you." She turned to Peter. "What is this?"

Peter kept his voice gentle as he spoke to Stacy. "We have a photo of you holding a package on a porch on Haight Avenue. What were you going to do with it?"

Stacy shrugged. "I was just looking at it. I didn't take it."

"No, you dropped it after a neighbor took your

picture. He said you were with an African American girl. Was that Taneesha?" Taneesha was Stacy's best friend, according to Ms. Freeman.

Stacy's head jerked up, mouth gaping.

Joyce Bender exploded, her arm drawing back as if to administer a slap, then dropping as her eyes sneaked a look at Peter. He wondered if her outrage was due to Taneesha's character or the color of her skin.

"I told you to stay away from them!" Joyce glared at Kim, whose skin was darker than Taneesha's. "What kind of school are you running here?" Her chair shrieked as she shoved it back. "I have no time for this. Do what you want with her."

Ms. Bender slammed the door as she exited, the sound releasing the tension in the room like the popping of a balloon.

Stacy muttered miserably, "Take me to Twenty-Twenty. Anything is better than home."

Twenty-Twenty was the juvenile facility located at 2020 Martin Luther King Boulevard. Stacy was probably right.

After Peter had broken the ring of copper thieves wrecking older homes in Northside, he'd been assigned to chase down the assholes stealing Amazon deliveries off porches. He'd made little traction in the case until an alert neighbor caught Stacy in the act and took her picture.

The clerks at the Northside UDF recognized her picture but didn't know her name or where she lived. She wasn't known at the branch library. His next stop had been Happen, Inc., a neighborhood organization with empowerment programs for teens. The kids said they didn't know her, but he'd caught their sideways glances.

His quarry might attend any school in Cincinnati's Byzantine system. Knowing which one would save him days. He'd shrugged, put his phone away, and let them show off the T-shirts they were printing. Then he asked where they went to school.

Kim had been a mine of information, providing background not only on Stacy, but on Taneesha and Taneesha's family.

Peter did quick mental calculations. A parent had to be present when questioning a minor unless they gave permission otherwise. They had something resembling consent on tape. In addition, schools served in loco parentis when parents were not available. Kim could fill that position. He caught Kim's eye and quirked a brow. Kim twisted her mouth, shrugged.

Stacy dropped her head onto the table, wrapped her arms around it. "My life is over."

Peter gentled his voice. "I know you didn't want Mrs. Robinson's support hose. What were you going to do with it?"

Stacy moved her head back and forth in negation while keeping her face to the table.

Peter played a hunch.

"Did Jamal ask you to take those packages?" Jamal was Taneesha's nineteen-year-old brother.

Stacy's head shot up again, her face white. She said nothing, but her eyes affirmed Peter's suspicions. Jamal probably had a stable of young girls ripping off packages for him. He wondered how long it would take Jamal to turn those same girls into prostitutes.

"How many of Taneesha's friends are stealing packages for Jamal?"

Stacy was shaking. "I don't know anything. I didn't say anything. You can't say I said anything!"

"Did Jamal threaten to hurt you if you told anyone?" he asked.

She stared at him with big eyes, her mouth quivering. Peter could fill in the blanks. It was possible Jamal fed someone with a flea market table, but flea markets were going out of style. More likely he or someone he knew sold the stolen items on eBay or Facebook.

She'd dropped the package, which meant he didn't have grounds to take her into custody. Too bad. Considering the home situation, that might be the best thing for her. A confession would make it easy to get the search warrant he wanted, but Stacy was too scared to talk. He wondered if he'd blown the case by interviewing her.

Maybe not.

"I'll make you a deal, Stacy. Did Taneesha see Mr. Weston take your picture?"

She gave him a cautious look and shook her head.

"Did you tell her about it?"

"No."

"Nobody knows you're talking to me. They just know you had to see Ms. Freeman." He turned to the guidance counselor. "What's a legitimate reason for you to see Stacy?"

"Aren't you on the health technician track, Stacy?" Kim asked.

"That's what Mom wants. I want the zoo program."

"Getting arrested will ruin your chances for an internship at the zoo," Kim said.

Peter followed Kim's lead. "I bet Jamal has a lot of kids like you stealing for him. I bet he told you if you got caught, it was no big deal. You'd only get a slap on the wrist because you're a minor and your record would be clean when you reached eighteen. I bet he didn't tell you it could ruin your education and your chances for having a career you want."

"He's right," Kim said. "What you do in high school affects the rest of your life."

Stacy's lip trembled.

"Maybe Stacy can still get that internship," Peter said. "Maybe Stacy can say she was talking to you about the zoo program. We just spoke about it, so it's not a lie."

He caught a flicker of hope on Stacy's face. He gave her a deliberate look as if he were considering something new.

"Maybe Stacy can tell Taneesha her mom is angry with her and she can't go around with her for now. That wouldn't be a lie, would it?"

Stacy worked her mouth.

"I don't think you'd be a very good liar and I don't want you to have any trouble with Jamal or Taneesha. I need you to stay out of the way while I do my job. Can you do that?"

Stacy gave him a suspicious look. "I don't want to get anyone into trouble."

"I'll be straight with you. Trouble is coming. You can't

stop it. I think you might be a decent kid with the wrong friends."

Stacy opened her mouth to protest. Peter barreled on. "Anyone who asks you to do something that could get you arrested isn't a friend. Whatever they promised you, it will never make up for what it will cost you.

"If you don't tell anyone about talking to me and you stay out of the way, I can give you a pass. You'll still have a chance to get into that internship program. If you go back to helping Jamal, you'll be caught in a criminal conspiracy and I won't be able to help you. If Jamal moves his operation because you told him about me, I won't want to."

"All I have to do is keep quiet?"

"And wait. I have to gather evidence. That could take weeks. You might find yourself under pressure."

Stacy squirmed.

"If I knew more about Jamal's operation, I could pick him up within forty-eight hours, maybe tomorrow. It would be over."

"People would know. They'd come after me."

"We protect confidential informants. Your name won't show up anywhere. The only person who knows I'm talking to you is Ms. Freeman. You can trust Ms. Freeman, can't you?"

Stacy looked at Kim, eyes troubled.

Peter continued, "A guy like Jamal, I bet he brags to too many people for him to know who talked. But we can set it up so it doesn't look like we got inside information."

Peter waited while Stacy did the mental math. She spilled. When they finished, Kim escorted Stacy out of the room, sending her back to class.

"You're a kind man," Kim said when Stacy was out of earshot.

Peter shrugged. "My cousins shoplifted when they were in high school. I don't imagine Stacy thought this was any different."

"No, she probably didn't think about it at all. They don't at this age."

"You've been a big help."

"What will you do about her mother?"

Peter rubbed his jaw. "I don't want to be seen near Stacy or her mom, and Ms. Bender is just mad enough to go to Taneesha's house and blow everything. Think you can calm her down?"

Kim pursed her mouth, considering.

Peter continued, "Tell her it was a one-off, and Stacy was sufficiently terrified that we don't believe she'll do it again."

"You don't want her to know about your investigation?"

"You think Ms. Beer for Breakfast won't talk?"

Kim sighed. "I see your point." She followed Peter into the hall. "How's Sam?"

Detective Sam Robertson was Kim's uncle. "Sam's a riot. He tried to scam Brent into a desk pop."

"A desk pop? You mean from the Will Farrell movie?"

"Sam kept winking at me because Brent's all serious, asking him about desk pop protocol. Cynth is there, and she says, 'I did mine ages ago. I can't believe you haven't done it yet.' Brent pulls his gun and Sam thinks he's going to fire one into the ceiling. Then Brent says, 'I'm not real clear on this, you're the expert, you show me how it's done' and he tries to hand his gun to Sam. You should have seen Sam backpedal. Sam says, 'It's a rite of passage, you only do it once, but if you're not man enough—' and he backs out of the office. Brent follows him down the hall and he's whining, 'I need to do this, you gotta show me how.'"

"Good heavens. What did Sam do?"

"Sam ran. Almost crashed into Captain Parker."

"You cops and your practical jokes."

Peter retrieved the phone he'd silenced for the meeting. Four missed calls from his captain. "I've got to go. Can you handle it from here?"

Kim tilted her head, looking down her nose at a mock-imperious angle. "I can handle one terrified girl and her maniac mother."

"Send up a flag if her mom doesn't bite."

Peter strode toward the exit, taking a quick look at his voicemails while avoiding the tide of students. The four from his captain were less than ten seconds each. Probably "Call. In. Now." He waited until he reached the privacy of his car and turned off on a side street a few blocks from the school to check in.

Captain Ann Parker didn't bother with niceties. "What's your status?"

"Just finished interviewing a juvenile package thief. I think I have enough for a search warrant."

"Pick up the new issue of the *National Enquirer* on your way in."

Better not to ask. "Right away, sir."

HE FOUND THE CURRENT *NATIONAL ENQUIRER* TUCKED behind other magazines in the top shelf of the rack at UDF. He slid the top copy out. A grinning skull stared at him, the ragged remains of a collar barely visible in the nest of roots. The sixty-point, white on black headline read:

Elvis Murdered!

PETER SAT IN HIS CAR, POPPED THE TAB ON HIS PEPSI, THEN pulled the *Enquirer* out of the bag. Parker expected him five minutes ago, but taking time to find out the worst was the smartest thing. He flipped through to the photos splashed across the center spread.

Photos he hadn't known existed.

————————

Elvis' Shallow Grave Discovered!

Elvis Presley's death on August 16, 1977, may be the most hotly disputed event in history. Rumors abound, of conspiracies; of suicide; that the grave at Graceland is empty and the King still lives. A shocking discovery on Cincinnati's Mill Creek last week proves that only one of the above is true: The King's Graceland grave is empty. But Elvis' fate is wilder than anyone suspected.

Boaters on a float trip sponsored by the Mill Creek Yacht Club, an environmental group tasked with monitoring the health of the urban estuary, stumbled upon the skeletal remains in the roots of a toppled tree.

"When I saw the bones and the jumpsuit, I knew it was Elvis," our anonymous source said. "It's obvious he was murdered and buried in a shallow grave. I fear the people who have hidden the truth for so long will continue to cover it up. With the photos made public, the police must pursue this. Elvis deserves justice."

The photos show a skeleton dressed in a rotting jumpsuit bearing a distinctive pattern of metal studs, identical to one worn by Elvis when performing.

"His killer must have loved him, must have had regrets, because he buried Elvis dressed the way his fans loved him best," our source said.

Asked how Elvis could have been killed in Cincinnati when he was known to be at Graceland, our source speculates, "I imagine he died at Graceland, but the body had to disappear. The killer was connected to Cincinnati, so he brought Elvis here, where he could visit the grave in secret. Only a Graceland insider could smuggle the body out."

When contacted, Bruce Koehler, founder of the Mill Creek Yacht Club, declined to comment, except to say, "The Mill Creek Yacht Club will support police efforts to investigate this matter in whatever way we can."

———————

PETER SLUMPED BACK IN HIS SEAT. SHOOTING TERRY WOULD not be justifiable homicide, and that was a crying shame.

PETER OCCUPIED A VISITOR'S CHAIR IN CAPTAIN PARKER'S office, waiting for her to finish the phone call in progress when she waved him in. He held the bag with its damning contents, hands flexing as if to throttle the magazine. He forced them to relax. Parker wouldn't thank him for mangling the gossip rag, though he expected it had already served its purpose.

Parker commanded from a bland beige box identical to every other office in District Five's temporary home. She kept the fluorescents off, relying on the incandescent glow of a desk lamp instead. The space was further humanized with three giant snake plants on her credenza. When asked, she said they were there for the air quality. That, and they were impossible to kill.

As with all the other windows in the building, the mini blinds were permanently closed. The station had outgrown the Frank Lloyd Wright inspired building next to Mount Storm Park and relocated to a former social services agency in a College Hill strip mall. The front of the building abutted a heavily trafficked sidewalk. It wouldn't do for customers of the hip hop clothing store or the Family Dollar to peep in, thus the blinds.

No carpet could withstand traffic generated by more than a hundred officers. It and the baseboards had been ripped out, exposing abused linoleum that could not be replaced unless the CPD and city council committed to the College Hill location as their permanent home. On good days Peter said their new home was functional. On bad days the building pervaded with a depressing, Kafkaesque depersonalization.

A woman with strong, androgynous features, Parker wore her hair in a utilitarian ponytail and dressed like a member of the rank and file. She hung up the phone, raising an eyebrow at Peter.

He wished he could read her mood, but she had a talent for looking friendly while maintaining the most indecipherable cop face in the CPD. He laid the bag on her desk and waited.

She nodded at the bag. "You read it?"

"Yes, sir."

"How bad is it?"

"Hard to say, sir. Looks like a return to the alien baby stories they used to run."

"I suppose that's safer than politics these days. Any idea where the photos came from? You know the *Enquirer* won't tell us."

Peter had asked himself this question all the way up Hamilton Avenue. "My first thought was Terry Dunn, the reporting party. But I know him. I'm sure he took photos, but I don't believe he would sell them. Someone took them before we got there, or snuck behind us while the Yacht Club got everyone out. I take full responsibility for not protecting the scene."

Parker waved it off. "You're not responsible for anything that happened before you arrived. It's impossible to keep track of three dozen witnesses when half of them are out of sight and you're busy making sure nobody drowns.

"Safety always comes first. It's just unfortunate. The media is all over this. We have to get in front of it."

"Sir?"

"Captain Arseneault wants to borrow you for the Mill Creek remains. I reassigned your porch pirates to Davis."

Command was command. Training kicked in, suppressing the urge to protest. "I don't understand."

"Your bones were slated for the cold case unit. But that's only two men. Tucker just had an emergency triple bypass and Wallace is in the Bahamas. We expected the bones to keep until the anthropology report was complete and Wallace returned from vacation. With this idiotic story we can't wait. Everyone in Homicide is ass-deep in the club shooting and other cases.

"A dozen news agencies have called, wanting to know what progress we've made. With the press salivating and social media blowing up, we have to demonstrate we're on top of this."

Homicide was chasing gangbangers who'd killed two and injured seven more, but the media was blowing up over a polyester jumpsuit.

"But this isn't an immediate threat to the public."

"Even so. While we have our hand out to city council for funds to renovate this place, we need to play nice. Arseneault will owe us if we keep Channel 7 off his back. If I didn't know better, I'd suspect he planted the photos to get attention off the club shooting."

I not only have to find a killer who has been in the wind for forty years, I get to put on a dog and pony show to drum up twenty mil. Great opportunity for career advancement. Just great.

"I appreciate your confidence in me, sir, but I'm out of my depth. Why not someone who was around then? I'm not from Cincinnati. I'm flying blind."

"You're a good detective. All we expect is a good faith effort to show the public we're doing our job."

"It sounds like you want a cosmetic investigation."

"Not at all. But we're realists. Just do your job and find what you find."

Or not. "What resources will I have?"

"Homicide will field tips and forward them to you. Other than that, you're on your own. It's not ideal, but this isn't a case where we have to mobilize manpower before evidence and witnesses disappear. Our best bet will be the tip line.

"We'll be flooded with tips. Every one of them has to be vetted. The last thing we want is someone coming forward after we botch things to say they told us who our killer was on day two. You're thorough to the point of being a pain in the ass. That's what we need."

"Thank you, sir." Peter wondered if it had been a compliment. "Can I ask a question?"

"Go ahead."

"Is this assignment punitive, sir, for letting those photos out?"

She turned the supreme blankness of her exceptional cop face on him now. "Captain Arseneault and I agree that you are uniquely suited to pursue this. If anyone knows anything about our bones, they've kept quiet for decades and they may be three steps from the grave. Handling them will take a delicate touch. We need someone people will continue to talk to, the third, or even the tenth time we come calling. You're that guy. You're up on the case and you've met the folks at the Mill Creek Yacht Club. They could be useful."

"You don't need me for that. They'll talk to anyone."

Parker gave him a stern look. "Thank God Arseneault ran cadaver dogs through the site last week. We know this is a one-off. We'd have a disaster on our hands if there were more bones. You can be certain a half-dozen yahoos are on the creek, looking."

Peter surrendered. "What do you want me to do?"

"Check in with Jeffers at the morgue. Let's figure out who this guy is and put a stop to the Elvis nonsense. I've arranged an interview with Channel 7 for four o'clock. See that you have something by then."

"Sir?"

"We want your face on this thing. You'll do the interview with Aubrey Morse."

Translation: you're the messenger, in case anyone needs a target. "Yes, sir."

"You're on this full time for the next week. After that we'll reassess. You can catch Davis up on your package thieves once Morse gets her soundbite. And Dourson?"

"Sir?"

"Ditch the sport coat for a suit and get a haircut."

Not Elvis in situ had been a dark entity from the pages of Lovecraft, a demon drawing power from the earth as it slept. This demon would awaken in full control of the roots entwining it, using them as tentacles to capture and eat every human in sight.

In the cold light of laboratory LEDs, the stained and disarticulated remains were a sanitized thing, empty of even the memory of life or intelligence—more like a toy skeleton you could buy at the Cincinnati Museum Center. It made Peter sad.

He stood at the head of the steel autopsy table and scanned the reassembled remains. Gaps in the hands and one foot indicated missing bones. The other leg was missing below the knee. *Probably halfway to New Orleans.*

Assistant Coroner Amanda Jefferson, a sturdy black woman with a heavy mop of braids bundled behind her head, said, "It was nice of your guy to pop up the way he did. At least I didn't spend Saturday killing my knees over a shallow grave. Remains aren't usually that considerate."

"I see you got rid of the roots."

"Not me. I was under orders not to touch—after Junior and I did the dirty work hauling him through raw sewage to get him here."

"If it's any consolation, Commodore said you'll see condoms, lettuce, and toilet paper floating in the water when there's raw sewage in the creek. We didn't spot any of that, so I doubt you're harboring dangerous bacteria."

Amanda raised a neatly groomed eyebrow. "Lettuce. I feel so much better. Regardless, I was happy to let Dr. Fancy Pants figure out how to clean him up. That tree fed on those bones for decades. What's left is fragile as cigarette ash." She snorted. "The man thinks he's God,

Kathy Reichs, and Kay Scarpetta rolled into one. I didn't mind watching him pull his hair out."

"Sorry I missed him."

"No, you're not. I don't have the final report yet, but I can give you the highlights. Not Elvis was buried sometime between the mid-seventies and early nineties. We may know more when the lab is finished with his clothes."

"So he could be Elvis."

Amanda glowered at him. "Don't be funny. Elvis had enough trouble, though I imagine the King would have preferred murder and a shallow grave to the indignity of dying on a toilet seat."

Junior entered, rolling a steel cart full of supplies. "Don't disrespect the King."

"Fact is fact, Junior."

Peter's interest was piqued. "You studied Elvis Presley's death?"

"We all get asked about it. And so you don't have to ask, he died of a heart attack. Some say it was the emergence of punk rock that gave it to him but they would be wrong. Even if he had hypertrophic cardiomyopathy as others claim, the combination of drugs in his system tipped the scales. Crying shame it happened where it did."

"Huh."

"You'd think Michael Jackson and Heath Ledger would have learned from his example, but no. Losing them was bad enough. Tom Petty broke my heart, for real. Nothing like having a prescription to legitimize stupid."

"I didn't take you for a Tom Petty fan."

Amanda's face turned wistful. "The teeth on that man. You could see him smile from the nosebleed seats. The

American Dental Association went into mourning when he passed."

"And he could sing, too."

"That, he could."

Junior looked up from loading supplies into a cabinet. "Don't talk about Tom Petty in the same sentence as Elvis. That's sacrilege."

Peter nodded at the bones. "Any chance you can pull DNA?"

"I might be able to extract some from the teeth, but your best bet for identification is dental records."

"Can you run it anyway?"

"There's no need at this point."

"Humor me."

She shook her head. "Whatever."

"What did the anthropologist say?"

"Besides carping about my collection methods? Never mind he was in Toledo when Not Elvis popped up."

"Besides that. Cause of death?"

"No discernible cause of death. Not Elvis lacks the usual trauma associated with violent assault. Skull is intact, so no bludgeoning. Same for the vertebrae. Arnold Schwarzenegger did not snap his neck. No nicks, chips, or breaks associated with a knife or bullet.

"He could have bled out from a gut wound without incurring damage to his bones, but that only works if he sat still while someone carved up his intestines."

"Unlikely," Peter agreed.

"If he was gut shot, we would have found the bullet with the remains. Rats don't run off with slugs. My eagle eye spotted the hyoid bone in the dirt. It's intact, which means strangulation is ninety percent out, but it doesn't rule out suffocation."

"Electrocution?"

"Don't be cute. Could be poison, could have drowned in the creek, but I can't state either conclusively. Could have died from natural causes and been buried there for some reason."

"A sentimental attachment to toxic waste?"

"That does seem unlikely. He's a bona fide mystery."

"So the prime contenders are suffocation, poisoning, drowning, and natural causes. What can you tell me about him?"

"Best guess on age is sixty to eighty."

"And dressed for disco?"

"Takes all kinds. Caucasian, consistent with the British Isles. Five foot seven. Excellent dental work, that means middle or upper class. Excessive wear in the finger bones we recovered. He played piano or did something else that required hours of manipulation of his hands. With that jumpsuit, maybe he hung around with Liberace."

"Guitar? Maybe he really was an Elvis impersonator."

"Maybe. Maybe a typist, but that doesn't feel right. He came from a generation of men that didn't do their own typing."

"Unless he was Ernest Hemingway."

"Possibly a writer, I'll give you that, but he wasn't famous or we'd know about him. Inconclusive about his general health, the tree sucking on his bones thinned them out in a way that masks osteoporosis, diabetes, and a host of other issues."

"So far nothing you've said is very helpful."

"I saved the best for last." She moved down the table, nodding at the right leg. "Take a look at that."

Peter bent closer. He'd assumed the entire lower leg was missing, but a few inches of the tibia and fibula remained, ending in formations that looked like clumps of petrified angel hair pasta.

"What is that?"

"Your man isn't Elvis. He's a peg-legged pirate. That happens sometimes with amputated limbs. You get these crazy growths where the bone was sawed."

"Our guy is missing a leg."

"Diabetes, cancer, frostbite, injury. He might be a veteran. War is a popular cause of lost limbs."

Peter did the math. "World War II?"

"That would be my guess."

Peter thought about the figurehead on Terry's canoe. "I think I know how to identify him."

CARDBOARD BOXES FILLED TERRY AND STEVE'S LIVING room, a thin layer of dust confirming Peter's suspicion that they hadn't budged since Peter helped with the move more than a year earlier. He expected the boxes to remain where they were until the glue on the tape failed and any attempt to pick one up resulted in disaster.

In the middle of this cardboard obstacle course, Terry sat in his favorite chair, leaning over a box situated to function as a footstool. He adjusted his glasses as he examined the cover of the magazine resting on the box.

"The resolution is excellent," he said.

Peter kept his tone mild. "Where do you think it came from?"

"It's not Terry's," Steve said. "His didn't turn out this good."

Terry shot Steve a look promising revenge. "I took a few snaps for personal use. Not to show anyone. Check my phone."

"Who did you let back there?"

"No one, ... exactly."

"Who, not exactly?"

"It was Commodore's float trip. He had to see why we couldn't portage around the tree."

"He take photos?"

Terry sent Steve another look. "We left him for a minute to chase off a couple of the young guys. But Commodore wouldn't do something like this." Terry flipped to the center spread, pointed at the last paragraph. "It says right here. He refused to talk to them."

"That's just to give him plausible deniability," Steve said. "He wouldn't do it for the money."

"Why, then?" Peter asked.

"Commodore spent the last quarter century raising public awareness about regional watershed issues. He'd do it to get Mill Creek in the news. A sizable anonymous donation to the Mill Creek Alliance would just be a bonus."

"You can't accuse Bruce. Nobody was watching the tree when we were getting everyone out. Anyone could have snuck back."

Peter sighed. "If you see one of your yacht club buddies in a new car, you need to tell me."

Terry raised troubled eyes. "I let you down. I'm sorry."

"It was too much to expect it wouldn't leak. But there's something else. I need your figurehead."

Color flooded Terry's face. His mouth gaped in horror. "You can't take Smaug! He had nothing to do with Elvis."

Patience was required here. "Where did you get him—I mean it?"

"He pulled it out of a tree right before we spotted Elvis," Steve said.

"Smaug isn't part of your investigation," Terry blustered.

"How do you figure that?"

"He was upstream! If he belonged to Elvis, he would have been downstream."

"That's not strictly true," Steve said.

"Backstabber," Terry muttered.

Peter kept his eyes on Steve and said, "Explain."

"The Mill Creek barrier dam is in place to keep the creek from flooding when the Ohio River rises. It's set to close when the water gets to a certain level. Otherwise, the creek backs up and you have flooding miles upstream. That's how Northsiders wound up rowing boats on Hamilton Avenue in 1937."

"And?"

"There's a window of time before the dam closes where you get backwash in what Commodore calls the trash free zone."

"Trash-free zone? That's the opposite of what I saw Saturday."

"Not trash-free. A free zone for garbage, where the normal rules don't apply. There's a spot between the downtown viaducts and the old railroad trestles. Trash collects against the pilings, which makes the channel tighter. The water wants to move faster but it can't go anywhere. Then it eddies and circles around. Anything that floats can travel upstream when that happens. We might find Elvis' wristwatch hanging from a bridge on our next float."

"I can't believe you told him that," Terry groused.

"I can't believe you want to obstruct a police investigation," Steve said.

"But this is *Smaug.*"

"So get yourself a fake leg on eBay."

"It's not the same," Terry grumbled.

"I'll buy one and stick it in the rocks so you can find it in the creek. Will that make you happy?"

"He's too old."

Sometimes you had to let people work things out. "You know this, because?"

"They started using plastic decades before Elvis wound up under that tree."

"I have a skeleton with an amputated right leg. You found a prosthetic leg the same day. Is it right or left?"

"Right," Steve said.

"Some friend you are," Terry said.

"Don't be such a crybaby."

Peter continued, "If it has a serial number, it may tell us who our John Doe is."

"He's not John, he's Elvis. It said so in the paper. And there's no serial number. I looked."

"Technically, he's Not Elvis. I'll give you a receipt for the leg. If it turns out it's not connected with our bones,

83

you can have it back. If your leg belongs to my bones, you can make a case with the next of kin. They may not want it."

Terry stared at the opposite wall with a mulish expression on his face.

"Or I can get a warrant."

The sound emerging from Terry's throat resembled rumbling before an earthquake.

Steve stood. "It's in the garage. I wouldn't let him bring it in the house." He turned to Terry. "You coming? This is your chance to say goodbye."

Peter sat at his computer, rubbing the spot on his neck that always itched after a haircut. Amanda had cooed over the workmanship of the handmade leg but it had no serial number or other identifier. He'd wasted two hours on a lead that went nowhere. He hoped Parker was right and this week out of his life would contribute to the common good.

Forty-three minutes to show time. He stared at the seal of Ohio on his monitor, praying for something he could toss Aubrey Morse as he clicked through to the Attorney General's missing person data base.

Wonders of the digital age, the site listed cases going back more than fifty years. Unfortunately, the data base had 1001 pages. There was a search option for keywords, but not for date ranges.

Peter tapped his fingers in rapid hoofbeats while he thought. He doubted plugging "Elvis" into the search bar would net him anything. He noticed his tapping had segued into the theme for *The Lone Ranger*—he corrected himself—*William Tell Overture*—and forced himself to stop.

Entering individual years would take forever. Instead he keyed in 197. The database came up with three pages of results from the seventies, most of them young women.

He couldn't resist skimming the listing for a 20-year-old woman who disappeared from a locked law office in Toledo while the partners were away at a meeting. A romance novel lay on her desk, opened to a page detailing an abduction at knifepoint. She'd had an alarm buzzer under her desk but hadn't pressed it. They found her locked car in the parking lot. That one rang the bell on the weird-meter with Not Elvis.

None of the men fit.

He clicked the search bar again, entered 198. Three pages of results. Two-thirds down the first page, the photo of a cherub-faced older man stared out at him. He clicked the link for the report.

––––––––––

Andrew Heenan, Missing Adult
Missing from: Cincinnati, Ohio
Missing since: 5/16/1987
Missing age: 68
Current age: 98
Gender: Male
Race/Ethnicity: White

Height: 5'7"
Weight: 140
Hair color: White
Eye color: Blue

Details

Clifton resident Andrew Heenan was last seen wearing a black jumpsuit while performing magic tricks at a birthday party for a neighborhood child. He was scheduled to leave the following day for a trip to Europe. His car was found at the Cincinnati Airport and he was listed on the flight manifest for Delta flight 238 for New York City on 5/17/1987. A neighbor reported him missing four weeks later when he failed to return. Andrew's right leg has been amputated below the knee.

———————

Peter picked up his phone, buzzed Parker's office. "Our bones have a name, and it's not Elvis."

"LOVE THE SIDEWALLS," BRENT SAID, SLAPPING A HAND ON Peter's shoulder as he leaned forward to peer out the featureless glass door fronting District Five.

Four in the afternoon, and Brent still looked like he stepped off the cover of GQ.

"If I pay seventy bucks for a haircut, it better blow dry itself in the morning."

"I pay beautiful women to run their fingers through my hair. The cut is only a side benefit."

Three hours earlier, a fat, bald guy named Ernie ran clippers over Peter's head like a lawn mower. Unwilling to concede the point, Peter grunted and continued to stare across the sea of patrol cars between the station and Family Dollar. Months before, his view had been a wooded hillside and the occasional deer. Now he faced littered sidewalks and display windows full of cheap goods. He wasn't sure the extra room was worth the tradeoff.

"Any sign of Channel 7?" Brent asked.

"Nope. What do you suppose the locals think of having us here?"

"I suspect the resident shoplifters have stepped up activity to meet the challenge we present. They score points if they shove a second bag of potato chips in their pants when one of us stops in to pick up a candy bar. You, my man, do not look appropriately gratified about your up close and personal with the lovely Aubrey Morse."

Peter tugged the tie he saved for court, giving himself a quarter inch more breathing space. "Plenty of bodies pop up on Mill Creek and they barely rate a paragraph below the fold in the metro section. I'd murder the low-life who sold those photos, if I could figure out who it was."

"The *Enquirer* won't give him up."

"I love running an unsolvable murder while the entire country is watching."

"Who can resist an Elvis sighting?"

"You're only here to watch me make an ass out of myself."

"Like any right-thinking, red-blooded male, I am here to check out the slide of Aubrey's skirt when she gets out of her van."

"You're a true gentleman."

"That I am. I also have eyes, and I bless every day for them. But why are you so cranky?"

"I'm cranky because thirty minutes after this airs, crackpot calls will flood the lines. It's my job to investigate every tip, doesn't matter how questionable. Why aren't you out chasing down Jamal? Parker handed him to you on a platter."

"You haven't briefed me yet."

Peter turned narrowed eyes on his best friend. "You can read a file. You just want to give Aubrey a chance to seduce information out of you."

Brent grinned, unrepentant. "True that. The seducing part, not the information part. Ah, milady approaches."

A van equipped with a satellite dish and telescoping antenna passed the main parking lot entrance on Hamilton Avenue, disappearing behind the row of storefronts on the street.

"Think she's lost?" Peter asked.

"Nope. Circling to stage an entrance. ... And here she comes."

The van entered from a side street, parking across three spaces and positioning the passenger door directly opposite the entrance to District Five.

The door opened. Aubrey swung her legs around, showing more thigh than a professional hemline normally offered, the arched pumps she extended anything but demure. She tossed her head, sending her carefully coifed blond mane swinging as she emerged, smiling at the world with sculpted red lips. Her body-hugging purple suit made a bold statement compared to the navy favored by her sister reporters.

"She's doing that for our benefit," Peter said.

"And I do bless her for it."

Brent followed as Peter exited the building. They met Aubrey and her cameraman on the sidewalk.

"Detective Dourson, good to see you. Brent, am I interviewing you, too?"

"I'm just here to keep my man out of trouble."

Aubrey winked. "He's safe with me." She scanned the parking lot. "I guess there's no good place to do this. I miss the steps at the old station. They made such a nice visual with the flag." She tapped her foot, then pointed to a spot several feet away. "What do you think, Duff? Will that do?"

While Aubrey played the slick, sexy professional, Duff was pure counter-culture man candy, with rust-colored dreadlocks falling to the middle of his back and Celtic tattoos on both well-muscled arms. He shrugged, the camera tilting on a beefy shoulder.

"Brick walls all look the same."

Aubrey shot her last District Five story in the middle of a gravel parking lot. Since she'd been confronting detectives about irregularities in an investigation, Peter suspected it had been a deliberate choice to present a seedier impression of the department. CPD was currently in her good graces. Otherwise, she'd shoot their interview in front of the ugly yellow bollards sunk into the pavement to prevent drunks and criminals from driving through the door.

Once in place, she put on her I'm-serious-as-well-as-beautiful face and signaled Duff to start filming.

"This is Aubrey Morse, coming to you from District Five. Nine days ago, members of the Mill Creek Yacht Club discovered a human skeleton while on their annual float trip. Detective Peter Dourson, lead investigator in the case, is here to talk with us. Detective Dourson, have you identified the remains?"

Peter silently blessed Parker's efficiency. She'd raised hell in the archives until Heenan's file, never digitized, was unearthed. A harried clerk read critical details over Parker's speakerphone minutes before Morse arrived. With no next of kin listed, Parker okayed the release of Heenan's name. God willing, the Elvis business would die whimpering in the dark.

"We believe the remains are those of Andrew Heenan, a sixty-eight-year-old Clifton resident who went missing in 1987, after performing magic at a birthday party. Neighbors reported he had departed for a vacation. His car was found at Cincinnati Airport after he failed to return. The discovery of his remains by Mill Creek suggests he never left town."

Audrey's eye twitched, a tell. He'd taken the juice out of her story and she knew it. Too damn bad.

"How did you identify him so quickly?"

"The identification still needs to be confirmed, but the remains were clothed in a jumpsuit fitting the description of the costume Heenan wore for his last performance."

"This is the same jumpsuit that spawned viral Elvis conspiracy theories on the internet. Do you have any comment?"

"This is not Elvis Presley. Andrew Heenan was an older and much shorter man who needs justice. He had no known family at the time of his disappearance. We're hoping anyone who remembers Andrew will come forward to help us reconstruct his final days. It's the only way we'll learn what happened to him."

"There you have it, Cincinnati's own unsolved mystery. If you have any information regarding this case, please contact ..."

A white Caddy crawled down the parking lot behind Duff's back, same color, same model he'd seen outside the house hours earlier. It took every bit of Peter's training to maintain his cop face as Susan parked beside the Channel 7 van.

Brent must have noticed the stiffening in his cheeks, because he sent Peter a quizzical glance. There hadn't been time to tell Brent about Susan's stunt that morning. That morning? It felt like weeks since he left her with Cal.

Aubrey wrapped up the interview. "Nicely done. I think we can air all of it. You're a natural on camera. You could go into media relations."

Peter paused to frame a polite version of "I'd rather barbecue my own liver and eat it." Brent ambled up, mouth opening to issue some compliment or other. Aubrey's eyes narrowed, a predator preparing to take a bite out of the rival predator invading her territory.

"Peter," Susan called, staccato heels against concrete. "This is so exciting. I had no idea."

Please God, not now.

She stepped next to him and took his arm. "You must tell me all about it."

"Who's your friend?" Brent asked.

Peter forced his jaw to relax. "Brent, this is Susan Sweeney. She's an old friend from home. Susan, this is Brent Davis. And I'm sure you've seen Aubrey Morse on television."

Susan's face registered a purely southern veneer of apology over pity. "I'm sorry to say I haven't had the pleasure."

Aubrey no doubt ate a dozen Susans for breakfast. Her smile held.

They could have been gunslingers on a dusty Wyoming street. The vibration of one coral fingernail on Susan's clutch told Peter her mind was going a mile a minute, wondering how to unseat the alpha female she'd stumbled upon.

Brent slid in next to Susan. "Any friend of Peter's is a friend of mine. Let's take a stroll. You can tell me embarrassing stories about his childhood while he finishes with Aubrey."

Susan's expression turned uncertain for a microsecond. She lifted her chin, turning her Sunday-supplement, cheerleader smile on Brent as she allowed him to steer her away.

"Brent, we still have to schedule that lunch," Aubrey called after him.

"You bet, darlin'." Brent turned his head long enough to catch Peter's eye. He mouthed, "You owe me."

Don't I know it.

"Old friends are nice, aren't they?" Aubrey said, directing Peter's attention back to her. "I want to stay on top of this story, it's only going to get hotter. Can I call you for updates?"

What on earth is Susan doing here? Whatever she wanted, it was the last thing he needed. "Um, sure."

"Great! What's your cell phone number?"

Peter saw a dark abyss opening before him like the yawning hole he'd almost stepped into while caving in high school. He felt the same jolt now. *Back away from the edge. Slow and easy.*

He forced a smile. "Just call the station. They'll get a message to me."

"Is it your old friend? This is purely business."

"I'm sure it is. I can never keep track of my phone."

Aubrey would know the lame excuse for a brush off. He threw her a bone. "I bet Brent would appreciate a rescue."

Aubrey brightened. "You think?"

"Absolutely."

"Duff, let's load up." She clacked down the sidewalk, not waiting for Duff's reply.

Duff shook his head, the rusty dreads dragging across his back. "She'll eat him up."

"I think that's what he's hoping for."

Duff took his time packing up the van. Peter hung back, preferring to view the coming action from a distance.

Aubrey strolled up to Brent and slid a finger down his tie, cutting off his conversation with Susan. The move incited a flinty and determined look on Susan's face.

93

Peter wondered what Cynth would say about two women ready to engage in a cat fight over Brent just for form's sake. *Good thing she's not here to see this.*

Cynth appeared at his elbow, conjured like the Devil, by his thoughts. Unlike the high-maintenance women occupying Brent, Detective Cynth McFadden avoided drawing attention to her looks. It was a necessity in a male-dominated career. Loose clothes hid a Scarlett Johansson figure. Long, wheat-colored hair meant invisible brows and lashes, and a face that washed out without makeup. An unobservant man might not notice how beautiful she was.

She hissed in his ear. "He's such a man whore."

"Just passing time until you fall in love with him. Are you ever going to do that?"

"Not if he keeps this up."

"You two are something else. What do you intend to do?"

"I plan to stand here long enough for him to notice. Then I will scorn him. Better yet, I'll hit on Duff. He's got a Heath Ledger vibe and he's better looking."

"Don't blame Brent. He's distracting Susan as a favor to me. Aubrey just wants information."

Cynth's mouth fell open, her eyes wide. "Susan? *The* Susan?"

"*The* Susan. I need to find out what the heck she's doing in Cincinnati."

"Does Lia know?"

"Yes, Lia knows." He headed for the trio.

"Glad I'm not you," Cynth called after him.

Aubrey had cut Brent away from Susan by the time

Peter joined her. He bent over her shoulder and said, "You'll bloody your manicure if you scratch her eyes out."

Susan jolted, then turned to face him. "You're such a kidder. She's nice. I like her."

You like her fractionally more than a case of genital warts. "Why are you here?"

She pouted. "Don't be like that. We didn't get a chance to talk this morning. I just want to catch up."

"This isn't the time or the place."

"Peter Dourson, I drove six hours to get here. The least you can do is spare me five minutes."

Some things needed to be done, like ripping duct tape off your face. "Ruth's Parkside Cafe is two miles down the hill. Take a left at Blue Rock and follow the signs. I'll meet you there in thirty minutes."

She looked up at him with soft, serious eyes. "I've missed you, Peter."

Peter waited while Susan got in her car and drove away. Aubrey sat in the van with the door open, showing off her stupendous legs while she chatted with Brent. Cynth sauntered up, ignoring the tete-à-tete.

"Hasn't Brent seen you yet?" Peter asked.

"Brent can piss up a rope. Duff and I have a parkour date for Saturday. What will you do about Susan?"

"Damned if I know."

YOU'D THINK AN INDUSTRIAL SPACE WITH TWENTY-FOOT ceilings would be a cold place to dine, but Ruth's was the best venue for private conversation Peter knew. The hostess led Peter down the row of tall booths to one where Susan nibbled on a salad, her brow wrinkling at the edgy art on the walls.

She smiled at him, the hesitant smile she pasted on when she wanted to appear vulnerable.

"I hope you don't mind that I started. I felt funny just sitting here without ordering. Have you seen the menu? I don't know about this stir-fry vegan food. You'll have to tell me what's good."

Peter slid into the booth. "This isn't dinner."

A waiter appeared, hands clasped, face politely expectant.

"Just a Pepsi. I'm not eating."

"Yes, sir, right away."

Susan pouted. "It's dinnertime. You have to eat."

"I have plans."

"How important can they be? I haven't seen you in forever."

"What happened to the furniture king?"

"I came to my senses."

"Was that the day you found last year's homecoming queen with her nose in his zipper after he promised to put her in his new commercials?"

Susan's eyes dropped. "Don't be crude. I suppose you talked to your sisters."

"We do talk, every so often." *Here comes the brave front.*

She looked up, unshed tears glimmering. "Then you understand why I had to leave."

Like the sun rising on an overcast day, illumination arrived late. He said the words, not quite believing as they came from his mouth. "You're relocating."

Susan's smile was a shade too bright. "Isn't it wonderful?"

"And what do you expect to do with yourself?"

"I'm a reporter now."

"For whom?"

"For myself. People make big money on YouTube, and I know all about being on camera. I'm putting together a show."

She slid a business card out of an oversized designer bag, presenting it with a flourish. "Susan's Snippets" jumped out in fancy purple script surrounded by stylized daisies on a pale pink background.

"I designed it myself."

"You're serious."

"Why not? Cats and twelve-year-old kids are making a fortune on ad revenue. I can, too. If we'd had social media when we were in high school, I'd be a Kardashian by now."

"And you're doing this here?"

"Cincinnati is an active, exciting city. You'll help me, won't you?" Big brown eyes turned on him, making him think of Viola begging for pizza crusts.

"What could I possibly do for you?"

"You gave that Aubrey woman an interview. You could give me one to kick off the show."

Peter leaned back, took a sip of the Pepsi that had silently appeared on the table. Leveled his eyes at her.

"No."

The face Susan played like a Stradivarius showed confusion and hurt. "After all we've been to each other? Why ever not?"

Peter opened his mouth, knowing when the words

were out, they couldn't be recalled. "I have someone in my life."

Susan shrugged. "Can't be serious."

"Why not?"

"Because your mother doesn't know about her."

"And I'll thank you to let it stay that way."

Susan's brow wrinkled in confusion. "What are you hiding, Peter? Is she ... you know ..." her voice dropped to a whisper, "an *atheist?*"

"What?"

"There has to be a reason you haven't told your family." She sat bolt upright, genuine shock on her face. "No! You're *gay*. I knew there was something wrong when we were together."

Peter spoke through gritted teeth. "I am not gay."

"Then what is it?"

"Lia is none of your damn business."

"Lia?"

Dammit. I did not mean to say that.

Susan's eyes flicked around the table, a sign of rapid calculation.

Here it comes.

"Your landlady with that vicious little dog? You're *living* with her? *Out of wedlock?*"

For once, Peter appreciated Lia's fine distinctions about boundaries. "We are not living together. I have my apartment and she has hers."

"Under the same roof in a house she owns. Your mother has a right to know."

"And what gives her that right?"

"You caused excruciating pain when you passed

through her womb. She's entitled to pray for your eternal soul."

"And you're the one to share the happy news?"

Susan's brown eyes narrowed, as if she were preparing to kill a small, helpless creature. *More likely plotting a spot of blackmail.*

Blackmail went both ways. "I don't imagine you'd like the details of your impending divorce to be top of the page on Google every time someone plugs in your name. It might hurt the image you're trying to create."

"You'd never do a rotten thing like that."

"I have to go now." Peter scooted to the edge of the booth.

"You used to love me."

He hated this, hated the need to speak brutal truths. "When I was eight, I thought people who smoked grass were burning their lawn clippings. I grew out of that, too."

"Don't be ugly." She stared into her iced tea as she stirred it with her straw, then peeked up under her lashes. "Remember when you were prom king and I was queen? I still have the photograph dad took. That was the happiest day of my life."

Sad, and probably true. "Our relationship was nothing more than a foregone conclusion hatched by our mothers when we were in diapers. I was never the man you wanted me to be."

"Didn't you love me, even a bit?"

"I'm not sure if what we had counted as love, for either of us."

"It suited you well enough back then."

"What makes you think it wouldn't be us divorcing right now?"

"You would never leave me. I left you. I'll be sorry about that for the rest of my life."

He stood.

"Getting fingerprinted like a criminal was the second-biggest humiliation of my life."

Everything was the something-est for Susan.

"At least tell me you'll take care of the fine."

Peter shook his head and turned for the door, abandoning his Pepsi.

Susan's voice floated after him. "What about the check?"

WITH DAVID AND ZOE FINALLY OUT THE DOOR, LIA slumped in the leather Morris chair she'd bought for Peter in a defensive move to keep his unforgivably ugly Lazy Boy out of her living room. She sighed, waving Zoe's check to fan her face, or maybe to remember why she put herself through the meat grinder like this. Thank God it was over.

It took hours for Zoe to decide, after Lia pulled out everything she had, after David measured every canvas (as if Lia didn't know how big they were), after Zoe held paint chips and swatches next to each one, asking if Lia had the same thing, but with apricot accents, or maybe something in raspberry.

David knew Lia's limits, steering Zoe away from the cliff with pithy remarks and gossipy distractions. But when it came to the sticking point, Zoe would dig in her three-inch heels, tapping a lavender nail against her pouty bottom lip as she delivered a hesitant, "I don't know ..."

At the restaurant where Lia worked during college, a fellow waitress liked to hide in the soundproof walk-in and scream when things got crazy. When Zoe got on her nerves, Lia plastered a smile on her face and imagined screaming in that walk-in. As the afternoon dragged on, she'd replaced that image with one of Zoe padlocked in a freezer, bloody nails clawing the lid as she whimpered for help.

Zoe finally chose the trio of stargazer lilies on display when she walked in the door. Lia had known they were the best fit and wanted her to have the impact of seeing them as she entered the room. Zoe put them aside because finding the perfect dress on the first try meant you didn't get to put on every dress in the store. That or she loved the way David cajoled when she played hard to get and didn't want the fun to end.

Her next client, she'd save the perfect painting for third or fourth, or even tenth, to see if that made a difference.

Zoe signed her check with a large, loopy signature, handing it over with the understanding that Lia would hold the check while she lived with the paintings for a week. It was the usual arrangement, designed to avert buyer's remorse.

Zoe lagged like a kid being dragged out of a candy store, ooh-ing and ah-ing over the textured paint treatment Lia had given the interior of her "charming rehab" and wondering if Lia might do something similar for her.

David lured Zoe out the door with the promise of a lychee martini at The Hamilton. With Zoe's attention fixed on a new shiny, David doubled back to give Lia a quick shoulder squeeze.

Lia whispered, "If she doesn't keep those paintings, I'm coming after you with Peter's Taser."

"Once they're on the wall, you won't be able to pry them away from her."

"Your mouth, God's ear."

She followed David to the door, an excuse to check the curb. No white Cadillac. Susan had been and gone. Uber? Or had she sweet-talked Cal into bringing her back? At least Peter had texted her midway through the afternoon with a promise of Dewey's pizza and explanations.

Her eyes caught on Susan's scarf, stuffed in a ceramic pot when she'd heard David and Zoe at the door. She ran it through her hands, tracing a finger across the invisible dents Pup put in it that morning. The scarf featured fanciful mythological animals playing a variety of lawn games in muted pink and mauve and gray. Susan must have chosen it for the color. It couldn't be the subject matter.

Lia had succumbed to temptation and searched the Hermès website during one of Zoe's many private consultations with David that afternoon. The design was one of the year's signature styles, so Susan hadn't bought it at discount. Peter's ex had bucks, or someone who liked her did.

A tap on the kitchen door interrupted Lia's thoughts, followed by the scrabbling of claws on her wood floor. Chewy bounced in, leaping onto her lap, curling into a ball as if seeking sanctuary from nuclear attack in a sixties, kiss-your-ass-goodbye pose. Pup pursued and sat at her feet, whining and tugging on Lia's Boho maxi skirt.

"Hey, that's my good skirt!"

Good was relative. Bought for twenty dollars on sale, and with ten times the yardage of Susan's pricy designer scarf ... Lia was too tired to work the math but decided Susan would hand Lia's favorite skirt over to the maid—to clean grout.

She picked Pup up to rub noses. Chewy scrambled out of Lia's lap and sought refuge on the Mission couch, cowering in front of the prized art pillows Lia had on display for her visitors. Lia made a mental note to put them away before Pup realized they were there.

Alma entered, followed by Viola. She perched on the couch and gave Chewy a consoling pet. The bird-like woman with her stubbornly black cap of hair had seen everything in her seventy-plus years. She remained serene and sensible in spite of it.

Lia's stress vanished.

"I saw your visitors leaving and decided it was safe to bring them back."

Lia glanced at the mantel clock, a vintage Seth Thomas from Ruth's estate. When Lia bought the house, Alma insisted it couldn't be parted from the Rookwood fireplace and gave it to her as a housewarming present. Ten after six. Peter was late.

"Thanks, Alma. I was too pooped to come get them."

"I thought that might be the case. Your client was here much longer than you expected. I hope she spent oodles of money."

"Enough to keep the kids in kibble a while longer. I hate selling paintings to someone who cares more about her color scheme than whether she likes the art. Unfortunately, those are the people with money to buy."

"Sometimes I think buying art should be like adopting a dog from a rescue organization. You have to fill out an application and submit to a home visit to prove you'll be a good owner."

Lia snorted. "That's how I'll do it from now on. Throw up a few roadblocks to ownership to give my paintings some mystique. Double my prices while I'm at it."

"What was the business out in your yard this morning? I didn't ask earlier because you were in such a rush."

Lia huffed. "Peter's ex-fiancée popped into town and made herself at home in his apartment. I thought we had a burglar, so I called 911."

"Oh, my. What did Peter say about it?"

"Nothing. He was late for a meeting, so he left as soon as he knew there was no danger. I expect he'll tell me what's going on when he gets in." She glanced at the clock again. "Which should have been thirty minutes ago."

"Don't be too hard on him. If Luthor was alive, he'd cause all kinds of trouble with no encouragement from you."

"Truth. How did the fur kids do? Chewy looks traumatized."

"Your little girl wore him out. My kitchen floor is the cleanest it's been in years between mopping up the pee puddles and her splashing in the water dish. Every time I looked at the bowl, it was empty. I thought she was dehydrated until I realized I had a lake on my floor."

"I'm so sorry."

"I tried penning her in a corner, but she just howled and she's such a cute little thing I couldn't leave her there. Viola bullied her."

"Oh?"

"She laid down in the middle of the kitchen and wouldn't let your little girl out from under the kitchen table. I shut Viola in the living room. She liked having it all to herself just fine."

Pup, restless on Lia's lap, grabbed the hem of her blouse and tugged.

"Oh, no you don't."

Lia put Pup on the floor and knelt down to join her, hips in the air in a human play bow. She dangled Susan's scarf. Pup yipped and snapped.

"You are one classy pup. I'll have you know this is a four-hundred-dollar chew toy."

Alma raised a hand in protest. "Is that silk? She'll ruin it."

"It's Susan's. She left it behind after saying Pup should be put down. Destroying Susan's scarf is the only way girlfriend will recover her self-esteem."

Lia held the scarf high, jiggling to make the silk shimmy. Pup leapt, latching onto the scarf, growling and tugging. Lia let go. Pup tumbled, wrapping the scarf around her.

"Goodness," Alma said. "She's so colorful. Just like a little gypsy."

Lia unwound the scarf and started the game again. "Are you a gypsy? Is that your name?"

Gypsy growled and leapt, tearing a hole in the scarf.

THE AROMA OF PIZZA AND A SLAP ON LIA'S UPTURNED posterior announced Peter's arrival.

Lia dropped the scarf and gave Peter her best stink eye. "Seriously?"

"Couldn't resist. Hey, Alma. I brought dinner. Will you stick around for a slice?"

Alma stood. "No, thank you. The cheese doesn't agree with me and I think you two have things to talk about. I'll let myself out."

Peter watched her leave. "She catch the Susan show this morning?"

"You think? Yeah, she caught it." Lia disentangled scarf and dog and pushed herself up off the floor. "I was about to feed the kids."

"How did Pup do at Alma's?"

"She is Pup no more. Alma and I christened her. She's Gypsy."

"Did the christening have anything to do with Susan's scarf?"

"Only everything. I think I'll frame it."

"You looked like a scene from *Alien* when she lunged out of your chest."

"If only I had it on video. You left me holding the bag this morning."

"Couldn't be helped." He presented the still-warm pizza box and a stack of napkins. "I brought a peace offering."

Lia poured kibble for the dogs. They ignored it, staying glued to Peter and the box of amazing scents now residing on the coffee table. Gypsy—who had never experienced pizza in her brief life—whined at the box like a heroin addict in the presence of a loaded hypodermic.

Lia sat next to Peter on the couch, taking a napkin from the stack. "How can she possibly know about pizza?"

Peter opened the box and gently separated a slice, handing it to her. "Chewy told her."

"I refuse to believe that." She took a bite, humming with pleasure. "This is the first time you've brought Dewey's home since District Five moved."

"Desperate times, desperate measures."

"I'll think about forgiving you."

Lia had just fed the crust of her second slice to Gypsy and Chewy when Peter took her hand, chafing the knuckles with his thumb.

"I love you more than Pepsi and Pop Tarts."

"Sounds serious."

"Susan's off the rails right now. It has nothing to do with you or me, but I have to deal with her."

"What makes her your problem?"

"I've known her all my life. I can't ignore that."

It wasn't an argument Lia agreed with, but Peter's sense of responsibility made him who he was. She let it go.

"Why is she off the rails?"

"She caught the furniture king auditioning last fall's homecoming queen for his next batch of commercials. With his pants unzipped."

"I suppose I should feel sorry for her. Was it the adultery or the thought of being upstaged on television that did it?" She waved her free hand. "Forget I said that. I suppose she wants to pick up where you left off."

Peter sighed and squeezed the hand he still possessed, gave it a little shake. "She's humiliated, and she's starting over. She wants to do a local-interest video blog."

Lia's gut clenched. "She's moving to Cincinnati?"

"It's a big city. Nothing to do with us."

"Lexington is a big city. Louisville is a big city. And both of them are closer to Bowling Green than Cincinnati. Both have plenty of local interest."

Peter shrugged. "Maybe distance is the point."

"If she wants distance, there's Cleveland, Columbus, Indianapolis. Hell, she could shoot for the big time and go to Chicago. She came here because you're here."

"You and I are together. I made that clear."

"Well, okay then."

"You have no reason to feel jealous of Susan."

"Who says I'm jealous?"

"You're not?"

Lia's voice rose and took on an edge, slicing the air like a razor. The sound and what it implied mortified her. "I don't like that she's here with the misguided idea she can snap her fingers and have you back."

Peter gathered her in his arms. She hid her face in his chest, crumpling under the weight of the day.

He said nothing. He slid a finger down her neck to her collarbone, hooked the delicate gold chain that disappeared under her blouse and withdrew the token that hung next to her heart. He stroked a thumb across the surface of the opal, careful not to bend the bird's nest of gold wire that cradled it.

"If I gave Susan a rock I picked up off the ground, she'd throw it in my face. It wouldn't matter that it was pretty, less that it was a piece of me. I suspect you'd wear this if it was only a bit of polished gravel."

Lia sniffed. "Only if the shape was interesting."

Peter's chest quivered against her cheek with a silent laugh.

"Even if I'd never met you, I wouldn't go back to Susan."

"Oh?" It was a small and pitiful sound.

"Susan ... our parents are friends. We grew up together. They always hoped we'd marry. She was the prettiest girl in school and dated anyone she wanted. She wasn't interested in me until the basketball team won state."

"Were you interested in her? ... Don't answer that."

Peter stroked a soothing hand up and down her back. "I didn't have much experience with girls. My parents kept me busy with scouts and church and sports. Didn't want me to get into trouble, I expect. But Susan was the next thing to family, and it was a boost having the most popular girl in school cooing over me. I fell into it without thinking much about it. After we got engaged, she started trying to fix me. She called it supporting me so I could reach my potential."

"That makes it all right, then."

Peter laughed. "God love you. I can't blame her. She was raised to see a husband as a lump of clay and a wife as the driving force in his career. That's a plan that works for a lot of folks. It took me a while to realize it didn't matter to Susan who he was as long as he wound up with a fat wallet and a fine house. It was a harsh awakening."

"I imagine."

"I sat across from her at Ruth's—"

Lia's stomach twisted tighter. "You took her to Ruth's?"

"No, I met her there. And I only stayed long enough to let her know it wasn't happening. You know that saying they drilled into me at the academy?"

"'Know where the exits are'?"

"I was thinking of 'Be polite but plan how to kill them.'"

"You did not."

"Cross my heart. I had my eye on a steak knife on the next table."

"What will you do?"

"I have to keep saying no until she gets it. She has too much pride to push in where she's not wanted. Right now, she believes I'm making her suffer before I take her back."

"You'd never do that. Why would she think it?"

"First because she can't imagine I'm not secretly pining for her, second because that's what she would do. Are we okay?"

Lia saw the worry in Peter's eyes and her stomach relaxed. "We're fine. Let's not let her ruin any more of our evening."

"I wouldn't call you hanging on me a ruined evening."

She thumped his shoulder, gently. "Smart ass. Not to change the subject, but why do you have a spare key where anyone can find it?"

"Not anyone. Only someone I grew up with. My homies aren't thick on the ground here."

"It won't be an issue anymore. I trashed your rock."

"You didn't."

"Dig it out of the garbage if you want it for a paper-weight. We need a better solution."

"It was an acceptable solution that didn't cost a cent. You spent plenty on that security system. Why didn't it go off?"

Lia grimaced. "I didn't think I needed to set it while I was at the park. Who breaks in at 9 a.m.?"

"Apparently Susan does."

"She won't be doing it again."

"You know this because?"

"I took your key away from her."

Seeing Peter wince satisfied the same small part of herself that took pleasure in watching Gypsy chew Susan's designer scarf.

"Didn't think she'd waltz off with it, did you?"

"No, but I should have."

"Sounds like we both had an exciting day."

"You don't know the half."

"Oh?"

"I finally got the evidence I need for a warrant on a guy running kids to steal packages."

"That's great."

"Then Parker told me to hand the case over to Brent and assigned me to Not Elvis. Just me. No resources. Tomorrow my life will be whack-a-doodle city."

"No! I'm so sorry."

"It's a boost that they chose me, but it's frustrating. Jamal's running a half dozen juveniles or more, kids with lives headed in the wrong direction. If Jamal is part of a network, it could be a hundred kids across the city."

"Still, it's just packages."

"Mostly Amazon. You know who shops at Amazon?"

"Um, everyone?"

"Older people on fixed income, disabled people who can't get around. A fifty-dollar loss, not getting what they need when they need it, these are hardships for them. For some of them it's groceries."

"I'm sure Brent can handle it."

"Something will go wrong. I can feel it."

Lia toyed with a button on Peter's shirt. "Then you come home and I give you a tough time about Susan."

"You were very civil to her this morning, considering."

"I was also planning ways to kill her."

"Poor Cal. He's too polite to say, but he was hoping for a girl fight."

Lia's head popped up and her mouth gaped. "He was not!"

"It's been a long time since that YouTube video."

Lia shoved him away. "You're a jerk, Peter Dourson."

He pulled her back. She struggled for form's sake while he tipped her chin up and kissed her.

"But I'm your jerk."

A DREAM REALIZED

WEDNESDAY, MAY 5, 1937

MAL FOLLOWED PETE—MR. SCHMIDT SAID TO CALL HIM that—up the long stairs to the second floor of the newly remodeled Beverly Hills Country Club. A year ago, he'd watched it burn.

In a few hours, the first and finest carpet joint in the country would reopen. The rich and famous would return —for fine food, the best shows outside of New York, and wall-to-wall gambling.

Tonight, the Dublin gutter rat was inside.

Mal schooled his face to look like it was no big deal, the plush blue carpeting you could sink your feet into, gold-leaf patterned wallpaper, crystal chandeliers bigger than your average Packard.

Pete stepped through a door labeled "Trianon," then stopped at a landing overlooking tiers of linen-draped tables encircling a central dance floor. The only sounds were the clink of china and silver as silent waiters prepared for the first service. A large, empty stage loomed over all. Mal's mouth went dry. *I'll be on that stage, if I have to kill to make it happen.*

Pete, a broad man with a receding hairline and a double-breasted suit, dropped his usual worried expression and grinned. "You'll be in here. Nervous, kid?"

Mal shook his head.

Pete gave Mal a shrewd look. "You're stupid if you aren't."

Mal jerked a shoulder. "I can handle it."

"You're bold for a seventeen-year-old kid, I'll give you that. But a few nerves give you an edge. Just remember, they're only schmoes in fancy suits, like me. When you forget that, pretend you're back on the loading dock, showing me your tricks."

Since the fire, Mal had made it his business to learn about the big wheels who ran Newport. Pete was a smart guy, even if he called himself a schmoe. He'd spent years in prison protecting the money he made bootlegging with George Remus during Prohibition. When he got out, booze was legal and Pete was out of business. Instead of folding his tent, he built the Beverly Hills and got richer.

More joints opened up. Now Newport rolled in money. Enough money you could smell it all the way to Cleveland. The Cleveland Four—the most powerful gangsters in the Midwest—wanted in, but they didn't see the logic in opening their own joints when they could take over places that were already successful.

One of the Cleveland Four, a guy named Moe Dalitz, decided to buy the BH. Pete wasn't selling. Dalitz hired an operator named Red Masterson to set fire to the club, figuring this would make Mr. Schmidt—Pete—change his mind. Only the BH burned to the ground and the daughter of the caretaker died, outraging a police department used to looking the other way.

Pete rebuilt, making the BH bigger and better than ever. That made him Mal's hero.

Mal had spent weeks as a day laborer hauling debris from the burned-out shell. Later he spent more weeks unloading endless truckloads of furnishings for the renovated club before he found the right opportunity to show his tricks to Pete.

Mal wasn't nervous, but he knew not to contradict the guy giving him his big chance. "Thank you, sir. I will remember. Are the Andrews Sisters really on next month's bill?"

"It's not official yet. Cab Calloway not good enough for you?"

"I like him just fine, but he's not as pretty as they are."

Pete barked a laugh, the same laugh that had given Mal the confidence to show him his card tricks.

"There will be plenty of pretty ladies here, but don't notice them too much, no matter how much they notice you. No pulling coins out of cleavage. I don't want complaints."

"No, sir."

"You'll work the tables during dinner. You ever work in a restaurant?"

"Ate in a few."

"It gets tight between the tables. Don't bump the guests. See Bess about your clothes."

"Yes, sir."

"You need a stage name, something to get people excited." Pete pulled a cigar from his breast pocket and squinted. "What's Mal short for?"

"Just Mal, sir. It's not short for anything." Mal was what the gang called him in Dublin. It meant "chief," but it wouldn't do to let the boss know that.

"My wife has a Pomeranian named Malachi. Sharp little fellow and too big for his britches. Got red hair like you." Pete poked the cigar at Mal. "From now on, you're Marvelous Malachi."

Mal blinked. He wasn't sure how he felt about being named after a lapdog, but he suspected he'd wind up washing dishes if he wasn't grateful. "I don't know what to say. Thank you, sir."

Pete lit the cigar with a gold lighter, puffing to get it going. "Get something to eat in the kitchen and be ready to start at seven. We'll see how it goes after tonight. Do well and I've got a place for you."

MAL STOOD BESIDE THE STAGE IN HIS NEW SWALLOWTAIL tuxedo, his heart thumping pleasantly in his chest. He rubbed a thumb across the lucky Irish shilling in his pocket as he looked out across the ocean of fancy-dressed diners.

The jewelry in that room could set him up for life, and he had the hands to make much of it disappear. But Pete would cut those hands off if he touched one tiny rock. Anyway, fishing in this pond would be ungrateful after the opportunity he'd been given.

He allowed himself a minute to regret leaving those glittery treasures lying on their soft, pillowy breasts, then reminded himself to focus on the prize. No haul was worth giving up his shot at the limelight.

Mal, tonight your life changes.

DAY 11

TUESDAY, APRIL 30, 2019

Peter shoved the enormous stack of tip reports under one arm to open his office door. Elvis greeted him in the form of a life-sized plastic bust sitting next to his computer. This Elvis featured a grinning skull, Elvis hair, and a collar reaching to the skull's non-existent ears.

He dropped the reports on his desk and flicked the skull with his middle finger. The head bobbled and a tinny version of "Jail House Rock" blared out of the skull's mouth. Peter turned to glare at his office mate.

Brent threw his hands up in a don't-look-at-me gesture. "It was here when I got in. Someone already owned it, or they paid overnight shipping to get it here. My superior taste precludes the first, and I don't like you enough for the second."

Peter raised his voice over the music. "What idiot would own this piece of junk?"

"I'd vote for Junior, him being an Elvis fan. And he

works with dead people so the skull would appeal—only he'd think he was casting pearls before swine to pass it along to you."

The song stopped, thank the Lord. Peter dropped into his chair, stared at the now-silent King. "Maybe I'll give it to him."

"Won't that make Amanda do a happy dance."

Moving as if handling a live bomb, Peter turned Elvis to face the wall. He booted his computer and opened Heenan's newly scanned file. The original missing person file was thin, consisting of interviews with neighbors and ending with the discovery of Heenan's car at the airport and the assumption that whatever happened to Heenan, happened elsewhere. The file also included Heenan's fingerprints, courtesy of a record check for a children's organization.

With no next of kin to push the issue, Heenan's disappearance slid into obscurity. Now brass expected him to pull a rabbit out of his ass.

He shifted his gaze to the stack of tips with the wariness you give the rattlesnake that already bit you. Someone could send you down a rabbit hole for their own reasons. And biases often distorted information from legitimate sources. The quick glance he'd given the stack earlier suggested the usual time wasters, but they were all he had.

He bought a Pepsi from the machine in the hall, then used post-it notes to label sections of his desk as "Psychics," "Crackpots," "Nuisance," "Possible," or the hopeful "Priority." He popped the tab on the Pepsi and settled down to triage the information, scanning each call sheet before assigning it to its proper place.

Brent scooted his chair over. "I'd change those to 'Malicious,' 'Misguided,' 'Attention-Seeking,' and 'Deluded.'"

"That's helpful."

"Anything good in there?"

Peter snorted. "Only if you count entertainment value. I've got three psychics and a claim against Heenan's estate, along with accusations we're desecrating the King and demanding we return his bones to Graceland."

"You calling the psychics?"

"You never know. Bailey's come up with some spooky stuff with her Tarot readings."

"Only in a Monday morning quarterback kind of way. Her ju-ju never helps when you need it."

"Truth." He picked up the next report. "Here we go. 'Joe Thomas killed the magician. He lives at 4317 Glenmore Avenue.'"

"There you go. Case closed."

Peter set the page on the space marked "possible" then pulled Thomas' driver license up on his computer.

"Thomas was four when Heenan died. No criminal record."

"Who called it in?"

Peter checked the header information on the form. "Anonymous."

"I bet Joe let his dog piss on Anonymous' lawn."

Peter shifted the report from "possible," to "nuisance." "Only if Anonymous is a total psycho, which I won't discount. More likely Anonymous is Joe's ex-girlfriend, or Joe got a promotion Anonymous wanted."

History was full of tips that had been ignored to everyone's regret, so Parker's mandate to follow every tip—no matter how bogus—made sense. But he was in no mood to chase down cranks.

Peter's phone rang. He grabbed the handset with one hand while he scanned the map. "Dourson."

"Detective Dourson? My name is Sylvia Walsh." The voice was female, hesitant and reedy, likely middle aged or older.

"What can I do for you?"

"I saw you on the news. I'm calling about Andrew Heenan."

Right age. Doesn't sound like a crackpot. He grabbed his legal pad and a pen. "Did you know him?"

"No, I never met him. But—I don't know if you've heard of me, but I get messages."

Peter deflated. "You're a psychic."

"If you want to call it that. I have a message for you. I need you to write this down, exactly as I say it. Will you do that?"

Peter surrendered to the inevitable. "I'm ready."

"You will solve this. I want you to know that."

Peter caught Brent's eyes, shook his head. "Thank you, that's good to know."

"That's not the message."

"What's the message?"

"I had a vision of roots, a tangle of old roots."

Peter once read facial expressions transmit over the

phone. He didn't know if it was true, but he kept his eyes from rolling, just in case.

"Um, yeah, that's how Mr. Heenan was found."

"These roots stretch into the past."

Time to ease the nice psychic off the phone. "That certainly makes sense since he disappeared thirty years ago."

"It's more than that. I keep seeing a tree, with roots reaching into the past and branches reaching into the future. Andrew Heenan's death is the base of the trunk, where future meets past."

Peter dutifully scribbled this down. "Any idea what that means?"

"I'm just a conduit. The message was for you, not me."

"Anything else? A name, maybe how Mr. Heenan died?"

"Sorry, that's all they told me."

"Thank you for your civic-mindedness." Peter took her contact information for his records and disconnected the call. He made an explosive "puh" sound and slumped in his chair.

"I take it your psychic wasn't helpful."

"She said the murder is a tree."

"That's a valuable tip there. Who gave her this message?"

"I didn't ask. Probably a forty-thousand-year-old Inca warrior."

"There were no Inca forty thousand years ago."

"Exactly."

Three hours and thirty-seven phone calls later, Peter shoved away from his computer, tipped his head back and shut his eyes. The bland office walls closed in around him. He opened Google maps on his computer, switched to satellite view, and plugged in the GPS coordinates he'd taken at the site. On his left, Brent hammered at his keyboard.

"I have to get out of here. Want to be a sounding board?"

"Sorry, jammed up with the warrant you were supposed to write—"

Peter picked up his desk phone.

"—and Cynth's out on an active shooter simulation with SWAT."

Peter hesitated with the receiver frozen halfway between the phone and his face, then dialed nine for an outside line.

A WALL OF PARKED SEMI-TRAILERS PASSED BY LIA'S WINDOW, towering over Peter's Blazer as he navigated a narrow stretch of recently paved asphalt. Trees lined the other side of the road, looming over a barricade of honeysuckle bushes. The effect was tunnel-like and claustrophobic.

Two weeks earlier, honeysuckle blooms perfumed the air all over the city. Today, withered flowers littered the pavement. The bush was Ohio's version of kudzu and a target of those determined to eradicate invasive species. Of all the requests clients made, no one ever asked her to paint honeysuckle.

"Where are we, Boot?"

Peter responded to Lia's involvement in dangerous

situations by treating her like a rookie and coaching her in preparedness. This was much better than trying to keep her locked up, so she usually humored him. Today's game was a standard field training exercise intended to increase awareness and observation skills.

"We're in the middle of nowhere, headed for more nowhere."

"Cute. Do better."

"Somewhere in the West End. Please don't make me jump out to find a street sign. I haven't seen one since we turned off Gest."

"You won't find one. We're not on the map."

"Dirty trick, Dourson. How does a road that's not on the map rate fresh asphalt?"

"This is the back way to the academy."

"Where we did those shoot/don't shoot scenarios?"

"Yep."

"Explaining why an alley rates better maintenance than Hamilton Avenue. Someone buried Andrew Heenan behind the police academy? That's gutsy."

"Not exactly behind. A tick north. CPD took over the site in 2004. It was the Bengals training camp in the eighties, but I'm not sure if the Bengals or Heenan got here first. The site may have been under construction when Heenan went into the ground."

Peter checked his GPS app and pulled over to a patch of gravel. "This is as good as we'll get."

"Do you think Terry knew the road was so close?"

"Probably not. You can't tell from the creek what's at the top along this stretch. I found this spot on Google Earth, but I don't know if we can get down from here.

Hand me the water bottle and grab your hiking stick."

Once out of the car, Peter stashed the bottle in the cargo pocket of the pants he'd changed into when he picked her up. He pulled a machete and a backpack out of the rear, slinging the pack on his back. He led, shoving branches aside and whacking his way through the thicket.

"What exactly is our purpose today?"

"Parker expects me to deliver some kind of progress when I have nothing to work with. I thought another look at the scene would help."

The way Peter swung his machete, Lia wondered if he'd really come so he could take out his frustrations on the honeysuckle.

"There's nothing helpful in the file?"

"The file is useless. The detective who worked the case died of cancer years ago, so there go any private observations or personal notes."

"Do cops often keep notes out of their files?"

"Case files are for facts and evidence. We keep speculative stuff and impressions off paper, especially if they seem nutty. But I need crazy for this one.

"Everyone associated with the case is gone. I can't locate the neighbor who reported Heenan missing. The booking agency he worked with went out of business years ago. The neighbors said he was a nice man who kept to himself, except for one who thought he was a pervert because he performed for children—but there was no substance to that."

Peter gave a vicious thwack at a bush before he continued. "They might have found something—fingerprints, blood evidence, a freaking gum wrapper—if they'd bothered to consider his home a possible crime scene. They decided he left home under his own steam and only did a minimal search. Heenan didn't have anyone looking for him, and the assumption he ran into trouble elsewhere made it easy to let it go."

"Poor man. It would be awful to disappear and have no one looking for you."

"He was never formally declared dead. I kept getting more and more pissed about what hadn't been done thirty years ago. I had to get out and reboot."

"What do you hope to find?"

"I want to see what's involved in getting a body to the creek. That's the only clue I have to Heenan's killer. I need you to be a sounding board and devil's advocate."

"Won't Captain Parker care that you're consulting your girlfriend?"

"If she cares, she needs to assign more people to the case."

They emerged at a steep slope overlooking the creek. The bank was taller than she remembered, or rather, the water level had returned to normal. The ugly aftermath of the flood remained. Mud had yet to wash from the tree trunks. Detritus hung in the branches. She wondered how long it would stay there.

Peter scanned the slope.

"No easy way down." He nodded at a thin spot in the vegetation, a deer trail running along the top. "This way." He continued to mangle bushes until their path was blocked by the crown of the downed cottonwood.

"Where to now?"

"We hack our way back to the road and go around."

PETER RULED THE BANK ON THE FAR SIDE OF THE TREE
navigable, and they worked their way to the creek with
the aid of convenient saplings. The water, so muddy ten
days before, ran clear, the bottom visible through what
she guessed was two feet of water. He dug into his pack,
swapping his sneakers for waders.

"I don't suppose you brought a pair for me," Lia said.

"You get to ride piggyback."

Peter left his pack on the bank with his machete and
took Lia's hiking stick. She climbed on his back, his heat
penetrating her clothes as she hugged tightly, pressing her
cheek against his hair.

Touch was a simple thing people took for granted, a
luxury Lia only allowed with people she trusted. It was a
secret pleasure, one she relied upon Peter to provide
because initiating was still so hard for her. She sank into
that sense of comfort that was Peter as his body shifted
and lurched inside the circle of her arms and legs.

He eased into the creek and plowed through the water,
using her hiking stick to assure his footing on the sand
and rocks while her feet dangled inches above the surface.

On the other side, Peter turned his back to the bank
and let her slide to the ground. She felt a pang at the loss
of him, then turned. The trunk loomed beside her, the fan
of roots reaching over her head.

They climbed the bank to the root crater, mud sticking
to Lia's sneakers in clumps and smelling of wet basement.
The ends of severed roots glowed pale in the tangled wall

of roots and muck, marking a void where Andrew Heenan had been.

Lia sat on a log. "Hard to believe something that awful was right here."

Peter unhooked the bib of his waders, handed her the water bottle, and sat beside her. She drank and handed it back to him for a long pull. He wiped his face with the back of a forearm, smearing mud across his cheek. She rubbed it away with a thumb.

"Is this helping?" she asked.

"It's a sight better than talking to wackos on the phone while I'm chained to my desk. And now I know one thing about our murderer."

"What's that?"

"He's strong. Or he was thirty years ago. Heenan weighed 145 pounds when he disappeared. You could handle that with a fireman's carry, but it's rough going."

"What about Commodore's idea, that the killer came in on this side and buried him at the top?"

Peter shook his head. "I studied the satellite view on Google Maps. You'd have to hump the body across an obstacle course to get it here. There's a rail yard with two hundred feet of rough ground and tracks to cross between the top of the bank and the nearest place you could park a car. Beyond that you have a warren of warehouses covering more than a quarter mile before you find your way out to a street.

"A night watchman would spot the car and investigate before you could get in and out. If a train came through at the wrong time, Heenan's killer would be stuck with nowhere to go. Crossing the creek makes no sense, but coming from this side is idiocy."

"Not if it was the night watchman doing the dumping."

"That's possible. He kills Heenan, puts him in the trunk of Heenan's car and drives it to work. What if it's not the watchman?"

"I don't understand why he didn't dump the body off the side of I-74. There are places where the highway is fifty feet above the ground, spots only accessible to coyotes. He pulls over in the breakdown lane, tosses the body over the rail, and drives off in less than two minutes. No chance it would ever be discovered."

Peter frowned. "When was I-74 built? Maybe it wasn't around then."

"Sometime in the seventies."

"That tells us something about him. You use what you know, what you see. He didn't drive I-74 and wasn't aware of the potential for body disposal."

"He felt at home running around an open sewer? A toxic waste dump?"

"Maybe he explored the creek when he was a kid," Peter said.

"Then finding him will be easy. He's the guy with three arms, and ears that glow in the dark."

"Stink and danger would only make it more attractive to most boys."

"Why didn't he dump poor Andrew off the Eighth Street Viaduct? Andrew lands in the creek, washes down to the Ohio River, and winds up in the Gulf of Mexico."

Peter took another slug from the bottle. "Maybe the viaduct was too exposed. Too much traffic that night.

Then he got down here and this section of creek was too low to carry the body out to the river. It had to be low that night or he wouldn't have crossed it."

"And he found a shovel propped against the tree? He brought the shovel, so he had to carry the body *and* the shovel. If it was the watchman, he probably had some kind of cart."

Peter shook his head. "The ground by the tracks is too rough. Maybe if he had a Humvee."

"Now you're making fun of me. Humvees didn't exist until the nineties."

"Your night watchman had to be a real behemoth to hump Andrew two-thirds of the way across a football field. There are a lot of industrial jobs down here, jobs that build more muscle than being a night watchman. And I bet more than a few sports fans hung around to see the Bengals practice."

"A football player could haul a shovel and 145 pounds of dead weight with no problem."

"They built the training facility that year," Peter said. "A construction worker might be a better choice."

"Construction workers would be hard to track, wouldn't they?"

"They come and go. I don't think my guy came in from the rail yard, but he might have discovered the creek because he was hanging out to watch trains."

Lia took the bottle from Peter. "You're thinking someone who grew up here."

"Screams 'native' to me."

"I can see that."

"Most people aren't dumb enough to haul a dead body

around in daylight. My guy brought Heenan here in the middle of the night. He had to know this area to navigate it in the dark."

Lia ticked off points on her fingers. "So he was strong, he was local, and he didn't drive to Indiana since he didn't think of I-74. He was a mutant chemical zombie, a night watchman, a Bengal, or your basic blue collar muscle guy. Are you getting any other ideas about him?"

"I'm thinking he was twenty-five to forty."

"Why?"

"Statistics aren't always reliable but the sweet spot for homicide offenders is between twenty-five and thirty."

"You hear more and more about young killers these days."

"If you're not talking gang-banger executions, younger guys who kill, it's usually an impulse. It's violent and messy. We don't see that here. No signs of violence on the remains—"

"That you can see."

"Pretty slim that you stab or shoot someone and don't hit bone. No blood in the house, or they would have handled the case differently."

"He was killed elsewhere."

Peter retrieved the bottle and took another swallow, draining it. He screwed the cap back on and returned it to his pocket. "You're a heck of a devil's advocate."

"I do my best."

"Heenan died in his Elvis suit after performing for a bunch of kids at a party. If I had just spent two hours entertaining children, I wouldn't be wandering the streets in my Elvis costume. I'd head straight for a shower to wash off whatever sugary goo was sticking to me. I'd want a change of clothes."

"A mugger?"

"A garden variety mugger wouldn't have gone to so much trouble to hide the body, and I doubt he grabbed Heenan on the street outside a kiddie party. There would have been witnesses, parents picking up kids."

"A carjacking, then."

"If Heenan's killer hijacked the car to joyride or commit a crime, he would have dumped it at any one of a hundred high-volume parking lots in the city. The employee lots on Pill Hill are perfect. People come and go from the hospital at all hours. Plenty of buses, going all over the city. He'd have an easy way home. We would have found Heenan in the trunk of his car."

"Not a mugger or a car-jacking. How do you think it happened?"

"I think he was laying in wait at Heenan's house."

"And?"

"The killer knew Heenan was leaving town. He timed the attack and planted the car at the airport so everyone would think he left on schedule. Then he used Heenan's ticket. Question is whether he used the ticket to disappear because something went wrong, or if he used it to mislead everyone and snuck back into town. Either way, it was weeks before anyone started looking."

"How could he use the ticket?" Lia asked.

"Airlines didn't require identification back then. If you had a ticket, you could board."

"Then he knew Heenan, he was a planner and he was an adult."

"He went to a lot of trouble. That means he had a purpose."

"What kind of purpose?"

"No clue. Why would anyone kill a third-rate magician?"

DAY 12

WEDNESDAY, MAY 1, 2019

THE MILL CREEK ALLIANCE WAS ONE OF SEVERAL organizations making its home in the rectory of Northside's decommissioned Saint Patrick's Church. The front door opened to a wide hall featuring kitchen cabinets and a coffee bar stocked with exotic herbal teas. Pale art faded into the walls.

In a room on the left, a man in baggy pants led a group of women through a tai chi form. Beyond an open door on the right, a frizzy-haired woman in soothing colors frowned at a laptop. A desktop fountain gurgled somewhere in the room.

Peter poked his head in the office, knocked on the jamb.

"Mill Creek Alliance?"

The woman looked up, the reflection on her glasses giving her an empty-eyed, Little Orphan Annie look. "End of the hall, turn right. You'll see the stairs."

The steps creaked as he ascended, which was likely why Bruce Koehler met him on the landing.

"That's some advance warning system you have," Peter said.

"It works for us. Come on back."

Bruce led him to an office cluttered with maps and literature, and much more comfortable than the determinedly tranquil decor of the first floor.

"Have a seat. Can I get you something to drink?"

"I'm fine. Thanks for agreeing to meet with me."

Peter sat on an old, sturdy couch, one he imagined to be the site of many naps.

"I was surprised to hear from you. Last time I saw you, you said your attachment to our find was temporary."

"The *National Enquirer* changed that. How did they get your name?"

Bruce frowned. "Shame about the article. I supposed the person who sent them the photos gave it to them."

You old pirate. I bet my pension it was you. "You have any idea who that was?"

Bruce made a mistake liars often made, holding eye contact a beat too long while resisting the urge to look away.

Yep, you were the source.

"I'm sure it wasn't Terry or Steve."

Smart, because I wouldn't believe you.

"Lot of young folks on that trip. Impossible to monitor all of them."

Peter sighed, deliberately. "Water under the tree."

"Literally. How can I help you today?"

"We believe Heenan's killer knew the creek."

"A reasonable assumption. I can't see a man with a body in the trunk of his car getting a sudden urge to pull over behind Bengal's field."

"Everyone says you know Mill Creek better than anyone."

Bruce shrugged. "I don't know about better. Maybe longer. What would you like to know?"

"I wonder if you ran into our man on the creek."

Bruce leaned forward, eyes lit with interest. "You don't say?"

"Andrew Heenan went missing in 1987."

Bruce shook his head. "Before my time. I started exploring the creek in the nineties."

"We think he might have been hanging around."

"Returning to the scene of the crime? Interesting thought."

"Can you think of anyone from back then? He would have been strong enough to move a body—"

"Down that gully and across the creek? Quite a feat, even when the water is low."

"Exactly."

"I met plenty of people on the creek. I rarely got their names. I suppose some of them were strong enough, but there's no one who sticks out. I can't even remember their faces."

"What about your old timers? Any of them around in the eighties?"

Bruce rubbed his chin, thinking. "I can check the rosters, but I doubt I'll find anything. Terry was in Alaska back then, and Dick—Dick Brewer, you met him—was in the Army, career military. He retired here and started his business." Commodore rubbing his chin, thinking. "2004, 2005?"

"He put in his full twenty?"

"I'm sure he did. No pension if you leave early, at least back then. I understand that's changing. Steve Reams grew up here. I imagine he was in better shape thirty years ago."

"You think Steve might have done this?"

"No, I think Steve was working for the sewer district in the eighties and he was probably fit enough back then to haul a dead body. That's what you asked. I also think he's constitutionally incapable of killing."

"He doesn't seem like the type, does he?"

"I may have seen your guy, but I can't think of anyone who registered on my creep-o-meter. I think it's a real long shot that your guy is still around."

"You have a creep-o-meter?"

"Every paddler who saw *Deliverance* has a creep-o-meter."

THE *X-FILES* THEME DRIFTED OVER FROM THE PHONE ON Lia's drafting table, signaling a call from Bailey. Peter had set the ring tone as a joke. She'd left it because it served its purpose.

"What's up?"

"Promise not to shoot the messenger?"

Gypsy's teeth sank into Lia's foot, an increasingly common occurrence. She picked up Susan's scarf, dangled it to distract the little demon. "Will I want to?"

"You might. But you'll hear about this anyway."

"Someone put naked pictures of me on the internet?"

"Not you. Peter."

"You can't be serious."

"At least he's not naked. Susan posted her first video. I'm texting you a link."

"Do I want to see this?"

"Probably not."

"Hang on." Lia checked her messages and found the YouTube link. "I've got it."

"Call me back after you watch it."

Lia followed the link to a video clip with the white "play" arrow covering Susan's mouth. She tapped the arrow, and tiny Susan spoke.

"Welcome to the premiere episode of *Susan's Snippets*. I'm Susan Sweeney coming to you from Cincinnati, here to share with you the happenings of one of America's most intriguing cities. Today, nothing is more fascinating than the discovery on Cincinnati's Mill Creek, of a long-buried skeleton rumored to be the bones of Elvis Presley himself."

Susan displayed a copy of the *National Enquirer* with the grisly cover photo.

"Heading the investigation into this mystery is Detective Peter Dourson of the Cincinnati Police Department."

The scene switched to a clip of Peter standing in front of District Five. Peter did not appear to be aware of the camera.

"Few people know that Peter grew up next door to me in Cave City, Kentucky. We've been friends since we were in diapers. He's smart, he's dedicated, and girls, he's single.

I bet he'll figure out how the King ended up on the muddy banks of an open sewer in no time."

Lia paused the video and called Bailey. She did not wait for Bailey to speak.

"Tell me again about the Wicca Rule of Three."

"Energy is an amped-up metaphysical boomerang. Whatever you put out, positive or negative, comes back to you, multiplied by three."

"Is there a loophole that allows me to murder Susan as a public service?"

"Nope. You can kill her, but you won't enjoy the fallout. Do I have to talk you down off a ledge?"

Lia sighed. "I'd like to throw something but I value my stuff too much to break any of it because of her."

"There you go. Peter will probably get a few propositions out of it."

"I can't imagine he'll like that any better than I do."

"I wonder why she didn't say they were engaged."

"A failed engagement? Being a loser doesn't suit her brand."

"Love and light, Lia, love and light."

GRIZZLED VETERAN DETECTIVE SAM ROBERTSON ENTERED Peter's office, wreathed in the seductive aroma of hot pork in all its manifestations. He set the extra-large Buddy Deluxe pizza on the edge of Peter's desk, swiped the five-dollar bill waiting there, then curled his hand in the universal "gimme" sign. Cynth and Brent opened their wallets.

Peter flipped up the lid of the box. His hand hovered over the steaming pie when his extension rang. That same hand detoured to the receiver while his tastebuds mourned the first bite of hot-from-the-oven pizza.

Cynth slapped a bill on his desk. "Five dollars says it's a fake tip."

Brent laid a five on top of hers. "Nutcase confession."

Sam grabbed a slice. "I'm in. Psychic."

They could joke. They got a floorshow while his lunch turned into cement. Peter shook his head as he raised the receiver. "Dourson speaking."

Susan's voice, sweet as cotton candy. "My, don't you sound professional."

"Hold a minute." He punched the hold button, swiping bills off his desk. "Ex-fiancée. I win."

"Hey! You can't do that. You weren't in on the bet," Robertson said.

"My office, my rules. Scram."

Nobody moved.

Robertson said, "We paid, we get to play."

Peter gave Brent a pointed look.

"I'm not leaving when you're about to have such an entertaining phone call."

"Asshat."

Cynth folded her arms. "They stay, I stay."

Peter turned his back and took Susan's call off hold. "Sorry, I wasn't alone."

"I guess I won't be mad, then."

"I'm busy, Susan."

Susan huffed. "I just called to let you know I posted my first video."

"I saw it. I'm not amused."

"I know you said you wouldn't interview with me—"

"Not happening. Not in this world. Not in the next."

"I can help. People tell me things."

Peter closed his eyes and imagined banging his head on the desk. He knew better than to let her hear him sigh. "If, as a public-spirited citizen, you care to share information relevant to this case you are welcome to call the homicide unit, and they will take a report."

"Why must you make it so hard? Why won't you talk to me?"

"I'm assuming this is police business, because otherwise you shouldn't be on this line. We have a procedure. Homicide processes all tips about Andrew Heenan."

"I'm on this line, Peter Dourson, because you don't have the courtesy to give me your cell phone number."

"You're on this line because you couldn't wheedle my number out of Abby."

"I should call your captain and tell him you're discriminating against a member of the press for personal reasons."

"If she considers you a member of the press, which I doubt, she'll say you're welcome to attend press conferences like everyone else. If she sees your arrest report, she'll be more likely to think you're a stalker and ban you. Goodbye, Susan."

As Peter lowered the receiver to the cradle, the words, "You're positively evil, Peter Dourson" sputtered from the handset. He reached for his abandoned slice. The cheese, thank God, retained heat, pulling in strings as he lifted it from the box.

Brent tossed the crust of the slice he'd consumed while Peter was on the phone. "Rude, Dourson, after she was kind enough to pimp you out to the ladies of Cincinnati."

Robertson snickered.

"Brent, You're such an ass," Cynth said. "She did that to cause trouble with Lia."

Peter continued to chew, then swallowed. "Lia's not like that."

"Every woman is like that," Robertson said.

PETER STOOD IN FRONT OF HEENAN'S CLIFTON HILLS home, a Tudor style, half-timbered bungalow with mullioned windows, a steeply pitched slate roof, and fieldstone masonry covered with ivy that was likely well-established when Andrew lived there.

The property featured neat brick walkways and a spreading oak in the front yard. Pansies spilled from concrete urns while lilac bushes scented the air. The Tudor influence was strong on the quiet street, with no two houses alike. Peter suspected the original residents would not have stood for it.

Nice house. Way above a cop's salary. That was the Gaslight district: one mile and a world away from the street crimes that plagued Northside. Hard to imagine anything bad happening here, though Peter knew better.

Lia found the combination of academia, culture, and discreet old money stuffy, with ladies who never left the house without their face on, filling their days with charity obligations and their evenings hosting dinner parties enlivened with elevated conversation.

Susan would adopt the wardrobe and mannerisms. After a suitable period, she'd deny she'd ever heard of Cave City.

The Johnsons took possession of the house seven months after Heenan died. How had that happened? If someone had power of attorney to sell the house, why didn't they follow up with the missing person case? So far, the current owners were his best bet for finding a thread to pull that might take him somewhere. He wondered if they knew their house was connected with the *Enquirer* article, and how long they'd be able to maintain their privacy.

No one answered the bell. No sound of activity inside. He scribbled a note on a business card and stuck it in the door, then scanned the street for signs of life.

A woman wearing a broad-brimmed hat and espadrilles knelt on a rubber pad, tending a bed of iris next door. Peter thought about the ancient T-shirts and stained jeans Bailey wore for her gardening jobs. This woman was no laborer. The owner, then, who'd occupied the house a dozen years according to property records. She wouldn't have known Andrew, but he had to start somewhere.

Peter called out as he approached. The woman looked up with an expression of polite inquiry. She was attractive, as any woman in this neighborhood would be. If she didn't come by it naturally, she'd patronize the pricier salons on the east side of town to get the desired effect. In her case, the mandatory matron bob had been given a discreet boost to maintain a rich mink brown.

Her gardening clothes—and likely the tools scattered on the grass—came from L.L. Bean. Peter knew because he'd sent the same shirt to his mother for Christmas. But his mother didn't muck around with weeds when she wore it.

Peter handed her a business card. "Detective Dourson, from District Five."

"You must be here about poor Mr. Heenan. I'm Donna Merrill." She removed a glove and held out a manicured hand to shake. "I've been expecting someone since I saw the story on Channel 7. That was you in the interview, wasn't it?"

"You knew Andrew Heenan?"

"Oh, my, yes. This was my grandmother's house. My husband and I moved in after she went into assisted living, but you don't care about that. I was six when he went missing. I overheard my grandparents talking about it. It fascinated me, a magician disappearing like one of his rabbits. So sad he's been dead all this time."

Peter pulled out his notebook and flipped through the most recent items. "Your grandmother is Peggy Redfern? She made the missing person report?"

"Yes, that's right."

"Is she still in the facility? I'd like to talk to her."

"Talking to her won't help you. Alzheimer's. Nana doesn't know me anymore, though she still cheats the same way when we play Scrabble."

Just my luck. "Is there anyone who remembers him?"

"There's Marilyn Edling across the street." She nodded

at the opposite house. "But I don't think you'll get much sense from her."

"Alzheimers?"

"Her brain is fine. It's what she thinks with it. The woman has a deplorable worldview."

Peter's only witness had been a child with an active imagination when Heenan vanished. He looked back at the former Heenan residence, calculating his next step.

"It was the most exciting thing that ever happened during my childhood. I grew up with the stories."

Hope rose.

"I imagine you want to hear the gossip. I could use a cup of coffee. Will you join me?"

Peter did not care for coffee but it would be unproductive to refuse. Enough milk and sugar and he'd deal.

Donna showed him to a sunny breakfast nook overlooking the back yard.

At some point her kitchen had acquired aftermarket granite countertops and an assortment of chi chi appliances, including a thermal beverage dispenser, the kind you saw at gas stations and seminars. She pumped coffee into a pair of hand-thrown mugs and handed one to Peter. He doctored his cup and tasted. Better than decent, a different animal than the burnt sludge that stank up District Five.

She seated herself across from him, pushing a plate of oatmeal cookies in his direction. "What would you like to know?"

Peter took a cookie and bit in, tasting cranberries and walnuts. "What do you remember about the days before Andrew Heenan disappeared?"

Donna folded her lips inward, pressing them together as she thought.

"We weren't paying attention at that point. No one knew he was missing until he didn't return from his trip."

"I understand. How much were you around back then?"

"Both my parents worked, so I stayed here after school every day. There was nothing out of the ordinary, nothing I noticed, nothing anyone talked about later."

"He was last seen at a birthday party," Peter primed.

"I saw him leave that morning. I was in the yard, and I was pouting because I wanted to see his tricks. He promised he'd put on a show just for me after he got back from Europe."

"Did he say where in Europe?"

"No. At that age, I didn't think to ask. I thought Europe was its own country."

Peter felt his eyebrows raise.

Donna broke off a corner of cookie, nibbled. "I *was* only six."

"Did anything unusual happen while he was gone? Did you see anyone coming and going?"

"There was a chubby boy looking for lawns to mow. I don't think he had any takers. Nana wouldn't hire him because he charged too much. Besides him there was only Jenny. She came every day to pick up the mail."

"Jenny?" No mention of a Jenny in the reports.

"She kept house for him. She'd come over and push me on my tire swing sometimes."

"Do you remember her last name?"

Donna shook her head. "She was just Jenny. She

worked for him after school. If she saw me in the yard, she always stopped to talk to me."

"What happened to her?"

"I never knew. We never saw her after Nana reported Andrew missing."

"How did your grandmother find out he was missing?"

"Jenny told her, said he'd been due back a week earlier and she was worried. She asked Nana to make the report because she didn't think the police would take her seriously."

"Your grandmother didn't mention Jenny in her report."

"Jenny left a key with Nana and asked her to pretend she'd been watching the house. She gave Nana the name of Mr. Heenan's lawyer so she could call him."

"Didn't your grandmother think this was unusual?"

"In later years, yes. But Jenny was so sweet. It was impossible to imagine she had anything to do with his disappearance, and grandma couldn't see putting her through a police interrogation."

"How old was Jenny?"

"I don't know. She talked about wanting to go to college, so she was still in high school. Sixteen? Eighteen?"

"One of the neighbors mentioned a prostitute who came and went."

Donna huffed. "That would be Marilyn and her charitable view of mankind."

"Oh?"

"She thought my parents were unfit because my mother worked. Used to drive Granddad crazy. He said there was nothing wrong with Marilyn a lobotomy wouldn't fix. Nana said tolerance meant being tolerant of intolerant people. But she never invited Marilyn over for coffee."

"Why would Marilyn think Jenny was a prostitute? Was it the way she dressed?"

Donna sighed. "That woman sees evil everywhere. Jenny was sweet enough for a Doris Day movie. She mostly wore jeans—not tight ones—and polo shirts."

"Do you remember anything else about her?"

"I wish I could help. She had such long, pretty hair. I wanted to be her when I grew up."

Peter jotted "housekeeper Jenny high school long hair" in his notebook. "How about your parents? Would they know anything about Jenny?"

"Doubtful. They're RVing in Oregon right now. I can ask them for you."

"Thank you. I'd appreciate that." Peter glanced at his notes. "I have one more question for you."

"Sure."

"The house sold months after Andrew Heenan disappeared. I'm trying to figure out how a missing person could sell a house."

"That was the lawyer, and it scandalized Nana. She said she wished she'd never called him."

THE FRONT DOOR OPENED, THEN CLOSED. PETER WAS HOME. Lia stepped back from her canvas and gave the iris a critical look. It had been perfectly fine before, but after showing it to Zoe and David, she'd decided it needed more layers. She wiped her brush and her hands, then headed for the living room with Chewy and the oh-so-innocent Gypsy trailing behind her.

Peter sprawled on the mission couch, head back, eyes closed, Viola curled on the floor beside him. Unaware she was in the room, he yelled, "Why are your shoes in the bookcase?"

Lia sat next to him, leaned in and pressed her lips to his for a substantial hello kiss. His mouth curved, smiling under hers.

"You're a detective and you can't figure that one out?"

He opened his eyes, toyed with a lock of hair that had slipped the bun she always wore when painting. "What did she get into?"

She sighed. "I stepped out to get the mail and came back to find the entrails of Honey's bed everywhere." She'd cried over that. "You'd have fluffy white stuff all over your apartment if she knew how to climb stairs."

"Busy girl."

"Then the furry piranha decided my shoes and ankles are high-value prey. Did you know they make kevlar socks for hockey players?"

"Sounds uncomfortable."

"I'm saving it as a last resort."

Peter sat up, wrinkled his nose. "What's that I smell?"

"Bitter apple chewing deterrent. I sprayed it on my feet."

His eyebrows raised. "Does it work?"

Lia scowled. "She is now licking my feet instead of biting them. I suppose it's an improvement."

"Regrets?"

Lia held Gypsy up, eye to eye. She whispered, "Don't listen to the bad man." Gypsy wriggled out of Lia's hands and pounced on Peter's feet, worrying his laces. Viola gave Gypsy the evil eye while Peter removed his shoes, holding them out of reach. Gypsy tugged a sock.

"I see what you mean."

"I left you space on the shelf."

"You are a ruby among women."

Lia rescued Gypsy and imprisoned the little demon on her lap. "Only for you. How was your day? You look tired."

"Got a confession."

"That was fast. They must be calling you uber cop at the station."

Peter snorted. "The only one calling me uber cop is Susan. Did you see the video?"

"Between Facebook, text messages, and phone calls, seventeen people tagged me about it."

Peter winced. "Sorry."

Lia rubbed noses with Gypsy. Gypsy would never be Honey, but girlfriend was a great distraction from unpleasant realities. "In my happy little world, your former fiancée doesn't exist. You are welcome to join me in my happy little world. Tell me why getting a confession doesn't make you an uber cop."

"It was a false confession, which I knew before I went in. I had to waste ninety minutes interviewing him and writing it up."

"Why interview him if you knew he was bogus?"

"Most people who walk in off the street to make fake confessions are nutcases and it goes no further. This guy is an artist who self-publishes graphic novels about zombies. According to his bio he wasn't even in the area when Heenan died. He wants publicity."

"Someone like that deserves less of your time than some poor guy who's mentally ill."

"Pure CYA. I'm sure he was hoping I'd arrest him so he could have his very own Twitterstorm. But you can lay money on him having a backup social media campaign ready to—" Peter made air quotes. "—leak if I blew him off. So I made him go over every stinking detail, backwards, forwards, and sideways. His story was full of holes. If he paid attention while I took it apart, he realized any attempt to capitalize on Heenan will only make him look stupid. Repairing the damage and explaining things to the powers that be after he went ahead with his publicity stunt would take a lot longer."

Lia shook her head. "First Susan, then this jerk. I hope the rest of your day went better."

"I talked to Commodore. I hoped he might remember seeing our guy on the creek back when."

"Any luck?"

"If you consider Steve a viable suspect."

"That bad?"

"Pretty much. I took a field trip to Heenan's house and lucked out. One of the neighbors bought the house from her grandmother and remembers Heenan."

Peter summed up his visit to the neighborhood.

"So the lawyer had power of attorney and sold the house? That's cold. Probably stole all his money, too."

"Could be."

"Do you think he had anything to do with Heenan's disappearance?"

"I can't rule it out."

Lia pulled Susan's mangled scarf out of her pocket and dangled it in front of Gypsy's muzzle. Gypsy snarled and snapped at it. "Good girl," Lia crooned.

"I wish you'd stop that."

"Certainly." She jerked the scarf. It quivered like a small, desperate creature. "As soon as the woman who doesn't exist in my happy little world leaves town."

"Lia—"

"Peter, I'm trying. I know you have no control over anything she does, but I have to deal with this in my own way. I imagine the statute of limitations has expired on anything illegal the lawyer did."

Peter was silent for a beat, then pulled her into a hug, apparently deciding to join her in the happy little world where Susan did not exist. "Which is to my advantage."

Lia dropped the scarf. Gypsy pawed at it, then snorted and walked away. "How so?"

"If the lawyer is still alive, he has no reason not to talk to me. Not unless he killed Heenan. No statute of limitations on murder."

ROSE

FRIDAY, APRIL 22, 1938

MAL STOOD ON THE TRIANON STAGE, SMOKING A CIGARETTE
while he polished the swords he used with his trick cabinet. It was a subtle thing to sell the act. The brilliant
reflection of spotlights on the blades sent a message of
deadly danger as he inserted them into the cabinet,
drawing involuntary gasps from the audience.

It had taken six months for Mal to graduate from
working tables to setting up his act. It could have been
sooner, but Mal wanted to get it right: the right act, the
right girl, the right equipment. His table-side card tricks
were amusing enough, but patrons—that's what Pete
called them—wanted some real flash on stage. People
didn't know table magic, close-up sleight of hand,
required more skill than the illusions that got the big
applause. Those were all staging and misdirection.

He'd bought a decommissioned hearse to haul equipment
and built his own pieces, guided by the man who'd taught

him. Now he opened for the biggest names in showbiz. After a year in the BH, it was still heady stuff for an Irish gutter rat.

A girl with a pale face and long, black curls slipped into the dining room and crossed the sea of empty tables, ducking around to the side of the stage.

Her Betty Boop mouth gave a mew of distress as she struggled with her hat, a frilly pouf the cigarette girls wore as a uniform along with the puritanical black dress with its prim lace collar. Pete hired good-looking gals to please the men, but he put them in drab plumage so they didn't outshine the female customers.

She hadn't seen him. Mal clanked the sword against his trick cabinet, making her jump. She looked up with a sad twist of a smile.

"I'm absolutely hopeless."

Mal checked the clock. Thirty minutes before dinner was seated, another thirty before the curtain rose on his stage show. For now they were alone. He set the sword down and knelt at the edge of the stage.

"A bit early, aren't you?"

"First day. I was too nervous to sit at home."

"What are you doing in here?"

She looked around, as if uncertain where she was or how she got there. "I didn't want anyone to see me with my hat falling off, so I ducked back here. It's not a problem, is it?"

"Nah. Come over here, I'll fix that for you."

She came to the edge of the stage. Mal tucked his cigarette in the corner of his mouth and made quick work of the silly pouf with nimble hands. "There you go."

She tilted her head experimentally. The hat stayed in place. "My hero."

The smile she gave him was sunny, lacking the sly, brassy veneer too many of the girls had. He wondered how long she'd stay so innocent. He cocked his head.

"Why aren't you teaching kiddies in school?"

"I'd like that, but jobs are scarce. I was lucky to get this."

"What's your name?"

The head ducked. "I'm Rose."

"Nice to meet you, Rose. I'm Mal. Anyone gives you a hard time, you let me know."

Mal's heart gave a pleasant tug as he watched her walk away.

"That was an affecting little scene," Esme whispered in his ear, jerking Mal out of his thoughts.

"She's just a kid with first-day jitters."

Esme, his stage assistant, was one of the perks that came with his promotion to stage magician. He gave Esme's spangled bottom a pat, knowing she expected it.

Esme humphed. "She's like a zebra in a henhouse. She doesn't belong here."

That was probably what he liked about Rose. She didn't belong. "What have you got against her? She's a cigarette girl. You're a star."

Esme's eyes narrowed. "Misdirection doesn't work on me, buster. Something about her smells."

Mal returned to the sword, mentally shaking his head. *Dames. Some of them are just plain nuts.*

That night, and every night after, Mal had to fight to

keep his eyes from following the little pouf as it moved between the tables.

He was smart enough to hide his interest in Rose. Esme was a dame with a capital D. Like everyone else in this place, Esme had her eye on the brass ring. She might be biding her time with him until she caught the eye of one of the high rollers, but she'd make him pay if she thought he was interested in another woman. That was fine with him. A gal like Rose needed wedding bells before she climbed into bed with a fella.

He found himself coming in early to catch Rose before shift. She liked to sit at a table in the empty dining room before the bustle started. Their conversations were about nothing: her sick mother, the pregnant cat, kids she babysat. As looks went, Rose wasn't a stunner like most of the girls Pete hired, but she had a sweetness about her, and a love of small things unusual in a place that catered to the high life and impossible dreams.

Mal never wanted the straight life. That meant church, kids, and a back-breaking job that barely paid enough to keep a roof over your head. But Rose almost made living like a sap seem like a good idea. He wondered how long it would take before something happened to grind the sweetness out of her.

DAY 13

THURSDAY, MAY 2, 2019

BAILEY HELD HER HANDS OUT AS LIA AND HER WIGGLY passenger approached their usual picnic table. "Come to Auntie Bailey, you gorgeous thing."

Lia set her travel mug on the table and good-naturedly removed Gypsy from the Moby wrap, handing her over. Kita, lying prone on the tabletop, lifted her head, gave Gypsy a sniff, snorted, then laid her muzzle on her paws. Chewy butted Lia's leg, looking for attention. Lia dropped a hand without thinking and scratched the base of his ear.

Bailey stroked Gypsy's head. "Since you're not halfway to Canada, I assume Susan lives."

Lia inhaled the spicy scent of her chai latte, took a sip, and admired her own zen calm. "Can't kill her if I don't know where to find her. Seriously, I refuse to let that woman mess with my head."

"Good plan."

"She is less than the buzzing of insects in my world."

"Attagirl."

"May she find happiness, wherever she is."

Bailey frowned at the parking lot. "Who do you suppose that is?"

Lia caught a flash of blue from the corner of her eye. "Who do you think it is? That's Terry's truck."

"Not Terry. Behind him."

Lia lifted her head to see a white Cadillac pulling up to the fence.

"Geezle-freaking-pete. That's Susan's car."

"What's she doing here?"

"The video wasn't enough. She wants to insult me in person."

"Forget what I said about the Rule of Three. Do you want me to sic Kita on her?"

Kita, who was about seventy-eleven in dog years, looked up at the mention of her name. A four-inch tendril of drool hung dangerously from her muzzle.

"You'd have Kita slime her for me? You're a true friend."

Susan exited her car and joined Terry and Steve.

Bailey cocked her head. "She's wearing an Ann Taylor suit to a dog park. Goddess, she's wearing pumps. That's reason enough to slime her."

Napa, Jackson, and Penny crowded around Susan, sniffing. Susan took a stiff step back. Terry said something to the dogs and they retreated.

"Don't," Lia said. "If Kita goes near her, she'll swear out a complaint against you and try to get Kita put down."

"She can't do that unless Kita bites her."

Kita gave Bailey a mournful look.

160

Lia snorted. "She'll bite herself and say Kita did it."

Bailey tickled Gypsy's chin with a calloused finger. "I have a screwdriver. We could puncture her tires."

"She won't be able to leave. We'll be stuck with her."

"That's no good. How did she find you?"

"I don't think she did. She's talking to Terry and Steve like she knows them. I bet she wants to interview them about the bones."

"What are you going to do?"

Gypsy wandered across the table. Lia picked her up, holding her like a baby as she rubbed the fat tummy. "Nothing. I refuse to let her get a rise out of me. And I'm not leaving my own damn dog park."

The trio progressed up the service road. They parted at the picnic shelter with Terry and Susan remaining behind while Steve brought the dogs into the park.

Bailey waved to catch Steve's eye. "We need intel," she explained.

Steve ambled back to their table, opening his arms to Gypsy. "Come to papa, you vixen."

Lia surrendered the pup. "I'm going to start renting her out by the quarter hour."

Bailey nodded at the pair now assembling a tripod in the picnic shelter. "What's with the overdressed blonde?"

Steve cradled Gypsy as he looked over his shoulder. "Susan's a video blogger. She saw the story Aubrey Morse did with the guys at Boswell's and called Terry to set up an interview. He offered to meet her here."

Bailey's protuberant eyes widened for an alarming effect. "Didn't you get the memo? That's Peter's old girl-friend. I can't believe you brought her here."

Steve's eyebrow raised as he turned to Lia. "Peter's ex? I saw you take out Desiree in that video. You plan to put her down?"

"Don't ever joke about Desiree. I won't plow into Susan however much she deserves it. She'd cry fake tears while she asks Peter how I could be so mean to her."

"What will you do?" Steve asked.

Lia lifted her head to a virtuous angle. "She's Peter's problem. I plan to let him handle it."

Bailey bit her lip. "Are you sure you want to do that?"

"Why wouldn't I?"

Steve and Bailey exchanged glances.

"What?" Lia demanded.

Bailey folded her arms. "You think she'll ignore you and go on her way?"

Steve said, "We know that's not happening." He eyed Lia shrewdly. "Question is, if Lia can handle someone with obvious mean-girl chops when Susan decides to get under her skin."

Lia's back went up. "What mean-girl chops?"

Inside the shelter, Susan and Terry stood in front of the tripod, an iPhone serving as camera. Daylight bled into the darkened space, illuminating the pair while the shadowed background created a natural chiaroscuro effect. It was a sophisticated choice. *Has to be an accident.* Lia shoved the thought away as petty and mean-spirited.

Terry removed his camo cap and flipped an index finger skyward, making some point. Susan tilted her head and clapped her hands, clasping them between her breasts.

Steve interrupted her thoughts. "Former cheerleader, right?"

"How can you tell?"

"You saw her clap her hands and toss her head," he said. "Classic cheerleader moves. All cheerleaders have serious mean-girl chops. You can't make the squad without them. But there's something else you should consider."

Lia's temples pulsed with an incipient headache. "And that is?"

"None of us will admit it, but guys like it when a woman shows a little jealousy."

Lia's mouth dropped open. "You think making an ass out of myself would please Peter?" She turned to Bailey. "Tell me this isn't a thing."

Bailey's expression filled with pity. "It's a thing."

"Would you do it?"

"No, but John isn't like other men."

Lia looked from Bailey to Steve. "And Peter is?"

Steve cradled Gypsy with one hand and held the other palm up in defense. "Don't look at me. But you might want to consider how many hits that video got before it came down."

Like children banging on an out-of-tune piano, Lia's friends gleefully punched all the buttons she didn't know she had. It was something friends did—usually at the worst possible time—and she'd never understood it. She dedicated herself to picking stray twigs out of Chewy's fur.

"I refuse to lose my dignity over a woman Peter doesn't want."

"Famous last words." Steve nudged Bailey, whispering, "I bet she makes Lia blow up."

Lia stuffed her irritation and maintained an even voice. "I heard that."

Bailey poked her tongue in her cheek, considering. "What qualifies as a blowup?"

Steve rubbed his chin. "Screaming, profanity in a raised voice, anything that meets the requirements for assault under the law."

"You're on. We need a deadline."

"I say she loses it within a week."

"Up the stakes and make it two." Bailey placed a hand on Lia's. "You can avoid hitting Susan for fourteen days, can't you? You won't even see her for most of them."

The pulse in Lia's temples became a throb. She ground out, "I don't plan to hit anyone. Ever."

"Good girl." Bailey turned back to Steve. "What's at stake?"

"Steak sounds good. If I win, you can buy me one."

"That's low, expecting a vegan to buy you a steak."

"Why do you think I chose it?"

Head beating like a drum, Lia pretended she was far, far away. Somewhere without people. The Mojave would do, or that vacant beach Jody Foster found herself on in *Contact*. The one on the other side of the intergalactic wormhole.

Bailey said, "All right then. If I win, you detail my truck."

Steve's eyes tracked over the fifteen-year-old Toyota Bailey used to haul mulch. "What would be the point?"

"You want dead cow. I want a clean truck."

"Doesn't matter, since I'm going to win."

Her skull pounding, Lia snapped, "I'm not here so you can abuse me for entertainment value."

"See? Short fuse," Steve said.

Bailey didn't miss a beat. "What if Chewy attacks Susan? Does that count?"

"We'll take that on a case-by-case basis. Depends on whether Susan does something that would make any dog respond aggressively, or if Lia instigates the attack. Can't have loopholes."

Lia screeched, "You think Chewy would bite someone, even if I told him to?"

Chewy whimpered and hid under the table. Gypsy whined and squirmed in Steve's arms, desperate to get to Lia. She jumped onto the table and burrowed into Lia, seeking reassurance, giving solace. Lia's headache faded.

Steve tsked, shaking his head. "Short fuse. Still think you're going to win?"

Lia held Gypsy to her chest, glaring at Steve. "I won't punch Susan, but I may give you a good smack. Why aren't you interviewing with her? You found the bones."

Steve removed his Panama hat, scratched his bald scalp. "I spent enough time talking to the press when I was a union rep. No matter what you say, they find a way to make you look bad."

Lia forgot her pique. "You didn't warn Terry?"

"This is Terry we're talking about. The women he knows are either Mensa nerds or former hookers court-ordered to A.A." He finger-quoted the "former" part. "You think he won't invite public humiliation to hang with a classy blonde?"

On the far side of the park, Susan leaned over her tripod and removed the phone. Terry collapsed the tripod and presented it to Susan, who tucked it into her hobo bag. The pair strolled across the park to Lia's table, Susan's manicured hand resting lightly on Terry's arm.

Terry, at his most gallant, nodded to the group. "Susan, I'd like you to meet my friends."

Susan's eyes met Lia's and her practiced smile froze. Those eyes dropped to Gypsy, still in Lia's arms.

"I see you have that *adorable* puppy with you."

Lia bared her teeth in a parody of Susan's smile. "Always. She's my bodyguard. She's so enjoying the scarf you gave her."

"Delighted to hear it."

Underneath the table, Chewy sensed Lia's tension and whined. She dropped a hand and rubbed his neck.

Terry's face brightened. "You know each other? Excellent!"

Bailey cleared her throat. "Susan's an old friend of Peter's from high school."

"Really?"

Lia saw gears turning in Terry's head. Steve planted a foot on Terry's camo-patterned Croc. She wondered if Terry felt the pressure through the spongy synthetic. Probably wouldn't matter if he did.

"Peter and I were engaged for years. I can't believe I let him get away." Susan addressed Lia. "We got off on the wrong foot the other day. I hope we can start over. Do you mind if I sit?"

Bailey stood and Kita jumped down. "We're going for a

walk." She nudged Steve. He and Terry followed, three rats deserting a sinking ship.

Susan took a faded bandana from her hobo bag and laid it across the bench before she sat. Not Hermès. Terry must have given it to her.

"Peter says you're an artist—"

Not bloody likely he said anything to you about me.

"—It must be tough, making a living that way. Did he tell you about my video show? Maybe I can help you."

Gypsy squirmed, wanting to explore the table. Lia stuffed her in the Moby wrap to keep her away from Susan and a possible case of rabies.

"What did you have in mind?" She didn't know why she bothered asking. She knew what was coming.

"It would be fun to interview a local artist, and it would give you exposure."

Exposure: code for "something for nothing."

"Thanks, but I don't need the help."

Susan scanned Lia's paint-spattered shorts, took a side trip to stare pointedly at her bare left hand. Her eyes softened with pity as she took in Gypsy and the rumpled Moby wrap slung across Lia's chest like bandoliers.

Lia saw herself through Susan's eyes, saw Gypsy as a poor substitute for the infant the wrap was designed to hold, saw the studio clothes as a pathetic lack of personal pride. She understood in that moment how the right clothes provide armor. Today, in her safest of safe places, she had none.

Susan's eyes completed their circuit, meeting Lia's, oozing sympathy like too much maple syrup drowning a stack of pancakes.

"Artists are so independent. I admire that. Really."

"Let's not pretend. You're in Cincinnati because of Peter. You have no interest in me."

Susan tilted her head, blinked, made a little frown. The sequence made Lia think of android Nicole Kidman in *The Stepford Wives*. "Honey, you're selling yourself short. I find artists fascinat—"

"Peter and I are together. You can't waltz in here and snap him up like a purse at Nordstrom's."

Chewy's head butted Lia's leg, demanding reassurance. She dropped her hand again. Gypsy wiggled, trying to climb out of the wrap. Lia kept her eyes on Susan, restraining Gypsy with her free hand.

Susan's eyes hardened to cold, stone disks. "Believe what you want. I've known Peter all his life. You don't mean a thing to him, no matter what he tells you."

"And what makes you say that?"

"If you mattered, he'd marry you. You don't even have a ring."

Lia's hand flew to the lump under her shirt, the bit of Peter's heart she wore on a chain, precious and personal to her. Her fingers curled around it, drawing on it for strength and dignity. Chewy butted her leg and whined.

"You had a ring. You had more than one, and here you are. I guess a ring isn't everything."

The stone disks turned mean, snakelike. "If Peter loves you, why doesn't his family know about you? All he wants from you is easy sex and cheap rent. Or maybe that's cheap sex and easy rent. You're what we call a free-range dairy cow back home."

Lia blinked, speechless.

Susan resumed her cheerful expression. "Get a clue. You and your pathetic dogs mean nothing to him." She strolled away, abandoning Terry's bandana on the bench. Then she stopped, looked back, lifted her chin.

"Nothing."

Pride kept the hit from showing on Lia's face, but there was something smug in Susan's walk as she left the park. Chewy came out from under the table. Lia ruffled his ears with both hands.

"You, little man, can be very inconvenient."

Bailey hoisted herself onto the table top. "Are you okay?"

"You heard that?"

"It's all crap."

"I don't think so. Not the part about Peter not telling his family about me. I bet that's true."

"Then he has a reason. Peter loves you. You know that."

Lia said nothing. She dropped her face to rub her cheek against Gypsy's head.

"Peter would marry you in a minute. Not getting married was your idea."

Lia climbed onto the table and curled into Bailey. Chewy jumped up beside her, pressing against her hip. Gypsy struggled to reach Lia's face, the bright pink tongue flicking at her chin. In this moment, Lia missed Honey's soothing presence ferociously.

"It's not that."

"Why are you crying?"

"I'm not crying." Because she hadn't let tears come. "It was all bullshit, but it was so ugly. She wanted to make me feel like nothing and she succeeded."

"You got hit with a psychic zap."

"A what?"

"Thoughts can hurt, even, especially, when they aren't true."

"What are you talking about?"

"If your barriers aren't solid, people can impose their thoughts and feelings on you. And when those thoughts are hateful, it can make you sick." She took Lia's shoulders, pushing her into an upright position. "Cuddle Gypsy and close your eyes."

"You're going to do puppy woo-woo on me?"

"I use whatever is available."

Lia plucked Gypsy out of the wrap and laid the pup against her shoulder, shutting her eyes as she stroked the tiny body. Felt Gypsy's butter-soft fur against her cheek, the muzzle poking around her neck, in her hair. Inhaled the warm, sweet animal scent.

"Tickles."

"Feel better?"

"A little."

"Keep your eyes shut. Plant your feet firmly on the bench. Breathe in.... Now breathe out and feel all the poison and hatred flowing through you, out the bottom of your feet. It's not yours, it doesn't belong to you. She gave it to you but you don't need to keep it. Give it to the earth.... Breathe in through the top of your head. There's a gold light surrounding you. Breathe it in."

Lia didn't hold with Bailey's New Age mumbo, but the pit in her stomach was now large enough for her to fall in. She inhaled, having no clue how to do it through the top of her head.

"Keep breathing. When you exhale, imagine all the poison is dark smoke, leaving through the bottom of your feet, going into the earth where it will be purified. Breathe in the gold light. Fill yourself with it."

Lia kept her eyes shut. Gypsy squirmed and licked her nose.

"I want in on that bet."

"No can do."

"Why not? If you can bet on me, I can bet on me."

Bailey, her voice firm, said, "Lia, look at me."

Lia opened her eyes. "What?"

"We were yanking your chain. There is no bet."

THANKS TO CELL PHONES, TONY PIRAINO JR., ESQ. CAUGHT Tony Piraino Sr. at the eleventh hole of the Losantiville Country Club, where the old man now practiced golf instead of law. He agreed to meet with Peter, stating this was likely to be more entertaining than his usual round of lies at the bar.

Piraino stood when the hostess delivered Peter to his table of cronies, shaking Peter's hand with an impressive grip for a man well into his seventies. Trim build, excellent posture, and a full head of well-tended hair. Alma would call him a silver fox.

"Maggie, let Carmen know I need another scotch and water, and—" he turned to Peter "What's your poison?"

Peter wanted Pepsi, but that wouldn't win him points with Piraino. "Sweet tea, Thanks."

"Sweet tea it is." Piraino turned back to Maggie. "Pete and I will be over in the corner."

He nodded at an empty table in a sea of empty tables, then took the seat in the corner, giving Peter a view of the golf course. It made Peter nervous, not being able to see the door. He imagined Piraino put his back to the wall for the same reason he would, to ensure they were not overheard.

Piraino leaned back in his chair. "I was wondering when you'd get to me."

"You remember Andrew Heenan, then."

"It's hard to forget a client who goes missing." Piraino lifted his chin, eyes focused over Peter's shoulder. A waitress arrived, setting down their drinks. "Thank you Carmen." He waited for Carmen to leave before he resumed speaking. "You sure it's him?"

"He was wearing an Elvis jumpsuit and absent the lower half of one leg. Who else would it be?"

Piraino sighed. "I'm sorry to hear it. I liked Andrew. Any chance it was a natural death?"

"Unlikely."

"Damn shame. I think he expected something like this —not the shallow grave, precisely, but something."

"What makes you say that?"

"Our arrangement. As his attorney I can't talk to you, but as his agent under power of attorney I can say whatever I want. Andrew traveled overseas for extended periods. He hired me to pay the bills."

"He didn't have an accountant for that?"

"He did. One I hired for him. I had specific instructions in the event he disappeared."

"Did he have a will?"

"It was the same as his instructions."

"Which were?"

"If he went missing for ninety days, I was to sell his house and liquidate his assets."

"What happened to the proceeds?"

"Everything went to Our Blessed Lady Church."

Peter ran through the list of churches he knew. Our Blessed Lady had to be one of several lined up on Clifton Avenue, one-stop shopping for the soul. "You have an excellent memory."

"It was an odd situation. Hard to forget."

"Andrew strike you as a religious man?"

"Not particularly. As far as I know, he never set foot in the place. I'm sure I have the name of the priest I dealt with in my files. I'll look it up for you after I get home."

"How much money was involved?"

"Between the house and his financial assets, in the neighborhood of a quarter mil."

"That house has to be worth half a million."

"Today, sure. A fraction of that thirty years ago. But I always wondered about his finances."

"How so?"

"Andrew's lifestyle was modest. Modest people accumulate assets, janitors you hear about who squirrel away a million dollars. And he was no janitor. He was always vague about what he did, just said he was a businessman with interests overseas."

"In my experience, people who say things like that are usually posers living off someone else."

"I know what you're talking about. Someone who talks

a good game without ever saying anything. That kind of person, there's a feel, something behind the facade. Gold diggers, social climbers, con men. In my business you learn to spot them. That wasn't Andrew.

"Most people are nervous when they deal with lawyers. Andrew could have been ordering a Big Mac. He didn't need to impress anyone. You get a feel for that, too. The guy who walks into your office wearing stained overalls with forty grand in his pocket and forty million in real estate."

"You pegged Heenan as money under the radar."

"I did. But his accounts maintained a reasonable cushion and nothing more. Funny thing, the foreign interests, his travel expenses, they never came through me."

"How do you explain the theoretical missing money?"

Piraino eyed Peter while he took another sip of scotch. "I am unhappy with the prospect of any speculations I make becoming public."

"This is between you, me, and your scotch. And we both know the scotch will never make it out of this room."

Piraino barked a laugh. "You're all right, Pete. My dealings with Andrew were aboveboard, but your typical businessman doesn't make contingency plans for their sudden disappearance. I wondered if I was maintaining a front for him, and my purpose was to fold his tent when the time came."

"A front for what?"

"That's the question, isn't it? Whatever it was, there had to be other assets, and none of them in the name Andrew Heenan."

KIM FREEMAN PULLED TWO MORE VOLUMES FROM THE Hughes High School library shelf and added them to the pile Peter held.

"That should do it. If Jenny was here, she'll be in one of these."

The stack of yearbooks Peter carried had to weigh more than twenty pounds. He hoped Kim wasn't feeling chatty. "It will be just like looking at mugshots."

"I suspect more than a few of these kids wound up in your books. Our records don't go back to the eighties, but if you find your Jenny, the alumni association might have a current address."

"This will do for a start."

Kim ran her fingers over the spines of the books Peter held, confirming dates. "I'll check these out for you. Call me if I can do anything else."

Kim headed for the desk. Peter turned for the door. A timid whisper came from the next row of shelves.

"Detective Dourson?"

Stacy Bender leaned against the shelves in the ancient history section, arms wrapped around herself as if she had a stomach ache. She looked as miserable as she had the last time he'd seen her.

Peter set the books on a convenient table. He spoke quietly, as much to soothe her as to avoid attracting attention. "Hey. How are you getting on?"

Her bottom lip trembled. "Not so good. When will you arrest Jamal? You said two days."

Peter sighed. "They reassigned the case. I'm not in charge anymore."

Stacy's face froze in a deer-in-headlights, oh-my-god-I'm-gonna-die look.

"They're still working it, but it's taking a little longer than expected. We need you to hang in there."

"Are they gonna arrest me?"

"Stay out of it and you're clear. I promise."

"Taneesha's coming around. She doesn't understand why I won't let her in, since mom works evenings and wouldn't know. Last night she was yelling through the door. I don't know what to do."

"I know it's tough. Look—" He pulled out his wallet, removed a slightly bent business card. "You can go here. There's safety in numbers."

Stacy frowned at the card and rubbed at an acne scab on her chin. "Happen? Isn't that the place where kids make Easter eggs and weird toys?"

"They have programs for teens. It's a place where kids like you are taking steps to make something of themselves." He grabbed for a straw. "You'll learn how to make T-shirts."

Stacy snorted. "Mine will say 'loser' on the front in big fat letters."

"It will be over soon. Just keep your head down."

"Can't I warn Taneesha? She's still my friend. I don't want her to get arrested."

"Does Jamal own a gun?"

Stacy's mouth popped open, forming an "O."

"There's your answer. Bad things will happen if you tell Taneesha. Jamal's her brother. She'll tell him, just like you want to tell her. Jamal will get mad and do something to you or your family. Then he'll change his operation and I'll have to explain why the taxpayer money we spent building a case to get him off the street got us nothing. And because you warned him, I can't keep you out of it. You'll get it from both sides."

The lip trembled again, violently. "You're scaring me."

"I don't want to scare you, but I need to scare you. Talk to nobody. Tell Taneesha you're grounded for the rest of your life if you have to. Tell her your sisters will rat you out if you let her in. Your choices are to stay out of it or wind up in more trouble than you ever imagined."

Stacy's eyes blazed, furious. She hissed. "I thought you'd help me. I'm sorry I ever talked to you."

Cheap sneakers squeaked as Stacy spun on her heels, the unspoken "I hate you" hanging in the air.

CHEWY BUTTED LIA'S HAND AS SHE SKIMMED EMAILS ON HER laptop. Obliging, she scratched behind his ears while she read an update from David. Zoe liked the paintings but wanted to have friends for dinner to see what they thought.

Typical, needing a committee to tell you if you wanted something or not. Either that, or Zoe had David install the paintings to dress up her house for a dinner party she planned weeks ago, and she'd tell David to return them Monday with some lame reason why they didn't fit, like her husband was allergic to lilies and looking at them made him sneeze.

It was a trick certain people used to make themselves look wealthier than they were, and it applied to clothing, jewelry, art, and even cars. It didn't happen often, but every time it did left an indelible memory. If that was Zoe's plan, her machinations would cost David money as well as waste his time. David would smile and nod because any sign of censure would cost him business.

Here's hoping Zoe lives among the well-meaning and flighty, not the sneaking and social-climbing.

Thinking of Zoe reminded her of the morning's ugliness with Susan. She chucked Chewy under the chin. "What do you think, little man? Is it time to talk to Peter?"

Peter's voice drifted in from the living room. "Get away, rat."

Peter had a man cave in his apartment where he could concentrate without distractions, but he'd bonded with the leather Morris chair and it was now his preferred place to review files after dinner.

"Lia! Come get the swamp monster."

Lia rolled her eyes and closed the laptop.

"Coming, dearest."

Peter sat with a stack of yearbooks in his lap and a beer in one hand, shooing Gypsy away with the other. Unconcerned, Gypsy propped her feet on the coffee table and sniffed a pile of neatly cut paper slips. She licked the pile, then started chewing. She looked up at Lia, confusion in her eyes and paper stuck to her muzzle. Viola snorted from her spot on the floor.

"Lia!" Peter yelled again, eyes glued to Gypsy and unaware Lia was already in the room.

"Watch your beer."

Peter's hand jerked up. Chewy sat innocently under-neath as if the bottle had never been in danger, though everyone in the room knew he didn't care what you had in your hand when he head-butted you for a pet.

Lia scooped Gypsy up. "What do you expect? Puppies explore everything with their mouths." She grabbed a pencil cup off the phone table and handed it to Peter, nodding at the molested paper slips. "You can put those in here." She settled on the sofa, snuggling Gypsy in her lap. "Can I help?"

Peter gave Gypsy an evil look. "Not if Jaws is a member of your team."

She held Gypsy up, nose to nose, and was rewarded with a puppy kiss. "He doesn't understand. Floor for you, girlfriend." She pulled Susan's tormented scarf from a basket, dangled it long enough to get Gypsy's attention and dropped it to the gaping maw. Divested of puppy, she turned expectantly to Peter. "What are we looking for?"

He handed her a book. "Jennys, Jennifers, Jeans, Ginnys, Virginias, or other derivatives. If she has long brown hair, put a star on the bookmark. Two stars if it's Jenny or Jennifer." He pointed to a legal pad next to the mauled bookmarks. "Note the year, name, and page number on the master list. I'll show the matches to Heenan's neighbor. Maybe she can identify our housekeeper."

"Sounds like a long shot."

"It's a place to start."

It was companionable, soothing work, requiring concentration and marked only by the sound of turning pages. Lia wondered if every third girl child was named

Jennifer when these kids were born, or if it was like your friend buying a red Datsun and suddenly you saw red Datsuns everywhere.

She ran her fingers through the forest of bookmarks sprouting from the top of her current volume. Two dozen? Three? Eyes frying from the tiny type, she flipped absently through the back of the book, stopping when she saw the damage. She made a disgusted sound as she turned a few more pages.

"Kids can be so thoughtless."

"Graffiti?"

"Someone sliced out random pages."

"Let me look at that."

She tilted the book so Peter could see where a page in the activities section had been removed near the spine. It had been a neat job, almost invisible. The shallow cut in the next page indicated it had been done with a stencil knife. Peter took the book, thumbed through the rest of it.

"Four more pages. Wonder if Kim knows about this."

"Some people hate photos of themselves. I bet if we hunt up the missing pages, we'll find the same person on each page. Some poor girl immortalized with fake big hair like Melanie Griffith in *Working Girl.*"

Peter puffed out his cheeks, blew audibly. "I didn't bother with the activities section." He looked at the stack of completed volumes. "Guess I ought to go through these again."

"What for? It can't have anything to do with your case."

"Just to alert the school to the vandalism. Up to them what they do about it."

"Speaking of juvenile delinquents, how is your package thief doing?"

Peter took a long pull from his beer. "I saw Stacy today. She hates me."

"I'm so sorry. Is there anything you can do?"

"Jamal is on Brent now. I'm out of it until Parker sends these bones to Cold Case where they belong, which I'm hoping she'll do Monday. I laid out the realities for Stacy as gently as I could, and I think she'll hold. It's her mother I'm worried about. People who drink as their life's avocation have big mouths."

Lia was silent for a moment. Time to bite the bullet. "Speaking of mothers ..."

Peter looked up, a question on his face. She dropped her eyes. A fierce Indian chief glared at her from the cover of the yearbook in her lap, an artifact from pre-politically correct times. She traced an index finger around the feathers in his bonnet while Peter waited. Chewy, sensing tension, curled by her feet.

"Susan came to the park today."

"You didn't say."

"I needed time to marinate."

"What happened?"

"She came to interview Terry about finding the bones. I don't think she knew I would be there. She was friendly at first. Then she said some things."

He set his beer aside and joined her on the sofa. His hand was gentle as he pulled hers away from the book. Gentle as he stroked her knuckles with a thumb.

Anger lurked under the calm of his voice. "What things?"

"Look, most of it was silly. She offered to put me on her show—"

Peter's look of horror made Lia choke on a laugh. "Don't worry, I turned her down. Then she said I didn't matter to you because we weren't married."

He opened his mouth to protest. She placed the fingers of her free hand to his lips. "That's the silly part, and I didn't buy it, not for a minute—" The rest came out in a rush. "—but then she said you never told your family about us, and that meant you didn't care about me. Only she wasn't so nice about it."

Peter squeezed her hand and sighed. "I hope this hasn't been eating at you."

"Not exactly.... Maybe a little, partly because I knew she meant to hurt me."

"And partly because I never told my family about you."

"I never thought about it before because I never tell my mother anything. But we're estranged. You talk to your family all the time."

"If it helps, Abby knows about you."

"That's a start."

"She runs interference for me."

"She's a good sister."

He tapped their clasped hands against his leg, gathering thoughts. "Sometimes ... sometimes being the fruit of someone's loins makes them believe they have proprietary rights over your life, ordained by God. The only defense is distance and silence."

A long pause, punctuated by the tapping of their joined hands. "I promised to always tell you everything. That doesn't work with my parents. There's no way to tell

Mom about you that she'll accept. If I say we're committed to each other, she'll wonder why I'm not good enough to pledge your life to.

"If I tell her you have legitimate reasons to distrust marriage as an institution and I'm fine with that, not only would that entail telling her things that are none of her business, it won't make a dent in her ability to accept our situation. Worst case, she'll decide you're broken and nothing will ever change her mind."

"What's the best case?"

"She'll show up for a come to Jesus meeting and she won't be satisfied until we're married or she succeeds in grabbing me by my ear and dragging me home."

"Ouch."

"As far as Mom is concerned, the only acceptable state of affairs is me married to a nice Christian girl who pumps out babies. And in her book, you hardly qualify as Christian."

"What about your dad?"

"Dad's more flexible, but he's not inclined to get in the way when Mom has the bit in her teeth."

Something shifted, like a Magic Eye picture—when the big blur of nothing suddenly becomes the Statue of Liberty, or maybe a race car.

"I grew up aching for a nice, normal family. I guess being the scion of a nice, normal family isn't always wonderful."

Peter kissed her knuckles, shrugged. They were past the difficult part.

"Only son, oldest child, good student, athlete. They had huge expectations, beyond wanting me to marry a girl they approved of so I could go forth and multiply.

"You had to fight for everything you ever got. I had my life handed to me. I was just fine with it until I realized I hadn't bothered to think about where I was being led.

"Their plan wasn't a bad plan, just not right for me. But how do you tell people who love you that you don't want the best they have to offer? It's like saying their love isn't good enough."

"I thought you left Cave City because Susan dumped you."

"Everyone thinks that, and I let them. Susan just provided convenient timing. I wasn't getting with the program, so she went out and found what she wanted. If she hadn't dumped me, I would have left her. It just would have taken longer."

"What made you change your mind about her?"

"I didn't change my mind about her so much as I changed it about myself. Mom's the church secretary. Dad's an elder. They raised us on Adam's rib and everything that goes with it. Then I got a basketball scholarship to UC."

Peter paused to grab his abandoned beer. "A teammate invited me to his brother's wedding—this was when Susan was pressuring me long distance about law school. They had a reading full of flowery mixed metaphors that I mostly ignored the way you do when a sermon goes on too long. But one sentence stuck with me: 'Make not a bond of love.' It made so little sense to me that someone would read that at a wedding, I had to find out what it meant."

"Kahlil Gibran."

"You know it."

"I read it years ago. He wasn't a member of the 'two hearts that beat as one' school."

"I got a copy of it. The part that struck me was the end, where he talks about the oak and cypress not growing in each other's shadow. I asked myself why he didn't say 'two oaks' or 'two trees,' since the rest of it uses generic images.

"I realized that was the point, that they *were* different, that he saw strength in the differences. And I thought about how, if trees are too close, one of the trees gets stunted. He was saying it was wrong to want your spouse to be like you, and you had to give each other room to be who you are."

"I never thought about it so deeply."

"I showed it to Dad."

"Not your mother?"

"Like I said, Dad's more flexible. He said no matter what, never show it to Mom. He said most couples build space in their marriage, even if they don't know that's what they're doing and never admit it.

"I told him Susan was pressuring me about law school, and the longer I was at college, the less I liked the idea of being a lawyer. He said most women feel it's their mission in life to save men from themselves and mostly it's okay but a smart man knows when to put his foot down."

"What did you think when he said that?"

Peter laughed. "I didn't know what to think except I knew I wasn't going to like fifty years of Susan saving me from myself. It wasn't long after that the furniture king lured her away and it was a moot point."

"A narrow escape."

"True, that. It's a bad sign when you feel the walls closing in and you aren't married yet. When I first saw you, you were so nakedly real, vulnerable in a way Susan would never allow herself to be."

"I thought she played the fragile southern belle quite well."

"Susan's as helpless as Rambo with a rocket launcher. When I saw you on that picnic table, you were so devastated, it made all of Susan's pouts and hurts look as trivial as me pitching a fit because I had to drink Coke instead of Pepsi.

"Then I saw how you made your own life, your way. For the first time I wanted to know all the corners of someone, inside and out. I've never felt about anyone the way I feel about you."

"Back atcha, Kentucky Boy. You're my rock. I never had a rock before." Lia leaned against Peter's chest, her head against his shoulder. "What happens when Susan tells everyone you're sinning it up in Cincinnati?"

"I blackmailed her into keeping her mouth shut. No telling how long that will last. Maybe we can spread a rumor on the internet that I died in the line of duty."

"Died *tragically* in the line of duty. If we're going to do it, we need to get it right. Did you interrupt a convenience store robbery on your day off, or get crushed shoving a child away from a runaway semi?"

"Let's go with number two. If we have to produce a body, it won't have to look like me."

DAY 14

FRIDAY, MAY 3, 2019

BAILEY'S PHONE LAY IN THE CENTER OF THE USUAL DOG park table, surrounded by a dozen avid human and canine faces. Gypsy, given the run of the table top, sniffed the phone and pawed at the screen, where Susan sat between Commodore and Dick Brewer, her elegant suit an anomaly in the comfortable jumble of the Mill Creek Alliance office.

Lia scooped Gypsy up and handed her to Jim. "Keep her out of trouble, will you?"

On the screen, Susan said, "Commodore, tell my viewers what you have in store for them."

Commodore grinned. "Tomorrow we're retracing our steps down Mill Creek to the shallow grave we discovered two weeks ago—"

Terry bellowed. "Foul betrayers!"

Kita yelped and leapt off the table. Gypsy objected

with puppy ferocity from her perch in Jim's arms, barking and struggling.

"Shhh!" Bailey hissed. "You're upsetting the dogs."

Terry grumbled. "It was my idea. I suggested it to Susan. Now they're doing it without me. Cretins!"

Susan traced Dick's biceps with a manicured finger. "I can tell you've done your share of paddling."

On the screen, Dick's chest expanded. He gave Susan an aw-shucks head duck. Today he'd ditched the straw hat and silver medallion for a neat golf shirt. Lia wondered if Susan would still flirt with him if he had on sweaty creek clothes.

"I hate to break it to you," Lia said. "Susan has her sights on bigger game."

"The perfidy of women!"

Bailey tilted her head, considered Terry's competition. "Younger, better looking. Didn't you say he owns a business?"

"Bah! Man think's he's God's gift to the universe." Terry stormed off, Jackson and Napa trotting behind.

Steve sighed. "My weekend is ruined. If he stays home, I get to listen to him sulk. If he goes with them, I'll get to hear all about it after he gets back."

Jim scratched his beard. "Sounds like she used Terry. Can't blame him for being upset."

José, maintenance supervisor and lifelong Westsider, stared after Terry. His biker mustache added a mournful note to his perplexed expression. "Woman like that, how'd he think he had a chance?"

Lia snorted. "I'm sure she cooed all over him before she dug her stilettos in his back. I hear it's her specialty."

Bailey tilted her head. "Do you think she's really after Dick? Maybe she wants to make Peter jealous."

ELVIS GRINNED AT PETER AS HE ENTERED HIS OFFICE. PETER turned the ghoulish bust to face the wall every evening before he left. Every morning, Elvis greeted him when he arrived, like an evil, animate doll that moved in the night. He couldn't decide if he should continue facing Elvis to the wall, ignore the prank, or pitch Elvis in the trash. He narrowed his eyes, searching Brent for signs of guilt.

Brent threw up his hands. "Not my problem if you're too stubborn to toss it out."

"Cynth?"

"Maybe. She'd think it was funny. She say where she and the caveman are going for their parkour date?"

"What possible reason could you have for wanting to know?"

Brent lifted a shoulder and looked at the permanently closed blinds. "The park's too tame for Cynth. I'm sure it's a route known only to counter-culture types, involving chain-link fences and condemned buildings. Hypodermics and discarded condoms will be involved."

"If it matters so much, ask her."

"The woman disdains me."

"Try apologizing for whatever idiot thing you did five years ago to piss her off."

"Think I haven't? Woman holds a grudge longer than anyone I know."

Peter's phone beeped. The desk sergeant didn't bother

with niceties when he picked up the receiver. "You got another one. Line four. Why can't these folks go through the tip line? I have actual work to do."

"Your mouth, God's ear." Peter annoyed himself by looking at Elvis' mocking leer as he punched the extension. "Detective Dourson speaking. How may I help you?"

"Hi. My name is April. April Howard. I saw your interview with Aubrey Morse."

It was hard to tell about voices, but the woman on the line sounded too young to know anything relevant. "Are you calling about Andrew Heenan?"

"Do you watch *Midsommer Murders?*"

Huh? "I caught an episode or two."

"You remind me of Ben Jones. He was my favorite Detective Sergeant on the show."

"Umm ... thank you?"

"All earnest and buttoned up—"

"Ma'am—"

The voice turned breathy. "You're really cute. Like a Beatle before they went psychedelic."

Peter schooled the impatience from his voice before he spoke. "Do you have information about Andrew Heenan?"

"Ask me to lunch and find out."

Peter remembered his mandate to promote community relations and resisted hanging up the phone. "Can I bring my girlfriend along?"

Dead air. Peter counted to three, then hung up. *It should be illegal to sell phones that don't make a noise when you disconnect.*

At the other desk, Brent lifted an eyebrow. "Now

they're hitting on you? Sure you don't want to trade cases?"

"In a heartbeat, but Parker won't allow it. What's going on with Jamal?"

"I've been watching him all week. He never carries anything into his crib, so it's a good thing I didn't get that warrant. I have to figure out where he's taking the packages after little sis hands them off. I can't backtrack him because he never comes home the same way twice. I zig, he zags. If Bender was still involved, she could tell us where they're going to be."

Peter caught the hopeful look and shook his head. "She's out of it. Period."

Brent sighed. "I'm tempted to put a GPS tracker on his car, but that way lies madness."

"Unauthorized, illegal surveillance. Definite career-killing move. Social media?"

"No photos of Jamal sitting on a pile of Amazon boxes. If he's bragging, it's in code."

MAYBE SHE WANTS TO MAKE PETER JEALOUS. PETER WOULDN'T be manipulated by such silliness. Even so, more than twelve hours after her talk with Peter, Lia had a knot in her stomach the size of—well, bigger than Gypsy if not as big as her favorite schnauzer. Which was why she found herself climbing the steps of the repurposed clapboard house where her therapist, Asia Lewis, practiced.

Asia met Lia on the porch, embracing her tightly and without regard for her jewel-toned silk caftan or the gravity-and-logic-defying edifice of her hair. Lia continually marveled over Asia's hairdressing adventures, assembled through some mysterious process that could survive mortar fire and qualifying as an art form.

Despite a level of personal maintenance that suggested they did not live in the same universe, Asia was comfortable in her skin and easy to be with. Lia appreciated her combination of empathy and straight talk.

She'd relied on the therapist to carry her through acute stress disorder after Luthor died. Now she made the occasional appointment when the support of friends wasn't enough.

Like today.

Once inside her office, Asia eyed the paper shopping bag Lia carried and pressed a mocha hand against her chest. "For me?"

Asia's fine eye and weakness for color led to the women trading services. Both felt they came out ahead.

Lia held the bag out. "Absolutely."

Asia took it and removed the twelve-inch canvas square, holding it at arm's length. Her mouth made a moue as she studied the dragon's mouth orchid, an exotic fuchsia flame in a dark, misty forest.

"It reminded me of you."

Asia's face went soft. She propped the painting against her desk lamp. "It's lovely. Have a seat and tell me what's going on."

Lia sat on the edge of the cushy visitor's chair, her mouth suddenly dry. She looked down at her hands, twisting together like something apart from herself.

"Thank you for finding time to see me." She

consciously stilled her fingers before continuing. "I feel so ridiculous." It took time to recount the Susan saga, but she felt better afterward. "Peter and I talked last night and we were fine. Today, I have this knot in my stomach. I don't know what to do about it."

Asia leaned back in her chair. Between the angle of her head and the towering hair, she reminded Lia of Nefertiti.

"Do you know the difference between envy and jealousy?"

"Aren't they the same thing?"

"In fact, they're opposite. Jealousy is the feeling you get when someone threatens something that belongs to you. It's protective."

"Jealousy is healthy?"

"In tiny doses, applied to something that genuinely belongs to you."

"Getting angry because Susan is going after Peter is a good thing?"

"Depends on how you handle your anger. The anger itself is natural. Anger is healthiest when it motivates positive action. You have a tendency to turn anger inward, and it eats at you."

Not something Lia wanted to think about. "How is envy different?"

"Envy is wanting something someone else has. It can be healthy if it's used to motivate someone to work toward the things they desire."

"But?"

"Envy becomes toxic if a person operates from a poverty mindset. She assumes there are a limited amount of goodies to go around. Toss in a sense of entitlement, and instead of saying, 'I want a wonderful husband like Julie's. I'm going to work on my relationship so I can have a brilliant marriage,' this person says, 'Julie has a great husband. I deserve a great husband, so I'm taking Julie's husband and to hell with Julie and the husband I already have.'"

"That's rude."

"At the very least. They prefer to tear down the people they envy and steal what they want instead of creating it for themselves, not understanding the value in the fabulous job or the wonderful marriage comes from what they put into it. She might steal Julie's husband or job, but they will never be the same in her hands. In fact they might never have been what she thought they were to begin with."

"So Susan envies my relationship with Peter and wants to take him and I feel the threat and get jealous?"

"It's possible. She may blame you for her failures: if Peter wasn't with you, he'd be with her. The next step is the decision to tear you down, which she tried to do with that scene at the park.

"Meanwhile, you tend to avoid intense feelings, and you just lost Honey. Honey was your family before Peter. I suspect being hit with her rage and another potential loss at the same time has tossed you for a loop."

"I don't know what to do about it."

"What do you want to do?"

"I want to rip her internal organs out and feed them to the Mount Airy vultures."

"Your feelings are natural, even if the plan isn't practical."

"What can I do that won't land me in prison?"

"You can't control Susan, but you can change the way you think about her."

"How so?"

"The threat is a mirage, and it only exists in Susan's mind. She can't take Peter from you. If she can, Peter isn't yours and you're better off without him."

Lia folded her arms. "That makes me feel *so* much better."

"Let's put this another way. Think of everything you know about Susan, everything you feel from her when she's around. Do you want a man who prefers her to you?"

Lia pictured herself in three-inch heels, scolding Chewy because he put nose prints on her car windows. She thought about wearing lipstick, or worse, hair goop, and clothes you could never wipe your hands on. "Ugh. No."

"Exactly. Has Peter ever given you any indication that he'd like you to be more like her? Expressed a desire for you to dress less casually, for example?"

"He was engaged to her. Doesn't that mean anything?"

"And he left. Is there any reason to think he regretted it?"

"He never talked about it before now."

"Does he seem dissatisfied with you now that she's here?"

"He's frustrated, but that's work."

"Any truth to the things she said to you?"

"By her terms, I'm pathetic."

"Forget her terms. This is your life, your terms."

"I wouldn't want her life if you handed it to me on a platter."

"There you go."

"I still don't understand why I'm feeling this way. I never felt this way with Luthor, and plenty of women fawned over him. They irritated me, but I didn't feel gut-punched."

"That relationship was very different. Luthor was fungible."

"What?"

"Fungible. Fungible items are easily interchanged with like objects. Your paintings are not fungible, but car parts are."

"You're saying I treated Luthor like a human widget?"

"Essentially, yes. A penis widget. You needed a boyfriend, someone who would give you your space, someone you didn't need to invest emotions in. Other women may have irritated you, but they also served to reinforce the idea that Luthor was not your Mr. Right, only your Mr. Right Now. In a way, they made you feel safe."

Fungible. An ugly description of the parade of Mr. Right Nows in Lia's life before she met Peter. But the men in her life felt no differently about her, had they? Did that make it better or worse?

"Peter is not fungible. For the first time you've let someone in emotionally. You've allowed yourself to trust Peter. If Susan can take him from you, it undermines your foundations. Luthor was never your foundation, so losing him was never a threat. And, in your heart of hearts, you didn't want the relationship to last."

"That makes me sound like an awful person."

"Not awful. Human. And you had your reasons. You've been navigating new territory since you met Peter, healthier territory. The fact that a threat to this relationship is affecting you so much is proof. I think part of what you are experiencing is the shadow of grief, the realization of what loss of Peter would mean to you."

"And?"

"What does Peter mean to you? One word."

Unexpected and right, the word presented itself with a warm glow.

"Home."

"A very big word for a woman who never had one."

"But what do I do? How do I handle Susan?"

"You don't. You handle you. What are your options?"

"I can blow up and look like an idiot…"

"Or?"

"Keep my cool and try not to burst a blood vessel."

"There's a middle option. You can let Peter know how you're feeling. Let him help you through this."

"This is the shoe on the other foot, isn't it?"

"How so?"

"I want to resolve this by myself. It hasn't been that long since I was upset because Peter kept things from me, things he felt would make him look bad in my eyes."

"Funny how that works. There's another thing you can do."

"Oh?"

"Keep reminding yourself she's chasing Peter because her husband humiliated her. And if you can smile and be gracious, it will drive her nuts."

FATHER MARK WAVED PETER INTO HIS OFFICE AT OUR Blessed Lady, standing up behind his desk to shake Peter's hand.

"Thank you for seeing me, Father."

"Happy to do whatever I can to help. I'm fascinated by the idea that an anonymous donation thirty years ago might be connected with a murder case. I had my secretary dig through our records for a year before and after the date you gave me. She found nothing over a hundred thousand dollars from an anonymous donor, or anything under the name Andrew Heenan or Tony Piraino."

"How about under any name?"

"I can't give you names of donors, but I will tell you there was nothing for that time period that wasn't from a known source. I imagine you can get a court order, but you would be wasting your time."

Another dead end.

"Cash donations of that size don't occur, even back then."

"What about this Father Dismas who signed the paperwork?"

"The archdiocese has no record of a Father Dismas attached to any parish in the Midwest. Your Father Dismas doesn't exist."

"Troubling."

"Quite. I'm sure the church would love to know how such a significant donation was derailed."

Peter sighed. "I'm not sure it was. Andrew Heenan named Father Dismas in the instructions he gave Tony

Piraino, to be contacted through a post office box. If there is no Father Dismas, perhaps the plan was to dispose of the money without leaving a paper trail, and it was never intended for the church."

"That would be fitting."

"How so?"

"Dismas was one of the thieves crucified with Christ. You said Mr. Heenan was a magician. This would be a bit of misdirection?"

"In light of what you've said, that's how it appears."

Father Mark steepled long fingers and considered. "He picked Our Blessed Lady out of a hat, slapped a clerical collar on someone or other, and it had nothing to do with us."

"Very likely."

"It's just as well I didn't discuss your visit with anyone. There are those who would feel we were robbed of a substantial donation and want to pursue the matter."

"If someone diverted that money, they could announce it on network television and I couldn't arrest them. Statute of limitations expired years ago."

"Then I'll forget this conversation until you have some reason to remind me of it."

"That would be best. I wonder if there was a reason he chose your church. Is there anyone around who was here back then?"

"Father Nicholas is the only one left. He's ninety-four and sharp as a tack." Father Mark looked at his watch. "He likes to sit in the garden. If you'll follow me?"

They found Father Nicholas sitting on a bench, his

bearded face turned sunward. Cataracts clouded the blue eyes, but they remained bright with intelligence.

"The name isn't familiar. A magician during the eighties?" Father Nicholas pursed his lips, thinking. "That would have been ... Ronnie Reagan was president, there was the *Challenger* tragedy ... that awful Madonna woman."

His face lit up. "Little man, performed for the children during our festivals. You should have seen him, Father Mark. He did the most wonderful tricks, cards and coins and scarves. Some of our members didn't think magic was appropriate for a church event—some nonsense about devil worship—but the children loved him. Anything that brings a sense of joy and wonder to children is good to my mind. We could use more of it these days. Why are you inquiring about him?"

"He went missing back then. We recently discovered his remains."

The clouded eyes closed as Father Nicholas' face crumpled in on itself. "I'm very sorry to hear that."

"What do you remember about him?"

Father Nicholas stroked his beard. "Not much. He wasn't a church member. Can't recall that I ever saw him at Mass. Betty must have booked him for the festivals."

"Betty?"

"Betty Zabinski. Church secretary for more years than I care to count. Kept us together. I was sorry when she passed."

"Was there a festival committee? Someone who might have known him?"

Nicholas shook his head, slowly. "Betty handled that.

We had a parade of volunteers. They'd last a few years and someone else would take their place. I rarely needed to pay attention."

Father Mark said, "I'll have my secretary hunt through our files. We may still have paperwork tucked away somewhere."

"Thank you," Peter said. "That would be helpful."

Nicholas turned his milky eyes on Peter. "Detective?"

"Yes, Father?"

"Great evil was done to a man who took joy in making children happy. I will pray you find the man who killed him."

CHEWY, GYPSY, AND VIOLA STARED EXPECTANTLY AT LIA AS she stirred the simmering pot of chicken and vegetables. Gypsy still couldn't climb steps, but girlfriend could now drool like a champ. *Comes from having Olympic-class mentors.*

Chewy ate anything, but Viola was picky. And Gypsy was too young for spicy stuff, even if Peter said they'd cut her stomach open one day and find a license plate and a set of partially digested tires. Lia checked the clock. Ten minutes to go on the rice. Time enough to sauté carrots for the fur kids.

The front door closed as she tossed sliced carrots in her egg skillet. Approaching footfalls on the wood floor, then rapid squeaks, like the death throes of a small animal.

Gypsy jolted, then raced down the hall. More squeaks. Peter entered the kitchen with Gypsy in his arms, ignoring his ear scratches as she chewed away on a bleating, balled-up, child's sock.

Lia spoke over the cacophony. "You found Bailey's present."

"And you say she's your friend. I didn't know they made squeaky socks."

"Assembly required. Bailey provided the squeakers. I got the socks. That one should die in about three seconds."

Silence fell. Gypsy, clutching an unresponsive and now-mangled sock, gave Lia a distressed look and struggled to get down.

Peter set her on the floor. Gypsy abandoned the sock and returned to drooling by the stove. "Looks like she killed it."

"They don't last long. She's been through five already."

"How many did Bailey give you?"

Lia gave the curry a stir, checked the carrots. "The sack said a hundred."

Peter slid a hand around her waist, dropped a kiss on the back of her neck. "You need new friends. I'll pick up a set of used tires for her to chew on."

"Oh, stop it. How did it go today?"

Peter stuck his head in the fridge, emerged with a beer, sat at the table. "Good news, bad news. Smells like coconut. What's for dinner?"

Lia checked the clock again, turned off the burners. "I have no clue what to call it, but it involves curry. What's the good news?"

"Donna Merrill identified Jenny from the photos I showed her."

"Sounds like a win."

"It would be if we had an address. Jenny Olson fell off the map after Heenan disappeared."

"Do you think it's connected?"

"Unlikely. It's not like she went missing. Today you have a digital footprint and it's hard to go off grid. It wasn't like that back then. I would track down her old neighbors and see what they remember, but her street was mowed down for commercial expansion. There are no doors left to knock on."

"Maybe Alma can find her on Ancestry.com."

"There were three hundred thousand people named Olson in the last census. I checked."

"Ouch."

"And that's if she kept the name. If I have to pursue it, I could chase down her classmates and see if anyone remembers her, but that's more than a hundred people."

"And the bad news?"

"I got an earful from a woman across the street who swears Heenan was a pedophile in the style of John Wayne Gacy."

"They both played with balloons. Maybe you'd better run your cadaver dogs through the crawl space."

"This is Clifton Hills. There are no crawl spaces."

Lia scooped carrot slices into dog bowls. "How about the priest? Weren't you going to talk to him today?"

"Smoke and mirrors. The priest named in Heenan's documents never existed. Looks like a scam that allowed Heenan to liquidate without leaving a money trail."

"Where do you think the money went?"

"I think Heenan was up to something he didn't want people to know about, and this was his exit strategy."

Lia dished up a plate of curry and rice, set it in front of Peter. "How would that work?"

"He runs into trouble, he lays low. After a specified period of time, his lawyer liquidates and passes the cash on to the fake priest. The fake priest then passes the money on to Heenan, then they both disappear."

Lia filled her own plate and joined Peter at the table, followed by salivating dogs who refused to be fobbed off with carrots.

"Only Heenan isn't at the rendezvous point, because he's already in a shallow grave?"

"Could be. We don't know if he disappeared because he died, or if he disappeared first and the person he was running from caught up with him when he came back to pick up the cash."

"Maybe the phony priest killed him for it. He's the one guy who would have known where to find him. Or the fake priest was Heenan."

Peter chewed and swallowed, shaking his head. "Piraino is a sharp guy. He would have picked up on it."

"Jim has been active in the Catholic church for decades. If anyone knows anything about your fake priest, he could find out."

"I can't involve your friends."

"Why not? You know they're happy to help. They could track Jennifer Olson's classmates for you."

Peter set his fork down, his face serious. "I can get fired for talking about a case."

"You talk to them all the time."

"It's a one-way street. I can ask for information and I

can discuss anything that's public. I can't share confidential information."

"I don't understand. You're sharing confidential information with me. Why are you talking to me if it could get you fired?"

Peter tapped the shallow dent in Lia's chin. "Because I love you."

"Don't evade, Dourson."

"I'm not. I don't want to be that guy who comes home and pretends his day didn't happen. Some women would be fine with it. That's not you."

"You're right. I think we'd lose each other."

Peter snuck a sliver of chicken under the table to Viola. Chewy whined, head-butting Lia's leg, a reminder that fair was fair. She scraped sauce off two pieces of chicken and held them out for Chewy and Gypsy.

"And I figure you fall under the wife exclusion."

"There's a wife exclusion?"

"Not in writing, but everyone knows it happens. You're a good sounding board and I can trust you. And God willing, Parker will pull me off this on Monday so I can get back to Jamal."

"How do you figure that?"

"It's a budgetary thing. Going further means investing a lot of man hours against diminishing returns. Let's forget about Andrew Heenan. Tell me about your day. What did you and Alma find in the attic?"

Lia laughed. "We catalogued Ruth's Beanie Baby collection."

"Beanie Babies?"

"An army of them in pristine condition, with the heart-shaped tags. Alma lined them up on a plastic tarp. They look like they're getting ready to invade Disney World."

"Are they worth anything?"

"She's researching that right now. She plans to find herself a boy toy and move to Myrtle Beach."

"Anything else good?"

Lia tapped a tarnished candlestick sitting in the center of the table. "Alma insisted I keep this."

"That will shine up nice."

"I'm not sure I want to shine it up. Look at this." She held it up so Peter could see a black thumbprint on the base. "It tarnished that way. It's like a bit of Ruth remaining behind."

"So shine selective parts of it. What else?"

"Some seriously ugly Rookwood era pottery—not Rookwood, this is from a rival studio. It's worth something. I love this house, but I'll never understand some of the things people put on their mantels back then. Lots of old photos. Antique side tables, a ton of books. We only got through half the boxes."

Lia took a bite of chicken. "I got a call from David. Zoe is dithering, but her sister wants to see paintings."

"If this keeps up, you might want to reconsider getting a space at the Pendleton."

"I like working at home. I can't see paying all that money for window dressing when the people I work with are happy to come here."

"I see your point."

Lia kept her eyes on the dogs as she hand-fed them more chicken. "I saw Susan's new video."

"With Commodore and Brewer? What about it?"

"They're taking a canoe trip to your crime scene. Doesn't that bother you?"

Peter shrugged. "The scene's been released."

"I was wondering if you might want to go along for damage control."

"Susan invited me. I declined. Too many ugly ways it could go wrong."

The last remnants of the knot in Lia's stomach loosened.

Peter squeezed her knee. "Susan's making a last-ditch effort to get traction for her video show. That's all this is, and it's nothing to worry about."

DING DONG

SATURDAY, JUNE 11, 1938

MAL LOOKED OUT OVER THE SEA OF UPTURNED FACES, ALL eyes riveted to the stage, his stage. Not a cough, not a whisper, not the clinking of a single fork broke the tension. With a flourish, he thrust the fourth sword into the cabinet.

Inside the cabinet, Esme screamed. He had to give it to her, the lady had lungs.

The crowd gasped. Mal waited for the audience to die down.

Instead, a murmur grew, rippling across the crowd with the sound of chairs moving and patrons shifting in their seats. It wasn't in response to his act. Something else was happening. Annoyed, Mal broke a cardinal rule and stopped the act to look past the glare of the stage lights, searching for the disturbance.

A dozen men stood on chairs scattered across the room. As one, they unzipped their expensive trousers, withdrew their penises, and urinated on the crowd. They turned as they emptied their overfull bladders, splashing every diner in reach. Shrieks—genuine this time—pierced the air as diners shied away. China crashed and patrons fell on one another as they attempted to evade the offensive streams.

Cool as cucumbers, the men zipped up, walking out before security could react.

It had been a disaster. Stu, Pete's chief of security, asked Mal to continue performing while they attended to the customers who'd been "ding-donged"—that's what Stu called it—but the people who stayed were too upset by the attack to watch and he couldn't find his rhythm.

He found himself playing to a room that was three-quarters empty, the remaining diners huddled in pockets of intense conversation. For the first time, he was relieved to leave the stage.

Hours later he sat in Pete's office, Pete behind the enormous oak desk, Stu standing behind him. Mal stuck a hand in his pocket, felt for his shilling, rubbed a frustrated thumb across the face. "What's happening, Pete?"

"Moe Dalitz is back."

"Dalitz? The guy who burned you out?"

"He wants the club. I expect I'll get a new offer in a few days."

"And what? He pisses on the guests until you let him have it?"

"That's what he thinks. I'd rather burn this place down myself than sell—to him or anyone."

"You built this place. Nobody should be able to take it from you."

"You got that right."

"What's the plan?"

"We hold on. Things may get bumpy. I need to know if you're up for a scrap."

Years defending himself from gangs of larger boys in the alleys of Dublin taught Mal a thing or two. He hated bullies.

"You put me where I am. I'm in. Whatever you need."

DAY 15

SATURDAY, MAY 4, 2019

Susan's Snippets with Bobbi Johnson and Marilyn Edling
1.1K Views
Thumbs up: 253
Thumbs down: 147

SUSAN'S FACE FILLED THE TINY SCREEN LYING ON THE USUAL picnic table. She winked at the camera, slowly backing away to reveal her surroundings.

"I'm standing in front of the gorgeous Tudor home where Andrew Heenan lived before his mysterious disappearance in 1987. The house currently belongs to Don and Bobbi Johnson, who took ownership mere months after Andrew went missing."

She stepped aside, sweeping an arm in a Vanna White flourish as if the house was a game show prize. "Look at the beautiful stonework and handsome landscaping. Wouldn't you *kill* for a home like this?"

She turned her head and gave the camera a coy, confiding look. "Don is a retired realtor. I bet the deal they got was a *steal*. I hoped to talk to the Johnsons this morning, but they haven't responded to my requests for an interview."

Susan extended a hand and drew an elderly woman on screen. The woman peered at Susan, then turned tiny, raisin eyes to the camera, setting a bulldog mouth.

"With me today is Marilyn Edling. Say hello to our viewers, Marilyn."

Marilyn pursed her lips and gave a half-hearted queen's wave to the camera, peering as if she thought Susan's viewers were inside.

"Marilyn has lived across the street since 1974, years before Andrew Heenan moved in. She's the only person alive who remembers the missing magician. Marilyn, have the police interviewed you about Andrew?"

"I talked to that detective, but I could tell he wasn't interested in what I had to say."

Susan crinkled her brow in reporterly concern. "Why do you say he wasn't interested?"

"He scribbled some words in a little book and that was it. I've heard none of it on the news. They're hiding the truth about that man."

Wide eyes from Susan. "What are the police hiding? What does the public need to know about Andrew Heenan?"

Marilyn stared into the camera, her face trembling in outrage. "The man was a pervert."

Susan's eyes widened in fake shock. "No!"

"He had that young girl coming around all the time,

staying for hours. I know they weren't related because he had no family. She was barely old enough to drive!"

"It was an improper relationship?"

Marilyn huffed, "A man that age, pulling coins out of the ears of children. If you ask me, that was just an excuse to put his hands on them. That's what John Gacy did, dressed up as a clown to lure young boys to their doom. They should be checking the back yard for buried bodies."

"Mrs. Edling—"

A door slammed, loud and sharp as a gunshot. A woman stormed across the yard, fury emanating from her broad face. Susan turned to the woman with a welcoming smile. "Mrs. Johnson! This is a treat. I'd hoped to talk to you today."

"I will thank you not to record your seedy videos on my lawn."

Susan took a step back, her voice prim. "As you can see, we are standing on the sidewalk, which is a public thoroughfare. I know my rights, Mrs. Johnson. But if you have something you'd like to say to my viewers—" Susan paused and smiled. "—we're dying to hear it."

"What I have to say about this invasion of privacy is not fit for public consumption." She retreated. Lia thought she could see steam coming from Bobbi's ears, but that might have been a trick of the light.

Susan returned to the camera with wide eyes and a simpering laugh. "We've touched a nerve with that one. Wonder what she'll think when—"

Behind her, Bobbi Johnson opened her front door. A pair of barking maniacs charged into the yard, twin blurs of multi-colored fur, the lead dog all wild blue eyes and snarling teeth.

"Lily, Danny, down!"

The larger dog dropped with a happy grin. The other stood, snapping and growling an arm's reach from Susan.

Susan squealed, "Get away, get away."

Bobbi Johnson called again, "Lily, down!"

Lily gave Bobbi a resentful look and eased herself, grumbling, onto the grass. She turned her crazed blue eyes back to Susan, accompanied by a thuggish canine sneer. Bobbi joined the dogs, leashes dangling from one hand.

"If you don't mind, my dogs and I are availing ourselves of the public thoroughfare. As I understand it, your rights do not include blocking my way." She jerked her chin at the street. "Is that your Cadillac? Danny needs a place to—"

The screen went black.

Susan reappeared in closeup. "The Johnsons clearly have something to hide. Don't worry, I'll be back. Next time I'll bring pepper spray."

––––––––––

Bailey tapped the screen, sending Susan into the mysterious reaches of the internet, or maybe perdition.

Lia stroked the head of the pup currently snoozing in her Moby wrap, thankful she had yet to show signs of aggression. "Handsome aussies, even if the little girl has a temper."

"She's reacting to Bobbi Johnson's feelings," Bailey said.

"Protecting her territory, and I can't blame her," Jim said.

"I won't worry about Susan anymore. Bobbi Johnson will take care of her for me. Lily will dine on long pork for months."

"Shades of John Wayne Gacy," Steve said.

"Not Gacy," Terry said. "Dahmer. If Ms. Johnson invites you over for barbecue, I suggest you decline."

LIA STRETCHED OUT WITH PETER ON HIS ENORMOUS SOFA, her head against his shoulder. Gypsy sat on his stomach, snapping at the kernel of popcorn Lia waved in front of her nose. Viola curled on her dog bed, placed where Peter could drop a hand and give her a rub. Chewy sat, head cocked, eyes on the images running across the silent forty-eight inch flat screen TV hanging on the wall.

Peter's phone dinged. Lia craned her head as he pulled up a text. "Who is it?"

"Cynth. She sent me a photo of her parkour date."

"Oooh, let me see."

"I don't think I should. He's a manly man."

"If he was that manly, she'd be swooning in his arms instead of texting you."

"Good point."

Peter tilted the screen to show her a sweaty hunk vaulting over a rail, muscles bulging and rust-colored dreadlocks flying, his exposed limbs covered with an array of Celtic tattoos.

Lia took the phone, pinched out the photo so she could examine the ink. "Looks like he escaped from Asgard. I hope you don't mind if I fantasize about him tonight."

"Fantasize all you want in your cold, lonely bed."

"Seriously, aren't you going to text her back?"

"No. She's hoping that photo will make its way to Brent. I refuse to participate in their sick, twisted mind games."

Lia tapped a reply:

Stop pointing out my inadequacies to my girlfriend.

She showed the screen to Peter, her finger poised over the send arrow. "What do you think?"

Peter twisted as he grabbed for the phone. Gypsy yelped, tumbling from her perch on his stomach.

Lia caught Gypsy before she fell off the sofa and cuddled her, apologizing to the stricken puppy eyes. Gypsy looked over her shoulder and barked.

On the TV screen, a montage of shots followed Aubrey Morse and an entourage of Yacht Club members as they paddled down Mill Creek, ending in front of the crater with the exposed roots of the downed tree behind them.

Susan and Terry were nowhere in sight. The screen cut away to a commercial.

"I notice they didn't show Aubrey getting out of the canoe."

"You're a cruel woman."

"Just pointing out facts."

"I thought the float trip was for Susan's video blog," Peter said.

Lia fed popcorn to Chewy and Gypsy. "That was the original plan. Terry said Commodore decided to maximize their exposure. He took over the whole thing and sent Terry's romantic canoe trip off the rails."

Peter laughed. "That wasn't ever going to happen."

"Worse, Susan made a date with Dick Brewer. Terry's heart is broken."

Aubrey returned, standing in front of the crater with a short, bearded man. Peter pointed the remote at the screen, unmuting it.

"We're on the banks of Mill Creek with local crime historian Jay Overstreet, who has a shocking theory about the man whose bones were uncovered after a recent storm. Jay, Andrew Heenan was buried here more than thirty years ago, but you believe this story goes back much further than that."

Peter groaned. "This can't be good."

"I do, Aubrey. Andrew Heenan has ties to Newport's Sin City gambling days."

Peter snorted, making his chest jerk under Lia's cheek. "Public spirited of him to come forward."

"Many Cincinnatians are not aware that before Las Vegas, Newport, Kentucky was *the* national hotspot for gambling and adult entertainment. Frank Sinatra, Marilyn Monroe, and Dean Martin are a few of the big stars who spent their weekends on and off the stages of Newport's clubs.

"Before they died, old-timers from Sin City told a story about a magician named Marvelous Malachi who stole millions of dollars in gold, gems, and priceless art from the Beverly Hills Country Club, then fell afoul of the mob."

"Damn!" The sound exploded out of Peter's chest, causing Gypsy to startle.

"Shhhh!" Lia said. "I want to hear."

Aubrey continued, "Why do you believe Andrew Heenan was Marvelous Malachi?"

"One of the stories about Malachi claimed he Houdinied his way out of a leg manacle that had been riveted shut and no one knew how he did it."

Aubry's mouth dropped. "You think he cut off his own foot?"

"Simple explanations are often the best. Andrew Heenan was a magician. He was the right age, with no past and no known family. The amputated leg paints a compelling picture."

"What do you believe happened to him?"

"It's obvious, isn't it? Someone killed him to get the money."

"Do you think they succeeded?"

"It's been eighty years since the theft and the stolen art never reappeared. Marvelous Malachi's haul is still out there."

Peter zapped Aubrey's faux-astonished face into oblivion. "Susan hates being upstaged. Somewhere there's an Aubrey Morse doll with its head twisted off."

"They make Aubrey Morse dolls?"

"If they don't, Susan stitched one up. I may borrow it and feed it to the garbage disposal. We can forget that lazy Sunday."

DAY 16

SUNDAY, MAY 5, 2019

THE SUN HAD BARELY RISEN WHEN PETER PULLED UP IN front of the square, Price Hill fourplex where Overstreet lived. Glass block sidelights, brick patterns, and a concrete inset cast with chevrons decorated the facade—features Lia said marked the building as pre-World War II Art Deco. The apartments would be solid and spacious, the kind of construction that didn't happen anymore, places renters hung onto for decades.

He detoured to the parking lot behind the building and found the twelve-year-old Toyota Camry listed as Overstreet's on a recent speeding ticket, its condition hardly better than Lia's thirty-year-old Volvo. Being a crime historian didn't appear to be a big-money gig.

Having confirmed Overstreet's presence, he returned to the front of the building. The door bumped open. In the foyer, a woman with a toddler in tow wrestled with a stroller and a diaper bag.

Peter took two long steps and grabbed the door. She smiled in gratitude as he held it for her. He sent a mental thank you heavenward and took this opportunity to enter the building without buzzing Overstreet first.

Peter's knock went unanswered. He knocked again, this time eliciting a hollered, "Hold your horses." A long minute later, Overstreet's door cracked open, leaking stale tobacco smoke.

Overstreet, barefoot in striped boxers and a stained v-neck T-shirt, looked a decade older than he had on the screen. This put him firmly in the sweet spot for Heenan's killer. Blood-shot eyes suggested he'd either been drinking or smoking dope. No hint of sickly-sweet ganja under the tobacco. Alcohol, then.

He blinked owlishly. "Whaddya want?"

Peter flipped open his badge case, displaying his shield. "Detective Dourson. Do you have time for a few questions?"

Overstreet shut his eyes and mouthed, "Shit." The man's head bobbed a few times, computing. He opened his eyes and stepped aside.

"Come on in. Place is a wreck."

The living room opened into a dining area, the table stacked with books and periodicals, forming a wall around a laptop and an industrial-sized scanner. Crumpled paper littered the floor around full wastebaskets. Overflowing ashtrays sat on various surfaces. A coffee table held a three-quarters empty bottle of cheap scotch and a pair of glass tumblers sticky from the previous night's excesses.

Overstreet scooped a pile of clothes off the couch and

dumped it on top of a cardboard box. "Have a seat. Do you mind if I make coffee and get dressed?"

"No problem."

Peter had chosen to catch Overstreet off guard. Now he'd gain more cooperation if he gave the guy a chance to settle himself. Often pure sincerity was the best route to getting information. And if that didn't work, it was better to play subjects like fish, letting them think they had some measure of control while he set the hook.

Overstreet crossed the dining area and out of sight. Smoke from Overstreet's morning cigarette drifted in the air, followed by kitchen sounds: a freezer door opened, then shut; a faucet running; a coffee grinder; the hiss and gurgle of a coffee maker. Overstreet returned, passing through the living room to a tiny hall, muttering to himself as the cigarette dangled precariously from his lip.

As soon as Peter heard the shower, he moved to the dining table and scanned the piles. A paper-clipped stack of pages torn from a legal pad tugged at him. He ignored it. People who looked disorganized often knew exactly where everything was and noticed if anything was a hair out of place. And anyone with half a hungover brain wouldn't leave him alone with anything of value.

Instead, he studied the seven-foot bookcases lining one wall. History and reference books, with a shelf dedicated to multiple copies of Overstreet's own titles, *Sin City Crime* and *Cincinnati Cold Cases*. He'd downloaded digital versions of both books the night before and ran searches for "Malachi." He'd gotten zip.

Overstreet, in fresh jeans and T-shirt, feet still bare, passed through the living room on the way to the kitchen.

"Want some coffee?"

"I'm good, thanks."

He returned to the living room, steaming mug in hand, and dropped into an armchair.

"Sorry, Dick Brewer brought a bottle of scotch over and we had a late night. You know him?"

"Sure. Mill Creek Yacht Club."

"I saw you on the news. I should have recognized you right away. You're wondering why I didn't come to you first."

"Among other things."

Overstreet took a sip of coffee. "I knew I could get more bang from Aubrey Morse if I gave her something you didn't have."

"And bang outranks civic duty?"

Overstreet sent Peter a rueful smile. "Bang is everything. I knew you'd get to me sooner or later. Wish it wasn't at the crack of dawn."

"Payback is hell."

"Yeah, yeah. What would you like to know?"

"Where were you in the summer of 1987?"

"You don't mess around, do you?"

"Just getting it out of the way."

"That's one way to do it. I was at OSU. Didn't move back until I got my degree."

"Good enough. Tell me about Marvelous Malachi."

Overstreet lit a cigarette, waved it in the air. "Channel 7 ran the sound bite version. I guess you want the full story?"

"Background first. I'm not from here."

"Okay. Be patient with me if I repeat myself. How much do you know about Newport?"

"Conventioneers go there to see strippers and get unlicensed massages."

"The shady reputation goes back more than a century. Newport was the center of bootlegging on a national scale during prohibition."

"You're kidding."

"No interstates back then. The river connected Newport with the rest of the country. The locals hated authority and were desperate for jobs. It was great for everyone until Prohibition ended. The players needed a new enterprise. They leveraged existing channels for local graft and moved on to adult entertainment. They opened places they called carpet joints, gambling palaces dressed up with classy decor and high-end entertainment.

"These were the first casinos. The very first was the Beverly Hills Country Club, but gambling was everywhere. You could find slot machines in the corner grocery. Now hundreds of them are on the bottom of the Ohio River, courtesy of Robert F. Kennedy."

Peter snapped his fingers. "The Beverly Hills Supper Club, didn't it burn down in the seventies?"

"Yeah, they changed the name. Third-deadliest nightclub fire in US History. One hundred and sixty-five people died. That was a mob deal. It has nothing to do with your bones, though our story centers on the club."

Overstreet took a drag and another slug of coffee. "You have to understand, the men who turned Newport into a national hotspot weren't traditional mobsters. They were businessmen who exploited prohibition and engaged goons on the side for security. Then business exploded. Truckloads of money rolled out of those places every night."

"It's hard to imagine Newport as the center of anything."

"When I was a kid, Newport was a scruffy biker town across the river. It's coming back with the development of the riverfront. During its heyday, there were Hollywood A-listers on stage and walking the streets every weekend. Marilyn Monroe, Frank Sinatra, Dean Martin, they were all regulars."

"I remember that part from your interview. What happened?"

"The short version is, Nevada legalized prostitution and gambling and the mob figured taxes were cheaper than graft. They opened the big casinos out west. Then Robert Kennedy became Attorney General. He rolled through and busted everyone who remained.

"Without the mob to ensure the streets were safe for tourists, the adult entertainment industry fell to the bikers, and Newport devolved to the seedy scene it became by the eighties."

"How does this relate to Heenan?"

"Everything. Repeal of the Volstead Act crippled organized crime across the country. They were called the Syndicate back then. Newport's successful transition to adult entertainment drew their attention.

"Big players from Chicago and Cleveland wanted a piece. A group of players called the Cleveland Four came to town and didn't see the sense in building competing casinos when they could take over established clubs."

Overstreet lit a new cigarette from the butt of his dying one, taking quick puffs to get it going.

"The Beverly Hills Country Club was the most successful of the carpet joints. A guy named Pete Schmidt owned it, and he wasn't selling—not that Cleveland's offer was in any way attractive.

"Cleveland launched an intimidation campaign. Schmidt wouldn't budge. They burned the club down in 1936. Schmidt remodeled and opened back up. Cleveland escalated to robbing the money trucks. This is where we come to your mystery bones."

"He robbed a money truck?"

"In a way. Malachi worked for Schmidt, opening for the big name acts."

"Malachi have a last name?"

"Not that anyone knows. Nobody knows who he was or where he came from. Everything I've said up to this point is fact. What comes next is legend, handed down from guys who stayed here instead of moving out to Vegas. I heard versions of this story from a number of those guys before they died.

"Some said Malachi worked for the mob, some said he was working for himself. Everyone agrees he made money disappear. Malachi skimmed the receipts and smuggled out what he stole. I figure he decided Pete wouldn't know the difference, since the trucks were getting robbed anyway."

"Where did the money go?"

"That's the mystery."

"Spawning rumors of lost treasure."

Overstreet spread his arms. "Like Al Capone's vault."

"But Malachi fell out with the Syndicate."

"Rumor was they had Malachi in a basement on Monmouth Street, permanently manacled by the ankle."

"He chewed off his foot like a coyote in a trap?" *More likely Malachi paid someone to help him escape and they dummied up the manacle to confuse things.*

"Nobody ever saw him again. I always figured they killed Malachi and put out the story of his survival to provoke Pete. You know, that Malachi betrayed him and was living large on his money. I thought they made up the story about his impossible escape so it wouldn't look like some stooge got one over on the mob. Now we know the story was true."

"What makes you think they didn't find Malachi's haul?"

"Are you familiar with the history of Fabergé eggs?"

"Vaguely."

Overstreet stubbed his cigarette out and went to the shelves, removing an oversized book with a glossy dust jacket. He flipped through the pages, handing the open book to Peter as he pointed at an array of colorful eggs.

"Fabergé was the royal goldsmith in Russia before the Bolshevik revolution. He created fifty jeweled Easter eggs for family gifts. Eight of the eggs have been missing for decades. Those eggs are the Holy Grail to collectors."

Peter had seen similar tchotchkes on eBay but knew better than to say so. He set the book aside.

"What happened to them?"

"The Bolsheviks happened. When they executed the Romanovs, they buried the Imperial treasures in a vault in the Kremlin. Fast forward to the Depression. Russia was broke and Stalin decides to sell off the Imperial treasures. No one has laid eyes on them in decades, and the accounting was loose.

"Armand Hammer—he was like Warren Buffett back then—he brought thousands of Fabergé pieces to the US, acting as an agent for Stalin. Imperial Fabergé eggs were going dirt cheap because nobody had any money. Hammer obtained several of the eggs for his own collection, including *Cherub with Chariot*. I'm sure he saw it as an excellent investment.

"About the time the Cleveland Four moved in on the Beverly Hills, *Cherub with Chariot* fell out of sight. It's rumored Hammer sold it to Pete Schmidt for a paltry thousand or two."

"Interesting. Is there a photo in your book?"

"There's only one photo in existence, and it's useless. The egg appears as a blurred reflection behind another egg. Today, *Cherub with Chariot* would get fifty million, easy. It's been eighty years. If anyone had the egg, it would have shown up on the secondary market."

"A fifty-million-dollar trinket would burn a hell of a hole in your pocket."

"Exactly. The egg isn't the only artwork that went missing from the club, but it's the most famous."

Overstreet waved his cigarette as he talked. "Malachi steals the egg. Then he realizes selling it would get him killed. He hides the egg until it's safe to sell. Only, instead of cooling off, the egg gets hotter. Then he dies. And if he hid the egg, who knows what else he hid?"

"Why not pop the gems, melt the gold?"

"He'd need a jeweler. Too risky to trust anyone when

Malachi's whereabouts were worth a hundred times more to the big guys than Malachi would pay to dismantle the egg. And Malachi wasn't a cheap hood. I suspect he would have seen destroying the egg as sacrilegious."

"Why stay in the area if people wanted to kill him?"

"That's the question, isn't it?" Overstreet put his palms on his thighs and pushed up off his chair, signaling the end of their interview. "That's all I've got. You want my notes? I'm happy to scan them for you."

"That would be great." Peter returned to the bookcases while Overstreet booted up his laptop and unclipped the stack of yellow pages. The scanner hummed. "You writing a book about this?"

Overstreet shook his head. "It's a sexy story, but there's not enough meat on those bones, if you'll pardon the pun."

VIOLA LAY IN THE HALL OUTSIDE LIA'S STUDIO, MUZZLE ON paws as she sent evil looks through the new baby gate. Lia sighed. Despite the barrier, Gypsy huddled behind the huge easel for protection.

Lia set her palette on the drafting table and crouched, offering a treat. Gypsy bellied out, snagged the goodie. Lia caught her up, rubbing her cheek against the velvety fur, inhaling puppy scent.

Dog business was dog business, and Viola was making it clear she was queen bitch. There wasn't much Lia could do about the dynamics except keep them apart. She considered covering the gate with cardboard so Viola couldn't see in, but the two dogs could still smell each other and it probably wouldn't work. Moving the gate to the base of the stairs would keep Viola off the first floor, but Viola got along fine with Chewy and she hated to separate them.

"She doesn't like me, either, girlfriend. Just remember: You're younger, you're prettier, and in six months, you'll have bigger teeth."

Viola's ears perked. She bolted, scrambling for the front hall seconds before the doorknob rattled. Peter was home.

Lia stood, cradling Gypsy as she surveyed her newest iris. "Look what your mom did. Isn't it pretty? What's that? It needs a highlight on the top petal?"

From the hall, Peter said, "Everyone's a critic. Don't you hate that?"

"She can say what she wants, as long as she's constructive." Peter's face sagged, a sign of exhaustion. "You look bushed. Put some water on while I clean my brushes. I've got a stir-fry ready to go."

Water bubbled on the stove when Lia entered the kitchen. The wok was out, the table set. Peter sat, legs in a jock sprawl, sipping a beer while he fed biscuits to the dogs. He said, "I didn't see any rice."

Lia took a packet of dried noodles from the cabinet and turned on the heat under the wok. "We're having bean thread instead. How did it go with Jay Overstreet?"

"He was congenial for a man with a hangover."

"I bet you enjoyed ruining his morning." She dropped the tangle of noodles into the water, poking at it with a wooden spoon.

"I won't deny it."

"What did he say about the missing art?"

Peter tipped his beer back, took a long pull. "You know anything about Imperial Fabergé eggs?"

Lia poured a dollop of oil in the wok, added garlic and ginger, and retrieved shrimp and vegetables from the fridge. "He thinks Andrew Heenan had one of the missing eggs?"

"That's the theory."

She dropped shrimp onto the sizzling spices, chased them with the spoon. "I bet he made it up. Lost art treasures are more impressive than saying Andrew ran off with enough money to buy a three-bedroom house in today's market."

"The book he showed me had some wear on it. He didn't pick it up yesterday. True or not, he believes it."

Lia scooped the cooked shrimp into a bowl and dumped noodles in a strainer. "Rinse that while I cook. What kept you so busy today? I thought you'd be back hours ago."

Peter ambled to the sink, dealt with the noodles. "I need to be on top of the Malachi thing before I talk to Parker tomorrow. After I rousted Overstreet, I spent the day doing research. Then I decided the only person who might know about Andrew's past is Peggy Redfern, so I stopped by Twin Towers."

Lia splashed rice wine and soy sauce on top of her frying veggies, stirred in cornstarch, added the shrimp. "How did that go?"

Peter handed her plated noodles. "No better than last time. She asked if I was a Redfern. I said no. She patted my hand and said I looked like a very nice man anyway. Then

I asked if she remembered Andrew and she said, 'Does he work here? This is a very nice place.'"

Lia turned from the stove. "Will you try to talk to her again?"

Peter sighed. "I don't know if it's worth the effort."

PRETENDING LIA DIDN'T SEE HIM, PETER SNUCK A LAST scrap of bean thread to Viola under the table and pushed away from his empty plate.

"How was the gang this morning? Terry must have had something to say."

Lia sliced two bits off her last piece of shrimp, handing one to the puppy warming her lap and the other to Chewy where he lay at her feet. "I didn't go. I took the kids for a hike instead."

"Chicken."

"Yeah? Tell me Jay Overstreet wasn't a convenient excuse for you to avoid the park."

Peter shrugged. "Guilty."

"Did your research turn up anything?"

"Mostly that Newport's gambling days are a big tourist attraction. They even have gangster tours."

"Really? Sounds like fun."

"Maybe it was the way I was raised, but it rubs me the wrong way, glamorizing the murder and corruption that went along with gambling and prostitution as if it's something to be proud of. Nudging and winking at it all without considering the cost in human lives. I don't understand how anyone could consider something so shameful their glory days."

"Your moral compass is one of the things I adore about you."

Peter snorted.

"Will you look for Pete Schmidt's family?"

"According to Overstreet's notes, Schmidt outlived his only son. No evidence his son had children. There may be distant cousins, but they're not likely to be involved."

"Will you try to track them down?"

"Cincinnati Bell has over three hundred listings for Schmidt. That doesn't account for folks who ditched their landlines for cell phones, or female members of the family who changed names."

Lia forked up a bit of broccoli, holding it away from Gypsy. "Alma's a whiz on Ancestry.com and the Schmidt connection is public knowledge. I could ask her to look."

"Overstreet has been there and done that. I'd put money on it."

"Misdirection?"

"More like a snipe hunt."

"Why are you convinced he's misleading you?"

"He's a liar, for one."

"Oh?" With no more food forthcoming, Gypsy gave a disgruntled chuff and curled into Lia's lap.

"He made a production of copying his notes on a scanner and printing them out for me."

"And?"

"He wrote them on a yellow legal pad with the pages paper-clipped together. Paper fades over time. This was too yellow to be as old as he claimed, and paper that's been clipped for years will have a permanent dent. The penmanship is too uniform for notes he compiled over a period of years.

"He rewrote his notes after he called Channel 7. He knew someone would ask and he wanted to have something ready when that happened. I have to wonder what he left out."

"Why would he leave anything out?"

"The benign theory is he's protecting his research for the book he says he isn't writing. And the non-benign theory is he's up to something."

"Such as?"

"If Malachi's egg exists, he's in the best position of anyone to find it. He must have hundreds of hours of interviews and research. The answer might be in his files. He buys time by fobbing redacted notes off on me."

"If he wants the egg, he can have it."

"You don't want a fifty-million-dollar egg?"

"Have you seen one?"

"He showed me photos."

"Overly embellished and boring, like wedding cake. A triumph of craft over art. Tiffany stained glass is much prettier."

"I'll keep that in mind for Christmas. It'll be easier on my wallet."

"Could he be protecting someone?"

Peter raised an eyebrow. "The real killer?"

"What if it's more than that? What if he did it? He's old enough, isn't he? That would explain his interest in old crimes."

"Overstreet kills a man when he's barely out of school

and makes his life's work taunting the police with their failures, with this as his finest hour?"

"I see what you mean. Too Hollywood."

"You saw him on television. He's a skinny guy. You think he was ever capable of hauling a dead body over a hundred feet of rough terrain in the dark?"

A PLAN

SUNDAY, AUGUST 21, 1938

DING-DONGING BECAME A REGULAR EVENT AT THE BH. THE Cleveland Syndicate must have had an endless supply of goons willing to wag their willies because it was always a new crew that came to do the dirty deed. That meant Pete's security force never knew who it would be.

Pete turned the tables on them by comping dinner for everyone splattered with urine. The potential for harassment added a frisson of danger to an evening at the BH. Add a free meal and the BH drew record crowds. Record crowds meant heavy competition to play on BH stages, and a willingness for entertainers to tolerate the interruptions.

Mal was the first to instruct his lighting tech to spotlight any men getting on their chairs, at which point, Mal stopped his act and announced, "Who's getting a free dinner tonight?" Staff had to identify those customers quickly, because some folks attempted to splash themselves with urine they'd carried in with them in order to claim a meal. It became fashionable to sit near dangerous-looking stag men.

Pete was bearing up fine until the Syndicate decided to play hardball and hijacked one of the trucks his men shoveled money into after closing. Stu found the empty truck and the severely beaten driver and guards hours later.

The following afternoon, Mal sat in Pete's office. The big man puffed violently on his cigar while his gears turned. Finally he spoke.

"Stu, how much did we lose last night?"

Stu, leaning against the wall, lit a cigarette. "Over forty grand. It was a good night."

Pete pointed with his cigar. "They don't need to buy me out. They can let me do the work and take everything. We'll have to send more guards with the trucks."

"Someone will get killed that way," Mal said.

Stu snorted. "You got a better idea, kid?"

"Maybe."

Pete sat up, giving Mal a hard look. "Lay it out."

"Dalitz doesn't want the BH because it's classy—or that's not the main reason. He wants it because you rake in cash."

"Tell me something new."

"Until they robbed that truck, they had no way to know how much you were making. What if the trucks carry less money than they expect? What if we convince them the BH is a money pit, and the trucks are for show?"

Pete lifted his head. "Send out empty trucks? And what am I gonna do with the money?"

"I'm a magician. I make things disappear."

DAY 17

MONDAY, MAY 6, 2019

DAVID BOWIE'S *FAME* SOUNDED FROM LIA'S POCKET AS SHE opened the corral gate. Chewy shot off for his perimeter run while Gypsy squirmed in her Moby wrap. Lia juggled her travel mug and phone, tapping David's photo on the screen while continuing across the park.

"You're up early."

"You know me, I'm all about that worm."

She stroked Gypsy's head. "Stop bragging about your sex life."

"Speaking of which, when are you and Peter coming over for dinner? Bob is dying to meet you and I want to try my mac and cheese on someone who grew up with the genuine article."

Lia worried her lip as she thought. "Peter's tied up with his bones."

"Sounds kinky."

Not with Peter spending every evening tracking bogus tips. "It so isn't. Seriously."

"Your man works too hard."

"They're supposed to reassign that case today. Maybe we can come Saturday? I know you didn't call me up at—" Gypsy sniffed Lia's phone while she checked the time. "— Seven forty-three in the morning to invite us to dinner."

"Where is my head? Zoe called last night, but I didn't want to interrupt your weekend."

"Much appreciated."

"Good news or dubious news first?"

"Good news, please."

"You can cash that check."

"Yay. What made her highness decide?"

"Renée's admiration of Zoe's excellent taste sealed it. Our goddess expects her usual fee."

A woman of considerable influence, Renée Solomon promoted Lia whenever she could. Her usual fee was gossip.

"And the dubious news?"

"You know Renée. She rhapsodized about that portrait you painted of Dakini. Now Zoe wants one."

Dakini was Renée's champion collie. "Drop the other shoe, David."

"She has no pets, though Travis often behaves like an animal."

Travis was two.

"No."

"You can charge what you like. Toss in a nuisance fee. It's not like she'll notice."

"No children. It's in our contract."

"I'll forgo my commission. It will make my life ever so much easier."

"And if I do, it will get around that I paint children. No, and no. Your desperation is your problem."

"Sargent hated painting portraits and look what they did for him."

"She can adopt a cat. I'll paint a cat."

"Persian hair on her Persian rug? That won't happen."

"Bye, David."

She ended the call a few yards from the gang congregating at their usual table. Steve extended his hands with a gimme gesture. Lia set her mug down and extricated Gypsy, who snuggled in Steve's arms without a backward glance.

Bailey pouted. "Why does Steve always get her first?"

"You have a problem with sloppy puppy seconds?"

"I expect preference as your best friend and sometimes partner."

Terry reached over to tickle Gypsy's chin. "Where were you and Peter yesterday?"

Gypsy chewed on Terry's finger.

Steve set Gypsy on the portion of table not occupied by Bailey's hound, Kita. "Translation: Terry wants the dirt on Marvelous Malachi."

Gypsy wandered across the table to chew on Kita's tail. The tail thumped, creating a moving target. Gypsy pounced.

"I only know what I saw on TV. You spent Saturday with Jay Overstreet. Didn't you get it from him?"

Terry scowled. "I didn't know why he was there until

Aubrey Morse did her interview. After that, Dick button-holed him and they went drinking."

Bailey rescued Gypsy from Kita's tail, cradling the pup in her arms, cooing and stroking. "What does Peter think about Malachi, the mobster magician?"

Steve snorted. "It's a hoax. Overstreet knows enough to fake the story, and there's no way to call him on it because those old guys from Newport died years ago. You watch. Overstreet has a book in the works. He's after a payday."

Jim had been silent until now. "Malachi is real."

Lia asked, "What makes you say that?"

Jim tapped Gypsy's nose. Gypsy swatted his finger. "Because someone murdered Andrew Heenan. Until Steve found the bones, everyone thought he died overseas. Now you think the killer faked Heenan's departure to cover up the murder. That's not the reason."

Bailey relinquished Gypsy to José. "It's not?"

Jim said, "He was buying time."

José tickled Gypsy's belly. "You think this old guy who made balloon animals was a retired mobster?"

"I think someone *believed* he was."

Steve said, "How do you figure?"

Jim scowled, a sign they'd missed the obvious. "Thirty years ago, Mr. X decides Andrew Heenan is the missing Malachi. Mr. X wants the treasure. He thinks Heenan is an old guy and easy pickings. Mr. X forgets Malachi fought the mob and won."

Lia picked up the narrative. "If Andrew Heenan is Malachi, he had the guts to cut off his foot and escape the mob with his loot. He wouldn't just hand it over. He says

'You idiot, I spent it before World War II,' or 'I was in Peoria in 1940—'"

"Or 'piss up a rope, asshole,'" Terry said.

Jim nodded. "It goes wrong. Andrew Heenan dies without talking. What does he do?" Jim sat back, palms up and eyebrows raised.

Bailey made an "O" with her mouth. "He pretends to be Andrew and gets on the plane. Then he doubles back and spends weeks searching."

Jim tapped Bailey's forehead. "You get a gold star."

Bailey posed, head turned, hand to her cheek. "How does it look? Is it pretty?"

The missing housekeeper had been in the best position to pull this off, if she had a partner. But Jenny wasn't public knowledge and Lia couldn't talk about her.

José stroked his biker mustache. "Why would a guy with millions in stolen loot hang around here? Why wasn't he living it up in Cancun or Bimini?"

Terry jabbed a finger in the air. "Ninety percent humidity, cicada swarms, and crumbling roads. Why would anyone leave?"

Steve shook his head. "He stayed because he wasn't Malachi."

Exhausted by all the attention, Gypsy curled up next to Kita. The hound sighed.

Lia's brain felt the same way. "Interesting question, but it doesn't matter why Andrew Heenan chose to live in Cincinnati. If Jim's theory is correct, Mr. X found the money and he's long gone. Or he didn't find the money. What does he do now?"

Bailey stroked the sleeping puppy. "What do you mean?"

Lia ordered her thoughts. "You kill a guy, you get away with it, you get on with your life. Thirty years later the bones pop up—"

"Literally," Terry said.

"—If you found the money, nobody can prove where it came from. You're safe as long as you keep your head down. Say you live in Cleveland. Who's going to knock on your door? Nobody. Scenario number one is you laugh at the *Enquirer* with all your friends and life is good."

"What's the alternative?" Steve asked.

"You never found the money. It's been eating at you for thirty years. You see Andrew Heenan's skull at every checkout lane when you shop for groceries—"

"If he's married, his wife does the shopping," Jim said.

"Picky, picky. Okay, it stares him in the face at the convenience store where he gets his morning coffee. Even if he lives in New Zealand, Elvis' water-logged grave memes are cluttering his Twitter feed. Mr. X knows. It might eat at him, but the smart money stays home. Then Jay Overstreet goes on Channel 7 and says, 'Hey, world! Mob treasure here!'"

"So?" Bailey asked. "If he didn't find the money then, he won't now."

Steve turned a shrewd eye on Terry. "But now, every moron in a hundred miles is dusting off their metal detector."

Terry sent Steve a mutinous glare. Steve ignored him and continued, "Commodore's awareness campaign could backfire. If the idiots get it in their pointy heads Heenan's killer buried loot with those bones, Mill Creek will wind up looking like the aftermath of Woodstock."

"A ghastly thought, and illogical," Terry said.

"No accounting for stupid," José said.

Chewy returned from his daily expedition, butting Lia's hand. She fed him a treat from her pocket and scratched behind his ears.

"The police went over the entire area with a metal detector two weeks ago, looking for evidence. Can Commodore get the message out?"

Terry sighed. "Maybe Aubrey will run a follow-up."

José frowned, exaggerating the lines of his biker mustache. "Why do treasure hunters matter?"

Jim's voice turned gruff. "Mr. X killed someone to get that money in 1987. He won't let some yahoo walk off with it now."

Four phones sounded simultaneous alerts.

"Oooh," Bailey said. "Terry's girlfriend posted a video."

Terry perked up. "That's the interview we did by the tree. Let's see it."

Lia navigated to the video. The screen showed Susan standing on Clifton Hills Avenue. She snuck a peek at Terry as she laid her phone in the center of the table.

Susan's Snippets with Lena Ware

5.3K Views

Thumbs up: 743

Thumbs down: 109

Delicate, brightly intelligent, and wreathed with flyaway hair, the wrinkled face on the tiny screen brought to mind Geraldine McEwan as Miss Marple in the BBC series.

"Andrew was a charming man, and he took such lovely care of his house and garden. He could be mysterious. You always had the sense that he knew a secret and life amused him."

"Were you ..." Susan paused, a nod to sensitivity. "Intimate?"

Lena laughed. "Oh my, no. But he could make a woman wish she was single."

"How did you meet him?"

"My husband and I were in a dinner club. That month's host would pick a menu. Everyone cooked a dish and we'd spend the evening together. When it was Andrew's turn, he chose Lebanese food. We barely knew what that was back then. Our group was mostly couples, but Andrew always came alone. We'd have a few glasses of wine and he'd perform card tricks. He was always inventing new tricks. Or maybe he was recycling old ones. I'm sure we wouldn't have known the difference."

"What did you think when he disappeared?"

"It wasn't unusual for Andrew to be gone for weeks at a time. We thought he'd been delayed in one of those little countries where the phone service wasn't so good. This was before the internet. We didn't have Skype or Zoom or FaceTime. Months passed and he never came back. I thought, 'Well, they finally got him.'"

Susan's face took on an intense expression, reminding

Lia of Barbara Walters as the reporter went for the big revelation.

"Tell us, Mrs. Ware, who got him?"

"I thought it was the Russians. Really, it could have been anyone."

Susan's eyes widened and her Kentucky drawl deepened. "Why would the Russians murder your friend?"

"Dear, you don't think he did all that travel for pleasure, do you? He was an operative."

"An operative? You mean a *spy*? For whom?"

"I never knew. Our side, I hope. Israel, maybe. He sure enjoyed Middle Eastern food."

Lia scanned the park. In the distance, Napa and Jackson ran happy circles around Terry as he strode toward the gate, oblivious to the disappointment and humiliation driving him away from his friends.

Bailey's hand fluttered like an agitated bird. "What happened to Terry's interview?"

Steve stared after Terry, one hand absently stroking Gypsy's belly. "Don't know. He said she had trouble focusing. They had to redo parts of it. Maybe she couldn't make it work."

Bailey snorted. "I bet she trashed it because Aubrey Morse scooped her."

Terry's shoulders slumped as he made his way down the service road, making Lia's heart hurt.

Steve stood. "I'd better go. He'll be waiting for me in

the truck. This is the second time Susan interviewed him and didn't show it. After everything he does to help her, she should have told him."

"From what Peter says, empathy isn't her strong suit."

PETER DROPPED THE STACK OF TIPS GENERATED BY AUBREY Morse's story onto his desk. Elvis, facing the wall when Peter left the day before, grinned at him. A sticky note on the King's forehead read:

Kiss Me, You Fool

Peter crumpled the note, tossed it in the can for a two pointer.

Brent wheeled his chair around. "What did Cynth say about her date with the Neanderthal?"

"They're getting married Memorial Day weekend. He wants five kids, but she bargained him down to three, providing at least one is a boy."

"Bite me."

"You want to know, ask her yourself."

Brent nodded at the stack. "Anything good in there?"

"A guy who says he'll loan out his backhoe to dig up Heenan's treasure if he gets half."

"Generous of him."

"Some names of guys from the old days I should hunt up, but no contact info, and no guarantee they're still alive or that they know what happened in 1987."

"That's helpful."

"Thankfully, this mess will belong to Wallace before the end of the day."

"Does he get Elvis, too?"

"With a hunka burnin' love on top."

PETER PUNCHED THE BLINKING EXTENSION ON HIS PHONE for the tenth call that morning. Damn Jay Overstreet and the Toyota he rode in on. "Detective Dourson speaking."

The man spoke quickly, with an accent from one of the boroughs of New York City. Peter couldn't say which one. "My name is Billy Baker. I own a gallery in Tribeca. I've been following the Andrew Heenan story."

Of course you have.

"I'd like to donate my services."

In a pig's eye. "In what capacity, Mr. Baker?"

"I understand artworks may come into play. You'll need someone to authenticate them."

"That's a kind offer, but we have art dealers here."

"If I may say, you have no one with my reputation."

"Mr. Baker, are you hoping to broker the art if we find it?"

A hesitation.

"I have excellent connections."

"Those connections include Jay Overstreet?"

Another hesitation.

"We've spoken. I specialize in early twentieth century art."

Baker wanted a piece of pie in the sky, like every other yahoo calling him. Peter's normally polite manners frayed.

He took a nanosecond to remember Chief Isaac's latest mantra: Expect that you are always on camera. "Mr. Baker, if we uncover a priceless Easter egg, I'll pass your name along."

Peter's line beeped. "I have to take another call. But I'll keep your information handy." He switched lines before Baker could say he hadn't given Peter his number.

"Dourson."

Captain Parker did not bother to identify herself. "My office, five minutes. I need an update on Heenan."

Despite her inscrutability, Peter liked Captain Parker. She was smart, open-minded, and not inclined to the knee-jerk reactions of her predecessor. He respected her commitment to staying as fit as any of her men and didn't care to think about his chances if he had to meet her in hand-to-hand. She was also middle management. Parker might not originate crap, but rank obligated her to roll it downhill no matter how she felt about it.

Peter contemplated the landmine that was leadership as he walked the long, dreary hall to Parker's office. She sat at her desk, framed by the open door, scanning a report. He rapped on the jamb.

Her head lifted, face full of regret. "Have a seat, Dourson."

Peter settled into the visitor's chair. "Sir?"

"Tell me the Malachi story is a hoax."

"Eighteen years of research by Jay Overstreet weighs against it. There was a Malachi. Who knows about his cache, or whether he cut his leg off."

"I almost wish you hadn't identified Heenan's remains. Elvis conspiracy theories can be laughed off. Lost mob treasure is a disaster, unless it jogs someone's memory. Any chance of that?"

"Plenty of folks want to talk about the good old days when crime was king and life was a never-ending party. No one knows boo about who killed Heenan four decades later."

Parker sighed. "We planned for you to work Heenan until Wallace returned. That can't happen now."

"Sir?"

"His cruise ship was quarantined with an outbreak of some mystery virus."

Peter's heart sank into his stomach. "I'm sorry to hear that."

"We had five calls from the Johnsons yesterday, idiot trespassers with metal detectors."

"I didn't know."

"No point calling you. Bobbi Johnson sicced her dogs on them and they disappeared into the woods behind the property. She has some blurry photos on her phone, nothing that will give us an ID. It's a nuisance. Unlikely it has anything to do with Heenan's murder."

She ran a hand through hair that had taken the brunt of her frustrations. "Bobbi Johnson wants to file a complaint against Susan Sweeney. I explained that there was no law against Ms. Sweeney conducting interviews on the sidewalk as long as she didn't harass anyone or block access to the property. I did not tell her Susan was your ex-fiancée."

"Much appreciated, sir."

"Have you interviewed the Johnsons?"

"Not yet. I didn't consider them or the house relevant

until Overstreet told the world about Malachi's lost mob loot."

"Reputed lost mob loot, unless you have sound evidence it exists. I've already stepped up patrols and flagged the house. When you talk to the Johnsons, reinforce our commitment to protecting their safety and peace of mind."

"Yes, sir."

"And if you have any influence with your ex-fiancée, feel free to suggest she conduct her interviews elsewhere and stop putting videos of the house on the internet."

Peter felt tension building behind his eyes, a sure sign of a pending headache. "Honestly, sir, sometimes the only thing that will derail Susan is an oncoming train. I'll try, but my expectations are low."

"Understood. What did you get from Overstreet?"

"Nothing that points us in a productive direction. He may have the why of Heenan's death, but according to him, plenty of people knew about Malachi. Our guy could be five or six degrees of separation from the source. We'd have to track the Schmidts, anyone who worked for them, anyone connected with the Cleveland Syndicate, and three generations of descendants. Then we have to figure out who they talked to."

"I see your point. What did you think of Overstreet?"

"He's hiding something. It's a toss up whether he's writing a book or hunting the treasure."

"Maybe both. You run him?"

"He has a disorderly conduct from an animal rights protest at OSU from that summer. There's nothing to say he didn't sneak into town to kill Heenan, but there's nothing to connect him. His involvement with the animal rights group suggests his mind was elsewhere at the time. I'm not ruling him out, but he doesn't excite me."

"The burial site?"

"Between construction workers and Bengals fans, we're talking hundreds of unidentifiable men capable of hauling Heenan into that gully. The yacht club was a bust. The only possible is a friend of Lia's, but he didn't do it."

"Convince me."

"Nothing in Steve's history says he ever had money. If he killed Heenan, he didn't find the loot. He went through significant financial hardship a few years back. If he knew about Malachi, he would've been looking then."

"Who says he wasn't?"

"His roommate would have noticed and Lia would have heard about it. Respectfully, sir, Steve discovered the bones. Most guys would sweat bullets if they were standing between a cop and the unearthed bones of someone they killed. Something would have been off."

"Keep him on the list for now."

"Yes, sir."

"Do you have *any* avenues to pursue?"

"Whoever killed Heenan had to interact with him while he lived in Clifton Hills. Our best bet is to focus there. A neighbor identified the missing housekeeper as Jennifer Olson. She's the person most likely to know something, but she left the area shortly after Heenan disappeared.

"There are a hundred and fifty thousand Olsons in the US. If she married, who knows what she goes by now. We won't find her unless we put out a request for public assistance."

Parker paused, tapping a disjointed rhythm as she thought. Peter understood. You didn't publicly identify witnesses unless you had no other choice.

"See if you can dig up someone who knew Ms. Olson. If you don't find anyone in the next forty-eight hours, put a call in to Aubrey Morse."

Peter sighed. "Yes, sir."

FIRST RUN

WEDNESDAY, AUGUST 24, 1938

Mal sat behind the wheel of the Cadillac hearse he used to haul his equipment, watching a pair of guards wheel a cart loaded with sacks of cash onto the loading dock. Stu unlocked the back of the armored truck. When the guards had their heads in the truck, Stu jerked his chin at Mal.

Time to go.

Only Pete and Stu knew part of the take now resided in Mal's disappearing cabinet. It had been easy to pull off: stopping by the money room for a palaver, parking the dolly with the cabinet outside the door, keeping the guards laughing while Stu slid bags in the secret compartment, wheeling the cabinet to the hearse and humping it into the back as if it were nothing more than a cheap stage prop.

Stage one had been diverting the cash. Now for stage two, getting it away from the club.

Mal turned the key in the ignition and put the hearse in gear, his senses hyper-alert as he eased down the drive to Route 27 five minutes ahead of the truck's scheduled departure. The truck would turn north on its regular route. Mal turned south. If he escaped notice for the next twenty minutes, he'd be scot-free.

The country road grew pitch black as he pulled away, the narrow slice of his headlights blinding him to everything else. If Dalitz was smart, he'd have a second crew of goons waiting on the south road in case Pete re-routed his truck. In the black void surrounding him, they'd be invisible until it was too late.

Mal felt his heart beating like it hadn't since his days picking pockets under the nose of the Garda, when a fumbled dip or the unexpected turn of a head would mean a beating.

The road rose and fell in gentle rolls. Mal searched the side of the road, looking for a telltale glint, a reflection, movement, something to let him know someone was there. He wouldn't find them on the rises, where they'd be silhouetted against the sky. Instead, he focused on the dells and copses while keeping a steady rate of speed to suggest he wasn't looking for anything at all.

Three miles from the club, he'd almost decided they weren't there when he caught a flicker of movement up on the left, a shaking branch on the edge of a copse. He maintained his speed, splitting his attention between the road and the trees, expecting a car full of goons to come roaring out.

He counted, topping the next rise at five. His was the

only motor he heard. When he reached ten, he exhaled, not realizing until then he'd stopped breathing.

At the count of twenty, Mal reached McMurtry's farm and relaxed. McMurtry managed to hang onto his cows during the recession, but he'd never recovered and the place showed it. Mal drove another seven miles with nothing to set off alarm bells, then wheeled the Caddy onto the track to the barn where he built his tricks.

Unlike most barns in the area, this one had a cellar below a wood floor. He stashed the money bags and parked the hearse on top of the trapdoor.

Pete had skimmed as much as he dared, wanting to look like a slow night, not wanting the goons to realize he was shorting them. That was twenty grand Dalitz wouldn't get his paws on.

Now that their experiment had worked, they'd slowly increase the skim to make it look like business was going down the tubes. And they needed a solid plan for what to do with the money to keep it hidden. The barn was fine for overnight, but it wouldn't do for long term.

DAY 18

TUESDAY, MAY 7, 2019

Sonya Trent appeared on Susan's show with her tall, rail-thin frame arrayed in a riot of paisley scarves left over from the seventies, her fluttering hand flashing enough diamonds to signal passing aircraft. A bush of wild, white hair made Lia think of a gaudy dandelion going to seed.

"Sonya, what were your thoughts when you read about the discovery of Andrew Heenan's bones last week?"

Sonya blinked through oversized glasses that gave her a bug-eyed appearance and sighed, head tilted at a dramatic angle, the diamond-encrusted, butterfly hand landing on her chest.

Kita, a streamer of drool dangling dangerously, hung

her head over the tiny screen on the picnic table. Bailey nudged Lia's phone out of reach.

On-screen, Sonya said, "My dear, it was only to be expected."

A nonplussed Susan asked, "You expected him to be buried in a shallow grave under a cottonwood tree?"

"Andrew Heenan trafficked with evil."

"You mean the Cleveland Syndicate?"

The dandelion head shook slowly from side to side. "No dear. Andrew was more than a stage magician. I'm talking about—" Sonya delivered her next words with an ominous vibrato. "—Daaaarrrk magic."

———————

Bailey cackled. Steve guffawed. Jim shook his head and smiled. Terry sat, uncharacteristically silent. Startled by the noise, Gypsy jumped out of the Moby wrap and onto the picnic table. All hands dove to corral her before she leapt to the potentially parvo-infected ground. Lia hit the pause button on her phone and searched the faces around her.

"What?"

Bailey stopped laughing long enough to wipe tears from her eyes. "She hasn't seen it yet. Steve, you tell her."

Steve lifted his head from nuzzling Gypsy. "When was the last time you visited the Westwood library?"

"Not since Desiree. What does that have to do—?" She took a long look at Susan's guest. "Oh my God, that's the children's librarian."

Bailey filled in the blanks "—Doing her very best Professor Trelawney."

"It's her go-to costume for Halloween," Steve said. "The kids go crazy when she does the 'You are in grave danger' bit."

"Sybill Trelawney, Sonya Trent," Bailey giggled. "I love it."

"Not funny," Terry grumbled. "She should know better than to mock Susan publicly, and I'll say so next time I see her.

HOME FROM THE PARK, GYPSY WIGGLED TO GET OUT OF THE Moby wrap as Lia inserted her key into the front door.

"Ouch, girlfriend, chill for a minute."

Chewy whined.

"Breakfast is coming, little man."

The dogs bolted through the opened door to the sound of her alarm panel beeping. *Like they're in* Mission Impossible *or something.* She keyed in the alarm code and headed to the kitchen, dropping her phone and keys on the table. Gypsy ran to the door leading to the rear stairs, barking viciously. Chewy stared at it and whined.

"What is your problem?"

Above, a door closed.

If Susan thought she could waltz into Peter's apartment any time she wanted, she had another thing coming. Lia shoved a palm at the dogs, commanding, "Wait!" She slammed the door behind her and raced up the stairs, two at a time.

The door at the top banged into the attic door as she burst through. Something heavy and soft fell over her as muscular arms banded around her. She screamed and kicked. Connected with a shin. Dug fingers into a pressure point on a thigh.

He grunted.

Something smashed the top of her head. A hard shove. Pain, shooting through her hip and skull as she landed on the attic steps.

The skeleton key that stayed in the lock snicked.

"Hurt my dogs and I'll kill you!" she screamed as she wrestled out of the enveloping shroud. She pounded the door, helpless as feet raced down the stairs, her dogs barking, the sound growing fainter as they chased him outside.

Please, God, don't let them run into the street. Fear for her dogs drove out all other thoughts until the sound of paws thundering up the steps brought relief. Both dogs whined as Gypsy's puppy claws scrabbled against the attic door.

Dammit, dammit, dammit. Lia sat on the steps and took a deep breath, reminding herself that her burglar left after he locked her in, when he could have taken his sweet time ransacking the house. And he *was* gone.

"Sorry, kids. Unless you can pick locks, you can forget breakfast."

Gypsy howled.

She picked up the thing that had blinded her, a fleece throw Peter used to protect his couch from Viola's hair and other indignities. She sniffed. Fake flowers, not dog. He'd washed it, and it had been conveniently lying in his laundry basket when she charged up the stairs.

None of which explained who had been in Peter's

apartment or what they wanted. Not Susan, unless Susan had morphed into the Hulk since her last video.

Lia eyed the lock. Old locks with skeleton keys were easy to pick. If she'd had any foresight, she would have gone on YouTube when she bought the house and learned how. Keeping the key in the lock had obviously been a stupid idea, but the door was weighted wrong and swung open. And who expected to be attacked in their own home?

She sighed and climbed the stairs. Alma would be working in her garden at some point. If Lia could find a window that wasn't painted shut, she could holler for help and Alma would rescue her.

PETER FOUND LIA SITTING ON ALMA'S MANY-TIMES reupholstered sofa. An aromatic cup of herbal tea— chamomile?—sat untouched as she held a towel-wrapped bag of frozen peas above her ear with one hand and corralled Gypsy and Chewy on her lap with the other. Viola sulked in her preferred corner.

She looked down, hair falling over her face. Peter was reminded of the day they met, the way he couldn't see her eyes. She'd been traumatized then, too.

Months earlier it would have been Honey's head on Lia's lap, Lia's fingers combing the silky fur for comfort. He didn't imagine the pair of wiggle balls she now owned provided the same degree of emotional support. Chewy sniffed her face as if he could smell her distress and it worried him. He probably could, and it probably did.

He pulled Lia's hand with the bundled peas away from her head, set the peas on the coffee table, and probed gently at the lump on her skull.

"Ow."

He handed her the peas. "You'll live."

"On the bright side, Gypsy learned how to climb stairs."

He pulled a chair over and sat, facing her. "Dammit, Lia, what did you get that fancy alarm system for if you don't use it?"

"I don't know Peter, I—" Her head jerked up, green eyes damp and confused. "I turned the alarm off when I got home. I'd swear to it."

The red mark on Lia's cheek—put there when she landed on the steps, Alma had said—made him crazy. One more time he hadn't been there when she needed him. He wanted to gather her in his arms and rock her until she cried it all out, but he had to focus and be a cop.

"I *know* I did. We can call the alarm company. They keep a record."

"We'll do that. Whoever our visitor was, he's a fast thinker and he's cool headed. Whatever he wanted, he didn't want us to know he'd been there. He didn't leave a mess, and when you showed up, he kept you from seeing him and got out of there. You're bruised, but you aren't dead. I'm betting he didn't have a gun."

Lia removed the peas and took a sip of tea. "I suppose I should be grateful for that."

"Any thoughts about what he wanted?"

"Not a clue. All my electronics are still there. It doesn't look like he rifled through any of the places you told me people look for cash and valuables. He was in your apartment. Is there a chance Susan is behind this?"

"Popping in to surprise me is one thing. Sending some creep to burgle the place isn't in her playbook."

Lia's championship-quality fish eye was interrupted when Alma led Cal Hinkle into the room.

"I checked all the doors. No signs of forced entry. All the windows are nice and tight."

Lia rubbed noses with Chewy, ignoring Peter. "It's been warm out. Maybe I left one of the studio windows open and he locked it after he came in."

"Unlikely he'd bother," Peter said. "Check the outside again. He got in somehow."

Five minutes later, Peter and Lia stood behind Cal as he pointed to broken branches on one of the overgrown lilac bushes concealing the foundation of the house. Peter knelt in the grass. He prayed for a footprint, but it hadn't rained for more than a week and the ground was hard.

Gypsy nosed in beside him, sniffing, then disappearing into the bush. Peter pushed through to find Gypsy up on her hind legs, tail wagging furiously, her front paws against an iron hatch embedded in the wall. The hatch read:

MAJESTIC
COAL CHUTE
NO 101.

"I'll be damned." He counted the bricks around the hatch, making rough calculations to confirm what his eyes told him. The opening was eighteen by twenty-four inches, easily accommodating an adult male. Peeling paint scabbed the rusty metal. *Fat chance lifting prints.*

Hinges screeched as he pulled the hatch up. Dim light bled through the bushes, revealing nothing in the room below. He backed out on his hands and knees, then held branches aside so Lia and Cal could see.

"Excellent work, Cal."

"Thank you, sir. What now?"

Peter looked around. He didn't know as much as he would like about his neighbors, but Alma knew everyone.

"Check in with Alma. Find out who's likely to be home and knock on doors. Keep your eyes peeled for security cameras. If we're lucky, someone has our visitor in the cloud."

Lia stood by silently until Cal reached the sidewalk. "All those months you slept in the basement waiting for copper thieves and you never noticed the coal chute?"

Peter rubbed the back of his neck while he mentally slapped himself across the face several times. "It was dark down there."

"That's your excuse?"

Lia must be over her fright if she was giving him a hard time.

"We've got to make the house more secure. We need cameras, but first I'm bolting the chute shut."

"That's original. You're not drilling holes in it."

"It's insecure. You're not safe."

"We can screw plywood over the opening from the inside, anchor it to the brick."

"I can secure it with a bolt from the outside right now. I won't be able to pick up plywood for a couple days."

"I've got a length of one by six I can bolt across the opening and no one will be able to fit through."

"One good kick will fix that."

Temper flashed, turning her eyes hard as jade. "You'd prefer steel sheet?"

"You sure you don't mind me drilling into your *original brick?*"

"Don't worry about it. Bailey and I will install it."

Peter huffed, annoyed, and annoyed with himself for being annoyed. The last thing either of them needed right now was a battle of the sexes. *Dial it back, Dourson.*

Lia continued, "We're perfectly capable. But if you insist, you can play carpenter. Bailey and I will go looking for the bad guy. I'm sure Terry would love to help."

Peter wrapped his arms around her, softened his voice. "Point taken. You and Bailey make our castle safe. Before you call her, I want to look at the basement."

LIA STOOD AT PETER'S BACK AS HE UNLOCKED THE PADLOCK on the crypt-like bulkhead doors. Cool air drifted out as he lifted one panel.

"What are you going to do?" Lia asked.

"Your intruder was smart enough to get away without letting you see him. He was probably smart enough to wear gloves. But there's one kind of evidence he couldn't get around."

"What would that be?"

"Unless he can levitate, he left footprints."

"We're going through here because he didn't come this way?"

"What was your first clue, Tonto?"

"Duh. Padlock."

"Correct. But you haven't earned the chops to snark at a crime scene."

"My crime scene," Lia said. "I'll snark if I want."

"I'll give you a pass since you're traumatized."

He stopped at the bottom of the short flight of steps to unlock the door, then stooped, surveying the floor.

"I don't see anything," Lia said. "Don't you need an alternate light source for something like this?"

Peter pulled a mag light from his pocket. "Watch this." He switched on the light, holding it a few inches above the concrete at an oblique angle. A layer of dust Lia would have sworn wasn't there appeared, marred by scuffs and footprints. A clear path led from the interior basement steps to her washing machine.

"There are hundreds of them. How will you know which are his?"

Peter aimed the light to the right, where one set of footprints emerged from the room containing the coal chute, crossing the floor to merge with the morass of prints leading to the steps.

"That's him. Hard to tell from here, but I'll bet our man wears a size eleven."

"What do we do now?"

"We back out and lock the door. You go nowhere near the basement or the attic. Unfortunately, our break-in isn't important enough to rate a visit from the crime scene techs."

"Not important? But—"

"Budgets and manpower. It's not personal. I'll photograph these puppies and peel them off the floor with gel lifters, if I can beg some off Junior. Be a good girl and I'll let you help."

PETER PULLED INTO THE SMALL PARKING LOT BESIDE Overstreet's car, still fuming. Junior had gel lifters waiting for him, tacky plastic sheets designed to pick up footprints and other fragile evidence. But he had to make this detour first for his peace of mind.

He'd made a mental leap, one worthy of an action film where the star jumps from one building to the next and grabs the gutter with his fingernails, clawing his way up from certain death. But his hunch had been right. He needed to follow up now or implode.

It hadn't occurred to Lia yet that her attacker couldn't unlock the attic door while he was restraining her. The attic door had already been unlocked, which meant the intruder hadn't been in Peter's apartment, he'd been in the attic.

The only things in the attic were the remnants of Ruth Peltier's estate. Lia would have noticed if the Beanie Baby army had been disturbed. Whatever he'd been after had been in the boxes they had yet to sort. Boxes a historian might want to get his hands on.

Terry, whose photo was next to "open source" in the dictionary, had spent several hours with an expert on local history three days before, an expert whose ethics Peter suspected were on the sleazy side.

He shouldn't blame Terry. Their house was two blocks from Millionaire's Corner, where four of the richest men in Cincinnati once made their homes. It was natural to mention a potentially historic house to a historian.

Terry had told Overstreet he'd been wondering if the original owners of the property might also have been important. Overstreet had asked if the original owners left anything behind, and Terry told him about the boxes of cherry-picked items José and Alma culled from tons of junk one step ahead of the crowd that ran through the house like Sherman in Atlanta.

The story of Lia and Alma disposing of a hoarder's lifetime achievement in less than a day had been told and retold often enough. No reason for Terry to keep quiet about it.

Peter sat in his department-issue Taurus and took several deep, cleansing breaths to drain the anger building since he'd gotten Alma's call. He couldn't afford to go gonzo on Overstreet, not when all he had was the timing of a conversation. If he kept his cool, he'd know in a few minutes if Overstreet was his guy.

Peter rounded the building and badged the man mowing the lawn—the manager, it turned out—who then let him in.

He restrained the urge to pound Overstreet's door, opting instead for a friendly rap. Overstreet responded, opening the door with a question on his face. Curiosity, not fear.

"Hey, Detective. What's up?"

"I have a couple quick questions you could help me with."

"Sure, whatever you need." He stepped aside, inviting Peter in. Overstreet scanned the pile of work on his dining room table, likely ensuring he'd left nothing important in plain view.

"Have a seat. Can I get you something to drink? I think I have water and, uh, water, unless you're off duty."

"I'm good, thanks."

Ashtrays and wastebaskets still overflowed, but a new load of laundry piled on the end of the couch. No scotch bottle on the coffee table. Peter sat next to the heap of clothes.

Overstreet sat opposite, his face relaxed. "What can I help you with?"

During Peter's prior visit, Overstreet had displayed a number of micro expressions, tics that told Peter Overstreet was holding out on him about Heenan. Not a guy who could fool his aunt Sally, much less a lie detector.

"You been in all day?"

Puzzlement showed on Overstreet's face. "What happened? Is this about Heenan?"

"Maybe, maybe not. Humor me and I can rule out a troubling possibility."

"No problem. I took a run. On the way home I stopped for breakfast at Price Hill Chili. You can check, they know me there."

"What time did you get back?"

"Around ten, give or take. What was I supposed to have done?"

Something loosened in Peter's chest. "Nothing as far as I know. This is exclusionary."

"If you made a report, I'll figure it out by Friday."

Peter ran the math in his head. Overstreet was smarter than the average bear about accessing public records. Might as well win points with the guy since he'd find out anyway. "First tell me your shoe size."

"Nine."

He pulled off an ancient sneaker and handed it to Peter. The aroma it exuded reminded Peter of a drying swamp.

"Go ahead, check."

Peter already knew it was too small for the prints in Lia's basement. Still, he examined the shoe. Overstreet could have worn a larger pair and stuffed the toes to throw off investigators, but if the waitresses remembered Overstreet, he was off the hook.

"Last weekend you spoke with Terry Dunn about items of historical interest at a Victorian house that was burgled today."

"Yeah, by Millionaire's Corner. What was taken?"

"We don't know yet."

Overstreet remained relaxed. "Wasn't me. Stuff I want, most folks are happy to give to anyone who has a use for it. That way they don't feel guilty about throwing it out."

"What kind of stuff do you mean?"

"Old papers, photos. Say something happened on Glenway Avenue fifty years ago. The area's changed since then, more than once. Someone entirely unrelated to the crime might have a photo that shows how it was at the time, and that helps me understand what might have happened. It gives context and can produce leads. Business names, license plates."

He waved at a row of archival boxes on the bottom shelf of the nearest bookcase. "I have hundreds of old photos, organized by neighborhood and date."

"Anything that pertains to Heenan?"

"No photos of Malachi. Clifton Hills hasn't changed. As for Mill Creek, you might check the Bengals to see if they have construction photos of the area.

"The Mill Creek Alliance are the only folks interested in old photos of the creek, for comparison. You might luck out with the Metropolitan Sewer District. Everyone else just wants to forget the bad old days."

"It occurs to me there's a lot I don't know about investigating cold cases."

"Threw you into the deep end, huh? I can help."

Peter stood to leave. "I'll talk to the homeowner and pass along your phone number. If she has old photos she doesn't want, she might call you."

"That would be great." Overstreet accompanied him to the door. "Detective? Be sure to tell your girlfriend I'm sorry she was burgled."

Peter changed his mind. He was going to kill Terry.

RAIN DRUMMED THE DARKENED WINDOWS OF PETER'S MAN cave as he stretched, his back cracking vertebrae by vertebrae. The time he'd spent dealing with the break-in meant hours hunched over his laptop that evening, following dubious Heenan tips and writing reports. Pure busywork to satisfy the powers that be when he itched to find the dirtbag who violated his home and attacked Lia. It didn't help that there were no witnesses, no cameras, and nothing to pursue.

By his feet, Viola lifted her head. Peter looked at the clock. 11:43 p.m. Lia had to be asleep.

She'd been a trooper, holding the light while he photographed and lifted footprints. Later, she and Bailey installed a steel plate over the coal chute. His Lia did not get the vapors, though she was more fragile than she acted.

Figuring she wouldn't be up for much, he'd brought Kung Pao chicken and rainbow shrimp for dinner. Bailey had stayed, and when he'd come upstairs to work, they were looking for a rom-com to download.

He ghosted barefoot through the dark house with Viola a shapeless black blob padding behind him. Lia's bedroom door stood open, a signal for him to join her. Gypsy curled on the pillow, snuggled in the curve where Lia's shoulder met her neck, her face in repose.

Gypsy lifted her head and yawned. She stood and came to the edge of the bed, wagging her tail, asking him to let her down. Chewy woke and all three dogs followed him into the kitchen for late night biscuits.

Viola snorted as Gypsy pawed the water in her bowl, splashing it on the floor. Peter shook his head and poured a glass of water from the jug in the fridge, carrying it to the kitchen door to watch the deluge. He stepped in something warm and wet, the scent of urine drifting up. Gypsy paused her splashing and cocked her head.

Peter pointed at the dog door. "You're a freaking

menace. Can't you go outside?" The rain continued to pound. He sighed. "I wouldn't want to pee in that, either."

He hopped over to Gypsy's bowl, swished his soiled foot in the puddle of water on the floor, then swiped the bottom of his foot on the rag rug in front of the sink to dry it off.

"I'm not enabling you. You'll have to work this out with her."

Gypsy tipped her head the other way, looking at him as if he spoke a foreign language. He thought about Lia's day, sighed again, and pulled two pee pads out from under the sink to soak up the mess.

THE MATTRESS SHIFTED, WAKING LIA. SHE EMERGED FROM sleep as Peter spooned behind her, one arm pulling her against him.

He enfolded her: love, wrapped in a blanket with chicken soup and all the boo-boo kisses and attagirls she'd never received. He was rain in the desert, while she ached with thirst and feared drowning.

The edifice she'd held in place since a stranger threw a blanket over her head crumbled. She shook, hiccuping soundless sobs. Peter's arms tightened, containing her spasms until they passed.

His breath whispered against her ear. "Thank God."

"For what?"

He ran a hand up and down her arm, comforting himself as much as her. "You've been such a trooper, I was beginning to think you didn't need me."

She stopped his hand, laced their fingers together. "I'll always need you. I just wait till it's safe to fall apart."

"Very considerate of you."

"It's not like I do it on purpose." He'd said nothing over dinner. Now she was afraid of the answer, but had to ask. "What's happening with the break-in?"

"Besides getting chewed out for handling it myself? Nothing."

Lia turned in his arms, read frustration in his face. "Tell me."

"The footprints are worthless until I find the shoes they came from, and there's nothing else to work with. I filed it. Now we forget it until something comes up. It's the best I can do."

"It's hard, isn't it, not being able to do more?" He said nothing and she continued, "I ordered security cameras, one for each side of the house."

"I thought we were going to talk about it."

"The movie was boring so Bailey and I did research instead. We found cameras that alert your phone when anyone moves in the yard. We can both watch the house from anywhere. They're so cheap it seemed silly to wait. They'll be here by Friday. Bailey and I can install them."

Peter chuffed a laugh. "There's my stand-up girl. I feel my balls shriveling as we speak."

"You can be manly anytime upper-body strength is required."

"I feel so much better."

She became aware of her hand on his chest and flexed her fingers, enjoying the slide of hair between them. She dropped her eyes.

"Peter?"

"Hmm?"

"You know that life-affirming thing people do after near death experiences?"

"You have a near death experience lately?"

"More of a mugging, really."

"Not much of a mugging. No mace, no duct tape, no guns, no blood. Hardly worth mentioning."

"I got an owie on my head. That counts for something."

His lips pressed against her hair. "There. I kissed it."

"That life-affirming thing? Do they do it after muggings, too?"

He rolled onto his back, folding his arms. "I'm not sure what life-affirming thing you mean. You'll have to show me."

AT THE BARN

THURSDAY, AUGUST 25, 1938

THE SOUND OF A CAR HORN WOKE MAL. SUNLIGHT SLICED between the boards of the barn, heating the air in the hayloft. It had to be noon, at least. Mal stretched joints achy from sleeping on the cot he kept for late nights. The horn tooted again, impatient.

"Hold your damn horses."

He sat up, spat on the dirty floor, pulled on his pants and shoes, then stuffed his flask and cigarettes in his pocket before he climbed down the ladder. The horn sounded a third time as he reached the door and peered through the gap.

Pete was alone.

There were too many ways they could be found out. Pete's driver talks to his girl after sex and one of Dalitz's goons grabs her and puts the squeeze on her. Maybe her granny needs an operation, so she sells out. They beat the driver with a tire iron until he squeals. Or the story about how Pete's pulling a fast one on Dalitz is too good not to repeat, and it gets around.

So Pete left his driver at home.

Mal pulled the barn door wide. He took a slug from his flask and lit a cigarette while Pete drove into the barn.

The first words out of Pete's mouth as he hopped out of his car were, "Where is it?"

Mal nodded at the hearse. "Under the floor. Nobody can get to it until I move the car."

Pete stared at the hearse as if willing it to levitate. "I thought you were nuts when you said I should put the Chinese squeeze on my own take, but this takes the sting out of getting hit last night." He pointed a thick finger at Mal and grinned. "You're the bee's knees. Let me see my money."

"Let's talk first," Mal said. "We're safe as long as it stays where it is. We'll load it when you're ready to leave."

Pete gave him a long, steady look, then sat on a crate, unconcerned about the state of his suit. "You've been thinking."

"Yeah. This gag could work half a dozen, a dozen, maybe two dozen times before they start wondering. We have to stay ahead of them."

"What do you have in mind?"

"Cash takes up too much space. We need to turn it into something else."

"How do you propose we do that?"

"More misdirection. I heard sometimes customers want to sell their watches and cufflinks to keep playing."

"Go on."

"You turn your cash into something else and let other people walk out the front door with the money. You have big rollers from all over the country coming in every weekend with briefcases full of money they plan to lose in your casino."

He took a long drag as he read Pete's face. So far, so good.

"Get a handful of middlemen from outside the Syndicate's turf to play big rollers, only instead of money, they bring in small things that are valuable: gold coins, rubies, even art. They blow some cash at the tables, then you conduct a private transaction in your office like you usually do."

He took another drag, drawing out the reveal to allow Pete time to think about this new proposal.

"It's business as usual to anyone watching. Only instead of grandpa's watch, they sell you loose stones, a lot of them. Your money leaves with one of those fine patrons Dalitz doesn't want to upset. Instead of a truckload of money, you only have to hide a handful of stones. Then you have lots of options."

Mal deliberately didn't mention the guests who came straight from the airport, leaving suitcases in Stu's custody while they disappeared into back rooms for high-stakes poker.

It was better if Pete didn't realize how much Mal knew about the operation. But it hadn't taken long to figure out a few of the private poker games were shams to cover a money laundering operation, with the dirty cash they brought in run through the casino and returned—minus a percentage—in winnings.

Pete would make the jump without Mal's help, that Dalitz had no desire to disturb one of the BH's cash cows, that what looked like men bringing in money to launder could be couriers with pretty baubles to sell. Dalitz would be none the wiser.

Pete pulled on his chin. "Doesn't have to be loose stones."

"Anything smaller than a breadbox will be easy to hide. I build secret compartments in my tricks. I can put some in the hearse, in places they won't look because they're looking for a truckload of cash."

Mal's people had been smugglers back in Ireland. Before Da died, he'd told Mal all the old stories and gambits. But Pete didn't need to know he came from a long line of criminals. Better for him to think Mal came up with the scheme because he was a magician.

Pete frowned, shook his head. "That means bringing in outsiders. Outsiders who might talk."

"They don't have to know what's going on. You pretend you're a middleman for someone else. You don't tell them you're stealing from the jerks who are stealing from you before they get a chance to do it."

"This is complicated. I like things simple."

"Confuse and conquer. That's what I do every night on stage. It's either that or get on your knees every day and pray no one finds the warehouse you have to buy to keep all the cash hidden, because before long it's gonna be like hiding an elephant."

Pete pulled out a cigar, tucked it in the side of his mouth. Pete whipped out his lighter and lit it without thinking. Pete looked at the rafters, blew a smoke ring.

"Confuse and conquer, huh?"

"Just like magic."

DAY 19

WEDNESDAY, MAY 8, 2019

Susan's Snippets with Walter Miller

7.4K Views

Thumbs up: 1,014

Thumbs down: 109

THE TALL, STOOP-SHOULDERED MAN RESTING A GNARLED hand on a tripod cane appeared desiccated next to Susan's vibrant, unlined youth.

"Walter, who do you believe killed Andrew Heenan?"

Walter lifted his head, fierce eyes boring through the screens of thousands of electronic devices as he growled a single word. "Aliens."

"Illegal immigrants?"

Walter gave Susan an incredulous look. "Aliens in UFOs." The phrase "stupid woman" hung in the air, implied and unsaid.

Susan blinked, her television smile turning brittle.

"What makes you say it was aliens?"

"I managed a Radio Shack back in the eighties. Andy bought a lot of special order components designed for the most powerful ham radios. One day I joked and asked him what planet he was trying to reach."

"And what did he say?"

Walter ducked his head conspiratorially. "He said, 'Not a planet, Walter. Alpha Centauri.' Disappeared a week after he told me that."

"That's an amazing story, Walter. How do you suppose he ended up buried on Mill Creek?"

"Simple to beam his body underground from their ship. How do you think he wound up under a fully grown tree?"

"Why do you suppose they wanted to kill him?"

"Isn't it obvious? He intercepted transmissions about their invasion plans. They had to kill him."

"But it's been thirty years. There has been no invasion."

"Do you know how long it takes to assemble a fleet of a million alien warcraft and transport it 1.3 parsecs? Longer than thirty years. But you can bet they're coming."

"Walter, if Earth is in danger, why didn't you come forward back then?"

"You know how it is. People would have thought I was crazy."

Lia tapped the screen, pausing the video with Susan's mouth mid-gape. She took a sip of chai, thinking it might be fun to leave Susan like that for a while, or even forever.

Across the kitchen table, Peter fed the end of his Pop-Tart to Viola.

"Walter come to you with his theory?" Lia asked.

"Sorry to say he hasn't."

Lia eyed Peter's bland face. "No, you're not. Suppose he ever met Andrew Heenan?"

"No mention of a ham radio at Heenan's house back then. The aliens must have beamed it up with him."

"Will you follow up?"

"With him or with Susan? They pulled Heenan's credit card records during the original investigation. He made purchases from a mail-order magic emporium. Nothing from Radio Shack. Unless Heenan used his magic wand to call up Alpha Centauri, there's nothing to it." Peter stood and carried his plate to the sink.

"What if it's something else?"

"Like what?"

"A disinformation campaign. A distraction."

"Then investigating Walter would play into their evil plans." He rubbed Lia's shoulders. "Relax. Walter is a bored senior citizen seeking internet fame. There's nothing more to it than that."

PETER'S EYES SKIMMED PAST A FORWARD-FACING, SMIRKING Elvis as he made his way to his desk, landing on Brent's monitor. Dots peppered a map of Northside. An overlay of colored shapes divided the area, with a key associating each color with a list of dates. He moved behind Brent to review the diagram.

"What've you got?"

"Surveilling Jamal's crib didn't work. He dumps his stolen booty and heads out for the evening instead of coming home with it. So now I'm being smart."

"And the map?"

"Each dot represents a package theft, culled from police reports and rants on the NextDoor bulletin board. I have overlays of Amazon and UPS delivery routes along with typical time frames, but that made the whole thing too busy. Most porch pirates follow the trucks. Per Stacy, Jamal's band of barely pubescent thieves lay in wait at different points along the route on different days. I'm looking for a pattern so I can predict his moves."

A strategy Peter hadn't considered. "You intend to pick him up after a handoff?"

"One Amazon shipment does not a felony make. We need quantity. I want his stash house ." Brent kept his face in his monitor. "Your ex called last night. She said she was in a quandary. I agreed to meet her for a drink."

Peter flicked Elvis' bony chin, making the skull jitter. Now battery-less, Elvis remained blessedly silent and unable to comment.

"Do I want to know what Susan has on her mind?"

Brent swiveled his chair to face Peter. "As an old friend concerned only with your happiness, she was distressed to discover your woman murdered a friend and was never arrested. I told her it was a shame how the media twisted events to suit their purposes and she apparently didn't get the memo that Lia was defending herself against a serial killer. She got a little gleam in her eye and said, 'I can't *imagine* what kind of woman gets mixed up in such things.' That's verbatim."

Peter heard it in his head, that troubled tone of concern used by Southern ladies as they moved in for the kill. "Did you have to dump gasoline on my fire?"

"Pre-emptive damage control, brother. I was anxious on her behalf, that others would misconstrue her good intentions if she followed her current line of inquiry. I understood it might not bother her if our brothers in blue refused to talk to her after she made a spectacle out of a nice woman you cared about, but it would be a godawful shame if Lia's big-deal, socialite clients took a dislike to her just when she was trying to get her show off the ground. I shook my head and said it wasn't fair, but rubbing certain people the wrong way could be a career killer in a town like Cincinnati."

"I bet she loved that."

"She went all huffy about the public's right to know. I said, 'Find out what war you're in before you pick your battles. Check out the article about Renée Solomon on the *Cincinnati Magazine* website. While you look at the pretty photos of Renée's home, ask yourself who created her garden sculpture and painted the gorgeous collie hanging over the fireplace.' Then I left."

"You're a rare friend."

"You telling Lia?"

"Only if I have to. She doesn't need this after yesterday's break-in." His desk phone rang. He grabbed the receiver, his voice sharper than he meant it to be. "Dourson."

The voice on the phone was tentative. "Detective

Dourson? My name is Jenny Olson. I knew Andrew Heenan."

Peter leaned back in his chair. It couldn't be this easy, but it was best to treat everyone as if you believed them.

"You're a hard lady to find."

Silence. Then, "You were looking for me?"

"A woman whose grandparents lived next door to Andrew gave us your name. She thought you might be able to help us."

"Oh."

"She remembers you fondly."

"Donna was a cute kid. I don't know how much help I'll be."

The woman knew about Merrill, a good sign. "Probably more than you think. But you called me. What can I do for you?"

"Can we meet?"

Peter looked at his watch. 9:20 a.m. "Where are you calling from, Ms. Olson?"

She paused before answering, "I'm in town."

Something was off with Jenny's sudden appearance, and under her even tone, that fraction of a second hesitation said she was skittish.

"Do you know where District Five is? We've moved since you lived here."

Another hesitation. "I don't want to put you out, but can you come to my hotel?"

JENNY OLSON ANSWERED PETER'S KNOCK AT QUALITY INN room 321 dressed in functional navy slacks and a white oxford shirt, her blonde hair pulled back in a simple ponytail. She had a healthy, medium build and was slightly shorter than average.

Peter saw both strength and compassion in a broad face that leaned toward heart-shaped and had few lines for a woman nearing fifty. Jenny Olson appeared to be an attractive, practical woman, free of vanity.

"Detective Dourson? Thank you for coming." She nodded at a long couch, the only seating in a bare-bones room designed for business travelers. "Can I get you something from the honor bar?"

"A glass of tap water would be fine." Peter seated himself as she disappeared into the bathroom, raising his voice so she could hear him. "You've been gone a long time. What brought you back?"

Jenny emerged with two glasses of water, handing one to him as she sat at the other end of the couch. "I'm a home hospice nurse. One of my patients reads the *National Enquirer.*"

"I'm sure that was a shock. Before we get started, can I see some ID?" He didn't need it. He could see the girl she'd been in the shape of her features, but it never hurt to cross your t's.

Jenny reached for her purse. "I guess you have no way to know who I am, do you?" She rooted in her purse, producing an Arizona driver license for Jennifer C. Olson, residing in Phoenix.

"You're a long way from home."

"Andrew meant a lot to us."

"Us?"

"My gran and me."

"You never talked to the police."

Jenny stared into her glass, her thumb scraping the rim. "I didn't know anything that would help."

Peter raised an eyebrow. "And?"

"I was ten when my parents died in a car crash. It was just me and gran and she was dying of Lou Gehrig's disease. It upset her enough that Andrew was missing. I couldn't bring the stress of an investigation into the house. I asked Peggy to make the report and keep me out of it."

"You're here now."

Jenny turned her head to look out the window. There was nothing to see but a blank, blue square of sky.

"You get older, you feel a responsibility to close the gaps if you can. Andrew was good to me. I've always felt like I ran out on him, even if I didn't have a choice."

The woman needed to tell her story, a sign she felt guilty about something. He could help by easing her into it.

"How did you meet Mr. Heenan?"

"You can call him Andrew. That's how I remember him."

"You liked him."

"I did. Gran's medical bills were enormous. The money I made working for him allowed me to finish high school. He was always sending stuff home with me. He'd have me buy pounds of peaches when I did his shopping. Then he'd say he couldn't eat them all and send most of them home with me. Gran loved peaches."

"How did you come to work for him?"

"He performed at our church festivals. Someone told Gran he needed help. By then Gran was sick. We knew we would be struggling, so I called him. I was young and had no experience, but I guess he liked me."

"Your gran didn't worry about you spending so much time with him?"

Jenny turned wide eyes on Peter. "He was sixty-eight. Should she have?"

Her astonished expression suggested the thought had never occurred to her.

"What did you do for Andrew?"

"Housekeeping, laundry, shopping. I stopped by after school three times a week. He didn't need me that often. I think he enjoyed the company."

"Tell me about him."

Jenny smiled at some memory. "He wanted things a certain way, but he was nice about it. He was kind. I don't think many people understood that about him."

"Were you aware of any friends or associates?"

"As the English say, he kept himself to himself. He liked to attend events at the museum and the library, but he went alone."

"He ever perform magic for you, outside of church?"

"Sure. He tried to teach me card tricks, but everything I did turned into fifty-two card pick up. He had a coin he was always pulling out of the air. Did you find it?"

"A coin? What kind of coin?"

"Irish, with a harp on the face." Jenny's face softened. "He made puzzle boxes. I still have the one he gave me."

Time to move into delicate territory.

"The original investigation concluded Andrew met with foul play after he left Cincinnati. Now we believe he never made it to the airport. What do you remember about that time? Anything unusual about the trip, or the way he was acting?"

"Nothing at all. I saw that story on the Channel 7 website. They said Andrew was hiding mob money. That's impossible. Andrew was a nice man who never hurt a fly."

Peter wasn't so sure. "Andrew was wearing his magician costume when he died. Would he be likely to go somewhere in his costume after a performance?"

"He didn't go out in costume. He said it diluted the effect when he was performing. Something about keeping his different selves separate. He would have come straight home from that party."

Kidnapped on the way home, or killed soon after he arrived. "You watch the house while he traveled?"

"I brought in the paper and the mail. He never discontinued the paper when he left town. I told him he could pay for another vacation every year if he'd cancel the paper while he was gone, but he'd just smile and tell me not to worry about it."

"Notice anything out of place while he was away? Say, when you brought in the mail?"

Jenny's brow crinkled. "We didn't know anything was wrong, so I wasn't paying attention. It could have been nothing."

"What could have been nothing?"

"Just an odd feeling, maybe the stack of mail didn't look right, or a chair was an inch further from the table than the day before, like that."

"Only in the kitchen?"

"I can't say. I could have imagined it."

"When did you realize Andrew was missing?"

"I stopped by the day after he was due back—there was always laundry from his trips. There was no sign he'd returned. I waited a week. When he didn't call, I asked Peggy to file the missing person report."

"What did you think when he didn't return?"

"I thought what everyone did, that something happened overseas. When they found his car at the airport, we knew that's what happened."

"You left Cincinnati not long after that. Isn't it unusual to disrupt medical care for someone as ill as your grandmother?"

"Gran worried about money, and she was determined to give me an education. When Andrew disappeared, we lost that income and she worried even more. We moved to Texas because instate tuition to the University of Texas was dirt cheap compared to other schools back then. She figured if we were lucky, she'd leave behind enough so I could manage an education if I got a part-time job and saved my pennies."

"And did you?"

"After she died. I refused to start school while she needed me."

"And you studied nursing."

She traced the rim of her glass with a finger. "Being so helpless while I watched Gran die had a big impact on me."

"It must not have been easy for you to come here on short notice."

She blinked, hard, then cleared her throat. "All these stories, people making fun of him, and there was no one here who cared about him."

Peter leaned forward, elbows on knees, hands clasped. He held her eyes. "You came here to tell me something. So far nothing you've said is worth a cross-country trip."

Jenny stood and turned to the window, taking a drink as she stared down at the traffic on I-75. "Not much of a view. I had a choice of the highway or the cemetery. This part of Cincinnati, everywhere you go you trip over a cemetery. Andrew didn't have any family. It would mean a lot to me if I could see to his remains."

Peter gentled his voice and hoped the rapport they'd built would be enough. "That shouldn't be a problem. I'll give you the number for the coroner's office so you can get the ball rolling. But that's not the only reason you came back."

Peter watched Jenny's back and waited.

"This may not be anything, you understand."

"Okay."

"Andrew wasn't hiding a million dollars."

"I suspect you're right."

She turned, searching his face. "As soon as the media got hold of the story of a one-legged magician, that crime expert thought Andrew was a mob magician. What if someone heard about his leg back then and thought the same thing?"

"Wasn't his leg common knowledge? It was in the missing person report."

Jenny shook her head. "I don't believe anyone knew. I

told Peggy for the report. I thought it might be important."

"It was. That's how we identified him. How did you know about his leg?"

She leaned against the sill. Her finger returned to the rim of her glass. "It was his socks."

Not what he expected. "Socks?"

"He always limped a little. He was getting old so I thought nothing of it. But I did his laundry and you know how socks get, they smell a bit and they're limp. He'd have pairs of dirty socks and one wouldn't have any smell to it. One afternoon he was napping on the sofa and I touched his leg, through his slacks. It was hard and cold, no give to it like skin would have."

"When did you figure this out?"

Jenny's eyes went to the ceiling as she pursed her lips. "It wasn't snowing anymore. It had to be after February. Not by much, because he disappeared in May."

"Did you talk to him about it?"

"No. He'd kept it private. I didn't want to upset him."

"Who did you tell?"

Jenny blushed. "Some friends at school. I had no business doing that and I felt terrible about it later. What if one of my friends said something to someone who'd heard the old stories, and I'm the reason they killed him?"

"That's a long shot, but we'll check it out. Who were they?"

"They were my drama club friends."

"You did drama club on top of school, a job, and a sick grandmother? That's quite a load."

Jenny must have seen something in Peter's face,

because she rushed to explain. "Gran insisted. She said it made her feel better to know I was involved in something fun, and she liked seeing the plays. I've been racking my brains, but I can't remember any names."

"Your drama club have a photo in the yearbook?"

"I'm sure it did."

"Maybe we can find your friends."

A BOVINE ENCOUNTER

SATURDAY, MARCH 9, 1940

THE WEDGE OF MAL'S HEADLIGHTS CUT THROUGH THE black void, leading him on while concealing everything outside its reach. In a way it was like stage lights. You couldn't see beyond them either, unless you put your mind to it.

It used to make him nervous. But he'd learned every inch of road, every farm, and he found the dark and quiet relaxing after the adrenaline rush of performing.

Tonight he carried emeralds and gold coins in the compartment under his chassis, accessible through the floorboard if you knew it was there and how to open it.

Good luck finding it if you didn't.

This booty would join the growing stash of jewelry and gold bits under his barn. Last night he'd added a strange little statue of an angel pulling a Roman chariot. Only instead of an ancient soldier, the chariot held an egg.

The thing reminded him of dust collectors littering his

grandmother's house. But diamonds and sapphires smothered the little chariot, and Pete said it once belonged to Russian royalty. Mal supposed if you were that rich, you didn't need taste.

It had been an excellent night, both shows flawless. He'd sent Rose a wink when he caught her gaping at him with the puppy dog eyes that irritated Esme so much. Her mouth made an "O" when he removed the scarf draped over a bottle of champagne to reveal an army boot. He wondered how it would feel to press his mouth against those astonished lips.

Rose was just a kid, easily impressed. Pete's crowd saw shows in Manhattan and Paris. They were always looking for new thrills, and he needed new tricks.

Houdini did his escapes. That wasn't Mal's bag, but maybe he could set Esme up for an escape and turn it into something else, say tie her up and handcuff her and lock her in a chest, then Esme shows up on the other side of the club, still tied up. He'd have her cuss him out for laughs. She'd like that.

He was still smiling when two trucks roared out of a stand of trees, blinding him with their lights as they blocked the road. Mal whipped his eyes up to his rear-view mirror. Two more cars cut onto the road behind him. No way through the woods on his right. With a mental apology to McMurtry and his cows, Mal whipped the steering wheel hard to the left and plowed through a split-rail fence.

Shouts from the trucks. He slowed before he hit a cow and killed his hearse. Cross the field or cut back to the pavement? They'd see him coming and their cars were faster than his. He might get out in front of them, but they had the horsepower to catch up. Now that all bets were off, they'd just run him into a ditch. The field, then.

His passing disturbed the sleeping cows, who obliged by milling in his wake, mooing distress as he worked his way through the herd. Two trucks drove through the hole he'd made in the fence, stopping when faced with the cows. If he was fast and agile, he'd make the road on the far side of the field while the herd stalled Dalitz's men.

Kill the lights? He'd be safer in the dark, unless he drove into a cow and wrecked the hearse. Or drove over a rock and punctured a tire. Lights on then, even if meant the goons knew exactly where he was.

Could he use that? Get a bit further ahead, leave the car with the lights on and take off on foot? It would be hell to find him in the dark, but he wouldn't have time to retrieve Pete's package. Too big a risk they'd catch up to him before he got the goods and got gone.

Unless he lucked on a dirt track, it was a mile over rough ground to the next road. Mal shoved away all thoughts of the men chasing him and the chaos in his wake, keeping his eyes on the narrow slice of light. It didn't matter who they were or how they knew what he was carrying. He'd worry about that after he lost them.

Ahead, silhouettes of McMurtry's barn, outbuildings, house. The road would be a few hundred feet beyond. His lights struck the hoped-for dirt track. He cut his lights, drove fifty feet, then made a hard right, chancing a glance in his mirror as he wheeled onto the track.

A truck emerged from the throng of cows, picking up speed. A shotgun blast. Someone standing in the truck bed, aiming over the top. Purely for show. He was too far ahead for them to hit him. That would change if they caught up. He gauged the distance to the house. A minute, ninety seconds. If luck held, he'd make it.

The mooing cows, the gun blast. Lights should be coming on in the farmhouse. Alarm prickling his senses, he goosed the accelerator, roared around the house.

A tractor loomed, blocking his path. He braked hard. A thump on the running board. A figure clung to the top of the passenger window, a revolver aimed at Mal's head.

In a more nimble car, Mal might have swerved to throw the goon off, dodged the tractor and escaped. But the man had his arm inside the window, and the Caddy's running board made a sturdy platform.

Mal dove for the passenger door and shoved it open, into the goon's gut.

MAL FOUND HIMSELF STRIPPED TO HIS SHORTS AND HOGTIED on the floor of McMurtry's barn. Goons swarmed his beloved hearse by the light of oil lamps. He ached where he'd been manhandled, but surrender saved him the broken ribs and worse resistance would have bought him. Goons loved pounding flesh and breaking bones. They needed little provocation.

Hot breath in his face, stinking of bad rye, the light too dim to see the goon's face. A voice, angry and hoarse.

"Where is it?"

"Where's what?"

"Whaddya take us for? Where did you hide it?"

Mal mustered indignation. "I don't know what you're talking about. Can't a fellow drive down the road without getting waylaid?"

A boot in the ribs, searing agony.

Mal forced words past the pain. "Moe Dalitz can't just rob trucks, he has to terrify staff? Some boss he'll make if he gets his hands on the BH."

Snorts all around. He'd said something funny. What? The sound of a knife, ripping into his leather seats.

"Hey, hey, stop that!"

Agony exploded in his head.

DAY 20

THURSDAY, MAY 9, 2019

Lia restrained Gypsy in the Moby wrap while Peter knelt to unhook Chewy and Viola inside the dog park corral. The dogs shot through the gate, Chewy on his daily perimeter patrol, Viola to their usual table for pets.

Peter grumbled. "I hate doing this."

"It will be fine."

"Famous last words."

"You have a better option?"

Peter sighed. "No."

"Then buck up, buttercup."

He placed a hand on the small of Lia's back, escorting her into the park. "Thank you for your support."

Bailey and José waved from the table. Viola simpered at Steve and Terry, wagging her tail as she begged for treats. Lia extracted Gypsy from her papoose, placing her next to Kita's reclining bulk on the table. Gypsy's head swiveled, overwhelmed by reaching hands. She curled into Kita's side. Kita grunted.

"Hail," Terry said. "What brings our esteemed detective here on a weekday?"

Peter sat by Terry, clasping his hands in a position that was almost prayerful. "I could use a favor. A friend of Andrew Heenan's is in town. She wants to see the tree. Can you take her?"

Terry scratched his beard. "Is she attractive?"

Bailey grabbed Terry's camo cap, smacking his head with it.

Terry winced. "Ah, anything to help a damsel in distress. We can go tomorrow if she wants."

Peter gave Terry a direct look. "She doesn't want attention. I'm trusting you not to tell anyone. "

"Moi? Discretion is my middle name."

"That means no poking her for information," Steve said.

Terry muttered to himself, the words "no respect" audible to everyone at the table.

Lia sat, coaxing, "She's taking charge of his remains. You'll have the entire trip to make your case for Smaug. Just be sensitive. Don't make Peter regret asking you."

Terry's face turned mulish. "I am the soul of subtlety."

"Subtle like a freight train," Bailey cracked.

"José," Lia said, "remember the day you helped us with Ruth's things?"

"You kidding? I still have nightmares."

"Sorry about that. Alma said Ruth had a complete set of yearbooks. Did anyone get to them before you?"

José tapped a finger in front of Gypsy's muzzle, trying

to get her attention. "Too much going on. Bigfoot coulda made love to a unicorn and I woulda missed it."

Terry perked up. "Are the yearbooks for your mystery lady?"

Peter opened his mouth to speak. Every phone at the table chimed. Bailey checked hers first.

"Susan posted a video. I wonder who the lucky kook is today."

Lia patted Peter's leg. "We might as well get it over with."

Susan's Snippets with :X
84 Views
Thumbs up: 29
Thumbs down: 43

Jim leaned over Lia's shoulder, rubbing his beard as he squinted at Bailey's phone. "Who's colon X?"

"That's emoticon for 'keeping my mouth shut,'" Steve said. "It's a surprise guest."

Susan's face filled the tiny screen, her surroundings blocked by the floppy brim of an oversized hat. Wide-eyed, she tilted her face coyly and raised a finger to her lips.

"Shhh. I'm sitting in the lobby of Quality Inn on Mitchell Avenue."

The screen cut to an exterior view of the hotel.

"Detective Peter Dourson, lead investigator in the

1987 death of magician Andrew Heenan, passed through these doors an hour ago."

The growl was not a dog. It was Peter. "I'll kill her."

"Hush," Bailey said. "We're watching."

Lia squeezed his hand.

Susan returned. "What possible reason could Detective Dourson have for spending so much time at a hotel in the middle of his investigation? Stick around and find out."

Susan's face faded away, replaced by Peter crossing the lobby with a small woman in dark slacks.

"Who is this attractive mystery woman? Why is Detective Dourson closeted with her in a hotel room on city time?"

––––––––––

Peter shoved off the picnic table and stalked away, Viola trailing behind him. No way around it. He had to call Susan. He said a small prayer of thanks that he'd kept her card in his wallet, then took a minute to block his number before he punched in hers.

Susan's voice was chipper. "Susan Sweeney."

"You've gone too far."

"Goodness, Peter, can't you even say hello? Where *are* your manners?"

"I have plenty of manners. You know this because I have not reached through the phone to throttle you."

"My, my, is that a threat?"

Peter took a deep breath.

"You need to take that video down. Now."

"Which video? I have many."

"Don't play games, Susan. I don't care about your kooks and their goofy stories, but this one has to go."

"Don't want your girlfriend to see what you're up to when you're supposed to be fighting crime? Really, Peter, that woman has to be your mother's age."

"That was police business and not for public consumption."

"Says you. I know my rights. You were in a public place. I wonder what Lia will think when she sees it."

"Lia has seen it, and she doesn't think what you want her to think. If that video isn't down in the next ten minutes, I will arrest you for interfering with official business. That's ninety days. In jail."

"You're determined to lock me up. I wonder why."

"Clock's ticking." Peter jabbed the tiny red handset and stuffed his phone back in his pocket, desperate for a sheetrock wall to ram his fist through.

As he stared into the surrounding woods, a hand touched his sleeve. Lia.

"Will you be okay?"

"Ask me after I tell Parker. Do me a favor. Refresh that video and see if it's still online."

"You don't want to do it?"

"I don't trust myself not to break the phone if she hasn't pulled it."

Fifty yards ahead of him, Lia opened the corral gate for Chewy. She shot Peter a worried look, adjusting

Gypsy in the Moby wrap as she waited for him to catch up.

Phone to his ear, he snapped his fingers at Viola—currently sniffing who knew what—and lengthened his stride. Back at the table, José laughed. Terry's supply of cougar jokes must be holding out.

Parker sighed audibly through Peter's phone. "Just for the record, how did your ex-fiancée catch you on camera with Ms. Olson?"

"She wanted lunch. We left the hotel at the same time."

"We don't need an investigation into cops dating on the job."

"It wasn't a date."

"Won't matter. Tell me the worst. At least tell me she didn't look like a hooker."

"Jenny Olson dresses like a nun. The video came down inside fifteen minutes. There were two hundred and twenty-three hits the last time I refreshed my screen."

"Could be worse. Ignoring your ex isn't working. What can we do about her?"

"Can't arrest her. She hasn't broken any laws."

"Yet. Is she a reasonable woman?"

"Not often, sir."

"I'll have a chat with her about boundaries. Then she does what she does. If an actual reporter calls, you were on official business and cannot comment on the nature of that business."

"It's nothing but the truth, sir."

"That's an advantage. I can't imagine there's any risk to Ms. Olson as a result of this exposure, but encourage her to change hotels."

"Immediately, sir."

"How did your interview go yesterday?"

"Ms. Olson was forthcoming and provided an avenue for investigation, but right now, I'm stuck."

"What's the problem?"

"We need to identify students in her drama club, but pages are missing from the relevant yearbook."

"Are there no other copies?"

He and Lia had spent Wednesday evening unboxing Ruth's junk in a hot, sweaty attic because Alma said Ruth had a full set. Two dozen yearbooks. None of them from 1987.

"No, sir. We tried Classmates.com, but the most recent volume they have is 1979."

"Eight years too early."

"Yes, sir."

EARTH AND IRON

SUNDAY, MARCH 10, 1940

MAL'S NEARLY NAKED BODY SHIVERED IN THE COLD, WAKING him. He kept his eyes closed as he assessed his condition: packed earth beneath his cheek, an ache in his skull, arms wrenched behind and tied so tightly he had no sensation in his hands. Mouth parched. A weight on his ankle. Everything he could feel hurt.

Silence told him he was alone, but he didn't dare trust it.

Mal kept his breathing even, cracking his eyes a nearly invisible slit to find unrelenting black. He gusted a loud, frustrated sigh, wishing he could roll onto his back. Tried to lick his lips but couldn't work up enough saliva. Something clanked. That weight on his ankle. Iron. A shackle.

He was somewhere light didn't reach, a cave or a basement. They hadn't bothered to gag him. Wherever he was, no one could hear him scream, at least no one who would help him.

He sent his mind back to the last thing he remembered. Pain, in his head. Before that, snorts and chuckles. He'd said something—what had he said? About their boss, Moe Dalitz, and they'd laughed. Their boss wasn't Dalitz. Who, then?

Someone else had been watching. Not Dalitz's cronies —there wasn't a goon whose life would be worth a plugged nickel if they pulled this stunt behind his back. Someone thought they would get away with it, someone who either bribed or intimidated McMurtry to keep silent, because the farm was part of the setup.

Why involve McMurtry? Smarter to ambush him at the barn after he unloaded. Except Mal was careful, never driving to the barn if there was a car behind him. Easy enough to see headlights in the wee hours and too dangerous to risk driving with the lights off on the rolling, twisty Kentucky back roads.

He remembered the sound of a knife ripping into his upholstery. *Good luck with that.*

As thoughts chased around his injured head, two facts emerged. This was someone close enough to Pete to know about the skim, and they hadn't found his barn. He'd make sure the bastards never did.

DAY 21

FRIDAY, MAY 10, 2019

As a bleary-eyed Lia poured the morning kibble, a rap at the kitchen door set Gypsy barking. Alma stood on the porch, silhouetted by the barely risen sun as she held up her phone.

At the table, Peter said, "The swamp monster won't be much of a watchdog if she waits for people to knock before she barks."

"Hush." Lia waved Alma in. "I'm making eggs. Are you hungry?"

Alma took the seat opposite Peter. "I ate hours ago. But I thought you should see this."

Gypsy sniffed at Alma's ankles, then ran back to her dish before Chewy could start in on it.

Lia paused long enough to ensure canine mayhem did not erupt, then sat. "What is it?"

Alma tapped her phone and set it in the middle of the table. "Susan's kook of the day."

Dixie Langford's ancient cat's eye glasses and fuchsia lipstick dominated the screen, clashing with a carrot-colored beehive that had to be a bad wig. Or roadkill. A patchwork jacket in screaming primary colors made faux-Trelawney's scarves look tastefully subdued. Susan appeared unconcerned that her guest's multiple assaults against fashion might crack the camera lens.

"Mrs. Mitchell, what did you think when you read about the discovery of Andrew Heenan's bones last week?"

"Aaron, dear. There's no such person as Andrew Heenan."

"Excuse me?"

"His name was Aaron, not Andrew. That's what his intimate friends called him. To the world he was Elvis, but he asked the people he loved to call him Aaron."

Susan blinked.

Dixie continued, "I always knew that toilet story was a coverup. Disgraceful, too. Hateful, spreading that around. Of course they had to make something up with his body missing all these years, but they should have been more dignified about it."

She sniffed, wiping her eyes with a lace handkerchief. Susan patted her arm and made soothing noises.

Alma snorted, turning her phone face down. "If Miss Dixie was on speaking terms with Elvis, I have Buddy Holly in my closet."

"You know her?" Lia asked.

"You know her, too. She lives at Twin Towers. She was there when you painted your murals. Her name is Margaret, and that's not her hair."

Lia thought back. "Saffron jogging suit? She didn't seem dotty."

"Sharp as a tack, unless she had a stroke since last month—which she maybe did, considering the train wreck she's wearing."

"Could she have known Andrew Heenan?" Peter asked.

"Your guess is good as mine."

"How do you think she hooked up with Susan? Do senior citizens watch YouTube?"

Alma sat back and folded her arms, giving Peter a steady look.

"Point taken," Peter said. "So Dixie's a fraud. Poor Susan."

Lia gaped. "She exposed Jenny yesterday, and now you feel sorry for her?"

"This will blow up in her face, but warning her would be pointless. She has 9,000 hits. That's all she cares about."

AT THE END OF A LONG DAY, JENNY AND TERRY PADDLED TO the foot of a dam soaring a hundred feet over her head.

The volume of water it was designed to restrain boggled the mind of someone who'd spent the last twenty years in the desert. The need for this giant gate unsettled her. It spoke of lurking menace, danger she expected very few locals ever thought about or were even aware of.

Steve waved to them from the landing, a patch of dirt at the bottom of a long, steep bank. Thank God for him; the canoe was heavy and she dreaded hauling herself up the rutted path. As soon as he'd helped her out of the canoe, he and Terry resumed the good-natured bickering that she suspected was their default form of communication.

When they'd launched the canoe, it had amused her. Now she craved silence and the privacy of her room. She'd promised Detective Dourson to change hotels, but hadn't had time earlier and was too tired to think about it now. One more day wouldn't hurt.

Fifteen, twenty minutes in the truck and they'd be back at the launch site. It would be another ten minutes to the hotel, plus five minutes to pick up dinner at Popeye's. Half an hour, forty-five minutes before she could crash.

She made these calculations, considering the state of her bladder as she examined the cluster of neglected porta potties at the top of the bank. Terry said they were for the workers who periodically dredged silt from the base of the dam.

She could handle another forty-five minutes.

It had been a peaceful afternoon on the water. She hadn't minded getting out to help Terry drag the canoe over shallow spots, though her sneakers were now a sopping mess.

When they reached the cottonwood, Terry lodged the canoe in the rocks and helped her onto the bank, waiting in the boat. When she returned, he said nothing about her tear-streaked face and continued to say nothing until she broke the silence.

She hadn't expected delicacy from him.

The death of a man she'd known slightly more than a year should not have affected her so much. But with her grandmother's failing health, Andrew had provided stability and normality. Everything changed after he went missing, leaving her friendless in an unfamiliar city while gran died.

It was comforting to think of the poisoned creek healing around Andrew while he lay buried on its banks. She would have wished for him to remain undiscovered in the peaceful spot, if not for the unanswered questions. The questions had always been there, but coping with gran pushed them into the background, where they'd stayed for thirty years.

Terry said the city would remove the cottonwood at some point. The earth would settle, the wounded ground would teem with life again, and all trace of Andrew would disappear. The thought upset her.

Now she sat between Terry and Steve as Terry pulled his truck next to Jenny's rented Kia in the city garage parking lot. She stared at the deserted lot. *Nothing is so desolate as an industrial area after hours.*

Her bladder gave her a nudge. *Damn gran's genes.* She needed a bathroom. Urgently. Still, manners were required. She turned to Terry.

"Thank you for making this possible. I suppose I'm

morbid for wanting to see where Andrew was buried all these years."

"You're the only person with a legitimate reason for wanting to see it."

"You gave me the privacy I needed, especially after that awful woman posted that video." Jenny scanned the tree-lined creek bank. No porta potties here. "The curse of a middle-aged bladder. Is there a public restroom near here?"

Steve's tone was apologetic. "Nothing between here and the highway. You might as well drive back to your hotel."

The increasingly insistent pressure on her bladder told Jenny that wasn't an option.

Terry nodded at the blocky building. "They rarely lock the glass door. The ladies' locker room is halfway down."

"Will they mind? I don't want to trespass."

"It's not officially sanctioned, but they know. I can show you where it is."

If she couldn't get in, Jenny didn't want two men standing around while she squatted in the bushes. "I've caused you enough bother. I'm sure I can find it."

Terry looked pointedly at the empty lot. "We'll wait until you get back."

"Please don't. I'll be fine. If the car doesn't start, I'll call."

Jenny waved as they drove off, then approached the entrance, minuscule next to the giant overhead doors. A tiny lobby opened onto an interior sidewalk running the length of the football field-sized garage, fronting offices and utility rooms.

The interior smelled overpoweringly of grease and gasoline, generated by rows of garbage trucks filling the building. Sunlight slanted through high windows, illuminating rivers of dust motes in the gloom. The space hummed with a low, mechanical noise she couldn't identify.

If parking garages were cause for caution, this was a nightmare. The enormous trucks could conceal a battalion of rapists.

Something clattered.

"Hello? Is anyone here?"

Startled birds flew out of the high eaves as her voice echoed off the walls. Somewhere, water dripped. In the corner of her eye, something darted in the shadows. Cat? Raccoon? Rat?

Too small to worry about.

She called again, louder. "Hello?"

The big bellied trucks sat, silent and ominous, crushing mechanisms stilled, their capacious maws shut.

She crouched, looking under the vehicles for signs of movement, or maybe a pair of legs.

Nothing.

Just her imagination. She walked swiftly, wishing she'd opted for the bushes as she peered in office windows and scanned between vehicles.

Like many public restrooms, the entrance to the ladies' locker room was a doorless opening. A free-standing wall shielded the room from view, forcing visitors to detour around.

Rows of lockers filled the room, with long benches down the middle of each aisle. Jenny poked her head between the rows as she passed. No one there, though she spotted evidence of human presence: a stuffed bunny atop a locker, a T-shirt draped over a bench, a forgotten jacket tossed on a broken chair.

At the far end of the room she found an opening hung with mismatched, flowered shower curtains. She pushed through to find a maze of curtains in an empty room lined with shower heads, a jury-rigged arrangement to create privacy in a space originally designed for none.

Claustrophobia choked her.

She backed out and found another open doorway. On the far side of a half-dozen sinks, the toilet stalls she'd been so desperately seeking lined the wall, the doors shut or barely ajar.

A noise to her left startled her. She froze, heart pounding, then slowly turned to find her own anxious eyes staring back at her from a mirror.

Has to be rats.

She passed down the long row of stalls, slapping doors open as she went. Empty. Empty. Empty. Feeling silly and with relief seconds away, she stepped into the last stall and locked the door.

VIOLA, CHEWY AND GYPSY SAT IN A ROW WHEN PETER opened the front door, Chewy no doubt serving as a buffer between the two girls. He bent to pet Viola. Gypsy wriggled her head under his hand, Susan's damp, mangled scarf dangling from her jaws.

"You have no clue how much joy you give your mom every time you chomp on that thing, do you?"

He straightened, lured by the murmur of voices in the kitchen. Lia sat at the table with Alma, huddled over Alma's tablet and a pair of steaming mugs. A row of squat electronic devices—had to be the new cameras—sat on the counter. They were nondescript, easy to ignore. If he had one of these in his office he could catch the jerk who kept messing with Elvis.

"Should Gypsy be sucking on that scarf? The dyes could be toxic."

Alma looked up, her face full of concern.

Lia kept her eyes on the tablet. "He's baiting me, Alma. Ignore him." She scooped Gypsy up, extricated the sodden mess from her jaws and dropped it on the floor, then snuggled the pup under her chin. "You can have your binky back in a minute, baby girl."

Peter heaved an exaggerated sigh, ducked his head into the fridge for a beer. "Upstaged by an incontinent ball of fur."

Lia said, "Do you know the difference between a puppy and a boyfriend?"

Peter twisted the top off his Pearly Gates IPA. "Besides the tail?"

Lia rubbed noses with Gypsy. "I'll still hug the puppy after she pees in my shoes."

Peter checked the pots warming on the stove. Lentils and greens were on the menu. "There go my plans for the evening."

Alma frowned. "I have to ask—"

Lia put her hand on Alma's. "Don't. We don't want to know what he meant by that."

Peter took a long pull on his beer. Pup wiggled from under Lia's chin and stared at him over her shoulder. The dog was laughing at him. He wandered over to the table.

"What have you got there?"

Lia grinned and tapped the screen. "Alma found the missing pages from the Hughes 1987 yearbook."

Peter toasted Alma with his bottle. "Including you in the circle of trust was a good move. How'd you manage that?"

Alma tilted her head modestly. "I posted a request on several bulletin boards. Someone scanned the pages and send them to me. And no, I didn't explain why I wanted them."

Peter dropped into the chair next to Lia so he could see the tablet. "God bless retirees and the time on their hands. So this is the drama club."

"What do you think?" Lia asked.

Peter pinched out a photo, the requisite group shot of a dozen kids lined up in two rows according to height. He dragged the screen to others, staged shots on production sets, adolescent faces looking twice their age in theatrical makeup, mugging with exaggerated expressions.

The drama teacher stuck with the classics: *The Music Man, Our Town, The Crucible*. In an egalitarian move, a photo showed stagehands painting a backdrop.

"Big hair, shoulder pads. Madonna and Johnny Depp wannabes. Looks about right to me."

Lia rubbed the bottom of her chin over Gypsy's head.

"Do any of them look like they hang out with murderous mobsters to you?"

Peter squinted his eyes and pointed at a skinny, freckled boy, "That guy is thinking about the joint in his pocket." His finger moved to a sad-looking, obese boy painting a backdrop, "And this one is praying he gets to feel a naked breast before he dies. The girl with the worried look is counting the days to her next period. Did you find Jenny?"

Lia returned to the group photo. "For some reason they didn't put names in the captions. I think that's her in the front row, third from the right."

A pretty girl with sad eyes. "She in any of the productions shots?"

"On the next page. Abigail Williams in *The Crucible*, who condemned John Proctor to death by hanging."

"Let's hope she was playing against type. I need to show these to her and see if it jogs her memory." He pulled out his phone and tapped Jenny's number. The phone went straight to voicemail. On another call, then. He left a message, hung up, checked the time. 7:20 p.m. "Have you talked to Terry?"

Lia set Gypsy on the floor. Gypsy pounced on the dead scarf, determined to make it deader.

"No, why?"

"Just wondering how the float trip went."

He helped Lia with the dinner dishes and they took the dogs—with the monster riding high in her papoose—for their evening walk.

"What will you do now?" Lia asked.

"Nothing until I have a chance to show the photos to Jenny." He checked the time. "Nine o'clock."

"I can't imagine why she hasn't called you back."

"She might not know I called, or she got distracted. I'm going to try her one more time."

Voicemail. Peter swiped the screen, ending the call.

A TROUBLING OFFER

SUNDAY, MARCH 10, 1940

ROSE STARED DOWN AT THE GLAZED HAM ON HER PLATE, wishing desperately to be elsewhere, especially if elsewhere had a bed or at least a sofa to nap on.

Uncle Stu was in one of his jolly moods, when the oddest thing might set him off. He'd gotten her the job at the Beverly Hills, paid for Mother's medical bills, and kept them in the tiny house. It would be unchristian not to invite him to Sunday dinner, even if she *had* worked until the wee hours and hardly slept before taking Mother to early mass.

But Sunday dinner meant hours cooking a fancy meal Mother would barely touch now that the cancer had stolen her appetite. It was little enough, Mother said, to thank her brother-in-law for all he did.

Rose toyed with her mashed potatoes while Stu tucked away enough ham to feed her and Mother for three days.

She recited a litany of God's blessings inside her head. It was the only way to fight resentment.

Stu forked up the last bite of apple pie on his plate, wiped his mouth with one of Mother's best linen napkins, and belched. "That was a fine meal, Rose, very fine."

She kept her eyes lowered. "Thank you."

"You don't mind if I borrow Rose, do you, Mary? I have a job for her, two dollars a day while it lasts, and she can still work her nights."

Rose's eyes shot up. Two dollars was a man's wage.

"She already works so hard, Stu. I don't want you wearing my girl out."

"Nothing she can't handle. I have a pair of men watching a property for me south of town. They need someone to cook for them and do a little cleaning. She can go with me when I drive out to check on them. I need her to fix a hot lunch and put on soup or stew for supper. It doesn't have to be fancy like this. It would put my mind to rest." He winked at Rose. "You can do that, can't you, Rose?"

Something about Stu's offer bothered her, but she couldn't say what, or why. She fought past the lump in her throat to swallow her potatoes.

"Certainly, Uncle Stu. When do you need me?"

"That's the spirit. We'll leave as soon as you clean up and put your mother back to bed."

ROSE STARED OUT THE WINDOW OF STU'S NEW PACKARD, watching cows and trees go by as she wondered why she felt so uneasy. This was Stu. He took care of them. Sure, he had a temper sometimes, but he never hurt her or Mother.

"... poor sucker survived the Depression, then lost the farm during the recession. I got two men there for the next few days, seeing what repairs it needs and how much it will cost me to get it going again."

Uncle Stu had never farmed a day in his life.

"We'll go after you tend to Mary in the mornings. You can see to the food while I talk to the men. You don't go back to work until Wednesday. If I still need you then, I'll bring you back in time to rest up for your shift."

Two dollars. It was too much.

"I need you to keep mum. If it got out I wanted this farm, someone might try to buy it out from under me, or they might start a bidding war. You wouldn't want that, would you?"

This was more about Stu's business than he'd ever said before.

"No, sir."

"You're a good girl. These men, they're rough. They know not to bother you, but stay in the kitchen. Don't go wandering off. You should have everything you need. If you don't, you tell me."

Stu pulled onto a dirt drive leading to a farmhouse badly in need of a coat of paint, the yard full of cows. Stu said a neighbor put his stock there to graze, figuring what the bank didn't know wouldn't hurt them. That would change when he bought the place. Then he winked at her.

Rose navigated around loose boards on the porch to get to the door. She expected the house to be empty, with maybe a card table and a few chairs. Instead, it was fully furnished with two men sitting at a dining room table playing cards and listening to a radio.

Stu cheerfully introduced her. Joe, a big, messy man in overalls, ducked his head and said a shy hello. Larry was skinny with his head thrust forward. He gave her a what the girls at the club called a "lizard look," like he wanted to lick his lips. Before he ate her. She resolved to stay out of sight and within reach of an iron skillet.

The electric refrigerator and well-stocked larder were a surprise after the house's deficiencies. Still, she had to make do without the gadgets she was used to.

She took a quick inventory, calculating how to cook two meals with only one skillet and not enough pans. She started by cutting up beef for stew. While it seared in the frying pan, she peeled and sliced potatoes—what man didn't love fried potatoes with onions? Especially with ketchup?

She put the browned meat into a pot, set the potatoes to frying, then started cleaning and cutting vegetables for the stew. She'd fry up bratwurst with the potatoes, served with sauerkraut and the loaf of bakery bread she'd found in the cupboard. Once the skillet was free, she'd use it to bake cornbread to go with the stew.

By the time the men ate and she cleaned up, the cornbread would be done. The stew could simmer on a low flame until they were ready for it. A few more pans would be nice. Maybe she'd ask Stu if he was in a pleasant mood.

Maybe not.

With the scent of frying onions and bratwurst in the air, she continued her inventory of the kitchen. No serving dishes, she'd have to fill plates off the stove. She set out flour and cornmeal for cornbread and lit the oven. Sounds drifted up through the heat register: low conversation, clanking, banging. The men must be in the basement.

When they returned, the two men were quiet. Stu's face flushed and his eyes glittered with something Rose didn't want to know about. She dished out plates and turned to mixing cornbread while the three of them ate in the next room.

As she stirred the batter—not too much or it would turn into a corn brick instead of cornbread—a muffled sound came up through the register.

Something in the basement was moving.

DAY 22, MORNING

SATURDAY, MAY 11, 2019

9:37 A.M.

CHEWY SAT AND STARED AT LIA WHILE SHE SIPPED HER Bengal spice latte, doing his best to send a telepathic message along the lines of, "It's time to go, Mom!" She'd normally be at the park by now, but Peter slept in on Saturdays and he wanted to come with her today to get Terry's take on Jenny.

Gypsy tugged on the hem of her jeans. Lia bent, caught the little demon's eyes and said, "No!" She tucked her legs under her chair while Gypsy curled in a ball and pouted.

Lia resisted the urge to pick her up and cuddle her, because you couldn't reward destructive behavior. Some trainers used compressed air as a gentle deterrent. Maybe she'd dig up the can she used to clean her keyboard and give it a shot, since nothing else was working.

Peter's phone rang. Less than a minute later he shuffled in, phone clamped to an ear, eyes on the floor—no doubt searching for puppy puddles. He ended the call, dropping the phone on the table on his way to the fridge and his first Pepsi of the day.

Lia dangled Susan's scarf under the table, wiggled it until Gypsy pounced. Gypsy tugged, growling despite a mouth stuffed with silk. Neat trick. Girlfriend had the makings of a ventriloquist.

"If you stopped drinking cola, you wouldn't wake up with a caffeine hangover and you wouldn't need more caffeine to fix it."

Peter poked his head in the fridge. "It's a vicious cycle."

He shut the refrigerator door with his foot as he popped the tab and took a long swallow, which Lia suspected was made more satisfying by her disapproval.

"One more time and you're officially nagging. I thought the reason we weren't married was so we wouldn't get caught up in clichéd arguments over crap that doesn't matter."

"Your health and well-being matters."

"Next year there will be an article on the web saying Pepsi is the new superfood and you'll be all over it."

Lia opened her mouth, decided rebuttal was pointless, and shrugged. "As long as I don't have to nurse you when you give yourself cancer."

"Tell you what. I'll give up Pepsi and start smoking."

Lia rolled her eyes but didn't comment. He'd feel his age soon enough, and pain often made people sensible. "Who was on the phone?"

"Amanda. Looking for Jenny Olson."

"A bit early, isn't it?"

"They had an appointment an hour ago to expedite the paperwork for Heenan's remains. Jenny didn't show and hasn't answered her phone the five times Amanda called her. Concern for Jenny's welfare has now eclipsed Amanda's annoyance at being stood up after she agreed to come in on a Saturday."

"What do you think?"

"I think I need to skip the park and hunt her down."

FRIDAY, LATE AFTERNOON

All Jenny had wanted to do was grab a chicken combo at Popeye's, ditch her wet shoes, and fall into bed. Spooking herself in the garage and feeling like an idiot had made her ignore any warning bells when, on that back road by the city garage, a man honked at her and pulled alongside.

He'd pointed at her car, yelling that the rear tire was going flat. She pulled over to look without thinking about how deserted the road was.

The tire was dangerously low, almost running on the rim. She knelt to take a closer look. She did not know the man with the friendly face in the nice car had also pulled over until the steel of a gun muzzle pressed against her kidney.

Before she could form a coherent thought, he threw a blanket over her head, strapping the blanket in place with what she later learned were bungee cords. A hand groped her hips. She freaked, shrieking, twisting and kicking. The gun came back, a hard, bruising jab in her side.

"Shut the fuck up or I'll kill you."

She froze.

"Where's your fucking phone?"

Her throat froze along with the rest of her. She pushed hard to force air past her vocal cords.

"Car."

Blind and helpless, he dumped her in the trunk of his car and shut the lid.

She was Houdini, handcuffed in a locked trunk. Only there was no key up her non-existent sleeve. Andrew talked about such things. If there was any evidence that he had been a death-defying headliner magician, it was this: he said focus was everything in a crisis, shutting out the woe is me, all the whys, and keeping your eyes on the here and now.

Gimme Shelter blasted from the stereo, cranked so loud motorists would attribute any screaming to Mick Jagger, any thumping to an over-active bass.

The car pulled forward.

She felt around with her feet, wiggled her shoulders, seeking an interior latch. But she had no clue where it would be or if this car even had one.

She rolled around to face the rear of the car and thought she detected pale areas through her shroud. Tail-lights? Could she kick one out? Difficult with sneakers, even if she could get leverage.

She continued to feel around, for a tire iron, a screw driver, anything. The trunk was bare. No weapon, no way to alert other motorists to her kidnapping-in-progress.

The pounding rock made it impossible to think, but

she had to focus. What did he want? Scratch that. Where was he going?

The car had made several quick turns, then accelerated. I-74. East to I-75, or west to Indiana? When the car didn't slow to merge onto 75, she decided they were heading west, then wondered if knowing this would be of any help.

She'd seen his face. That didn't worry him. In the movies it was always because they planned to kill you. But why? What could he possibly want with her?

Gimme Shelter faded, replaced by *Brown Sugar*, then *I Can't Get No (Satisfaction)*. The car slowed and entered normal traffic. Still in Cincinnati, on the west side.

Too many turns later, the car stopped. She heard the rumbling of an automatic garage door under *Sympathy for the Devil*. There would be no opportunity for her to run or call for help.

The car pulled forward. The door rumbled shut and the stereo cut off. Jenny's ears rang in the silence. A car door opened. Footsteps on concrete. A key fob chirped and a horizontal slash of dim light appeared inches from her nose, bleeding through the cloth around her head.

"You can get out now. My gun is pointed right at you. Don't think you can do anything smart."

Jenny struggled, rolling from side to side, sending pins and needles up her arms and legs. She sat up in the trunk. Pain speared through her skull as she banged her head on the lid.

She breathed slowly till the pain subsided to a manageable level. "How do you expect me to climb out when I can't see? Why bother letting me out at all? If you kill me here, you can just drive me to the river and toss me in."

The voice was too reasonable. "I don't want to kill you. I only want to talk to you."

"So you kidnap me?"

"Wasn't sure you'd agree to talk to me and didn't want anyone to see us together. Didn't want you to have a chance to tell anyone about me."

Jenny shrugged inside her cocoon. She wished she could see him. Andrew said to watch their eyes, they always told you what people were thinking. "You must not do this often, or you'd know I can't get my balance when I'm wrapped up like a burrito."

"I'll put the gun down and help you out. Do anything funny and I'll break your face."

"What an offer. How can I resist?"

Rough hands dragged her out of the trunk, standing her on numb feet. Her knees buckled. She dropped to the floor.

"I said don't fuck with me!"

"I can't stand. Don't hit me!"

Silence, then, "We do this the hard way." He scooped her into a fireman's carry, out of the garage, down steps, finally dumping her on something spongy and sagging. A basement couch?

"I have to leave you for a while. I'm going to tie your legs so you can't leave, but you'll be more comfortable. Don't bother calling for help, no one can hear you. If I hear you screaming when I come back, I will break your face. I won't want to, but I will. Then I'll duct tape your mouth."

In a few breathless seconds, he released the bungee cords, removed the blanket, and zipped tied her hands behind her back. He shoved her back on the couch, pulled her feet up in the air, and zip tied her ankles together like the calf in a rodeo event.

They were in a basement lit by a single bulb. He picked up a coiled steel cable, the kind used with bike locks, and ran the cable between her legs, giving her thigh a friendly squeeze and laughing when she jolted.

The couch butted against a vertical pipe. He locked the cable around a ceiling pipe, hauling her legs upright so the only way to rest them was against the vertical stack. It was brilliant, really. With her legs raised, she was no longer a roped calf. She was a turtle on its back. A turtle with cold, wet feet.

He turned to leave, turned back, grabbed a cushion and stuffed it under her shoulders and head, taking the pressure off her wrists and hands.

"You'll be comfortable enough until I get back. Then we'll talk. It will be okay, you'll see."

She very much doubted that.

SATURDAY, 10:13 A.M.

Jenny Olson's rented Kia Soul was a boxy car with rounded edges. It looked like a child's toy, except for a designer blue exterior that deserved a name like "dirty sky" or "polluted lagoon." It sat as far as you could get from the door of Quality Inn, in a nearly empty lot.

Peter wondered why.

One more call to Jenny's phone. Peter ended the call before Jenny's recorded voice made it past "Hi! I'm—"

He stared through the car windows, willing the Soul to give up its secrets. The interior yielded nothing out of the ordinary except smears of dirt in the back. Jenny had stowed something there. Her shoes from the canoe trip? Analysis of the dirt might yield something, but it was premature to be thinking in those terms.

It was difficult to tell, but the rearview mirror appeared angled for someone several inches taller than Jenny, with the seat positioned for longer legs.

Suggestive, not conclusive.

He resisted the urge to tug the handle. Not only did he not have a warrant or even an investigation, anything he touched would be compromised.

So he observed and kept his hands in his pockets.

10:24 A.M.

A stocky, middle-aged man emerged from the back office in response to a call from the desk clerk. His brass tag read D. Hollis, and he met Peter with a practiced expression of polite inquiry.

"Detective Dourson? I'm the manager. May I see your identification?"

Peter flipped his badge case open on the counter.

Hollis nudged his bifocals up to examine it, then nodded. "How may I help you?"

"You have a guest, Jenny Olson. Is she still checked in?"

"Your interest?"

"She's assisting with a case. Her car is in the lot, but she's been out of touch since yesterday afternoon and we're concerned."

"I see."

Hollis looked at the computer, then punched three numbers on the phone.

Calling Jenny's room.

Hollis' brow crinkled. He hung up the phone and attacked the keyboard of the computer with rapid-fire strokes. "The last time she used her keycard was 7:43 p.m."

"Yesterday?"

"Thursday. Of course she wouldn't have used it when she left on Friday."

Hollis rattled more keys. "Yesterday her room was serviced at 1:17 p.m. Perhaps she entered while the maid was there?"

Terry last saw Jenny after five the previous day. "She was elsewhere. I don't believe she ever came back."

"But her car is here?"

"Can you pull the security feed on the parking lot? I'd like to see when it showed up and who brought it."

Hollis escorted Peter into his office and brought up the feed on his computer. "I'll leave you here to look through it. I imagine you'll want to see her room. I'll be out front when you're ready."

He cued the video to 7:00 a.m. He fast-forwarded until he spotted Jenny crossing the parking lot, then paused the feed. 9:21 a.m. Nothing about her body language suggested anything was wrong as she got in her car and drove off.

He skipped to 5:00 p.m., then continued scrubbing the video. At 8:41 p.m., the blue Soul made a right-hand turn into the lot, disappearing behind a van as it pulled into the first parking space.

8:41 p.m. Three hours after Terry said good-bye to Jenny. Twenty minutes, max, from Millvale if she'd stayed on surface streets instead of hopping on the highway.

Peter stared at the screen, waiting in vain for someone to emerge from behind the van. He backed up and played the tape again, hunting for signs of movement anywhere near the van and the Soul.

Nothing.

The car had been driving west. Coming from Millvale, it should have turned left into the hotel from the eastbound lane. Peter backed up the recording to ten minutes before the Kia's arrival. This time he trained his eyes on the narrow slice of eastbound lane visible at the top of the screen. He caught a flash of the distinctive blue and hit pause. 8:39 p.m. The car left the screen, reappearing in the westbound lane a hair over two minutes later.

Quality Inn was the biggest building on the strip. The designated turn lane was hard to miss. Two minutes wasn't enough time to stop at a gas station or drive-through.

The driver had not wanted to be caught on camera while waiting for a break in traffic to make the turn. Instead, he drove past and circled around, turning into the lot at the edge of the video frame. For the few seconds the car faced the camera, the sun visor was down, obscuring his man's face.

He'd spent the minimum time possible on the feed, invisible on the far side of the car. Parked at the edge of the lot, the driver could exit from the passenger side and duck around the wall surrounding the property without ever appearing on screen. The van was a bonus.

It was a neat trick. And if someone put that much energy into staying out of sight, Jenny was in trouble.

FRIDAY EVENING

Jenny's shoulders ached and the bones of her wrists dug into the small of her back. Her middle-aged hips grew stiffer by the minute. Something tiny crawled on her skin. Dust mites, or her imagination? At least her legs had the pipe to rest against, even if her feet were still wet.

She wished she'd asked him to take her shoes off, though the last thing she'd wanted was him touching her. And if she had a chance to escape, she needed shoes. Better wet feet. *Wet feet are nothing.*

Not being able to move made her desperate to do so, magnifying discomforts until they overwhelmed her ability to think. To gain perspective, she imagined patients confined for months to full body casts.

Worse than a body cast, she could have her skin covered with third-degree burns. The itch from the cheap upholstery against the back of her neck was nothing compared to that kind of unrelenting agony. She shifted her shoulders and turned her head from side to side, scratching as best she could.

Stress was the enemy, draining resources desperately needed during a crisis. She drew on strategies she'd taught to hundreds of patients and their families, starting with slow, deep breaths.

Next came a reality check. She could change nothing about her situation, but she could manage her emotions and stay rational. And as long as he—whoever he was—was gone, she was safe and could rest.

Composed and fearless, that's how she wanted to be when he returned. She crafted her desire into an affirmation, then closed her eyes and mentally recited her progressive relaxation sequence, contracting and releasing muscles from her head to her toes.

She had the hysterical thought that the sequence sometimes put her to sleep and wondered if that would be a good or bad thing. Still, thousands of repetitions over the years meant her muscles responded automatically, and focus on the process calmed her mind. The hamsters in her brain slowed on their wheels, then curled into furry balls for a nap.

She pictured a heart beating strong and slow, then connected it with her own heart, counting as it beat. When she achieved clarity, she recited the affirmation she'd designed:

I am calm and alert. When the time comes, I will know what to do to achieve freedom and safety.

She continued to repeat this message to her subconscious, focusing on the words as she breathed, shutting out the room, the pain, her fears.

She drifted off.

A DOOR CLOSED, WAKING JENNY. A THOUSAND PINS AND needles raced through her aching body as a cheery voice called.

"Honey, I'm home."

Her heart accelerated as heavy boots thumped down the wood steps, accompanied by the aroma of grilled onions and sugary-sweet cola.

He placed a white takeout bag and a giant soft drink cup on a storage bin before settling into an armchair.

"I thought you might be hungry. In a minute, I'll unlock your feet so you can sit up. Your hands stay tied until we reach an agreement. Hope you like White Castle."

She struggled to keep irony out of her voice. "That's thoughtful of you."

He tilted his head with a puzzled look.

While drifting off, she'd remembered a workshop about diffusing aggression by imposing a reality of your choosing on a situation, changing the context of your interaction with a potential attacker. The presenter used the example of drafting hoodlums to walk you home with the idea that by treating them as protectors, they would become protectors.

She suspected most hoodlums would grin and bash her over the head anyway, but if she was trusting her subconscious to provide her with the avenue to freedom she had to go with it. Clarice Starling made it work with Hannibal

Lector. She'd make it work for her. She would play along, let him feed her, let him talk.

Not that she had much choice.

He unlocked the cable to free her legs, then pushed her upright on the couch. With a gallant move, he held the giant cup where she could reach the straw with her mouth.

"We'll have to share. I hope you don't mind."

Now was not the time to tell him she'd given up fast food and especially sugar. Anyway, the chemical boost might come in handy. She drew greedily on the straw to satisfy a system desperate for fluids, but the cola bite and overpowering sweetness almost made her choke. She swallowed hard, then leaned away from the cup.

"Thank you."

He watched her intently as he drank, then set the cup beside the bag. "Zesty Zing sauce, ketchup, or barbecue on your fries?"

Zesty Zing was almost entirely fat, while ketchup and barbecue sauce were mostly high-fructose corn syrup. The fat would serve her better.

"Zesty Zing, please."

He drew napkins from the bag, spreading them on the bin as if he were laying out table linens, stacked a half-dozen sliders in their cardboard sleeves on the napkins, and brought out the fries.

"Slider or fries first?"

She forced a smile. "Slider."

"I got cheese doubles. Singles hardly qualify as anything more than grease and bread."

He held a sandwich for her with one hand while he ate

with the other. She took small bites, chewing slowly, doing her best to ignore the pain in her back and arms. She'd leave most of the fries for him. If she was lucky, the carbs would make him sluggish and give her an edge.

He continued to feed her with solicitous dabs of a napkin and careful attention to saucing her fries while keeping them short of drippy.

"I thought about getting chili cheese fries but they would have been too messy," he explained.

His friendliness—out of kilter with the zip ties and car trunk—disturbed her.

He's not rational. I have to remember that.

He offered her the last fry. She shook her head and it disappeared into his mouth. He chewed ruminatively, wiped his mouth, sipped the coke, then smiled. "Now we can talk."

Make a request, something small. Get him to say yes. Her first thought was her damp shoes, but again, she needed them if—no, when—her opportunity came.

"My arms are numb. Makes it hard to think. Can you do something about that?"

"Fair enough." He reached for his pocket. "I'll cut the ties and let you stretch for a minute. But then I have to tie your wrists again. This time I'll do it in front and lock your hands to your waist. Will that do?"

She paused, hoping for a better concession.

"It's that or I hold the gun on you. I can't imagine we'll have a productive conversation that way."

"No, you're right. We'll do it your way."

With the bike cable affixing her hands to her waist, she asked, "What do you want to talk about?"

"I want to start by apologizing for all the precautions. In a minute you'll understand."

Jenny doubted that but maintained the pleasant expression she saved for deranged family members of the dying.

He held his hand up, thumb and forefinger a fraction of an inch apart. "You and I are this close to millions."

What would he expect? Jenny decided a bit of skepticism was in order and raised one eyebrow.

"What are you talking about?"

"The story on Channel 7 about Marvelous Malachi and Pete Schmidt, did you see it? It's true."

"And you think that was Andrew?"

"He hid valuables that are now worth millions. You can help me find them."

"Andrew made balloon animals at kid parties. He was no David Copperfield."

"Smoke and mirrors. Misdirection. That's how he hid it in the first place."

Jenny raised her hands, palms out in appeasement, as high as the cable would allow. "Even if he was this mythical Malachi, that was eighty years ago. The money is long gone."

"Some of those pieces never appeared after Pete Schmidt bought them, and they were too famous for their whereabouts not to be known."

Now was time to show some curiosity.

"Like what?"

"Like a Fabergé egg that would rake in fifty million in today's market."

"How do you know all this?"

"Jeff Overstreet has been following this story for years. I got him drunk the other night." He winked. "I acted skeptical, so he kept spilling to convince me."

"What does all this have to do with me?"

"Overstreet told me about Heenan's housekeeper. I knew it had to be you when I saw the YouTube video." His eyes narrowed. "But you can stop pretending you don't know any of this. There's no other reason for you to come back."

Detective Dourson said two hundred people saw the video. Just her luck this lunatic was one of them.

"Why not just talk to me?"

"I had to get to you before Overstreet did. He killed your boss. He'll do it again."

"What makes you say that?"

"His aunt lived across the street from Heenan. I think he tried to get the old man to talk and screwed up. Maybe his heart gave out."

There was something off, beyond the weirdness of him kidnapping her. *Go carefully. Make him believe you buy his story, but don't make it too easy.*

"I don't remember him at all. How could he know Andrew was this Malachi when nobody else did?"

"Overstreet knew all the old-timers from the Syndicate days. Who's to say he didn't start talking to them when he was a kid? I bet they knew more than they ever told the police, and guys like that can't resist talking about their glory days."

He picked up the cup and shook it, making the ice rattle. "There's some left. Want the last drink?"

She shook her head.

"The house was never searched. The answer is there, and we need to get in before Overstreet can convince the Johnsons to give him access."

"My gran suffered for years before she died. If I'd known about an egg or anything else Andrew had hidden, I would have used it to help her."

"You know things you don't realize you know. We need to put the pieces together."

"How are we supposed to do that? Someone lives there now."

"The Johnsons couldn't handle the attention and left town. I can get us in and we'll have the place to ourselves."

"And then what? Sell the egg on eBay?"

His eye twitched again. He rubbed his upper lip, a tell Andrew associated with deception, something he told Jenny while teaching her the fine points of poker.

"Once we have the egg we can decide what to do with it. And because I'm feeling generous, we'll go fifty-fifty."

Once we have the egg, you'll decide where to dump my body.
"If I know so much, why do I need you?"

He grinned. "Besides to get out of my basement? We have a few days before the Johnsons return. I have the tools to get in and do whatever we need to do. I have Overstreet's research, and I know what we're looking for."

You probably used those tools to get into Overstreet's place and help yourself to his notes.

"So my only way out of this basement is to commit burglary."

"A very low risk project."

"And if we don't find anything?"

"I drop you off and we go our separate ways."

Yep. Not getting out of this alive unless I come up with a brilliant plan.

"It's late. I'll let you think about this overnight, but I need an answer in the morning." He jerked his head at a door in the corner. "You can have a bathroom break. Then I'll lock you up for the night. Will you be able to manage those jeans, or do you need my help?"

SATURDAY, 12:51 P.M.

Peter found Terry and Steve on Lia's living room floor, teasing Gypsy and Chewy with Susan's tattered scarf while Lia sketched from the couch. Squeaker socks littered the area around them, turning the floor into a field of land mines.

All heads popped up when he entered the room, like so many worried jack-in-the boxes. He sat on the couch and shook his head. Chewy head-butted his leg. He dropped a hand to ruffle the furry ears and said nothing.

Lia laid a hand on his thigh. "Will you call Captain Parker?"

"If I take this to Parker now, she'll say there could be a dozen reasons Jenny's not in her room or returning calls. She won't devote resources to finding Jenny when nobody in her life says she's missing. I can't ask her friends if they know where she is because I don't know who they are."

Terry scowled. "Catch-22."

"It would be different if I knew of an actual threat to Jenny."

"It was Walter Miller. He's nutty enough," Terry said.

Peter frowned, not placing the name.

"Susan's UFO guy," Lia said. "Alpha Centuri? Little green men? Any chance this isn't about Andrew Heenan?"

"If that's the case, I'm screwed."

"How can we help?" Steve asked.

No point closing the barn door now. "Give me a minute. I have to make a call." He scrolled his contact list, tapped a number.

Overstreet answered on the third ring. "What can I do you for, Detective Dourson?"

"Where were you between five and nine last night?"

"Ah, man. How did I turn into your usual suspect?"

"It's your obsession with my old crime. Humor me so I can go do something useful."

"All right, all right. I was writing blogs until seven. Then I met friends for beers."

"Names and numbers."

"Anything for the cops. What's this about?"

"I'm pushed for time right now. If I can, I'll tell you later."

"I'll hold you to that."

Peter pointed at Lia's sketchbook and made a gimme gesture. He scrawled several contacts on a clean page and ended the call.

Lia leaned over to review the list. "Do you think it was him?"

"He rattled off those names so fast, I doubt it. Gave me the waitress, too. He's the only person with a motive. Now I'm stuck." He turned to Terry and Steve. "She say what her plans were?"

Gypsy abandoned her scarf to paw at Terry. He ignored her. "She said she was tired and going back to her hotel. I had the impression she was done for the day."

"Someone picked her up after you dropped her off."

Steve's mouth twisted with concern and regret. "Last we saw, she was heading into the garage to use the restroom. We would have waited, but she seemed anxious to get rid of us."

"Any other cars in the lot?"

"Not a one," Terry said.

He'd have heard about it if she'd still been in the garage when city workers arrived that morning. He might need to search the facility, check the cameras, but he hoped to find her before that became necessary.

Steve said, "If I wanted to kidnap her, the best place would be between the garage and Beekman Street, somewhere on Mill Creek Road or Fricke. No traffic to speak of after five."

Terry protested, "But that means someone knew she was there."

Peter raised his eyebrows. "Who did you tell?"

Terry's face reddened, his expression reminding Peter of an outraged rooster.

"Nobody."

Peter spoke slowly and deliberately. "Nobody in this room kidnapped Jenny, and we're the only people who knew. You said something to someone that tipped them off. Think."

Steve said, "You called Commodore."

"Only to make sure it was okay to launch from the garage, since it wasn't an official outing."

Peter kept his voice even. "What, exactly, did you say?"

"I may have intimated something about a beautiful lady. I did not share her name."

"You say anything about Elvis?"

"It's not Commodore. He and his wife are away this weekend."

"We'll check that out. Anyone with him when you called?"

Terry dropped his eyes, licked his lips. "Dick was with him."

"I don't understand," Lia said. "What would Dick want with Jenny?"

Steve snorted. "What would anyone want? Whoever took her thinks she's a million-dollar meal ticket."

Gypsy tugged on Lia's pants. Lia gathered the pup into her lap. "What could she possibly know?"

Peter sighed. "She knows the house, and the Johnsons are in Georgia."

Lia folded her arms, shot him an accusing look. "You're going after him without backup."

"I can't involve anyone else."

"I don't like it."

Neither do I.

DAY 22, AFTERNOON

SATURDAY, MAY 11, 2019

2:23 P.M.

JENNY SAT ON THE EDGE OF A CHAIR IN THE JOHNSON'S living room, her skin itching from sweat and dust collected during hours crawling in the Johnson's attic and moving stacks of boxes in the basement.

At least her feet were finally dry.

The man—who said his name was Dick—had gone over every wall with a stud finder, looking for gaps or inconsistencies that would indicate a hidden closet. They'd measured rooms. They'd moved cabinets and removed vent covers.

Placating the man who held her captive while her brain scrambled for a way out left her exhausted. And despite all evidence to the contrary, Dick remained convinced a lost Fabergé egg hid somewhere in the house, waiting just for him.

Dick had been friendly, even jovial on the drive over, even while showing her his gun. "I don't want to use this, but I will," he'd said with that easy affability. "We have a job to do. No fooling around."

"I want this just as much as you do," she'd lied, keeping her voice steady despite the gun pointed at her chest.

Getting to the house unseen had been ridiculously easy. A wooded green space ran behind the properties along Clifton Hills Avenue, ending at a school a half-mile from Andrew's house. Dick parked at the school, retrieved a canvas bag of tools, then walked her through a lovely space dappled with cool, early morning sun. They looked like any couple out for a pre-breakfast stroll.

The gun in his pocket pressed into her back as she prayed for joggers, for dog walkers, for off-duty Green Berets. If she was lucky, a competing gang of treasure seekers would distract Dick long enough for her to get away.

On this quiet Saturday morning, they saw no one.

The wall behind Andrew's house was decorative more than protective, and manageable to climb, though it meant trampling Peony beds that had been well-established when she'd last seen them.

At Andrew's side door, Dick pulled a device from the bag that looked something like a cross between a staple gun and an UZI. He grinned at her as he fitted something long and slender in the muzzle.

"Lock rake. It's handy for construction work. People expect burglars at night. They pay attention to lights in houses that are supposed to be vacant. We're searching by daylight. Even if we turn on the lights, no one will notice them against the sunlight."

His hands were full. She considered the distance to the street, but the gun was in his pocket and it would be too easy for him to shoot her before she got away.

"Smart," she'd said instead of running. She put a hint of admiration in her voice. Enough to mollify, not enough to set off alarms. There was acting, then there was over-playing your part. The wrong inflection, an involuntary grimace, a rigid expression, and he'd smash that lock pick across her face.

That had been several tension-filled hours ago, before his ebullience eroded into determination, and determination became a thin skin over frustration.

Now Dick's attention turned to a built-in cherry book-case. It was seven feet tall with ornate carvings, five shelves over a cupboard. He laid one ham-sized hand on Jenny's shoulder, still friendly.

"I should have thought of this from the beginning. Malachi did his own cabinet work. A secret compartment in a bookcase would be child's play for him. Andrew ever talk about that? About building stuff for his act?"

"He did card tricks at birthday parties. He pulled coins out of my ear. He never talked about cabinets." The hand flexed, biting into her shoulder. A tiny rill of cold sweat snaked down her back. "I'm sorry. I wish I could be more help."

Give him something. The enclosed base was a good six inches high, taller than typical.

"There's plenty of room for a hidey hole in the bottom."

The hand relaxed. "Empty it."

Jenny knelt and opened the cabinet doors. A hodge-podge of electronic detritus greeted her: chargers, defunct mini tablets, cords, and cables that went to who-knew-what. "At least no one will know we were in here. It would be good if we had a box."

He dumped a wastebasket on the carpet. "Use this."

She dragged handfuls of wire and plastic gobbledy-gook into the container, scooting back when the cubby was clear. Dick rapped the bottom, a pointless gesture. They already knew it was hollow.

"Joints are tight," he said. "No obvious way for the bottom to lift or retract."

"I suppose you can't pry it up."

"Not my first choice. I don't want to damage the contents."

Jenny scanned the leaves and vines decorating the face. "Maybe there's a hidden catch? That would be kind of Hollywood, but Andrew was a showman."

Dick gave a vine an experimental push. "The carvings are pegged on. See if they move."

Any catch was likely to be stuck after thirty years but it was safer not to say so. "Move how?"

"See if they depress or twist in either direction, or if they slide. Take the left. Start at the bottom and work up."

Jenny tugged the bits of wood, wondering what would happen when Dick didn't find what he expected, how long she could string things out, and if she would have any warning when he decided it was time to dispose of her.

"Ha!" Dick sat back on his heels, his grin triumphant.

"What did you find?" Jenny asked.

"This leaf twisted. Move out of the way. I need to see if anything changed."

The interior of the cabinet remained seamless .

"Maybe there's more than one catch you need to find?"

Dick jerked his chin at a leaf. "Check the matching carving on your side."

That one didn't twist, but the one above it did. No change. Dick's brow drew down, his eyes turning mean.

Jenny kept a deferential tone in her voice as she spoke. "Andrew had an odd sense of humor. No telling how many catches there are, or what combination is needed to open them."

"Combination?"

"You might need to twist them in a certain order, or make a pattern. Maybe the tips of the leaves need to point up, or right, or down. The possibilities are endless."

"Too much trouble. Time to break out the tools."

2:59 P.M.

Peter sat in his car, in a spot that allowed him to see the side door of the Johnson's house and a sizable portion of the back yard. Perfect for watching grass grow, his main activity for the past hour.

It had been a long shot to think Jenny was ransacking a house that looked perfectly fine on the outside. He'd kept telling himself that as he ran plates of cars parked on Clifton Hills Avenue, working his way down the half-mile to DePaul Cristo Rey High School. He stopped when a

Ford Fusion in the parking lot came back registered to Dick Brewer.

The high school abutted a greenway that ran behind the Johnson property, the perfect way to approach the house unseen. Jenny and Brewer were in there. He could smell it. But was Jenny operating under duress or her own steam?

He stared at the house. Tore open a Snickers bar and took a bite, followed it with a swig of flat, lukewarm Pepsi. His phone vibrated. Terry. He'd hated drafting the Scooby Gang for official business, but this wasn't official and Terry was his best shot at locating Brewer. "What've you got?"

"I called Commodore. He doesn't know where Dick is—"

"You didn't tell him why you were looking?"

"Of course not. He did say Dick was rehabbing a home off Blue Rock. Steve and I drove around and found it. Nice of him to put a company sign in the yard."

"Good work."

"Dick left a guy named Mike Weller working the site. I told him we need to talk to his boss. He says Dick drove out to Indiana to pick up custom cabinets and expected to be gone all day, and not to bother him."

"Can he get Brewer on the phone?"

"Mike says he's under instruction not to call."

"Put him on."

A rough, irritated voice said, "This guy says you're a cop. How do I know you aren't gassing me?"

"You can call District Five and ask them to patch you

through to me. That will waste at least five minutes I don't have. Why would your boss say not to bug him?"

"You ask your boss why he does things?"

"Good point. He gamble?"

"What business is that of yours?"

"If your cabinet maker is in Indiana, he had to drive past the casinos. That's the best reason I can think of to tell your crew not to call."

Mike was silent. He'd hit a nerve.

"I don't think your boss is at the slots. I think he's still in town, somewhere he shouldn't be, and it's very important that I find him."

"That's bullshit."

"Maybe. I'm betting you have a way to let him know there's an emergency on the job so he'll take a call even when he's not answering his phone."

"If you're so hot to find out where he is, why don't you get the phone company to trace him?"

"This isn't television. I only get to do that when your boss robs a bank. Your boss rob a bank?"

"What's this about, anyway?"

"Right now he's suspected of something seriously bad. If you contact him and we prove he's not where I believe he is, You'll clear him of any suspicion. You'd be doing him a favor."

"A favor that will get me fired."

"Tell you what. If you can come up with an emergency that would get him to your job site and I'm wrong, I'll tell him we pressured you, and I'll give you a hundred bucks." A safe bet since the Ford Fusion made it a thousand to one Brewer wasn't anywhere near Indiana.

"No shit? Do I still get the hundred bucks if he's where you think he is?"

"You'll be a hero and I'll hook you up with a hot reporter."

"I'd rather have the hundred bucks."

"Take what you can get, Weller. What would get him there in a hurry?"

There was silence on the line while Mike thought. "I could say someone stole his equipment when I ran to the store. That would do it."

"That'll work."

"Then I'll say I called the cops, but since it's not my equipment and I'm not the property owner, the asshole cop decided maybe I'm trespassing and he's trying to arrest me."

Weller was entitled to a minor revenge. "Even better. Tell him the asshole cop's name is Hodgkins."

"And if he arrests me, the job site will be unprotected because the door is busted open."

"I think you got it. Let me talk to Terry."

Terry came back on the line. Peter said, "You catch that?"

"We shall lure our quarry from his lair."

Peter hoped he wasn't making a colossal mistake. "I'm leaving him in your hands. Call me as soon as he talks to Brewer."

A white Caddy pulled in front of the Johnson house and parked. Peter bolted from his car, disastrous scenarios ripping through his brain faster than bullets in a firing squad. His execution if he didn't do something.

Susan opened the door, stretched her legs languidly

and stood, iPhone in hand. Peter had a millisecond to register someone in the passenger seat.

"Get back in your car and go. Now."

She smiled, tilting her head. "Officer Dourson. How pleasant to see you here."

"I mean it, Susan. You're interfering with a police operation."

Susan's eyes went wide, the way they did when she dug in her heels. She swiveled her head in a wide arc to make her point. "I don't see an operation. I only see you." Her iPhone came up. "Perhaps you'd like to tell my avid viewers all about it?"

3:06 P.M.

As Jenny handed Dick a chisel, his pocket buzzed. He drew out his phone, glanced at the screen, swore, tapped the screen, held the phone to his ear.

"You'd better be missing a limb.... You've got to be fucking kidding. Put him on the phone.... Look, asshole, Mike Waller works for me—What do you mean, 'who am I?' ... Hold your damn horses. I'll be there in twenty minutes, and I'll show you who I am, that's a promise."

He shoved the phone violently into his pocket.

Jenny held her breath, eyes down and motionless like a terrified forest creature in the path of an angry predator.

3:07 P.M.

Peter wanted to close his eyes and count to ten, or even three. His phone rang. He held up one finger in a "wait" gesture, keeping his eyes on Susan as he took the call.

"Mission accomplished," Steve said. "Mike wants to know when he gets his hundred bucks."

"He gets it when he sees his boss and his boss isn't wearing handcuffs. Hang around until I call back." He had less than thirty seconds before Brewer came tearing out the side door.

Something shifted in Peter's periphery. A wizened woman exited the Caddy, hung with enough jewelry to stock a pawn shop. She quavered, "Miss Susan, aren't we going to do my interview?"

Peter imagined a blank wall and schooled his expression into cop face, "Put the phone down."

Susan held the phone steady. "Public street, public servant. I have every right to be here. My viewers will love this."

A tiny dog snarled. A crotchety voice demanded, "This is a nice street. Take your ruckus elsewhere."

Tiny teeth tugged at Peter's slacks.

Marilyn Edling of the pedophile claims. With her killer Chihuahua.

3:08 P.M.

Jenny stood behind Dick at the side door, the harangue of an angry woman penetrating the walls. He thrust his canvas bag at her.

"Hold this. You don't talk to anyone. If we see anyone, you do anything funny, I shoot them, then you."

A hand clamped on Jenny's upper arm, he edged out, peered around a bush. Snorted.

"What is it?" She whispered.

"Nothing to worry about," he said, dragging Jenny behind the house. "Nice and easy, back the way we came." The gun's muzzle pressed through his jacket pocket and into her back, prodding her over the wall. "As soon as I take care of business, we'll come back."

After so many hours spent reading this lunatic, Jenny doubted that. Now that he believed they'd found Malachi's motherlode, she was a loose end, something to snip off.

They passed into the shadows under the trees, her heart pounding like a trapped sparrow in a net. She reminded herself that the houses were too close for him to kill her now. Too many people home on a Saturday. They'd hear the shot.

She was safe while they were in public, as long as no one forced his hand. Once they were back at the car, he'd zip tie her hands and her ankles again, and that would be all she wrote.

Whatever you do, don't get in the car.

3:19 P.M.

Jenny smelled asphalt beyond the trees. The parking lot had to be near. She wondered what time it was, and if anyone would be around.

If she was lucky, there would be people, lots of people, and she could act. But she didn't hear motors, she didn't hear voices. Too quiet.

The heavy canvas bag occupied her arms while Dick kept a proprietary hand at her back. Someone coming face to face with them might wonder why she carried the heavy load, but they wouldn't notice the gun. Dick could fire a shot into her spine and no one would know where it came from.

The trees thinned. Sunlight glinted off Dick's windshield, less than a hundred feet away.

Whatever you do, don't get in the car.

Right now, she didn't know how to avoid it.

You'll know when the time comes.

Believe it.

3:21 P.M.

Thank God Mrs. Edling had gone home once she recognized him. But Susan remained, arms folded, lipsticked mouth twisting in a full-on tirade. Peter's head pounded with an adrenaline-induced headache as he scrambled his brain for a way to remove her from his scene before she alerted Brewer.

"—enough that you've scared off half my prospects? Must you follow me around? I'm trying to make a living! I'm a member of the Fourth Estate! I have rights and—"

How long had it taken to send Edling and her vicious dog home? Two minutes? Three? He needed to end this, now. Explanations would take time and only inflame Susan's love of drama.

When all else fails, lie.

"If you get back in your car right now and leave, do your interview from anywhere but this neighborhood—"

"This location is my brand for this story—"

"I'll give you an exclusive when it's all over." Peter mentally crossed his fingers that Susan read detective novels and actually believed this was how it worked.

Susan closed her mouth on whatever she had been about to say and narrowed her eyes. "Promise? Tell-your-mother-on-you promise?"

Peter looked at his watch. "This offer expires in ten seconds."

"Get in the car, Ada Belle. You can tell me all about your nights of passion with Elvis at Starbucks. I'll buy you a latte."

"A caramel latte?"

"You can have unicorn sprinkles on it if you want."

During the course of this debacle, Peter had slowly circled Susan, forcing her to turn with him so he could look past her and keep an eye on Heenan's house. Now he could see the front, but he'd lost his unobstructed view of the side door.

Susan, with her cheerleader lungs in fighting form, made enough noise to raise the dead. Had Brewer been watching from inside the house? Peter hadn't seen the drapes move, but he'd been distracted.

Damn Susan. Brewer could still be inside, waiting him out, or he could have slipped out while Susan had her hissy fit. Peter had no way to know unless he returned to Brewer's car. But then he lost his chance to catch Brewer in the house red-handed. Brewer could say he'd been anywhere, doing anything, and there went probable cause for a search warrant. He'd owe Waller a hundred bucks for nothing.

Stay or go? If he were Brewer, he'd wait to see what Peter did. He'd wait all night, job site emergency or not. Peter's best bet was to drive away, circle around and wait for Brewer to poke his head up.

As he walked to his car, Susan pulled out. She wasn't heading back to Ludlow Avenue. She was driving toward the school.

As the white Caddy disappeared around a curve in the road, Peter's phone vibrated. The text from Lia read:

Dick @ car w/ Jenny

DAY 22, AFTERNOON, CONTINUED

SATURDAY, MAY 11, 2019

3:22 P.M.

SHE SHOULDN'T BE HERE, IN THIS PARKING LOT WITH CHEWY straining against his leash and whining for attention. Bringing the dogs had been a poor decision and it was too late to stash them in the car. Gypsy squirmed in the Moby wrap. Lia distracted her with a treat while she kept her eyes on the couple emerging from the woods.

Peter took too much on himself and he couldn't be everywhere. When he'd called to say he'd found Dick's car and was surveilling the house, she'd decided to watch his back. Just in case Dick sneaked past him.

Which he wouldn't. That's what she'd thought, foolishly. She hadn't told Peter, deciding in this case to ask forgiveness later because permission was out of the question.

Except for the Ford, the lot had been vacant when she arrived. Typical for a Saturday, she suspected. She'd scanned the woods, straining her eyes to penetrate the trees as she wondered how Peter handled hours of nothing on a stakeout.

He handled it by not being alone.

She'd brought the dogs for cover, with the parking lot as the perfect place to run Chewy through badly-needed obedience drills. And working Chewy saved her from dying of tedium, or at least it had. Then his concentration had blown.

Tired of performing, Chewy kept dragging her toward the Ford. She gave in, taking a quick look at the woods as they reached the driver's side. Chewy sniffed at a tire and lifted a leg.

She yanked the lead, harder than she intended. "Leave it!" Chewy gave her a wounded look. She knelt and ruffled the ears he kept shaggy because he hated the groomer.

"Sorry little man, but that's vandalism. And if this car becomes evidence, your DNA can't be on it."

Gypsy pawed at the Moby wrap, wanting down. Another month before she was safe from parvo, and it was becoming increasingly difficult to keep her strapped up. Lia reached into her back pocket and withdrew the remains of Susan's scarf.

It was the one thing guaranteed to keep Gypsy happy.

Movement in the trees caught the corner of her eye. "Heel," she commanded softly, leading Chewy behind a dumpster.

Dick Brewer emerged from the trees, accompanied by the woman in Susan's video. Jenny appeared to be fine, though she struggled with a large bag Dick could have easily carried with one hand.

Where was Peter? Lia grabbed her phone, fumbled the lock screen while resisting Chewy's leash tugs, got an error message.

Stupid fingerprint sensor.

The screen responded as Dick and Jenny approached the parking lot. She dashed off the text, knowing they'd be gone before Peter arrived. Stupid, stupid, stupid, she came to watch Peter's back but never made a plan.

What now?

Stall them. Brazen out a chance encounter. Pray Peter shows up before things go sideways. Brewer wouldn't hurt her in public, surely.

She slipped her pepper spray in the bottom fold of the Moby wrap where it would be easy to grab, then pulled the top fold over Gypsy's head, tucking the scarf in to keep her happy. With a smile pasted on her face, she struck out to meet them.

3:23 P.M.

A dog barked. Across the parking lot, a schnauzer dragged a woman. The woman waved.

"Hey, Dick, who's your friend?"

The gun jabbed Jenny's kidney. Dick's voice hissed in her ear, "One word, I shoot you both." He waved back.

The woman's chest was wrapped with some kind of cloth. As she walked toward them, it wiggled.

The barrel of the gun rode up and down Jenny's spine.

The woman with the wiggling chest stopped ten feet away. The schnauzer strained and whined.

"Funny running into you. I was just working Chewy. Are you connected to the school?"

"Lia, right?"

The wiggling thing popped a head out. A puppy, with odd, blotchy fur and bright blue eyes. Jenny gasped, a barely audible intake of breath. The puppy snarled, frantic to escape. The woman—Lia—clapped a hand on the pup and shushed her.

Behind Jenny, Dick tensed.

Lia smiled apologetically. "I don't know what's got into her."

Jenny held her breath. Beside her, Dick thrummed like an overwound guitar string. Anything would make him snap.

3:24 P.M.

Where's Peter?

Chewy tugged and whined, jerking Lia's attention from the couple in front of her. Alarm bells went off in her head as she felt the situation slipping out of control.

Bad idea, taking your eyes off a possible kidnapper.

She resisted the urge to whip her head back. "Chill, little man," she scolded, using Chewy as an excuse to keep Dick from seeing panic on her face.

Gypsy kept snarling.

Lia stooped by Chewy, watching Dick and Jenny with

her peripheral vision. The woman's eyes darted like a trapped bird while Dick's face took on a hard look.

Something was definitely wrong. Lia looked up with what she hoped was a placating smile.

"I'm really sorry, they usually love people."

3:25 P.M.

Ahead, Susan's Caddy rounded another curve.

Peter fought the urge to stomp the gas.

Forget the school and what in God's name Lia is doing there. It's Saturday. Don't kill a kid.

He swooped around an Amazon delivery van, braked for a dog walker. A Chrysler performed a three-point turn at a speed approximating continental drift. He drove on the sidewalk, wincing as hedges gouged his department vehicle and making a mental note to apologize for the ruts he put in two lawns.

Motion in a driveway.

He slammed his brakes. A lawn service truck backed an equipment trailer into the street, maneuvering awkwardly between parked cars.

3:27 P.M.

Jenny froze in an agony of indecision. This might be her only chance. But with the gun pressed against her back,

373

Dick would feel her move. He'd pull the trigger before she took a single step—with the woman named Lia and her dogs in the line of fire.

She prayed.

The sound of a motor. A car, cruising into the lot like a great white shark. As it pulled up to the little group, a blonde head leaned out, smiling and feral, dangerous as the great white.

Susan Sweeney, who'd outed her on YouTube and got her into this mess.

"Dick! I thought you were in Indiana. Who's your friend?"

As if she doesn't know.

Dick turned his head toward Susan, his voice curt. "You'll have to excuse us, we have somewhere to be, and we're late."

"Oh," Susan said. "I won't hold you up, but before ..."

Dick turned a little more. Pressure from the gun lessened, then vanished. Jenny spun away, slamming the tool bag in the back of Dick's head. The gun roared. She dropped the bag and ran.

3:27 P.M.

Lia continued to shush the dogs, her brain scrambling for a way to stall long enough for Peter to appear. The sound of a car motor sent relief flooding through her. She glanced up.

Not Peter. *Susan.*

He's working with Susan? But no, Susan yammered at Dick as her car idled, obviously clueless. Lia tried to catch Jenny's eye, but Jenny stared into the distance, looking at nothing.

Jenny's hands tensed around the bag. "Look at the hands," Peter had said during an impromptu training lecture, "The hands tell you what's about to happen. The eyes tell you when and where."

Lia dropped to the pavement, rolling onto a shrieking Gypsy as she dragged Chewy down.

A gun went off. Dick fell as Jenny flew across the lot, tools flying like shrapnel, a gun spinning across the pavement.

Susan leapt from the car. "You bitch! What did you shoot him for?"

Dick pushed up on his knees and shook his head, blood on his face and murder in his eyes. Susan bent over him. He shoved her aside, grabbed the gun, and jumped into the idling Caddy. Someone screamed.

The car took off in a screeching circle, heading for Jenny.

3:29 P.M.

Peter punched his steering wheel, mentally cursing the lawn service truck. When the truck finally straightened out, it backfired.

Not a backfire. A gunshot.

He floored the accelerator. A hundred yards from the

school, it came: the unmistakable sound of steel slamming into concrete.

Blood roaring in his ears, Peter whipped into the parking lot, shoved the transmission into park, vaulted from the car. Susan's Caddy sat, crumpled against a brick wall while Chewy and Gypsy's howls pierced the air like twin sirens.

Ada Belle of the nights of burning passion banged the Caddy's passenger door open, waving a small pink something over her head as she emerged. Her voice quavered with rage.

"Try to kidnap me, will you!"

Susan sat on the asphalt, wailing, "My car!"

Lia huddled behind a dumpster with an arm around Jenny, shushing the dogs. Gypsy ignored Lia, howling over a mouth full of scarf.

Dick was nowhere.

"Where's Dick?" Peter demanded.

Susan moaned, "My car—"

"The car," Lia yelled. "He's in the car."

Ada Belle remained by the Caddy, jabbing the phone-sized pink rectangle at the open door like she was poking a stick at a cottonmouth.

"I stunned him." Jab. "I'll do it again." Jab.

"Ada Belle, back away from the car. Now!"

Jenny called, "He has a gun."

Brewer had twenty years in the Army. He wouldn't hesitate to shoot. Peter edged up to the driver-side window, drawing his Glock. Dick lay across the seats, groping the passenger-side floorboard. Peter aimed as he slammed a fist on the Caddy's roof.

"Hands up!"

Dick jerked, turning, gun in hand.

Peter fired. Shreds of leather and foam rubber flew inches from Brewer's head as the gun clattered to the floor. Dick's hands swerved up, shaking.

"Don't shoot! Don't shoot!"

Peter kept his Glock trained on Brewer's face as the men stared at each other. With Brewer's gun in reach, they were at a stand off.

Brewer looked like he could piss his pants, but you couldn't trust that. Getting him out of the car could be a problem. If Peter had to physically haul him out, he'd have to holster his weapon, giving Brewer a chance to grab his gun.

Backup, he needed backup. The silence stretched out.

"This is a misunderstanding," Dick said.

"And I'm going to handcuff you until we sort it out. Get out of the car. Slowly."

Across the lot, Susan shrieked, "What did your nasty dog do to my scarf?"

DAY 23, THE WEE HOURS

SUNDAY, MAY 12, 2019

Outside the Wasabi Grill, the man who looked like Matthew McConaughey sat cross-legged on the pavement. He held chopsticks above a platter of sushi on the low table in front of him, the tips floating and quivering like a divining rod.

Lia knelt by him, placing a twenty in his tip jar as he held her with blue, blue eyes. The chopsticks dipped to a slice of dragon roll.

"Fame," he said. "Taste of the dragon, my love, and it will be yours."

He lifted the delicacy.

Viola woofed.

Damn dog. If she didn't open her eyes, maybe Matthew would come back.

"Viola, stop it. I'm here. Gypsy's here. It's my apartment and neither one of us is going away. Go upstairs if you don't like it."

A hand stroked Lia's cheek. Her annoyance melted away with the dream. Peter sat on the side of the bed, looking down at her.

She tugged on his shirt. "You can stay, but you gotta take your clothes off."

"I feel so cheap."

"I promise I won't look."

Peter groaned. "I wish. I'm not done for the night."

"Two minutes ago, Matthew McConaughey was in love with me. He told my fortune with sushi and said I would be famous if I ate the dragon roll. You woke me up. Now I'll never be famous. You gotta give me something."

"Eat the dragon roll? You *fell* for that?"

She elbowed his thigh.

"He's a little old for you, isn't he?"

"This was 1997 *Contact* McConaughey."

"Celebrity preacher? He didn't quite pull that one off."

"Millions of women across the globe don't care."

"You sure that wasn't *Texas Chainsaw Massacre* McConaughey? It's easy to get them confused."

"That's pathetic and unworthy of you." Lia glanced at the bedside clock. "It's after midnight. What do you need to do?"

Peter kicked off his shoes and slid in beside her. She sat up, leaning against his chest for a bit of normal in a day that had been anything but.

"I have to write the search warrant for Brewer's place if we want to get in first thing tomorrow. We need to prove he held Jenny against her will, and we have to nail it down before he sees a judge."

"How is Jenny holding up? I told her she could stay here if she didn't want to be alone, but she declined."

"Donna Merrill is with her. Jenny's tougher than she looks. She'll make a solid witness."

"You've had a long day. Did Dick have that much to say?"

Peter huffed a humorless laugh. "It took four hours to get cleared on the bullet I put in Susan's leather seat, and I had to explain to Parker how I missed center mass from three feet. Then there was the added complication of the shot in Susan's front fender. After that I got to talk to Brewer."

"Was Parker upset?"

"Unofficially, no. My bad aim saved us all from the mess that comes with a shooting."

"I've seen the videos. I know how fast things can go bad. You took a huge risk."

His chest shifted under her cheek when he shrugged. "He was face down on the seats. I had time to get off a second shot before he could aim."

She curled her hand into a fist and gently thumped his chest to emphasize each word. "Don't. Do. That. Again."

"Yes, Ma'am."

"How did it go with Dick?"

"We got Brewer for stealing Susan's car. The Davis kidnapping will probably get dropped because it's not clear he knew Davis was in the car when he took it."

Lia's mouth dropped open. "But—"

"I know and you know Brewer knew Davis was in the car, but there's what we know and what we can prove. If we try, some idiot jury will believe him and it will poison

381

the carjacking. Juries are like that. If one part of a case is bad, they're inclined to let them walk on the whole thing."

"But what about Jenny?"

"No one saw Jenny under duress."

"I said I couldn't see his hand. That doesn't mean he didn't have his gun on her."

"Speaking of which, don't *you* ever do that again."

"You had no backup. He might have gotten away if I hadn't delayed them."

Peter kissed the top of her head. "You could have been shot again. I'd rather let a hundred kidnappers escape than see you hurt."

Lia rubbed the dime-sized dimple in her thigh. "I won't sit home and knit when you're out on a limb like that."

"Since when do you knit?"

"Don't change the subject."

"I let the air out of two of his tires, Tonto. I had it covered."

"You could have told me that."

"I didn't know you were running to my rescue. But it didn't hurt having you on the scene as a witness, especially after the way Susan went on about Jenny."

"Does Dick deny being in the Johnsons' house?"

Peter snorted, shaking his head so that his chin brushed her hair. "You should have seen him in the interview room, all cocky like he was checking out the talent at happy hour instead of cooling his heels in police custody. Then he tells a story about Jenny picking him up for hot, kinky sex."

"You can't be serious."

"And it's my job to keep him talking. I have to make like we're just two guys and everything he says is reasonable. Then I had to walk him through it all, like how she wanted him to tie her up—"

"That's crazy!"

"It is, but I needed the details. That's what hangs you."

"And did he?"

"Hang himself? There were a number of inconsistencies in his story. I felt filthy after I came out of there."

"I'm sorry."

"Don't be. The payoff is, he thinks he pulled it off."

"How did he get from kinky sex to the Johnsons' house?"

"All her idea. He went along for the ride, hoping for more kinky sex. That's a B and E, but still no kidnapping. The prosecutor wanted to arrest Jenny, but agreed to hold off when I pointed out it was Brewer's lock rake and we needed to explore her claims of kidnapping before we went there."

Lia sat up, stretched and yawned. "Poor Jenny. What's his explanation for why she brained him?"

"Jealous because Susan showed up. That, or she's nuts. He barely knew her, so who knows?"

"And he stole the car because?"

"He thought she took off with his tools."

"As if they weren't all over the parking lot. He has an answer for everything, doesn't he?"

"Guy didn't turn a hair. Says he lied to Waller because it wasn't Waller's business if he was playing hooky with Jenny."

"Geezlepete. I'm still half asleep. Make coffee while I get up?"

"Coffee? You?"

"Someone needs to keep you company in your misery"

LIA GRABBED A ROBE AND SPLASHED WATER ON HER FACE before she joined Peter in the kitchen. A steaming cup of coffee with cream waited for her on the table. Peter sat on the other side, his face in his laptop and a hand under the table, feeding biscuits to Viola.

Chewy and Gypsy abandoned Lia in favor of treats. Viola growled, sending Gypsy behind Lia's robe. She scooped up the whimpering pup and cooed.

"There there, little girl. I won't let the mean, nasty bitch get you." She held Gypsy pinned to her lap as she took a sip of coffee. "You're pursuing Dick as an opportunistic fortune hunter, right?"

"That's the prevailing theory."

"I've been thinking about this all day. What if it's more? What do you know about Dick? When did he enlist?"

"He has no arrests. I put in the paperwork to get his military records, but that takes weeks unless you have contacts, which I don't. What are you thinking?"

"I'm thinking about those vandalized yearbooks and how those same years were missing from Ruth's set. I'm wondering if we had them but Dick took them."

"We have no reason to connect Brewer with our break in."

"Gypsy connects him."

"How do you figure that?"

"She went crazy in the parking lot today, just like she did during the break in. I think it was Dick, and she remembered his scent. If it *was* Dick, it means he had a reason to hide something from high school."

"Like a connection to Jenny? She didn't know him."

"People change in thirty years. I bet he wears size eleven shoes."

"It's a common size."

"Don't be a jerk."

"You're connecting dots that may not belong on the same page. He has a lock rake. Why go through the coal chute?"

"He saw the discrete 'this house is alarmed' sticker on the door? Tell me this. How old is he?"

Peter rubbed the emerging stubble on his chin. "I don't remember. Babe, I have a warrant to write and I need to catch whatever sleep I can. Can you play Scooby Doo tomorrow?"

Lia searched Peter's haggard face. "Can I see the year-book photos Alma sent you?"

Peter sighed. "If I let you look at them, will you let it go for tonight?"

"Unless I find something."

Peter punched up a file and pivoted his laptop so Lia could see.

He came around the table and stood behind her. She found Cowboy Dick on the third scanned page.

"Here." She pointed at the obese boy painting scenery. "Look at the eyes."

Peter bent over her shoulder. "Maybe, maybe not. Why didn't they put names in the caption?"

"Are the yearbooks you got from Hughes still in the living room? I bet we find him in the student portraits."

GREASY HAIR FELL INTO THE EYES OF THE BOY STARING sullenly at Lia. "That's Dick as a sophomore in 1987. No one would recognize him now."

Peter accepted the yearbook from her and examined the photo. "He definitely got the army makeover. If I'd done the math when I ran him, I would have realized he was too young to enlist when Heenan went missing." He inserted a slip of paper to mark the page, then set the book aside on the couch.

Lia yawned. The coffee wasn't working. Probably just as well. "Commodore got his dates wrong or Dick didn't retire with a pension. Do you think he got kicked out?"

"Maybe. You talk about the attic while you were at Boswell's?"

Lia tried to remember, couldn't. "It would be like Terry to tell a contractor about this place. Dick had to know Ruth. I bet he signed her yearbooks."

"It's a good bet Brewer knew Jenny, or knew of her. There's no way to know who vandalized the Hughes yearbooks, or when it was done. Unless we can tie him to the break-in, knowing Jenny only supports the fortune hunter angle."

"You'll check his shoes?"

"It'll be a stretch, but I'll work it into the search warrant. Anything else, Nancy Drew?"

LIA HAD THAT LOOK ON HER FACE, THE ONE WHERE SHE wanted to say something but wasn't sure how to say it. Peter raised an eyebrow and waited.

She took a sip of coffee, then held the cup against her chest. It was something she did, for the warmth, or maybe it helped her pull her thoughts together.

"I want to run something by you."

"Okay."

"Picture this: You're this kid nobody pays attention to, but you hear stuff. You hear about this old magician who doesn't want anyone to know he only has one leg and it reminds you of a story."

Reasonable assumptions. He'd go along for the ride. "Where'd he hear the story?"

"Who knows. If Jay Overstreet heard it, Dick could hear it. And Overstreet put it together as soon as the bones turned up. The point is, Dick knew about Malachi's missing loot, and later he overhears Jenny talking about the leg in drama club. You're a kid nobody notices, so what do you do?"

"You find the treasure and impress all the people who ignore you."

Lia flipped a palm over in a classic game show hostess gesture. "And how do you do that?"

"You're young and dumb. You figure you've got it all over an old guy with one leg and you'll make him tell you."

"Only it didn't work, or Brewer would still be living it up in Cancun or wherever the big party place was in the eighties. He never would have enlisted."

"Probably would have moved on to Cabo, but Cancun will do."

"Something goes wrong. He kills poor Andrew before he finds out where the treasure is and buries him by the creek. He's smart enough to use the plane ticket."

"This is some thread you're pulling. Why does our young killer return to the scene of the crime?"

"It was a seminal experience. It made him a man. He wonders about it, secretly relives it. Maybe he never gave up on finding the loot, and staring at the grave every so often keeps it alive for him."

"You *have* been thinking about this. How does the military fit in?"

"You kill someone. You do your best to hide the body, but in your head that shallow grave is flashing neon lights. Maybe you have bad dreams about it.

"You know you'll trip yourself up and get caught. You enlist in the army to get as far away as you can, so no one connects you when the body pops up."

"A modern version of Poe's telltale heart."

"Exactly. Only the body doesn't pop up. Nobody is looking for you. After twenty years you feel safe and you want to come home."

"You just wrote a great movie about an old yearbook photo and the possibility of a size eleven shoe. Even if we can match the shoe print to Brewer, that's just another B and E. We confront him about high school, and he says, 'Yeah, I went to Hughes, so what?'

"Neither of those things gets us a murder charge. I'm not saying you're wrong—though it's a monumental long shot—but it's not enough to even ask him about it. If Brewer killed Heenan, he won't roll over in interview, not after the performance I saw today."

Lia's shoulders sagged.

Peter squeezed her hand. "But you've painted a fascinating picture of the crime."

"What tattoos does he have?"

"That's a heck of a segue."

"You say he's cocky. I'm imagining this sly kid with a big secret he's really proud of. He needs to commemorate the event, even if he's the only one who knows what it means. Tattoos are great for that."

An interesting point, but a dead end. "He has a tattoo for his division. That's it."

"Military also runs to medals." Lia's eyes flew open. "You said Jenny asked if you found a coin with the bones. What was on the coin?"

"It was Irish. It had a harp on it."

"What was on the back?"

"I never asked."

"Dammit, dammit, dammit." She grabbed her phone and hit the tiny microphone on the Google bar. "Irish coin image."

Tapping impatiently, she scrolled through the results, turned the phone to Peter. "You've got him. The son of a bitch was wearing it the day Terry found the bones."

"I don't remember seeing this."

"It was in a mounting, hanging on a chain around his neck. I bet he hasn't had it on since I saw it. Maybe he was

389

so used to wearing it he didn't think about it until I said something at Boswell's."

"I'll be damned. If he was smart, he pitched it down the first sewer grate he came to."

"You think he's that smart?"

"No. I think he's dumb enough to think he's smarter than everyone else, and he still has it. Which means I need to put it in the search warrant."

"It's not evidence of Jenny's kidnapping. How will you justify it?"

"It would establish a connection between Brewer and Heenan, which would support Jenny's story."

"Won't his attorney laugh you out of court? There must be millions of Irish shillings."

"We build his coffin one nail at a time, Woman Who Thinks too Much." Peter looked at his watch. "Two o'clock. I can grab a few hours sleep before I chase down that warrant."

Lia narrowed her eyes. Peter followed her line of sight to the coffee table where the candlestick sat, now selectively polished to retain Ruth's fingerprint.

Lia stroked the silver base with her thumb. "I know how to catch him."

DAY 23

SUNDAY, MAY 12, 2019

Susan's Snippets with Ada Belle Davis
20.8K Views
Thumbs up: 7,843
Thumbs down: 381

"I'M HERE WITH ADA BELLE DAVIS AT THE DEPAUL CHRISTO Del Rey High School, where hours ago Cincinnati business owner Dick Brewer hijacked my car after putting a bullet in the side." Susan placed a soothing hand on Ada Belle's arm and proceeded confidingly, "Ada Belle was in the passenger seat when he took the car—"

Ada Belle, sporting a neck brace festooned with a dozen strands of beads, stared fiercely into the camera. "He kidnapped me!"

"Due to her quick thinking, the situation was resolved before police arrived. Ada Belle, show our viewers your stun gun."

Ada Belle brandished a flat, pink box. "It's a cell phone case. Best ninety-nine dollars I ever spent. I stuck him in the arm and let 'er rip. Next thing I knew we crashed into that wall."

The scene shifted to footage of the Caddy with its nose crumpled against the wall.

"Here's my car before they towed it away. You can see the bullet hole in the front fender." The camera zoomed in for a closeup of the hole. "Dick Brewer jumped into my car after a woman named Jenny Olson assaulted him, walloping him with a canvas bag full of tools. Makes my head hurt just to think about it. She claims he kidnapped her though she sure didn't look kidnapped to me."

The picture changed, now showing footage of Peter walking through the lobby of Quality Inn with Jenny. "Jenny Olson is connected to Detective Peter Dourson, who is in charge of the investigation into the thirty-year-old bones found on Mill Creek recently. As this is a developing situation, I'm sure more will be—"

Lia tapped the screen, freezing Susan with her mouth unattractively open.

Bailey turned her phone face down on the picnic table. "She just doesn't know when to quit, does she?"

Terry said, "We missed the fun."

"Didn't we just," Steve said.

Gypsy wandered across the tabletop, sniffed the phone, turned around and squatted. Bailey whipped the

phone out from under her just in time to avoid dese-
cration.

"Good girl," Lia said. "Extra biscuits for you when we
get home."

PETER AND CYNTH STOOD IN THE TINY CLOSET THEY
called the vestibule, observing Brewer on the video monitor. In a replay of the night before, an orange jump-suited
Brewer sat, a confident, spread-legged jock, his eyes
cruising the room as if he were checking out talent at his
favorite bar. Every bone in Brewer's body shouted, "Try to
prove it, assholes."

Peter had been skeptical when brass pulled conference
tables from interview rooms, leaving behind straight
backed chairs with small tables at the side. He now appreciated how much body language had been hidden with the
traditional setup.

"What an idiot," Cynth said. "I can't believe he doesn't
want a lawyer."

Peter tapped Brewer's smirking image on the monitor.
"That's an O.J. gotcha grin if I ever saw one. Thinks he's
playing us and doesn't want a lawyer to get in the way. He
isn't burdened by guilt. We'd never get a confession with
the usual techniques."

Cynth narrowed her eyes at Peter. "I'm only doing this
to see if something this stupid will work. You are so going
to owe me."

Peter gave Cynth a once-over. Uncharacteristically, she
wore makeup and her unbraided hair fell in loose waves to

her waist like a third millennium Lady Godiva. She'd dug up a skirt from somewhere, tucked in a tailored shirt, and undone an extra button. The combined effect showcased her amazing figure. He doubted Brewer would recognize her.

"You'll be famous. Departments all over the country will fly you in to teach seminars. Where'd you find lipstick?"

"Family Dollar. Parker paid for it out of petty cash."

Peter retrieved his phone. Before Cynth realized what he was doing, he snapped a photo. "What's Duff's number? I want to send this to him."

"Over my dead body."

"Your mother, then."

"I'm taking a hammer to your phone."

He switched the phone to Do Not Disturb, and shoved it back in his pocket. "Ready?"

"As I'll ever be."

Peter turned on the recording equipment and opened the door. He knew the moment Cynth stepped into the room behind him. Brewer sat up, chest expanding. His tongue slipped out and quickly withdrew as he curbed an unconscious attempt to lick his lips. He covered by leaning back and folding his arms.

Didn't expect her, did you big guy?

Peter took a seat, maintaining cop face so he wouldn't laugh. He'd told Cynth to cross her legs and let some thigh show. At this moment, he was sure she was repressing the urge to kick him.

"Detective McFadden is joining me for this interview."

Brewer grinned, happy hour at the meat market. If

Cynth was performing according to plan, she'd just dropped her eyes and allowed herself a hint of a smile.

Too bad she can't blush on cue.

A pitcher and glasses sat on the little table next to Peter. He poured himself a glass of water, held it up.

"Want some?"

That tongue, unable to help itself, flicked out again while the eyes tracked Cynth as she did one of the hundred subtle things women do to distract men.

Brewer's eyes returned, focused. "I'm good. Look, I told you what happened. When do I get out of here?"

Peter heaved an exaggerated sigh. "Man, you've been cooperative, but we have discrepancies that have to be resolved. One way or another, you'll see a judge tomorrow morning."

Brewer's eyes turned mean. "That's bullshit."

"That's the weekend. No court on Sundays. But if we can resolve these discrepancies, maybe we don't need court."

The chair next to Peter creaked, Cynth shifting. Possibly the skirt riding another inch up her thigh. Brewer's eyes darted over to check her out.

"What discrepancies?"

"Ms. Olson tells a different story about your date."

"Bitch is lying. I told you, she's nuts."

"I hear you, but we have to treat everything as valid until we know otherwise. So we sent a team to your house—"

Brewer jolted forward, hands on knees, ready to launch himself at Peter. "You *what*?"

Peter didn't flinch. Cynth made a faint, ladylike snort of disdain.

"We have a he said/she said situation. Gathering physical evidence is the only way to show Ms. Olson is lying. We analyze that, and Bob's your uncle."

"I didn't consent to a search."

"Didn't need to. We have probable cause and a warrant."

"What did you take?"

Peter patted his pockets, came up empty. "Cynth, you bring that search warrant return?"

"I left it on the kitchen counter, like we always do."

Peter flipped his hand palm up, an apology. "Sorry, man. It's there, waiting for you. It lists everything. We took stuff like bedding so we can look for her DNA. That will tell us what we need to know."

Peter took a sip of water—a manufactured pause to allow the thought of DNA to sink in—before he continued in his best, earnest voice, "It helps that you were so detailed in your report of the incident. We knew exactly where to look."

"What if she didn't leave any DNA."

Cynth spoke, a hint of amusement in her voice. "You always leave *something*."

Another pause, another sip of water. Out of the corner of Peter's eye, Cynth leaned over to pour a glass for herself, rolling her shoulders forward to let her neckline gap, just a little.

Peter directed his comments to Brewer while the man's eyes continued to slide over Cynth. "I don't have a crystal ball. I can't see into the future. But you already know what the outcome will be. Right now, before we have the certainty of physical evidence, you have an opportunity."

Brewer leaned back, folded his arms again, suspicious. "Yeah?"

"We ran across something that suggests you might have information that could help us solve Andrew Heenan's murder. You help us, the prosecutor will look more kindly on a low-profile kidnapping that maybe didn't happen and a carjacking that lasted less than two minutes. He might decide the charges aren't worth his time. If that's the case, you could be out of here today."

"I saw the bones. That's all I know about Andrew Heenan." Brewer's left leg jiggled as he said this. Nerves, and possible deception.

"You're a solid citizen without a smudge on your record. If you knew anything about Andrew Heenan's death, you would have come forward. We know that. We think you're connected and don't realize it."

"And how did you work that out?"

"Your bull medallion. You wore it the day you found the bones."

"What does my taste in jewelry have to do with the price of beans in China?"

Cynth cleared her throat, smiled. "It's not jewelry, exactly. It's a 1933 Irish shilling, and we're wondering where you got it."

That leg kept going. "I forgot. Why do you care?"

Cynth continued, "There aren't many Irish shillings from 1933 floating around this part of the world. Andrew

Heenan carried one. We believe the person you got it from either killed him or knew his killer."

A vein throbbed in Brewer's jaw. "That bitch tell you that? She'll say anything. You can't prove it belonged to him."

Peter kept his tone neutral. "Funny thing, coins pick up finger prints. Metal—especially silver—is vulnerable to etching from skin acids. Once a fingerprint sets in, it changes the metal and it's there forever. The etching may not be visible to the naked eye, but we can pull it out in the lab. It's a big deal with collectors because handling devalues coins. We have Heenan's prints from a background check in the eighties. Once we pop the coin out of the mounting, I'm betting we'll find a match."

Cynth leaned forward, sympathy oozing from her voice. "We know you had nothing to do with Andrew Heenan, but you can lead us to the person who killed him."

"If I tell you where I got the coin, you'll drop the charges?"

Peter shrugged, hoping his indifference was getting under Brewer's skin. "You know the drill. The prosecutor won't make an offer unless he's sure he's not getting a pig in a poke."

Brewer sneered. "What makes you think I didn't off the old man and take the coin?"

Cynth gave Brewer a pitying look.

Peter kept his voice friendly. "You were, what, fifteen in 1987? Fat, too. You can't expect us to believe you killed a man."

Jiggling leg, throbbing vein. Right hand balled into a

fist, knuckles white. Brewer was turning into a regular one-man band. *Nothing worse than having your man cred obliterated in front of a sexy lady.* One more push, two, and Brewer would blow.

"Screw that. I'm not saying I killed the old man, but I could have."

Cynth folded her arms and smirked.

Peter huffed, signaling disbelief. "No way you pulled this off. You couldn't even drive."

Brewer thrust his face forward, nostrils flaring. "I knew how to drive when I was eleven."

Peter smiled sadly, shook his head. "You were a wimp. You can't convince me you carried Heenan down that gully."

Saliva sprayed Peter's face as Brewer roared, "I didn't have to, moron! I rolled him down the hill!"

A FRIEND APPEARS

TUESDAY, MARCH 12, 1940

THE LOCK AT THE TOP OF THE STEPS RATTLED, PULLING MAL from uneasy sleep and waking the bruises covering most of his body. He stifled a moan as pain speared through cracked ribs. No sense letting Stu's goons know he was awake.

Cold seeped into his body from the dirt floor and he shivered. He breathed shallowly, trying not to inhale the stench of his own waste in the corner slop bucket. His leg twitched, knocking into the heavy leg iron.

That damn manacle—they'd poured lead into the lock so he couldn't pick it. That was the first clue he wasn't leaving this basement on his feet, a suspicion confirmed when Stu showed up. Stu, who was Pete's head of security and his main man until Mal came up with his grand plan.

Stu, who could not let Mal talk.

The lock rattled again. *The jerks must be drunk if they*

can't get the door open. What will it be this time? Another beating? Cigar burns? Will they finally kill me?

Creaking hinges. Mal shut his eyes, waiting for the lids to turn red when the bare bulb hanging overhead came on. He heard stealthy footsteps and cracked his eyes open. A faint beam of light bobbled on the stairs.

A flashlight. Not the goons.

The light wavered and stabbed through the dark as it came closer. It landed on him, blinding. A gasp, a frantic female whisper.

"Mal? What happened to you?"

"Lower the flashlight will you?" he hissed.

The light dropped away. "Sorry."

Mal blinked several times before a pale oval appeared over him. Rose.

"Are you crazy? What are you doing here?"

"I—I heard noises. I had to see."

"Where are they? They'll kill you."

"Uncle Stu won't kill me, but they're gone. We'll hear the car when they come back. I don't understand, Mal. Why are you here?"

Mal tipped his head back, gusted a sigh at the ceiling. Winced at the pain in his ribs. "Then there's no need to whisper. Get me some water and I'll tell you."

MAL SAT, PROPPED AGAINST THE STONE FOUNDATION, exhausted from explaining. But finally, understanding appeared in Rose's eyes.

"So you were helping Pete hide money before Moe

Dalitz could steal it? And Uncle Stu decided to help himself?"

"In a nutshell."

"But why are you here?"

"Because Pete hid the take and Stu wants to know where it is."

"If they're hurting you, why not tell them?"

Three days of torture and threats of dismemberment hadn't made him squeal, and here he was spilling to a dame. If he was Stu, he'd send a sweet-faced angel to soften him up. Even if Rose was as innocent as he thought, Stu could get her to blab in a hot minute.

"Because I don't know where it is. I could make something up, but talking won't get me out of this. I bet Pete thinks Dalitz waylaid me. Stu can't let Pete find out it was him."

The Betty Boop mouth made an "O." Emotions shifted across Rose's face like racing clouds across the moon.

"I have to get you out of here."

"No can do, doll." He shook his leg so the chain rattled. "They poured lead in the lock. The only way I'm getting out of here is in pieces when they cut me up with that saw."

He jerked his head at a workbench on the other side of the room. Rose turned her flashlight on the odd machine.

"What *is* that?"

"It's called a circular saw. It's electric. See that disk with the zig-zag edge? You press a button and it spins so fast you can't see it. It'll cut through me like butter."

"Will it cut through the chain?"

Oh, how he wished. The yearning for freedom was so sharp his voice turned hoarse as he grabbed her hand.

"Forget it doll. If the blade didn't snap, it'd take so long to cut through the chain you'd get caught. Go back up those stairs and pretend it's rats down here. Pretend I ran off to Mexico. Whatever you do, don't ever tell Pete what you know. Promise me."

"But—"

"Pete trusts Stu. You tell Pete, Pete will ask Stu what you're talking about, and Stu will kill you. You can't risk it."

DAY 26

WEDNESDAY, MAY 15, 2019

As Lia approached the gang at their usual table, Terry and Steve waved identical dog biscuits, hoping to catch Gypsy's attention. Gypsy squirmed in the Moby wrap, desperate to get out. Whether she wanted pets or treats, Lia couldn't say. She stroked the soft head, holding Gypsy in place with her other hand.

"It's a contest," Bailey said. "You're supposed to set Gypsy on the end of the table so we can see if she likes Terry or Steve better."

"Seriously?"

"It's scientific," Jim said.

Lia rolled her eyes and held out a hand. "No lures. Give me the biscuits."

"Told ya," Steve said.

Terry grumbled.

Lia took the biscuits and pointed. "Everybody on that side. Bailey and Jim, too."

Gypsy whined and wiggled. Lia fed her a biscuit while her friends lined up on the far side of the table. Kita lumbered up, drool hanging, begging for the remaining biscuit. Kita leaned against her as she crunched, sixty pounds of love bought on the cheap.

"No moving," Lia said. "No smiling or talking or coaxing of any kind."

"Spoil sport," Terry said.

"You want science, be scientific."

Lia stood in front of the stone-faced human wall and placed Gypsy on the table. Collective breaths held. Gypsy remained where she was.

Kita hung her muzzle over the edge of the table and nosed Gypsy's side. Gypsy ignored the prod, turned to Lia and barked. Lia did nothing. Gypsy wagged her tail and barked again.

Lia scooped Gypsy up, cradling her as she took a seat on the bench. She cooed, "Who's Mommy's little girl?"

"That answers that," Bailey said.

Jim tapped the tabletop, attempting to get Gypsy's attention. Gypsy looked at his finger with suspicion, then pounced. Jim whipped his finger up, starting a game of keep away.

"What did Dick say? How did he do it?"

Lia had seen the video on Peter's laptop, Dick bragging about knocking on Andrew's door under the guise of looking for lawns to mow and forcing his way into the house.

Andrew had been running a bath when the doorbell rang. For Dick, the tub was an invitation to torture

Andrew with a series of near drownings. Andrew's death had been an accident.

Dick had shrugged, saying, "It was the old man's fault. He kept pushing. He should have talked. I ended up with nothing."

Panic drove Dick to bury Andrew in the most inaccessible location he could think of, hauling Andrew's body across the creek because there was no level ground on the near side.

It was an obvious answer, and Peter was mortified he hadn't thought of it.

After Dick calmed down, he returned to search Andrew's house, finding packed luggage and airline tickets. Genius that he was, he realized he could throw everyone off and buy time to find the egg if he used the ticket and bussed back.

Most appalling was Dick Brewer's lack of empathy, framing Andrew's death as bad luck on par with hitting a knothole with your drill and nothing to do with repeatedly forcing the man's head under water. The helpful paddler was gone, leaving behind a heartless psychopath celebrating his own ingenuity.

The video would wind up on YouTube after it became part of the public record. For now, Lia needed to respect Peter's confidence.

"I can't say."

"Which means you could, but you won't," Terry pouted.

"At least tell us how he got Dick to confess," Steve said.

"Enquiring minds want to know," Bailey said.

Jim nodded.

Lia smiled. "I can tell you that. OCT."

Blank looks all around.

Bailey was the only one willing to admit ignorance. "What's that?"

"Old cop trick. Dick's a narcissist. First Peter fed Dick's ego and let him think he was controlling the interview."

"Namby-pamby waste of time," Terry grumbled.

"The more Dick spun out his story and the more lies he told, the easier it will be to convict him of kidnapping Jenny. Then Peter went back and made Dick implode."

"Implode how?" Jim asked.

"This is where the old cop trick comes in. Peter said you put a guy who think's he's the smartest guy in the room in front of a pretty woman and tell him he wasn't man enough to commit the crime. He'll confess just to keep his man cred."

Terry nodded. "A tried-and-true strategy."

Bailey huffed, "That is so sexist."

Steve shrugged. "We're simple creatures."

"Peter said getting him to confess was a piece of cake. The hard part was talking Cynth into wearing lipstick and flirting on camera. Now she owns him. He mumbled something about doing her paperwork for a month."

"He should have negotiated that part in advance," Jim said.

"He said he had no idea she was that vindictive."

Steve tickled Gypsy's chin. Pup bit his finger. "No new videos from Susan. Wonder what she thinks of all this."

Lia pulled a limp and ragged length of silk from her

pocket and dangled it in front of Gypsy's nose. Gypsy latched on and tugged.

"Don't know, don't care."

Fame sounded from Lia's pocket. She retrieved her phone, tapped the call. "Don't tell me. Zoe got a cat."

"Aren't you the psychic one," David said. "Not a cat, a guinea pig, for Travis. They named it Godzilla."

"You've got to be kidding."

"It was her husband's idea. Will you do it?"

Chewy returned from his daily peregrination and butted her leg. She scratched behind his ears while she considered.

"A guinea pig? Really?"

"He's very cute."

Lia said nothing.

"Please? For me?"

Lia sighed.

"You're a rock star. *My* rock star."

"Conditions?"

"She wants it as big as Dakini's portrait."

A three foot **guinea** pig. "Of course she does."

"Make it heroic. And no, Zoe does not possess the Millennial affection for irony."

Lia sighed. "I'll need photos."

"If you trust me to take them, I'll have them when you bring Peter over for dinner. Then you can meet Bob. Hold on, you must see this, it's delish."

Lia's phone dinged. The photo of a dreadlocked hunk had her double-checking the sender.

"You didn't tell me you were dating a Norse god."

"A Celtic god. There's a brain inside that brawn. We have actual conversations."

"A Celtic god named Bob."

"Robert McDuff is a respectable Scot name, but it's too white bread for media. He goes by Duff at Channel 7."

"You sound happy. Tell me about this photo."

"Duff and his friends spent a Saturday running an obstacle course through Over the Rhine. Bob's amazon cop friend took the photo and texted it to me when we met up for dinner at Zula's. You might know her. Cynth something. Doesn't she have a terrific eye? I'm blowing this up to life size for the loft. What do you think?"

Lia eyed the sweaty biceps and flying dreads. Cynth had omitted salient details about her parkours date. It would be fun to see the expression on Peter's face when he met Bob.

"She could put me out of business if she got tired of being a detective."

"People will always want flowers, darling."

Elvis sneered at Peter as he labored on reports. He narrowed his eyes, muttering low so Brent wouldn't hear.

"Don't you start."

"What did you say?"

Not low enough. "Talking to the skull."

"Get rid of that thing before it tanks my reputation as a man of taste."

"I don't know anyone I dislike enough to dump it on."

"Your mouth, God's ear, brother."

They returned to work, silence broken only by the clattering of Peter's keyboard as he typed, deleted, and retyped. Convinced Elvis' constant supervision was ruining his productivity, he faced Elvis to the wall and felt relief.

He'd kept the damn thing, hoping to smoke out the prankster who kept turning it around while Peter was gone. So far it hadn't worked. He'd take Elvis to Saint Vincent de Paul, but he was certain he'd find the skull on his desk when he returned.

Across the office, Brent crowed. "Hah. Gotcha, you mutha-lovin' son of a bitch!"

"What have you got?"

"Jamal, the sneaky bastard."

Peter swiveled his chair to see the photograph on Brent's monitor, a man in a hoodie with a huge dollar sign on the back, putting a garbage bag in the trunk of a parked car while a caucasian woman looked on. Corners poked the sides of the bag. It contained boxes, not garbage.

"What is that?"

"That, my friend, is Jamal at his staging area. We've got him."

"Explain."

"Your lovely neighbor, Alma, saw a post in the North-side Facebook group complaining about a car parked on Jerome, sans license plates and belonging to no one who lives there. The OP said people were stopping by every few days to put bags in the trunk, sometimes putting plates on it and driving off for a few hours.

"He was helpful enough to include this photograph of

the vehicle in question. Being a sharp old bird, Alma pegged it as a dubious situation. Knowing you were tied up with Brewer, she called me."

"I'm not familiar with Jerome."

"A dead end three very quick turns from the on-ramp to I-74, exactly the spot I'd choose if I wanted to stay out of the public eye while having rapid access to a highway. If we run the VIN on that car, I bet it comes up stolen and we can't tie it to anyone. The only risk is when someone is driving the car. If they drive nice, there's no reason to pull them over."

"Why drive the car when they could leave it parked and offload the packages there?"

"First, you have to move a car every few days if you don't want it towed. Second, I bet Jamal figures if he gets pulled over he'll make a run for it and leave us with a vehicle and loot we can't connect to him."

"You can't see his face. That could be anyone."

"I've tailed that hoodie enough times. It's him. I just need to ID the woman."

Peter leaned closer to the screen. "Well, I'll be."

"What?"

"A monkey's uncle. That's Joyce Bender."

"Stacy's mom?"

"The very one, explaining why Ms. Bender stormed out of that meeting. Either Stacy strung me along, or she doesn't know and that's why Mom didn't want her hanging out with Jamal's little sister."

"I imagine we'll know which it is soon enough."

Brent cracked Peter's case, and did it with help from

someone who should have come to him first. It was a stab to the heart that he would swallow.

"What's the plan?"

"I could nail him the next time he drops packages, but I'd rather follow the car to wherever the packages are going."

"Bigger fish."

"Exactly."

Peter's desk phone beeped.

"Dourson."

"Susan Sweeney to see you."

Peter sighed. "I'll be right up."

Susan stood in the lobby, studying a display dedicated to fallen officers. The fingers of her left hand rested against her jaw, angled for him to see her new wedding set when he came through the door.

If that's what it was. The diamonds were big enough to qualify as a set of brass knuckles.

"What can I do for you, Susan?"

She turned and smiled, waiting a second too long before she dropped the hand to clasp its mate in a demure pose.

"I wanted to see if you needed anything from me."

In a pig's eye.

"We have your statement. If the prosecuting attorney needs anything, she'll contact you."

"Will I need to testify?"

Peter looked, but couldn't find a telltale, isn't-this-exciting-gleam in her eyes. Maybe Susan *wasn't* trying to milk Brewer for more exposure.

"I wouldn't worry about it. Brewer will never make it to court."

Her hands balled up, popping to her hips, indignant. "Why ever not? That man—"

"Hold your horses. I hear his lawyer is pushing for a plea bargain, and it's the most sensible thing for Brewer to do. Don't worry, he'll pay for his crimes."

"It was stinky of you to renege on my exclusive interview."

"Parker nixed it." Or she would have if he'd asked her. "How's your car?"

Susan glanced toward the door, though you couldn't see the parking lot from where they stood. "Dwayne thought I should have a new one, after the trauma and all."

"Dwayne?"

"He flew up after he saw the story on Channel 7. He begged me to come home."

"Giving up fame and fortune in the big city?"

"People are nasty here. I thought Ada Belle was so nice. Yesterday I got a phone call from a lawyer. He said Ada Belle has whiplash and it's my fault. Then someone started tweeting that all my interviews were faked. Now people think I'm a joke. Can you believe that?"

Peter could, but thought it best not to say so. "Then I guess this is goodbye."

She bit her lip, took his hand. "I need to confess."

"Oh?" He flicked his eyes sideways. The desk sergeant's face dropped to her computer.

Susan looked away, at nothing, or maybe the water fountain. "All that stuff I said about relocating and wanting to be with you, it was just me making Dwayne jealous. I never meant to stay. It wasn't nice to use you that way."

That was Susan, revising history to create a more flattering narrative. Peter shrugged, slipping his hand out of hers and stuffing it in a pocket.

"Looks like you got what you wanted."

A glimmer appeared in her eyes now, an unexpected dampness above the cheerleader smile.

"I did, didn't I?"

INTO THIN AIR

WEDNESDAY, MARCH 13, 1940

THE FOOD HAD BEEN THE ONLY DECENT THING ABOUT Mal's captivity. It sent an odd twist through his guts to know Rose cooked it. They'd fed him black-eyed peas and greens after her visit. Then they'd kicked his broken ribs until he vomited Rose's greens all over the floor.

Joe told him they'd let him go, send him to California if he talked. Larry sent nervous, excited glances toward the circular saw.

Mal listened for Rose the next day, the clatter and bustle of a woman in the kitchen, comfortable sounds that sent longing through him when they came, and when they stopped, grief that he would never hear them again.

He'd held out longer than expected. Those looks Joe and Larry gave each other the night before told him Stu was ready to cut his losses.

Dinner never came. Snores drifted through the vents,

the heavy snores of passed out drunks. Underneath the snores, the quiet click of the lock.

This time the flashlight penetrated the darkness with more certainty, the light kindling twin frissons of hope and alarm. He worked spittle into his mouth and licked cracked lips.

The sweet face he never expected to see again hovered over him, a finger to the bow mouth, warning him to stay silent.

She whispered, "I can get you out, but you're leaving your foot behind."

"Are you out of your mind?"

She set down a carryall and withdrew a quart bottle, some kind of liquor. "I can't leave you here. Drink this, it will help."

Mal propped himself up and took the bottle. She sat on the dirt floor beside him and rummaged in the bag, her face averted.

"How do you expect to do this without getting both of us killed?"

Rose's voice was brisk. "I put Ma's morphine in the soup. Larry and Joe won't wake up until the second coming. Uncle Stu is at the club.

"My grandpa did field amputations in the Civil War. I know how he did it, only he didn't have an electric saw. I'll put a tourniquet on your leg to keep you from bleeding to death, and afterwards I'll cauterize the stump the way grandpa did."

"And how was that?"

"I sprinkle gunpowder on it and light a match."

Mal took a swig from the bottle and waited for the booze to burn its way to his stomach.

"How many of his patients survived?"

"More than half. What other chance do you have?"

If he died this way, at least Stu wouldn't win. "And how do you plan to carry me out of here?"

"My cousin Nick is waiting outside to help with the operation."

"What's he doing outside?"

"This is going to hurt more than you can stand. I had to use Ma's morphine to put Larry and Joe asleep. I've got a piece of leather for you to bite on and the gin will help, but it won't be enough."

"What do you plan to do? Hit me over the head with a skillet?"

"Grandpa was a plain-speaking man. He said making love was one of the best pain killers nature ever invented."

Mal choked, spraying gin.

Rose shifted coming closer, fidgeting with the top button of her blouse. The brisk voice held a slight tremor now. "You're hurt, so I expect I need to do most of it myself." She picked up his hand and placed it on a firm, full breast. "I've never done this before. Will you tell me what to do?"

DAY 27

THURSDAY, MAY 16, 2019

STACY'S GUTS TWISTED AS SHE KNOCKED ON THE DOOR TO Ms. Freeman's office. The summons could only mean one thing. Ms. Freeman *knew*. And if *she* knew, other people would know, and they'd all look at her that way people did.

She didn't want their pity or disgust. She wanted to be normal and pretend the last twenty-four hours had never happened.

They'd been eating supper, glued to the TiVo'ed Bachelorette premiere. Onscreen, a hot guy in a suit jumped out of a giant shipping box, showering packing peanuts everywhere.

"Too goofy," Ma had said, chewing mechanically.

As if a guy like that would look at you twice. This is so lame.

Stacy rolled her eyes at Lynn and Connie. Movement outside the living room window caught her eye. A cop car

421

eased into a space across the street. A second cop car parked in front of the house, followed by a van and an SUV.

She stopped breathing.

They're coming for me. I have to get out of here. She picked up her plate and stood. "I'll start on the dishes," she told the room.

Ma tore herself from stuck up Hannah Brown in her silver spangle dress, her eyes narrowing at the uneaten fish sticks on Stacy's plate.

"Sit your ass back down and finish your dinner. You're not throwing out good food."

Connie and Lynn kept their eyes on their TV trays, hoping to be forgotten if Ma's temper blew.

Behind Ma, red and blue lights flashed while a line of cops headed down the side yard. More cops, coming up the front walk, followed by two men in suits. Detective Dourson, and a cute guy who looked like he should be handing Hannah Brown a dozen roses.

I'm doomed. She couldn't stop the panic on her face, even knowing it would piss Ma off. On the screen, a guy wearing a tux handed a baby seat to Hannah.

"Sit down now or you won't—"

Banging on the door.

Too late.

"Joyce Bender, open up, we have a warrant."

Surprise, then fury on Ma's face. Stacy cringed.

"What the *hell* have you done?" Ma hissed, pasting a neutral face on as she stood. She cracked the door, leaving the chain in place.

"What seems to be the problem, officer?"

"Please step outside."

Ma frowning, calculating. Outside the window, the neighbors stood in their yards and lined the street, talking and elbowing each other. She was going to jail, and they were laughing. Prime time entertainment.

After a pause that lasted too long, Ma stepped out, pulling the door behind her. Voices too low to be understood, the sound of a scuffle.

Through the window, Ma shouting obscenities as they frog-marched her to the van in handcuffs, surrounded by cops like she was the Hulk or something and they thought she was going to break out an Uzi and shoot everyone.

The lights, flashing. Red, blue, red, blue.

Ma?

Asshole neighbors on the sidewalk, cheering as if this was an episode of *Cops*. A lady cop with a blank, zombie face, herding her and her sisters into the kitchen.

More cops tromping through the house. Connie and Lynn scared to death. Trying to calm them down while her heart pounded. She felt like bawling herself.

Then it got worse.

Detective Dourson came and said Ma was helping Jamal sell stolen goods, and they were going into foster care as soon as the social worker showed up.

Stacy couldn't wrap her head around it. She tried, choking down cold fish sticks with her sisters while the zombie cop lady stared at them, waiting for the social worker to arrive. She kept trying during the hours of limbo before they found a place for her.

It was after eleven when she'd been dumped at a stranger's house with mismatched clothes in a garbage bag. She didn't know where her sisters were. Maybe she'd never see them again.

Fussy Mrs. Gertz in her fussy house, fussing over her until she could scream. Mrs. Gertz said she didn't have to go to school. But Stacy didn't want to be stuck in the fussy house, and school was the only place she knew where she could pretend her world wasn't falling apart.

Taneesha in the hall, giving her a hard stare. She must have looked guilty because Taneesha mouthed, "I'll get you," before disappearing into class.

Then Ms. Freeman sent for her.

This is not happening. It's not happening. It's not.

The door opened.

Ms. Freeman, dressed in her pretty suit, smiling as if the world was a nice place.

"Stacy, come in and have a seat. There's someone I want you to meet."

The woman sitting in the visitor's chair was a drab sort of woman, overweight, with short, iron-gray hair of no particular style. Somehow she looked happy and worried at the same time.

Stacy sat, backing into the chair while she kept her eyes on the woman watching her so strangely. She looked up at Ms. Freeman, waiting for an explanation.

The woman said, "Do you remember me?"

Stacy, mute, could only shake her head.

"You were only three. Joyce hasn't spoken to me since then. I'm Dee. I'm your grandmother."

Stacy blinked. "You're dead."

The woman bit her lip. "Dead to Joyce, I'm sure. There's a lot of water under the bridge, but I want to look after you, if you'll let me. Your sisters, too. Will you let me?"

DAY 28

FRIDAY, MAY 17, 2019

JENNY SAT AT THE CROWDED KITCHEN TABLE. DETECTIVE Dourson's girlfriend, Lia, set a plate of steaming lasagna in front of her. Terry sat on her left, with Lia's redheaded friend and Steve across from her. The ends of the table were vacant while the detective and Lia served dinner.

A damp nose bumped insistently against her leg. Lia's schnauzer, looking for a handout before she had a chance to taste her food.

Lia scooped the dog up. "Chewy's default is 'pest.' How did you get past the baby gate, little man? Back to the kiddie room with you."

"He's no bother. I enjoy dogs."

Detective Dourson—Peter—handed her a glass of wine. "You'll change your mind about that if we let him stay. Dig in while it's hot. Lia will be back in a minute."

Terry offered a basket of garlic toast. "Thank you again for Andrew's leg. I shall treasure it always."

Jenny took a slice, handed the basket to Steve. She didn't know what to think about Terry's plan to mount the prothesis on his canoe, but her discovery of the false leg led to Andrew's death. She didn't think she could bear to have it around. Terry would enjoy it without the baggage.

"You're quite welcome."

Lia and Peter joined them, a signal for the group to attack their meal. Between bites, the redhead with the graceful hands—Bailey?—said, "It must have been nice seeing Mrs. Redfern after all these years."

"It was. She doesn't remember me, but she's still very sweet. She patted my hand and asked if I was a Merrill."

Bailey's overlarge Shelley Duvall eyes brimmed with compassion. "Dementia?"

"Yes, but she's doing well, considering. She has a very protective group of friends at Twin Towers. You might recognize them."

The table gave her a collective confused look.

Jenny explained. "From those silly videos—*Susan's Snippets?*"

"I don't understand," Lia said.

"With Ms. Snippets coming around the neighborhood, Donna knew someone would eventually tell her where to find Gran. She asked Gran's friends to watch out for her. They decided the best defense was a good offense and created a plan to distract her."

"They made it up?" Lia said. "They weren't random nuts?"

"Watch the videos again. You can tell they were determined to outdo each other."

Terry shook his head. "Poor Susan. I hope she never finds out."

Jenny saw Lia and Bailey trade looks over their wine. A change of subject was in order. "I heard from Jay Overstreet again."

"Again?" Lia asked. "How many times has he called?"

"Five, maybe six. He wants my memories of Andrew for his book."

"Will you do it?"

"I'm about ready to block him. It's idiotic to think Andrew was a mobster with his hands on a fifty million dollar egg."

Terry toyed with his lasagna. "Dick Brewer thought the same thing."

"He also said Jay Overstreet killed Andrew. I guess he made that up to string me along. Dick was such a putz in high school. No wonder I didn't recognize him. I can't believe he killed Andrew."

Bailey turned those sympathetic eyes on Jenny. "Even if Andrew isn't Malachi, aren't you wondering what's inside that compartment you found at the house?"

"There was no compartment. I was buying time until I could figure out how to get away from Dick."

"This is just like *The Maltese Falcon*," Bailey said. "Do you suppose Malachi's treasure ever existed?"

Steve snorted. "What businessman trusts a peon with that much money in the middle of a mob war?"

"That seems so obvious," Lia said. "Why do you suppose the mob bought it?"

Peter snagged the last piece of garlic toast. "I've thought about it a lot. Magicians are masters of misdirection, and between Malachi and Pete, they would have foreseen the need for a contingency plan. I bet the Syndicate had informants inside the club and Pete knew they were there.

"So Malachi disappears and Pete plants a story with his inner circle that Malachi hid the money even from him, knowing it would get back to the mob and they would think the trail ended with Malachi. If Malachi had a cache, I bet it was a fraction of what everyone said."

Words burned into Jenny's head, words she couldn't say: *Then Andrew died for nothing.*

Peter's phone buzzed. He looked down at the screen, then held it in front of Jenny so only she could see the text:

DNA results indicate a match for immediate family with two degrees of separation.

Jenny looked up at Peter. "What does this mean?"

Peter nodded at the avid faces surrounding them. "Would you like to talk in private?"

Jenny took a sip of her wine. "I think I need to stay near the bottle."

"We compared your DNA sample to Andrew's. You're related."

"That's not possible."

"Two degrees of separation. Sibling or grandparent."

"My grandfather died in the war. Grandma was a war widow."

"Did your mother have any memories of her father?"

Jenny shook her head. "He joined up the day after Pearl Harbor. She wasn't even a year old. He never came back."

"December 8, 1941. Malachi disappeared in 1940, right before Pete Schmidt sold the Beverly Hills. You ever see any photos of your grandfather? Meet his family?"

Again, Jenny shook her head.

"A lot of unwed mothers assumed identities as war widows back then."

Jenny blinked. "Why wouldn't she tell me?"

"If the stories are true, I imagine she thought the less you knew the safer you were."

"If it was so dangerous, why put me in his house?"

"A calculated risk? She was dying. I imagine she wanted you in a position where Andrew could help you and no one would think anything of it."

The tears fell now. "Except I shot my mouth off and got him killed."

"You didn't know. Everyone involved had been dead for decades. It was a one-in-a-million chance that someone who could make sense of it overheard you."

The room fell silent as Jenny collected herself. Lia's chair scraped the floor as she got up, announcing dessert and coffee while she gathered empty plates. Across the table, Steve stared hard at Terry.

Terry excused himself, returning a few minutes later with a towel-wrapped bundle cradled in his arms like an infant. He placed it in front of Jenny. "You didn't know he was family when you gave this to me. I think you should have it back."

Jenny ran a hand under her nose and sniffed. The side

of her mouth quirked up. "I don't know what I'll do with it."

"Make a lamp out of it, like in *A Christmas Story*," Steve cracked.

"I don't have the right stockings." Jenny pulled the towel aside and ran a hand over the wood, frowned.

"Is something wrong?" Terry asked.

Everyone leaned in closer.

She ran a finger along a hairline crack. "This wasn't here when I saw it at the coroner's office."

"It was damp for thirty years," Bailey said. "Now it's drying out. A little wood filler will fix that."

"It's not that. Andrew made puzzle boxes. He gave me one. I still have it."

"You think the leg is a puzzle box?" Lia asked.

Peter nodded at the leg. "Can you open it?"

"Maybe. He used a system of metal shims. Each shim has a hole drilled in it so they spin around on a nail. The holes are off center, so one side is heavier than the other. You have to rotate the box in a pattern to clear the shims from their latches. Then you can pull it open."

"I wonder if he showed you the secret of the box on purpose," Lia said.

Jenny held the prothesis by the ends. "Here goes nothing." She manipulated the leg in a series of moves as familiar to her as breathing, then set it on the table. "Grab the other end," she told Bailey.

They pulled.

Nothing.

"I have a rubber mallet in my truck," Bailey said.

"Maybe if you tap it a few times it will shake something loose."

Lia and Peter served cheesecake and coffee as the group watched Jenny tap, shake and gyrate the leg. On the fifth try, something shifted. Jenny paused, astonished, as everyone whooped.

"What do you suppose is inside?" Bailey asked.

Terry waved a forkful of cheesecake. "It's the egg."

"Get real." Steve said. "There isn't enough space for that."

Terry grinned. "This is better than *Storage Wars*."

"Why guess?" Jenny said. "Pull!" Bailey tugged. The top of the prothesis came free, revealing a compartment. In it was a gray, plastic tube, two inches in diameter.

"I expected something classier than plastic," Bailey said.

"Plastic is waterproof," Lia said.

Jenny tipped the tube out of the slot with one finger. The screw cap stuck. She handed it to Peter. "You give it a shot."

Peter placed the tube on the table and tapped the edge of the cap with the mallet. He grunted and gave a twist, handing it back to Jenny. Jenny unscrewed the lid and peered in.

"What is it?" Bailey asked.

"Something's wedged inside." Jenny used two fingers to ease out a stiffly curled booklet with a red leatherette cover. She pressed it flat. The gold leaf on the front was almost gone, but the embossed image of a harp remained. Above the harp, the words ÉIRE and IRELAND could still be read.

"It's a passport!" She opened the little booklet, turning it sideways. A photo of Andrew smiled at her. She turned it around so everyone could see.

"Hello, Grandpa," Peter said. "What name is on it?"

Jenny scanned the faded print. "Michael Collins, born May 28, 1919. Baile ... something, Dublin. That's the Irish version of John Smith. I'll never find the right family."

"You have a birthdate and place," Lia said. "It's enough. Add in your DNA and I bet you have relatives somewhere."

Jenny clutched the passport, blinking against incipient tears. "I have roots."

Bailey held the tube up, shook it gently. Something rattled. When she tipped it, three keys and a fat roll of bills slid out.

Peter nudged the keys apart with a long finger. "One of these is for a safe deposit box. I wonder what's in it."

"Has to be the egg," Terry said.

"If the bank still exists," Steve said.

"Don't be a spoilsport," Bailey said as she peered into the tube. "There's something else in here." She handed the tube to Jenny.

Jenny drew out a folded piece of paper covered with foxing. It was a page from a magazine, featuring a photo of Andrew wreathed in smoke. Under the photo, the ad listed European tour dates for a magician named Lazarus.

Lia peered over her shoulder. "Covent Garden, Palais Garnier, La Monnaie, the Colosseum. He must have been huge over there."

Jenny stared, unable to take it in. "He pulled quarters

434

out of my ears," she heard herself say. "He made balloon animals for kids."

Lia placed a hand on hers. "And I bet he enjoyed making children happy just as much as he enjoyed the big stages."

"He was a public figure," Peter said. "There's a record somewhere."

Steve examined the roll of bills. "That's a hundred on the outside. If they're all hundreds, you've got the money to go over there and track him down yourself."

FATHER NICHOLAS OPENED HIS EYES TO DARKNESS AND wondered what time it was. Two, three in the morning? He'd dreamt of the Sin City days again, as he had nightly since Mal's bones rose out of the creek in a mocking imitation of Christ's resurrection.

When the church secretary showed him the magazine cover with the hideous skull, he'd admonished her about the destructive nature of gossip—a conversation they'd had before and one with little effect. Then he'd prayed: for Mal's soul, for justice, for direction. He'd been praying ever since.

God had not answered. If Mal's reappearance was a sign, perhaps it was not meant for him. If he'd sinned— and that was questionable—perhaps it was not a large enough sin to follow him now at the end of his life.

The bible says, "Thou shall not steal." Nicholas hadn't stolen, not precisely, and while he'd confessed decades ago —at a church far from Cincinnati, to a priest who did not know him and did not know he was a member of the priesthood—in his heart he never repented his actions.

How could he, when those actions saved the life of a young man in over his head and delivered a devout young woman and her unborn child from mobsters who would destroy her future?

What a pompous boy he'd been: Nicholas, named for the saint of penitent thieves. In his hubris, he'd seen himself as the instrument of Mal's rehabilitation and demanded a promise from Mal to give up his criminal ways as a condition for abetting his escape.

Uncharitable of him, as only absolution required penitence. His assistance should have been free of conditions.

Rose's fury put a stop to Mal's forced conversion.

They'd completed the grisly amputation, spiriting Mal away while murderous criminals lay in a drunken stupor overhead. A veterinarian cut off several more inches of leg to correct the splintered mess he and Ruth had made of the job, then hid Mal in a barn. A mission to Canada provided the means to smuggle him out of the country, funded by the contents of a package hidden in the dismantled hearse.

In return, Mal asked for help disposing of his share of Pete Schmidt's gems and gold. A third went to Mal, another third went to getting Rose out of Newport and into nursing school. Nicholas donated the rest anonymously to the church.

Mal winked when he offered the share for the church, expecting Nicholas to take it for himself. He'd declined. He planned to enter the seminary and saw this temptation as the first test of his commitment to God.

A message he'd sent through circuitous channels months later turned their brief connection into an uneasy friendship. Rose, pregnant, needed help. For more than forty years, Nicholas served as the conduit through which Mal looked after the family he could not acknowledge.

Mal prospered under a variety of names, performing in Europe as Lazarus while acting as a smuggler and go-between in dealings involving powerful and dangerous men. He could have provided better for his secret family, but they'd all agreed too much prosperity would draw eyes and awaken memories.

This connection and the resulting donations had been a blessing for his church. He'd come to appreciate Nicholas as the patron saint of secret giving as well as penitent thieves. He liked to think of his name as a sign that God had a sense of humor, approving of his actions and the good that came from the bad.

And after all, Mal was not a thief or murderer, though he trafficked with those who were.

Mal returned to Cincinnati when Jenny was ten and her parents died in a car crash. By then Rose's health was already failing. He needed to be closer at hand, though he wished to remain a step removed. Nicholas thought it a foolish precaution.

Mal treasured his brief encounters with Jenny at church festivals. It had been Nicholas who suggested hiring her as a housekeeper, and he ached for Rose and Jenny when Mal disappeared. With that ache came fear that the past had refused to stay buried.

So Rose and Jenny disappeared as well.

He'd been right, in a sense. They'd arrested a man

named Brewer for Mal's murder. Rose's uncle Stu had a daughter who married a Brewer. This man must be Stu's great-grandson. Stu had been greedy and immoral. Not surprising his progeny was as well.

Nicholas recognized Jenny immediately when her photo appeared in the papers, despite the three decades since she'd left Cincinnati. He wondered if she knew this Brewer was a cousin of some sort to her or that Mal was her grandfather.

Stu's great-grandson killed Mal in pursuit of the treasure Stu lusted for. Mal's granddaughter caught his killer. Mysterious ways, indeed.

The paper said Jenny was a hospice nurse. Blood ran true there as well, this entire chain of events starting as it did while Rose nursed her dying mother.

How much had Rose told Jenny about her family tree? Nothing, or Jenny would not have returned. He was kin to her, if distant. She might like to know she had family left.

Perhaps he would contact her, tell her the whole story. Mal must have squirreled money away. Perhaps he could help her find it.

He would pray on it.

Nicholas shoved himself into a sitting position against the headboard and turned on the bedside lamp. He picked up the small box on his nightstand, holding it in his hands while repeating a small, private prayer he'd been saying for seventy years.

The box, Mal's gift, a way to safeguard their private matters. He hadn't removed the false bottom for more than a decade, hadn't felt the need, and his arthritic fingers struggled to release the catch.

Seventy years ago, Nicholas briefly felt the presence of the glory of God, embodied in the indescribable beauty of Fabergé's *Cherub and Chariot*.

He'd never been given to covetousness. This once, he'd yearned.

He could not keep it, could not give it to the church, not without endangering all of them. When Mal found a place for it in a private collection in Europe, he'd kept a photograph. Black and white, paling beside the original, but it remained unfaded so many years later.

He removed the photo from the shallow compartment and held it close to eyes that could barely make out the image, even in daylight. It was his last vanity, holding on to this remembrance.

He was long past the age when waking in the morning was a given. It would never do for his connection to the egg to come to light, regardless of the time that had passed or good that came from it. Not for his sake. That was in the hands of God, and he was reconciled to God's judgment. It was the church he thought of, and the many scandals suffered in recent years.

He set the photo down and fumbled in the drawer for the candle and matches he kept there. He lit the candle, staring into the bright flame while he prayed.

When he was done, he lifted the photo with a trembling hand, holding one corner to the hungry flame until it caught, held it as the glorious cherub darkened and rose to Heaven on a plume of smoke.

EPILOGUE

Slivers of daylight penetrated the bottom of the bandana tied around Peter's eyes. Enough light to tease, not enough to tell him where he was. Instead, he tracked the turns Lia's Volvo made as it twisted and looped, sloping gently up and down and up again.

There was only one place in Northside with roads this convoluted, where cars drove half the speed of your average turtle. The lack of traffic noise was another tip-off. Peter said nothing, not wanting to spoil Lia's surprise, whatever it was.

The Volvo pulled to the side and the motor died.

"We're here," she said.

"Can I take my blindfold off?"

"Not yet."

The driver's side door opened, then closed with its usual screech and thunk. His door opened. Her hand, warm and firm, took his.

"Please tell me this isn't some kind of touchy-feely trust exercise."

"Not in the usual sense. There are steps, and they're uneven. Take it slow. I'll tell you when."

He let her guide him out of the car, across a soft expanse of grass, then onto the crunch of a gravel path. Around him, wind whispered through trees. The top of his head cooled as the sliver of light at the bottom of the bandana dimmed. Shade, no doubt from the shushing trees.

Lia ushered him up several steps, then turned right onto a curving path that climbed a slope. Between Peter's blindness and the uneven ground, it took ten minutes to travel what he estimated as less than a hundred feet.

Lia halted. "Here." Her hands on his shoulders urged him to turn ninety degrees to the right. "You can take the blindfold off now."

They were in a familiar slice of faux forest, with small boulders peppering the hillside among the wildflowers and ferns. Each had a bronze plaque. He dropped his eyes.

A white rock the size of an ottoman sat in front of him. The bronze plaque read:

———————

Aurelia Amaryllis Anderson - Peter David Dourson
An oak, a cypress, and the moving sea

———————

"Aurelia?"

"I thought if we were going to spend eternity together, maybe you should know."

Peter took her hand, chafed the back with his thumb. "I've never had a girl give me a cemetery plot. I don't know what to say."

Lia rubbed the lump under her T-shirt, the necklace he'd given her that always rested against her heart. "You gave me a rock. I want to give you one. Do you like it? We're not stuck with that epitaph. We can come up with something together."

Peter pulled Lia into his arms, rested his chin on her head. "Aurelia: golden. Amaryllis: a strong, confident, and very beautiful woman."

"How on earth do you know that?"

"I ran you when Luthor died. I've known who you are for a long time, Aurelia."

"Don't start."

"Why? It's a lovely name."

"And the source of childhood trauma. If you ever call me Triple A, I will hurt you. Bad."

"Duly noted. Is it Aw-rel-y-uh or Aw-reel-ya?"

"Aw-rel-y-uh."

"Thus, the derivative."

"Yeah. Thus."

"Why the urge to see to our eternal rest?"

Lia was silent for a moment. She pulled back in his arms and looked up at him, her moss green eyes serious. "When I lost Honey, I realized, unless we died together in a freak highway pile-up, one of us will eventually leave the other. I don't believe in marriage—"

"With good reason, considering your upbringing."

"Marriage is 'till death do you part.' I don't want to let you off the hook that easy. Will you be my eternity?"

He pulled her back to his chest, shaking his head as he huffed a quiet laugh. "Mom will never understand."

"Ever since Sarah's funeral, I've thought you would enjoy becoming one with the woods."

Peter glanced across the rows of boulders under the canopy of trees. Spring Grove Cemetery's Woodland Walkway, not quite woods, not exactly. But it was a peaceful place. Sarah's ashes, interred in a biodegradable urn, had no doubt achieved new life in the young maple behind her marker.

"I do like it. Very much."

She handed him a wedge of white rock, no bigger than a half-dollar. He held it, his thumb rubbing the edges.

"I chipped it from the base. I thought you could use it as a worry stone."

Peter liked the idea of carrying his forever around with him. "It will make a great keychain."

THE SWAMP MONSTER SONG

She'll bite your toes and shred your clothes.

She's a four-legged demolition team.

Don't let the blue eyes fool you.

Her needle teeth will school you

in keeping things you value out of reach.

Swamp Monster.

Demon spawn.

Jaws' little sister.

Furry piranha.

Nothin's safe since

She came to live here.

Mop the floor, one time more.

My shoes are toast, this can't go on.

Keeping up is such a chore.

That helpless little ball of fur

Will keep you running, run some more!

AUTHOR'S NOTE

The biggest obstacle I faced in writing Swamp Monster was wringing a confession from Dick Brewer. Dick Brewer is a narcissistic sociopath, a quality that enabled him to cheerfully lie, manipulate, and maneuver throughout the book. It has been pounded into my head at multiple Writers' Police Academy sessions that narcissistic sociopaths like Dick are immune to standard interrogation techniques. Simply put, you can't play on remorse they don't feel.

I turned to Peter's virtual uncles, fellow mystery authors Nick Russell and Billy Kring, who are retired, old-school law enforcement. I'm still shaking my head over their answer, but that didn't stop me from using it.

My descriptions of Mill Creek come from personal experience, both from having a studio overlooking the creek in the eighties, and from Mill Creek Yacht Club events. Commodore's trash free zone is a thing.

If you are one of the thousand people who have traveled the creek on one of his float trips, you'll know I narrowed the creek where the cottonwood fell. I hope you'll forgive me. If I hadn't, Terry and Steve would have paddled around the tree and we would have no story (And for anyone who's wondering, MCYC no longer launches from the Millvale garage.)

Pete Schmidt, George Remus, Red Masterson and the Cleveland Four are all part of Sin City history. After I took the Newport Gangster Tour, I went down rabbit holes looking for details to make Mal's story real. There were discrepancies between various sources, but Pete Schmidt's battle with Moe Dalitz is well documented. I fudged the timeline to allow Mal time to become a stage magician before Dalitz resumed his attacks on the Beverly Hills.

Marvelous Malachi is a product of my imagination, as is his role in the conflict between Schmidt and Dalitz. To the best of my knowledge, that conflict ended when Pete sold to Dalitz a few months after Mal's fictional disappearance. In my mind, Mal's disappearance was the final straw.

I found no record of Cab Calloway performing at the BH but he was local and it would have been strange if he hadn't.

And while I do not know if anyone ever amputated a limb with a circular saw, Rose's gunpowder cauterization is a historical fact.

I visited the roadside Elvis museum and the gas station selling vials of Elvis's sweat on the fifth anniversary of Elvis's death. Graceland was overrun with the faithful that day, so the closest I got to the King's grave was a trip through the Graceland parking lot.

I originally planned to take weeks to identify Not Elvis. Then I signed on to the Ohio Missing Persons database and realized Peter would solve that part of the mystery in less than an hour.

The young woman missing from Toledo is real. I left out her name—Cynthia Jane Anderson—because Peter stumbling across a possible connection to Lia would have been a complication too far. Still, Cynthia's story is so bizarre, I had to indulge myself and include it.

I've been a fan of Ruth's proprietor David Tape since he ran Mullane's Parkside Cafe downtown in the nineties. It's my favorite restaurant for special meals. And as soon as this book is published, I plan to treat myself.

ACKNOWLEDGEMENTS

When I first visualized bones on Mill Creek, I didn't know why they were there. I held a contest through my mailing list. Andrew Heenan's entry about a retired crime lord offered fun territory for me to explore, dovetailing neatly with Sin City history. Andrew was a pleasure to work with as I fleshed out details of my fictional Andrew, though I saved surprises I hope he will enjoy.

Many, many thanks to the folks who served (knowingly or not) as technical advisors for Swamp Monster:

Commodore Bruce Koehler and friends in the Mill Creek Yacht Club, along with Linda Keller of the Mill Creek Alliance, provided more material about their work than I could fit into the book. I can't say enough about the amazing work they do to revitalize this important urban waterway and address regional watershed issues. The canoe trips are a delightful experience. If you have the chance, I urge you to take one (or several!).

Forensic anthropologist Breanne Lasorso answered bone questions, adding fascinating details to the story. Any errors are my own.

The Legacy Tours Gangster Tour provided the foundation for my gangster research.

Information about police procedures comes from multiple sources: Lee Lofland's Writers' Police Academy, which I have attended several times; Former law enforcement officers and fellow writers, Nick Russell (Big Lake mysteries) and Billy Kring (Hunter Kincaid); Cincinnati's Citizen Police Academy; and more recently, two Facebook groups dedicated to helping writers, B. Adam Richardson's Writers Detective Bureau and Patrick O'Donnell's Cops and Writers. I've done my best with what I've learned. Any inaccuracies are no reflection on them.

Taylor Stevens (*The Informationist* and *Liars' Paradox*) and editor Lee Burton are my craft gurus, and my Beta team keeps me on track.

As always, the inimitable Elizabeth Mackey is responsible for my graphic design.

ABOUT THE AUTHOR

Carol Ann "C. A." Newsome is an author and painter who lives in Cincinnati. She spends most mornings at the Mount Airy Dog Park with a zombie swamp monster named Gypsy Foo La Beenz, digging up her next mystery.

Carol loves to hear from readers.
Contact her at
gypsy@canewsome.com

Would you like to stay in touch?
Sign up for Carol's newsletter at
CANewsome.com

facebook.com/AShotInTheBark